I0634546

The Mirror of
Present Events

IN THE SAME SERIES

The Mirror of Present Events
and Other French
Scientific Romances

translated, annotated and introduced by
Brian Stableford

A Black Coat Press Book

ISBN 978-1-61227-486-7. First Printing. March 2016. Published by Black Coat Press, an imprint of Hollywood Comics.com, LLC, P.O. Box 17270, Encino, CA 91416.
The stories and characters depicted in this novel are entirely fictional. Printed in the United States of America.

TABLE OF CONTENTS

Introduction

This volume continues a series of Black Coat Press anthologies of French *roman scientifique* whose ensemble provides a cross-section of short stories, novellas and short novels illustrating the evolution of that genre from the 18th century to the period between the two world wars.

The first item translated in the present anthology, *Le Miroir des événemens actuels ou la Belle au plus offrant* by François-Félix Nogaret, here translated as "The Mirror of Present Events; or, Beauty to the Highest Bidder" was first published in 1790—a year after the Revolution that is "mirrored" therein with extraordinary eccentricity—has recently acquired a certain celebrity because of an essay and book by Julia V. Douthwaite, whose prize-winning article "The Frankenstein of the French Revolution: Nogaret's Automaton Tale of 1790" (2009, with Daniel Richter) made the claim, repeated in *The Frankenstein of 1790 and Other Lost Chapters from Revolutionary France* (2012) that it contains a character called Frankenstein. In fact, it does not—the character in Nogaret's story is called Frankestein—but the false allegation has been widely repeated on the world wide web, even making it into Nogaret's Wikipedia entry, although the British Library website's item on the text scrupulously points out the error, evidently having been composed by someone who actually bothered to consult the text.

Nogaret's novella was reprinted in 1800 in his collection *L'Antipode de Marmontel ou Nouvelles fictions, Ruses d'amour et Espiègleries de l'Aristénète français*, [The Opposite of Marmontel, or, New Fictions, Amorous Ruses and Mischiefs by the French Aristanaetus], under the title "Aglaonice, ou La Belle au concours" [Aglaonice; or The Beauty up for Competition] that subtitle having appeared as the title of the story in the actual text of the earlier volume, in contrast to the title page   As the title of the later volume observes, Nogaret had originally begun writing fiction under the by-line "l'Aristenète français," an appellation that demonstrated his extreme fondness for esoteric Classical references, Aristanaetus being the name apocryphally attached to two volumes of epistolatory mock-moralistic erotic tales published long after the death of the actual Aristanaetus of Niceaea in the fourth century A.D.

The name was chosen because Nogaret's tales are in the same slightly salacious vein, although the satirical aspects of their mock-moralistic pose are inevitably as Voltairean as they are Rabelaisian. They generated a certain amount of critical complaint in their day, and *L'Antipode de Marmontel* includes a few items cast in the form of letters from Nogaret in reply to his detractors, one of which objects strongly to comparison being made between himself and "the author of *Justine*" (the Marquis de Sade) on the grounds that, whereas the author of *Justine* obviously hates women, he, Nogaret, adores them. That claim seems to have been backed up, if rumor can be trusted, by the colorful libertine life he led, over an unusually long period, between his birth in 1740 and his death in 1831. He was active for most of his adult life as a civil servant, under governments of very different complexion, probably aided in various transitions by his status as a leading Freemason.

Nogaret was an enthusiastic supporter of the Revolution—the title page of *Le Miroir des événemens actuels* gives its date of publication as "En l'an de notre salut 1790, et le deuxième de la Liberté [the year of our salvation...and the second of liberty]—and he initially kept the pension he was awarded therein during the early years of the Empire, but he was eventually rendered destitute in 1807 after getting on the wrong side of Joseph Fouché, and was forced to make a living from his pen thereafter. Although he was never taken seriously by his contemporaries as a scholar because he was so witty, flippant and sarcastic, he was obviously an extraordinarily well-read and intelligent individual.

Le Miroir des événemens actuels is a remarkable work in several ways, and although it must have been a rather difficult text in 1790, as it is today, it is well worth the trouble of attempting to appreciate its intricacies and perversities. In essence, it is an irreverent political allegory in which France is represented by the Syracusan beauty Aglaonice, who, following the unfortunate death of the inventor Archimedes in the siege of Syracuse by the Romans, offers her hand in marriage to the inventor who can produce the most effective innovative homage to the great man's mechanical genius. A series of suitors present themselves, each offering a mechanical device ostensibly more marvelous than the last. Thus, in the subtext of the story, made explicit in the final chapter, Lutèce [Paris] offers herself consecutively to a series of political ideologies before discovering an ideal of sorts. It was typical of the author that he did not hesitate to reprint the story even after the Terror had destroyed the hopes of the happy ending, in which the text looks forward, above all else, to an end to massacres.

From the viewpoint of the present anthology and its context, the principal interest of the story is not so much its peculiar political allegorizing as its ingenuity in depicting the inventors and their inventions, which include a remarkable flying machine as well as two automata. Although not entirely innovative—the author includes a tongue-in-cheek list of precedents for the flying machine, and the first of the two automata has the same title as one of the devices constructed between 1737 and 1742 by the prolific maker of automata Jacques de Vaucanson—they are nevertheless marked improvements on their models, and they inevitably embody a great enthusiasm for technological progress and its potential social rewards. The automaton that eventually wins the prize is strikingly symbolic in that way as well as in its disguised political implication.

The next item in the anthology is a set of six humorous stories taken from a collection entitled *Fantasmagories: Histoires rapides* [Phantasmagorias: Fast-paced stories] (1887), which carry forward a rich tradition of humorous

9

speculative fiction begun by Pierre Véron and extended by Eugène Mouton. The collection appeared under the by-line Jean Rameau, the pseudonym of Laurent Labaigt (1858-1942), which had previously appeared on a volume of *Poèmes fantastiques* (1883), also featured on the novel *Le Satyre* (1887), and was subsequently to appear on many other novels, poems and short stories, mostly of an erotic tendency, more than a few of them fantastic. The present stories adopt a typically irreverent attitude to future possibilities, but are remarkable because of their frenetic minimalistic style, which aspires to a certain futurism in itself.

"L'Immortel," which appeared in the popular magazine *Nos Loisirs* in two parts in 1908 under the by-line Régis Vombal, is a far more extravagant story, somewhat crudely composed, as one might expect in a rather downmarket periodical. The by-line does not seem to appear anywhere else, and nothing is known as to the identity of the person behind the pseudonym. It is not implausible, given the awkwardness of its composition, that it was his only publication; if so, it was a remarkable one, in terms of the relentless development of its ironically lurid theme, and its final image is undeniably striking. Although it does not deviate from the essential perversity of the long literary tradition that insists on representing immortality as an exceedingly mixed blessing, it develops that notion with an unusually jovial zest, which makes it worthy of attention in spite of its flaws.

Le Machine à galoper by Georges de la Fouchardière (1874-1946), here translated as "The Galloping Machine," first appeared as a feuilleton in *Paris-Sport* and was reprinted in book form under that title by Albin Michel in 1910; it was reprinted in 1919 as *L'Affaire Peau-de-Balle*. The novella is in the same humorous vein as Jean Rameau's phantasmagorias, although its central theme is more reminiscent of Nogaret's story. Its humor and satire are both updated, relying on slightly off-color jokes and making abundant use of the extensive resources of double entendre supplied by contemporary argot. Racing newspapers were not known for their use of feuilleton fiction, but La Fouchardière was admirably qualified to adapt fiction to that milieu, and did so with considerable brio, its deliberately poor taste calculated to appeal to an audience nor renowned for literary interests. The story also fits neatly into the rich tradition of narratives featuring automata in a maliciously satirical fashion.

The short novel that concludes the anthology, "L'Aérobagne 32," is one of a series of futuristic fantasies featured in the popular periodical *Lectures Pour Tous* in the decade following the end of the Great War. Two early examples by Raoul Bigot are featured in the anthology *On the Brink of the World's End* (2016)[1], and Bigot went on to collaborate with one of the authors of "L'Aérobagne 32," E. M. Laumann, on another short novel, *L'Étrange matière*, in 1921 and on the novelette "Le Visage dans la glace" [The Face in the Mirror] in 1922. Another author featured in *On the Brink of the World's End*, "Colonel Royet," also contributed a fantastic serial to the periodical in 1926 under his other pseudonym, Max Colroy. Laumann's collaborator on "L'Aérobagne 32," the illustrator Henri Lanos, was also a contributor to *Nos Loisirs*, in which he published a novella in collaboration with Jules Perrin, "Un Monde sur le monde" (1910)[2]. The impression of a community and continuity of interests might be extended further, with regard to the present collection, by the observation that E. M. Laumann and "Jean Rameau" were both regulars at the Hydropathe meetings at Le Chat Noir in the 1880s—Laumann helped to decorate the café—and were probably acquainted.

"E. M. Laumann," who appears to have been baptized Charles-Ernest Laumann (1863-1928), was one of numerous writers whose literary ambitions began in the Hydropathe era, under the influence of that community, but who eventually lapsed into the production of commercial popular fiction, and

---

[1] Black Coat Press, ISBN 978-1-61227-474-4.
[2] tr. as "The World Above the World", Black Coat Press, ISBN 978-1-61227-002-9.

retained therefrom a strong interest in speculative material, as promoted at Le Chat Noir in performances by Charles Cros and Alphonse Allais, among others. Laumann wrote a great deal in collaboration, another occasional contributor to *roman scientifique* with whom he worked being René Jeanne. He appears to have made a living primarily as a journalist, although he participated in a scientific mission to Senegal in 1890 and also worked as a set-designer in theaters—probably including the Grand-Guignol, for which he adapted several stories into short plays—before adapting his skills in that métier to work in the cinema. Much of his fiction was pseudonymous, and its full extent probably remains unknown.

Laumann was presumably the principal author of the text of "L'Aérobagne 32," which was reprinted as a book in 1923, although Henri Lanos (1859-1929), a prolific producer of futuristic illustrations in the tradition of Albert Robida, presumably provided ideas for the narrative as well as the illustrations. The story is typical of the melodramatic adventure fiction in which Laumann specialized during the 1920s, being primarily distinguished by the graphic image of the eponymous airborne prison-hulk—a striking, if dubiously economical, suggestion for future penal reform. The plot is blatantly preposterous, clearly designed specifically to accommodate and elaborate that central image, and it suffers from the commonplace feuilleton fault of an exceedingly hurried ending—presumably produced as the copy-deadline loomed—but the story provides an interesting illustration of the impact made on the French imagination by the Great War, and the entanglement of attitudes to contemporary technological development with attitudes to the continuing threat of German political ambitions.

Although it does not hold up a mirror to contemporary events in the same way as Francois-Félix Nogaret's novella—indeed, it is difficult to imagine any greater stylistic dissimilarity—"L'Aérobagne 32" does reflect contemporary concerns in an equally dramatic fashion, with a conscientious bizarrerie that makes use in much the same fashion of emblematic technological artifacts. In both works, symbolic flying machines meet a similar dire fate, but in both works, too, the march of scientific and social progress continues its heroically relentless forward surge.

The translation of *Le miroir des événemens actuels* was made from the copy of the 1790 edition reproduced on the Bibliothèque nationale's *gallica* website. The translations from *Fantasmagories* were made from the *gallica* version of the second edition of the 1887 Ollendorff volume. The translation of "L'Immortel" was made from the version reproduced in the "Introuvables" section of Jean-Luc Boutel's invaluable website *Sur l'autre face du monde*. The translation of *Le Machine à galloper* was made from the London Library's copy of the 1919 Albin Michel reprint, entitled *L'Affaire Peau-de-Balle*. The translation of "L'Aérobagne 32" was made from the *gallica* copies of the relevant issues of *Lectures Pour Tous*.

Brian Stableford

François-Félix Nogaret: *The Mirror of Present Events, Or, Beauty to the Highest Bidder*
(1790)

If you only want to amuse yourselves, read me. If you want to enlighten people and serve them, skip to the final footnote to this work, read it and follow the advice that I give you. Thus, the blue penitents, the gray penitents, the white penitents, the green penitents and all the masks of that species will have less to fear.

To my Friend M. Lecheveau
Clerk in the Département des Boulets[3]

Be the patron of the lovely Orphan of whom there is question in this little erotico-politico-patriotic story, which happened in the year 4400 of the Julian period, or the vulgar year 3790, give or take a year,[4] which you can verify very easily. You are so modest that you will be very surprised to find yourself the object of a dedication, as if you lacked the entitlement to pretend to such an honor, but I know you have more than one. For a long time you have acquitted, with as much zeal as intelligence, the retail committed to your care, and yet I do not see you figuring in the red book. You are no more inscribed in the green book, although you have been very honorable at all times; apparently, the order is a treasure.

---

[3] Probably a joke referring to the Ministry of War.

[4] These dates are inconsistent. The Julian year 4400 would be 313 B.C., while the "vulgar year," counting from Archbishop Ussher's estimate, would be 214 B.C. Neither can be the date in which the story is set, that being after the end of the siege of Syracuse, which concluded in 212 B.C.

Finally, your name is not even found in the provincial ledgers for annual retributions, by virtue of services rendered…or to be rendered. An obliging pen-pusher, without having an entire part in the Proscenium, where you nevertheless figure as one of the principal actors, if you have received, here and there, a few petty trifles, which honesty could not refuse the recognition, you have rapidly rid yourself of them by offering them to your guests. We call that the tax-gatherer's crumbs. Large morsels would have made you blush… You can clearly see, therefore, my old comrade, that, honor always having served you as a guide, it is only just that I should prefer you to so many others I have known.

I have resembled you in my time; I have gloried in it; but in addition, I have told the truth bluntly. My little family has suffered in consequence; my superiors have taken me for an Ammonite and the god Moloch has swallowed my children. On my table, at that time, was displayed the touching letter, the golden letter of the worthy pastor of Sormery,[5] well framed under Bohemian glass, in the guise of a prayer or canon, containing the sacramental words that edify me and the same time as they invite me to sobriety. My philosophy is accommodated thereto, and patriotism is honored to serve you the dinner of Democritus in the vessel of Tuberon.[6]

Your friend,

Félix Nogaret

---

[5] The curé of Sormery gave up his salary for a year in order to assist the French financial crisis associated with the Revolution, and was held up by the new government as an example to others.

[6] Tuberon's provision of an unusually lavish serving-dish for a public feast in Rome is recorded in French translations of Livy. Democritus was renowned for his frugality as well as his cheerfulness.

Fortunate are the people who sleep when they do not have bad dreams! While the Camus, the Lameths, the Menous and the Goupils stroll in dreams in the midst of beauties placed by Montesquieu in the bouquets of Gnide, or on the flowery banks of limpid streams that wind through those beautiful places, the de Sezes, the Cazalès, the Maurys and Mirabeau the killer have rendezvous on the bank of the Styx with Alecto, Megaera and Tisiphone. Those latter marriages are lit by the torch of the Erinyes, so the children of one and the other are as different as black and white.

I, whom am invalid before my time, for having made my paradise, do not travel when I sleep with either Montesquieu or Machiavelli. My imagination, less active than in times past, no longer offers me any but dusty books, a table, and paper, with a hundred stupidities and all the intelligence of the world in a cornet; it is up to me to take one or the other. A sad condition!

No matter. You have seen lately that Solon has not disdained to appear to me. I was in bed then. It was a pleasure for him to find me at work this time. "It's going well now," he said to me—and then he maintained a bleak silence...

I, who had scarcely begun to put my thoughts into a beautiful oratory style, in accordance with the advice of the divine revenant, was slightly surprised to see that he was not saying anything to me. I looked him in the eyes; I waited impatiently for some of those sweet speeches to emerge from his mouth that inflates our self-esteem, but my excessive politeness, the result of an old habit of a subordinate courtier, had made me do something stupid, which he was holding against me.

"You appear to me," I said to him, "to have something on your mind..."

"Undoubtedly," he said. "Where have you got the idea that I was something less than a philosopher? What is this ridiculous address in which I find myself seriously or flippantly called Monseigneur? Monseigneur, me! Are you mad? Cato, who wasn't laughing, thought that the letter was for Sardanapalus. Can a man chosen by his fellows to enable them to enjoy the advantages of equality be ambitious for a title destructive of the services that he renders to them? Is there one more flattering for him than that of benefactor of humankind, or servant of the fatherland? Do you not know, then, that Minos, who gave the law to Crete, would have blushed to hear himself called Milord? Lycurgus made that observation to us and said, speaking of himself, that, having lost an eye for the good cause, he would rather have heard himself described as a disreputable villain."[7]

"Forgive me," I said to him. "I thought that a model legislator like you would not be overly concerned with the title I gave you, but I thought I owed it to the descendant of Codrus, the Kings of Pylos and the cousin of Pisistratus."

"Stupidity once again. I could have ruled, but I did not want that. Be without baseness as I was devoid of pride. My address is: Solon, merchant in Elysium. Remember that. Anyway, that subscription is very nearly the only thing that has made us laugh at your expense. It has been found in general that you have spoken well of the conscript Fathers."

"So much the better, for I feared that I might be reproached for not having distinguished Philippe from Jean-François,[8] since it's true that they're not all friends of the fatherland. But moderation is a good thing, so I applaud the protective guard that is opposed to the ways of action of the monomachites, and which, full of humanity, have preserved the lamp of the Chevalier Sans-Peur, the servant of the God of peace, ever armed, whose conduct in the Senate is, it's said,

---

[7] The last remark is an untranslatable pun: *borgne*, whose literal meaning is "one-eyed" is used metaphorically in French to mean disreputable.

[8] Possibly the dramatist Jean-François de La Harpe (1739-1803) and his august predecessor Philippe Quinault (1633-1688).

nothing less than evangelical. The people cried: 'Curtain!' I can't see, though, that there's much for which to reproach him. A philosopher has observed that while one people becomes civilized, another becomes barbaric. Since the Moors are losing their taste for piracy, since they're presently renouncing living at the expense of their enemies, and want to render liberty to slaves, the laws of equilibrium demanded that the most flourishing nation in Europe should return to slavery, that the divine men who cultivate the arts and the useful men who labor the earth are treated like dogs and that the country's corsairs take possession of all the galleons.

"But let's leave those honest folk to one side and talk about something else. Answer, please, one question that I have to put to you. If a poor people in distress, sighing after liberty, menaced with iron and death, had implored the help of the Athenians in the time when you were their adviser and no one acted without your approval, what would have done?"

"I would immediately have sent them the number of men they had requested."

"Yes, but what if you too had been in such terrible difficulties that you did not have more than enough people to watch over the defense of your hearths?"

"That changes the matter entirely. In such a case my heart would have suffered, because, the first of duties being love of the fatherland, I would not have been able to endanger mine without being criminal. But I would not have wanted the request of my brethren, left without response, to make them presume a murderous indifference on my part. I would probably have done what the Carthaginians did three hundred years after my death."

"And what was that?"

That question, which characterized my ignorance, caused Solon to blush from the base of the chin all the way to the occiput.

"Carthage," he told me, "afflicted by the intrepid Agathocles, was betrayed within by the unworthy Bomilcar, one of its generals. Tyr, besieged by Alexander, informed the Carthaginians of the extremity to which its inhabitants were reduced. Carthage immediately sent them a deputation of thirty of its principal citizens to explain the chagrin it felt in being unable to send them troops. 'At least preserve from the enemy sword,' the Tyrians said, 'that which is most dear to us in the world...'

"That language was understood. Carthage saw its envoys return with a party of women, children and old men from the suppliant city. The Gods did not take long to recompense them for that action. Agathocles withdrew and Bomilcar was crucified."

"Those are fine sentiments on either side," I said to Solon. "I am chagrined to see that that excellent example of centuries past did not offer itself to our memory, but it must be said that for some time, any history of ancient peoples, especially that of republics, has been treated by us virtually as fables. The fine arts have put us to sleep. Now that the sound of the trumpet of war, blown by the Abbé Mably, has succeeded the sweet music of Fontenelle's flageolet, people are generally beginning to think differently."

"I can believe it. At this moment, I have no doubt, you're writing once again about the advantages of livery; one can do nothing better, and I congratulate you for it..."

As I was occupied at that moment in something quite different from which Solon presumed, the good opinion that he had of me rendered me as ashamed as a young woman before whom one speaks of a treasure that she has lost.

"Such a felicitation," I said to him, "would not have found the Camilles and Prudhommes at a loss; as for me..."

"What! What are you doing, then?"

"I'm amusing myself proving that the Earth is an animal. Terentia did not disdain to smile at that philosophical bagatelle, and I'm taking it up."[9]

---

[9] Terentia was Cicero's wife, whom he eventually divorced. She features in an eponymous 1775 tragedy by François Tronchin, in which Denis Diderot also had a hand, but I do not

"Too bad. What's this other scribble?"

"Another tale. You seem very surprised. I'm not, however, the first to have amused himself writing them during public calamities, and even during the horrors of the plague. This one might perhaps have been of some interest; it was taking on a physiognomy not foreign to present circumstances. The intelligent reader would have found analogies therein more flattering to the mind than the raw truth; but I didn't have the courage to continue it."

"Why not?"

"Because the love of slavery is an epidemic disease among us. Since the goblins, specters, ghosts and all the infernal spirits have not able to prevent my recent writings from reaching you in the realms of Pluto, you know what I have done to cure the idle."

"Has their number not diminished?"

"I believe, on the contrary, that it's increasing. It put me in a bad mood; that was what made me set aside that instructive bagatelle."

Solon put out his hand in order to find out what I meant.

"Excuse me," I said to him, "the title will not predispose you in its favor. It's a matter of a virgin who offers herself to the highest bidder. Truly, though, I would be wrong to make a mystery about that article with you; the fair sex was not indifferent to you once. You have composed enough ribald songs, which proves that you loved both women...and wine!"

"Agreed. Both have formed mores by softening the passions; I have only ever criticized excess. You put a woman on the stage? So much the better: the truth will be more pleasant for it."

It did not take him long to satisfy his curiosity.

---

know whether the idea of the Earth as an animal features therein. It does, however, feature in Restif de La Bretonne's *La Découverte australe par un homme volant* (1781) (scheduled to be published by Black Coat Press), which Nogaret would surely have read.

"Mores are respected—good!" he said. "Read, reread, correct and yield to the printer."

Reader, I have obeyed. This is my tale.

BEAUTY UP FOR COMPETITION

*I. Aglaonice decides to marry and offers her hand
on the conditions to be seen.*

Is it a good or a bad thing for a woman to be her own mistress at the age of fifteen? While awaiting the solution to that question, which has its difficulties, by virtue, on the one hand, of the shackles of dependency, and on the other, of the abuses that a young person might make of her liberty, I shall tell you, my brothers, a story of times past, which it is necessary not to regard as apocryphal, for I obtained it from a genuine Traveler, whose great-grandfather heard it recounted by a sage, who had it from his grandfather, who had read it in the Serapeon before the books in that library were employed to heat the baths of Alexandria.[10]

Syracuse, after the memorable siege that it endured on the part of Marcellus, finally enjoyed, although included in the number of lands conquered by the Romans, a liberty submissive to the laws and the benefits of a profound peace. Like the birds of spring who recall verdure after the mortal breath of winter, the arts that the tyrants had frightened away returned to settle in that beautiful abode. The reputation that Archimedes has left behind attracted lovers of the higher sciences from far away, curious to see the debris of the instruments of war that had repelled the enemy for three years in succession, sometimes astonished by such considerable losses.

---

[10] The Serapeon, or, more usually, Serapion, was the temple of Serapis in Alexandria. The spelling employed by Nogaret is employed in Claude Guyon's *Histoire des empires et des républiques* (1736), in a passage that records that the building housed a library.

That city had never seen so many inventors of genius in its bosom, gathered from all the corners of the earth. They were all in an admiration that verged on amazement, all saying that there was no genius comparable with the celebrated Geometer who had defended Syracuse for so long; but that homage was accompanied by a certain discouragement, because none of those men, so lauded elsewhere, took the trouble to give the slightest idea of his talents here. Thus the brilliant light of the torch of day causes the feeble light of the stars of night to disappear.

Aglaonice, a young woman of seventeen, orphaned of her father and mother, having no other relatives than an older sister, whose only wealth was a beauty of which she might be able to take advantage, took it into her head to make all those handsome men of genius do something. All that was required, in order to succeed in that, was the consent of Marius Cornelius,[11] a Roman praetor, a worthy man of sixty for whom a pretty young woman was not yet indifferent, but of a probity

---

[11] Author's note: "*Marcus Cornelius, Praetor peregrinus.* Foreign Praetors governed for two years, one in the quality of Praetor, the other in the quality of Propraetor. They presided over all judgments, but did not judge; judgments were rendered by a certain number of elected citizens drawn from various bodies of State. It was in the Roman year 418 that the Plebeians finally succeeded in winning a victory over the Patricians in also having themselves named to the Praetorate. As I have found in Cornelius the excellent qualities of a good Plebeian, I was curious to know his extraction. Marcellus' expedition, made in the Roman year 540, more than a hundred and twenty years after that great conquest by the Plebeians, gave me grounds to hope that I might find in him a man of the people. My research has verified my presumption. There are honest people everywhere." The praetor in Sicily in 211 B.C., which is presumably the year in which the story is set, was Marcus Cornelius Dolabella, about whom very little is known, thus leaving space for Nogaret to improvise.

so recognized that the Senate, interested in capturing the hearts of the Syracusans, were convinced, with reason, that no better choice could have been made.

Aglaonice had seen the Praetor sitting in his curule chair more than once, but his imposing gravity, the ceremony resulting from a large number of Judges placed around him and perhaps also the crowd of the audience, had frightened her a little. There is, however, no way of keeping the magistracy out of the matter of marriage. One morning, therefore, without consulting the pontiffs as to whether or not it was a good day,[12] Aglaonice went to see Cornelius, and, as she found him much less serious and dressed up than with his long robe fringed with purple, she asked him cheerfully whether he would not see with pleasure all those great makers of machines, so long inactive, finally taking flight and leaving some monument to their knowledge in Syracuse.

"Certainly," Cornelius replied. "I agree that, out of a hundred things imagined by those gentlemen, ninety-nine are almost useless, but in the end, since it's recognized that one good one might be found among the hundred, it's an acquisition that is not to be disdained. What are your means, though? It's not you, presumably, who proposes to set these skillful laborers to work?"

"Excuse me," said Aglaonice.

The good magistrate started to laugh. He thought he had divined her secret, but that was an error on his part. Aglaonice was virtuous without prudishness; knowing that youth and beauty are inappreciable treasures, she thought of putting them

---

[12] Author's note: "The knowledge of that difference of days when one might go to ask for justice was, for a time, a mysterious science, in which the Pontiffs, or 'makers of bridges,' makers of religions, had rendered themselves the master, and which they kept carefully hidden in order to appear necessary and oblige litigants to have recourse to them. Learned citizens ended up making fun of that charlatanism." The untranslatable wordplay derives from the fact that *pont* is French for bridge.

in the balance with lucrative talents, in a way that would enable her to escape criticism.

Whatever the idea was that passed through the Praetor's head, as it is rare for a man to refuse anything to beauty, he replied: "Do as you please," and did not forbid himself to kiss her hand amorously.

The following day, Aglaonice, taxed for a long time by a youth as fickle as it was hasty, tormented and persecuted by the choice of a lover, or at least of a husband, had it published by a herald in Epipoli, in Ortygia, in Achradina and Neapolis—in sum, in all the quarters of Syracuse—that she was disposed to listen to proposals of marriage that anyone cared to make to her, but that she would only give her hand to a Mechanician who had invented some machine that would prove not only his skill but that he knew the heart of women well. As for the birth of the individual, that was the least of her concerns. *Nobilitas sub amore jacet.*[13]

II. Two aspirants present themselves; one offers a mobile tripod, the other a little ivory chariot and ship.

The original proposition of the beauty spread throughout Sicily and passed into Italy and beyond. It was not long before Aglaonice was besieged by visits. All those who believed that they had enough talent to compete wanted, before anything else, to judge the prize that was offered to them. In addition, however, the same artist appeared ten times a day; the beauty was at risk of being stifled by the crowd of her admirers. She made the decision to go and see the Praetor again, convinced that she would obtain there a lodgment that would be infinitely more secure.

Cornelius did not see without chagrin a beginning that presaged that Aglaonice would soon find a husband, but in the end, rendering justice to the thought that he was past the age

---

[13] Nobility gives way to love; the quotation comes from Ovid's *Epistles*.

of pretentions, he consoled himself with the pleasure of serving as her protector.

"I consent," he said, "to lodge you in my house and I promise to treat you as my daughter. Have no fear of the influx of a society that I understand the difficulty of keep away from you. They will be able to see you to the extent that you permit, but I shall be present and you shall have guards."[14]

She did, indeed, and did not go out without being accompanied. It was a further motive for increasing urgency and curiosity. No one was any longer talking about anything but the joy of seeing, and above all of espousing, Aglaonice.

I would never finish if I went into detail about all the things imagined in order to reach that much-desired objective. I shall pass in silence over all those that do not merit a certain attention.

The first one who came, after two long months, to present his masterpiece of Aglaonice was a species of imitator, a native of Pystira, an isle neighboring Smyrna and Petgama, who had constructed, in accordance with known descriptions, a polished steel tripod that walked on its own, so to speak, although it was necessary, beforehand, to set up the mechanisms hidden in each of its three legs.

Aglaonice, who was aiming for the useful, refused the fine present flatly, on the grounds that a tripod that did not flinch when carrying a saucepan is preferable to one that can move away from the fire.

That man was succeeded by a certain Mymecide of Miletus,[15] who offered the beauty an ivory chariot, wrought with so

---

[14] Author's note: "This attention on the part of Cornelius was great; it does not, however, offer anything so extraordinary as to expose it to criticism. It is well-known that the Vestals walked preceded by a Lictor when they appeared in public. Agalonice also had her treasure to guard."

[15] The term Mymecide is featured in Guillaume de Saluste du Bartras' dictionary of arcane words, where it is defined in the 1641 English translation as "a cunning and curious carver in

much artistry and so small that a medium-sized fly could cover it entirely with its wings. That was only half of his tribute; he also presented a pretty ship with three rows of oars, also made of ivory, with all its rigging, every bit as dainty as the chariot.

Aglaonice took great pleasure in considering those two marvels, but when she harnessed the chariot one day to a fly that was a little too big, the insect flew away, transporting the vehicle, through the window.

The ship, for which a font full of water was no less vast than the Atlantic Ocean, could no longer be found one evening when Aglaonice had invited her sister and a few of her friends to come and see it. The Praetor and the ladies were at supper in a room softly lit, not by candles but by the light of the full moon. Aglaonice, asked to show her ship, asked for the vase in which it had been deposited; the surface of the water presented filaments of a greenish hue, which extended from the center to the edges of the bowl, but there was no more ship; it had disappeared.

Aglaonice showed a great deal of ill-humor to the slaves that Cornelius had placed with her to serve her; she accused them of theft with considerable vivacity, adding nevertheless that if they had not stolen the ship, it was probable that they had been clumsy enough to throw it away thoughtlessly, since it was obvious that she was not being presented with the same water.

The Praetor, who was something of a naturalist said to her: "My lady, do not put any of those who are here to serve you on trial. The water you see in the bowl is the same in which you set your pretty trireme afloat a fortnight ago. The green filaments that cover the surface today are nothing but Polyps, a voracious animal species whose form is infinitely variable, which one tries to destroy but only multiply by chopping them up. It's a freshwater Polyp, an ogre in miniature,

---

small works." The etymology invented by Julia Douthwaite in her misleading account of Nogaret's story is wrong.

that has swallowed the ship."[16] He added, in a low voice: "Such a misfortune, could surely never happen to the large vessel of prudent Lutetia."

"Lutetia!" said Aglaonice. "That's a Gaulish city. Are there polyps in cities?"

Smiling, Cornelius took one of her plump little hands, which he squeezed in both of his, and only said, by way of reply: "Aglaonice, you are charming."

"I don't understand all this gibberish," she said.[17] "At any rate, the Miletian has not found the secret of preventing me from remaining a virgin; let him know, I beg you, that a polyp has swallowed half his hopes and that a fly has flown away with the rest."

III. *The story of Téraois-clouni-ca-law-bar-Cochébas; or, the telescope without lenses.*

The slave charged with that commission set out for Mymecide's house. He was stopped on the way and retraced his steps, announcing a Necromancer whose name was a mixture of Greek and Hebrew. His name was Téréos-clouni-ca-law-bar-Cochébas;[18] he had arrived from Egypt, where he had been initiated into the mysteries of the Great Goddess, and he was asking to speak to Aglaonice.

"Send him in," said the Praetor.

Meanwhile, the taps on two fountains were turned, which poured an excellent Greek wine into the cups.

---

[16] The particular freshwater polyp that Cornelius has in mind is presumably a hydra.

[17] Author's note: "The solution will be found in the last chapter."

[18] Author's note: "Théraois-téréos-clouni-ca-law-bar-cochébas is equivalent to false prophet, speculator, pickpocket, etc., etc." The Greek *tereo* can mean "observer"; Bar-Cochebas is a Latinized form of the name of Simon bar Kokhba, the leader of a Judean revolt against the Roman Empire in 132 A.D.

"What do you have to show us that is fine and beautiful?" asked Aglaonice.

"I could, my lady," Bar-Cochébas replied, "talk to you about the secret I have or making gold, but you would doubtless think more of a talent that serves to procure it deservedly and strike good coin. Such as you see me with my long beard and my rather modest accoutrement, I have the right to hope for an alliance to which others have aspired in vain before me. Metals follow me as the trees and rocks once followed the singer of Thrace. You see this long tube of beaten iron; it is my talisman. With the aid of this machine, I can make known to you a host of objects that escape your overly short sight, and of which neither you nor anyone else can have a perfect knowledge without my help. Take, for example, my lady, the moon, from which you are presently receiving such a soft light, which you prefer to the annoying light of a hundred resinous candles, simultaneously wounding to the senses of sight and smell. The moon can serve as proof of what I say. Do you believe it to be inhabited?"

"No, in truth," said Agalonice.

"It's something that it's necessary to suspect," said the Praetor. "Pythagoras thought that the moon is a world similar to ours, where there ought to be animals, the nature of which he could not determine."

"That is true," replied Bar-Cochébas, "and the necessary instrument that he lacked, I have devised. I will render sensible to you things even less probably that what was suspected by Pythagoras."

"That may be," replied Cornelius, whom these magnificent promises did not fail to inspire some interest. "You doubtless intend to talk about the stars, considered as so many suns, and the planetary bodies that are liberally placed around them? I'm a descendant of Anaximenes, who heard it said by Thales, who got it from Heraclitus, who had read it in the verses of Orpheus, that the stars are masses of fire, around which certain terrestrial bodies, which we cannot perceive, carry out periodic revolutions..."

29

"It is charming to listen to Lord Cornelius!" exclaimed Bar-Cochébas. "No one is more learned in Memphis or Babylon, and I'm tempted to believe..."

"In fact," said Aglaonice, "those are compliments indeed, but many things have been announced, and we haven't seen anything. Let's stick to the moon, Sir Mechanician, and hurry up."

Then the Israelite was seen to aim his long tube, composed of three sections devoid of lenses, whose unique property was that of directing the sight and rendering it clearer by separating the considered object from the surrounding objects.

"If the moon is inhabited," said Bar-Cochébas, "the other planetary bodies are too; whoever proves one, proves the other. Such a discovery is of incontestable utility; in any case my lady, take note of one thing: that the parts of the moon that cast the brightest light toward our eyes are massive mountains of silver; so that if we succeed, as I hope, in convincing ourselves that the planet has inhabitants, it will only need a good loudhailer to inform them of our needs. Now, if that is so, and if my lady obtains some pleasure in convincing herself of it, my rivals have nothing more to expect; it is me who will triumph; it is me..."

"Well yes," said Aglaonice, "that follows. Let's see, then."

"See, my lady."

Aglaonice then drew near to the rather broad aperture of the long tube, which hid more than a quarter of her lovely face. Her left hand provided support for the body of the telescope, while her right lowered the eyelid of the other eye; her attention was entirely focused on the object of her consideration.

The Praetor, who had heard talk of mountains of gold and silver, was almost sorry to have had a serious conversation with a man who was, in the final analysis, making mock of the company, or proffering errors in good faith, which has happened to more than one scholar to whom statues have nevertheless been erected. He regarded it as possible that Bar-

Cochébas had fallen into delirium, without being entirely exempt from reason in consequence.

The members of the company, including Cornelius, therefore awaited their turn impatiently to see the seas, the forests, the shiny masses, the rocks and precipices that Bar-Cochébas had advertised, and which Aglaonice had not succeeded in discovering. When each of them, one after another, had become weary of looking, someone wanted to speak to send the promise-maker away and advise him to go see whether, in all those supposed worlds, he could find a jewel similar to the one that he had dared to aspire, but they looked to the left and right and all the corners of the apartment in vain; the supposed inventor of the tube had disappeared. Aglaonice and the ladies found themselves, to their great astonishment, relieved of their purses and some of their jewelry.

The Praetor tried to catch up with the clever rogue and make sure that he never saw the pyramids again, but as his beard and cassock were found at the bottom of the stairs, it was thought that it would be a waste of time running after him. Aglaonice was not the woman of the company who had suffered most from that accident; Cornelius was not a man to let it go unrepaired.

IV. Apparent neglect on the part of physicians.
Serious conversation between the Praetor and old
Cyaxare, former secretary of good King Hyeron.

Meanwhile, it seemed that the orphan beauty's project had failed complete, for I count for little an heir of Euclid who talked to her about dioptrics and catoptrics and made her a long serious of propositions, the last of which—the only one that was intelligible to Aglaonice—was no more welcome than all the rest.

The days succeeded one another without any mention being heard of anything, and the beauty's self-esteem was suffering a little therefrom. She had time to think that her charms had not put such a large number of artists to work, and that they had not had the effect that she had promised herself at all.

One consoles oneself as best one can. The windows of her apartment overlooked the flowery banks of the Arethuse;[19] she frequently cast her eyes upon that spring, whose good fortune made her hope for another Alpheus. Prosperity came to her while she slept, she told herself, and she tried to go to sleep to the amorous murmur of its waves, surrendering herself to sweet thoughts and the void in her heart. She did not know that the appearances of inaction hide labor, most of it undertaken by skillful individuals, and that all of it was about to appear at once, one fine morning.

The Praetor, whose age and the sacred title of Protector had eliminated from the ranks, scarcely able to talk to Aglaonice about love, conversed with her about politics, and his grateful ward deigned to listen while waiting for something better.

The Senate had charged Cornelius with analyzing the character of the Syracusans in order to discover in what manner they could be managed without embittering minds so versatile and always less submissive than independent.

Cyaxare, a former secretary of the good King Hyeron[20] came to see the Praetor from time to time. That former servant

---

[19] Author's note: "A Sicilian spring that runs through Ortygia, the quarter of Syracuse in which Cornelius was lodged." It was named after the nymph Arethusa, the object of the lust of the river god Alpheus.

[20] Author's note: "Hyeron II. The historians who have mentioned that King, an honest man, have all praised his good taste for the science and his love for the public good. 'My subjects,' he said, 'are my children and the State is my family.' Remarkable words! He was mourned like a father. Time has not damaged his reputation." Hiero II ruled Syracuse from 270-215 B.C. His grandson Hieronymus, who took the throne after his death, was only fifteen at the time, and an instrument

had displeased the young Hyeronimus, the unworthy son of the best of princes, an insolent dissipater of the treasure destined for the embellishment of the city and to pay the defenders of the fatherland, a violator of old treaties and, in sum, a declared enemy of public wellbeing. The young insensate had perished not long before under the vengeful swords of citizens in revolt one day when he had left Syracuse to go to the land of the Leontines.

Cyaxare was no more satisfied with Hippocrates and Epycides, enterprising Praetors,[21] usurpers of limitless power, maladroit politicians whose seditious maneuvers had been the cause of the siege, because both had openly declared themselves for the Carthaginians.

The old servant spoke as an eye-witness of everything that had happened for many years; he also knew by tradition the mind and heart of the Syracusans, and, in more than one conversation with Cornelius he put his mind to giving the Senate an accurate idea of it.

"The Syracusans need a King," he told him. "They're capable of an extreme fidelity and a limitless attachment. This city has, at all times, been exposed to strange scenes. It can be compared to a sea, more often agitated by stormy winds than refreshed by the breath of zephyrs. Exposed to the most terrible revolutions, it has passed from liberty to slavery. It has groaned under the iron scepter of Denis,[22] and has breathed easy under the mild reign of the immortal Hyeron. It has sometimes been seen surrendered to the caprices of an unbri-

---

in a power-struggle between his two uncles, so the blackening of his name by historians might be a trifle unjust.

[21] Author's note: "Praetors of the Senate of Syracuse, in the fashion of the Carthaginians." The two were brothers educated in Carthage, who held off Marcellus' siege of Syracuse for some time before the Carthaginian fleet sent to relieve the siege turned back and left the city to its fate.

[22] Denis is the French form of the name of the Sicilian tyrant Dionysius I (432-367 B.C.)

dled populace and sometimes submissive to the authority of laws.

"Such opposite extremes could be attributed to the Syracusans themselves, whose levity was their dominant character, but the primary cause of so many evils is the form of government, composed of two ever-militant powers and deprived of a third whose counterweight might have established equilibrium; with the result that liberty, too often groaning under the hand of aristocrats, rose up more than once, and rendered Sicily witness to the bloodiest scenes.

"What also renders the government of the city less easy is that its citizens, bellicose although frivolous, have not forgotten the signal victories won in Africa by their ancestors and their advantages over the Athenians, too proud of a maritime power that our people successfully disputed more than once with those rivals jealous of their glory.

"Although one has the right to say that wealth has softened the heart of the Syracusans and given them a kind of distance from all that has no affinity with games and pleasures, it must be admitted that they are nevertheless resistant on occasions to the voice of their orators, and then become capable of the greatest enterprises. The same men who went to sleep in the bosom of confidence wake up terrible and threatening, with the most superb heads, and, in their frenetic transports, massacre everything that has contributed to harming them.

"I regard them, therefore, as men inappropriate to enjoy a complete liberty or to accustom themselves to an entire servitude. They need a King, and I want that; but it is also appropriate that they should always be the masters of their own revolutions, when the utility if it is generally recognized by the most sound minds. The Prince will then enjoy the fine advantage of facilitating its execution, and everyone will be happy; otherwise, Rome will probably not have in the Syracusans a people on whom they can reliably count."

That idea of Cyaxare, of giving them another King, did not please Cornelius; he tried to make that honest man, misled by the memory of the great virtues of Hyeron—as if such sovereigns were not phenomena, to whom nature took centuries to give birth!—abandon it.

"The Roman Senate does not think as you do," he told him. "I don't know who you would designate today to reign, but you, who scarcely think of it, would be on the throne now if Rome, which makes Kings, had judged it appropriate to its own interests and those of Syracuse that the constitution of the city should be other than that of a Republic.

"Sicily conserves its ancient rights and customs, as you know, and Rome does not extend that distinction to many its conquered lands. You are more her friends and confederates than a submissive people, as you also know, since it is true that Rome does not levy and tribute from you by the entitlement of monument and the price of victory.[23]

Sicily is Italy's neighbor; you regard yourselves as being part of it. Kings, Cyaxare, too often affect an absolute power; their procedures, stripped of the forms of justice, then become violent actions rather than. Do you count for nothing the advantage of only obeying laws that you have made yourself, and of choosing your magistrates annually? No more judges henceforth that the parties cannot remove; and it is the ad-

---

[23] Author's note: "Sicily, in becoming a Roman province, conserved its ancient rights and customs. The Sicilians were not treated like the Spaniards and Carthaginians, on whom the Romans imposed a tribute as the price of victory. *Quasi victoriae praemium ac poena belli.* Let us say everything, for the best things only last for a time. So long as Rome was only dominant in Italy, the people were governed as confederates; the laws of each republic were followed; and Sicily, which added a great deal to the strength of Rome, of which it was the storehouse and granary, was to enjoy that privilege for a long time. As Montesquieu says, however; 'Afterwards, that liberty, so vaunted, only existed at the center, and tyranny at the extremities.'" The quotation, from Cicero, translates loosely as "as if it were a reward for victory and a penalty of defeat."

vantage of the Valerian law, which ought to have all its force here as it does among us, that the people now have the right to pronounce the death penalty against the enemies of the state."

Cyaxare was not without a reply to those observations.

"As all Kings," he said, "do not resemble Hyeron, all Praetors do not resemble Cornelius, and Rome will only leave you here for a short time...but I do not want to anticipate the evils that your successors might occasion here subsequently. Let us enjoy the present; I yield to your arguments."

Thus reasoned the good Cornelius and old Cyaxare, and at those moments the Praetor scarcely thought about the annoyances of the beautiful Aglaonice, which were increasing every day, by virtue of the silence of the mechanicians on whom she had founded her hopes, and by the nature of those grave conversation, by which she was somewhat embarrassed. But Cyaxare had no sooner left the apartment than the keenest interest in favor of the lovely orphan was reborn in Cornelius' heart. He begged her pardon so obligingly for having talked in her presence about anything other than what might please her that the most passionate of men would have seemed less expressive and less amiable.

V. The Flying Chariot and the Conspirators

Thirty days had gone by since the adroit thief who made people read the stars in order to rummage in their pockets had dared, in the magistrate's own house and before his very eyes, to obtain such a good result from his villainous métier. Amour and the arts seemed to be sleeping lethargically, and the good Praetor was secretly laughing at the thought that the beauty might perhaps not succeed in finding an abode other than his own house.

As he was yielding to the deceptive charms of that pleasant reverie, however, a great ardelion arrived, a hasty valet dressed up to the nines. He came on behalf of Lord Lycaon-agrios-kai tyrannos akeirotos-kai apenès-kai polémios-Brogli-

Lam-Beden-Mail-Aristos,[24] and begged Cornelius to permit that a machine be brought into the largest and most open of his gardens, the marvelous effect of which Aglaonice would see in a few days' time. The emissary added that the public might enjoy the spectacle, because the machine surpassed the clouds.

The lord in question was a direct descendant of a Spartan, one of those who, having acquired so much glory a hundred years before under the leadership of Gylippus, has ended up, like the miser Polemarchus,[25] by tarnishing the reputation of Sparta. A considerable number of those Lacedemonians, obliged to flee, had taken refuge in Sicily.

Aristos, born in the country, had no lack of castles and fine lands. He was one of those who could not bear the idea of a perfect equality, and had not yet despaired of the success of a tyrannical plot. It did not seem credible to him that nature had given the people the same organs as patricians; he could not imagine that they were capable of governing without their help, and even less of forcing themselves to obey.

That identity of constitution with the Roman Republic did not appear to him, in any case, to be so well-established or so strongly supported that the Syracusans could not be recalled to their former regime. A daughter of the people, a poor young woman like Aglaonice, would surely not refuse to accept a sum of money or some other advantageous proposition to favor the project he had formed of entering Ortygia by night and slaughtering the garrison. However, the dangers of the project

---

[24] Author's note: "Lycaon etc. In Latin, *lupus crudelis, praestantissimus*; in French, *cruel and powerful beast*. The whole is abridged." Lycaon was a king of Arcadia who unwisely put the omniscience of Zeus to the test and was transformed into a wolf

[25] Not the Athenian Polemarchus featured in Plato but a Spartan mentioned by Pausanias, although the word was a title rather than a name and thus appears somewhat promiscuously in Greek writings.

sometimes enfeebled his hope. Then his sad joy was that of the guilty; he only laughed bitterly.

It will be remembered that the Praetor had said to Aglaonice that no one would speak to her except in his presence. That mark of attention, which only had beneficence for its objective, did not worry Aristos to the extent that he regarded it as impossible to replace Cornelius by some woman in Aglaonice's confidence. As he excelled in the art of composing his exterior, and the perfection of his hypocrisy shielded him from all suspicion, it was not difficult for him to make Cornelius understand that it was very embarrassing for a man when he had to talk about love before his fellow; that the resultant constraint made the suitor seem so awkward that it was not astonishing that no one had succeeded thus far with Aglaonice; otherwise, it was more than probable that someone would even have made her forget the conditions she had imposed.

"Oh, let that not be an obstacle," said the Praetor. "I know that she has a sister to whom she's very attached. I'll cede my place to her. I don't intend to embarrass either you or Aglaonice. If you think it advantageous to talk to her before showing her your discoveries, come tomorrow; you can chat entirely at your ease."

Aristos did not fail. The machine followed, guided by a Cantabrian, a worthy confidant of such a great lord. He too was a lord, an aristocrat of the low Pyrenees, a land of dancing where the humanity of his fellows had rendered a great many things utterly problematic. Neighbors were not neighbors. Brothers were not brothers. Fire and water only belonged to a small number of men more powerful than the rest, and although everything was common in the land, brothers and neighbors ate grass and died of thirst if they did not have the wherewithal to pay.[26] At any rate, that lord was merely the

---

[26] Author's note: "This horrible abuse has not yet been abolished; however, it is on a par with those of the chapter of Saint Claude." The chapter of St. Claude in the Jura was the object

valet of the other. Delegated to look after the machine, he had remained in the garden, accompanied by eight or ten Cyclopes, while Aristos tried to convert the two sisters to his opinions.

I cannot deny that Aristos was a man to fear in the art of tactics; he had given proof of it. As for mechanics, that was another matter; circumstance alone had made him a mechanician. One would, however, be forced to admit that he also possessed, to a certain degree, a knowledge of motive forces and equilibrium; but one would see at the same time that he was as reckless as he was vain, two great faults against which it is often good to guard.

Aglaonice, therefore, alerted to his visit, was awaiting him with no other witness than Bazilide, her sister. Aristos was introduced. It would have been stupid to open up straight away, so he adopted a light tone and only spoke at first about a discovery that promised him the advantage of meriting the hand of Aglaonice—whom he regarded as fundamentally impertinent, since she was nothing but a peasant.

"My ladies," he said, "I have learned that a rogue who aspired less to the honor of espousing you than to the profit he could obtain from his skill has robbed you of your jewels while amusing you with a telescope that he had stolen from the King of Egypt's museum,[27] which would have merited that

---

of a rebellion by the bondsmen of six parishes in 1770 and again in 1789.

[27] Author's note: "A learned Benedictine has rendered this probable. He is said to have read in an old manuscript that in the time of Ptolemy usage had been made of those optical substances by means of which hazard has since procured us the advantage of adapting lenses for approach magnification. I do not know why the quibbler L. Dutens casts doubt on the statement of that monk." The reference is to Louis Dutens (1730-1812), who published his *Recherches sur l'origine des découvertes attribuées aux modernes* [Research on the Origins

Lord Cornelius have him whipped by his lictors. In truth, ladies, I find the Praetor and you possessed of a confidence and generosity of soul…you have not heard the history, then, of these refugees from the land of the Pharaohs?

"Anyway, the thievery of Bar-Cochébas and the trouble he must have taken are foreign to my object; let us only speak of his imposture—I mean the hope that he falsely gave you of revealing to you that which he was sure that you would never see. Yes, my ladies, his talisman is devoid of virtue; its mechanism is imperfect; he knew that very well; and believe that, as for his loudhailer, if he had had one, he would only have used it for himself.

"But even if you had read the stars distinctly, you would still have the regret of being separated from them by a distance that no man has thus far been able to cross. Consider the moon, and see there…what? Light and shadow; it is not of any interest from which any great satisfaction might result. The beautiful, the marvelous thing, would be to transport oneself to the very heart of this planet, to see there with one's own eyes and touch with one's hands that which reason gives us the right to presume is there."

"That would be very fine, indeed," said Aglaonice, "but what means is there of getting there?"

"My lady, I flatter myself on succeeding in that; I will take you there, if you are curious to make the voyage, and if it pleases the twelve great gods, we shall marry up there."

The conversation was interrupted at that moment by the attention that each of them felt obliged to pay to a rather disagreeable sound that made itself heard, and was somewhat reminiscent of that of the friction to which the axle of a pulley that has not been greased for a long time is subject.

One could pause without error upon that conjecture; Cornelius, without anyone suspecting it, was present at the conversation, and even seated in a very comfortable armchair.

---

of Discoveries Attributed to the Moderns] in 1766; his skepticism was justified, as Nogaret undoubtedly knew.

A counterweight kept him suspended above floor level, in the middle of a thick section of stone wall once contrived or that purpose; a small opening made at the height of a man and masked by a light cedar-wood panel gave the listener the facility of hearing everything.

That balance, or whatever machine it might be, was not Cornelius' invention; it is easily believable that it had been used more than once when one considers that the house he occupied was the same one that had once been the residence of the tyrants. Cornelius was not one of them, but he had given some thought to Lord Aristos' proposition and, either by virtue of suspicion or pure curiosity, had made the effort to listen in.

Our three individuals were looking in all directions, anxiously, when a cat, which emerged from a neighboring room and appeared to their eyes, made them believe that the sound they had heard was merely that of the door, which the anima had caused to grate on its hinges by pushing it.

Aristos pretended to doubt that, however, and took advantage of the circumstance to explain the true objective of his visit.

"Do you feel completely secure, my ladies," he said, "in this part of the city where it is now not permitted for any Syracusan to live?"[28]

That reflection of a soldier, prompted by a cat, appeared to them to have a comical seriousness. They laughed at it wholeheartedly.

"Security is a fine thing," Aristos continued, undisconcerted. "Laugh as much as you please; for myself, I cannot accustom myself to the idea that this quarter of Syracuse is absolutely forbidden to us. It's a tyranny. For, after all, of what are they afraid? Supposing, in any case, that some

---

[28] Author's note: "As the isle of Ortygia was surrounded by two good ports, and also had a citadel, that part of the city became very important, and was reserved for the Praetor alone."

good Syracusan wanted to shake off the yoke of Roman domination, would that be such a bad thing? Don't you think that an oligarchical government, composed of a few nobles, who would act in the interests of the people, would be infinitely more agreeable? You're Syracusan, my ladies: it must cost your hearts a great deal to see all Sicily thus become a Roman province."

"I don't see anyone complaining about it," replied Bazilide.

"Neither do I," said Aglaonice, "And furthermore, from what I've heard said of Cornelius in several conversations he has had with the wisest of men, I conclude that Syracuse is infinitely more fortunate in being governed in accordance with the principles of the Roman constitution that when it was necessary to obey the absolute will of the nobles. Cyaxare, the sage to whom I'm referring, doesn't think differently today."

"In that case," said Aristos, "I bear in my heart for your Cyaxare all the amity that I have vowed to the Demagogues. What a citizen!"

"But Monsieur," said Bazilide, "If it were the case that the Syracusans wanted to change situation now, it would be necessary for rivers of blood to flow; the walls of the city would be stained by it; let us try to forget it..."

"The conversation has certainly changed direction," said Aglaonice, looking at Aristos. That is not, I think, the motive that brought you here, my lord?"

"No other than that of uniting himself with you could animate anyone who has the good fortune to know you, and although you live here in the Praetor's house, people think too well of you to presume the good fortune of that aged foreigner."

"He serves me as a father," said Aglaonice. "I beg you to speak better of him."

"Good—but the advantage is all on his side. You would have had no lack of men as hospitable."

"Let us talk," said Aglaonice, "about what your talent for the mechanical arts has led you to undertake, or break off the conversation..."

Aristos thought that the young woman, whatever she said, was not sufficiently grateful not to allow herself to be caught by the charms of vanity.

"Well, my lady," he said, "on the subject of the machine about which you are questioning me, I will confide a secret to you that you will doubtless keep for me, when you know that it was constructed by design to favor the passion that I have for you. Beautiful as you are, you are born to reign; and I shall think about that from now on. If one could do at a stroke everything that one would like to do...

"But before anything else, it is necessary for this city to shrug off the yoke.[29] What you have to do in that circumstance cannot be treated as rebellion. Rome has stolen our liberty; nothing is more natural than that we should recover it."

"It was to liberate us, and not to dominate us," said Bazilide, "that the Romans battled our tyrants, and with them the Carthaginians who served them as supporters. The majority of us, animated by a long resentment, hoped to be defeated in order not to remain forever enslaved..."

Aristos had said too much for the ladies not to be tempted to denounce him to Cornelius. Aglaonice thought that it would be as well to know everything. Pallor, however, had spread over her face...

"One could listen to you for a long time," she said, "if it were possible to have the slightest hope, but I foresee that too many citizens would be the futile victims of it."

---

[29] Author's note: "Although this is only a historiette—which is to say, a mixture of fiction and truth, I am not so very far from the truth, from the history that serves as my basis. After the capture of Syracuse by Marcellus, there really were residual wars on the part of the partisans of tyranny, and it is also true that those wars had no consequences."

"Don't be afraid," said Aristos. "It's not a matter of killing them all; a certain number would suffice. I can answer for a good third who are not as obdurate as your Cyaxare. Then again, we have a few intelligent men, especially the leaders. But the essential thing would be for me to be able to get in here under cover of darkness."

"And what would you do here?" asked Aglaonice.

"The salvation of Syracuse depends on the death of all the soldiers there are around this palace. Deliver them to my vengeance; immediately afterwards, I'll take you away. As for the Praetor, I consent to show him mercy if you still deign to take an interest in him..."

Aglaonice shivered.

"Then," he continued, "instead of only being the wife of an obscure citizen, you would command them all in the quality of the wife of one of the foremost in the State. Look...this machine that I've constructed can transport me to unknown regions. I've said more to you; I've spoken about the Moon, and I really don't despair of going as far as that..."

At this point, Aristos' eyes, and his entire physiognomy, no longer depicted anything but a man gone astray; his mind became unhinged at that moment.

"Now," he went on, "since the populace, whom we've tried in vain to seduce, is too stupid to listen to pour propositions; since even our soldiers refuse to obey us, it's not mountains of gold that I'll go to search for up there; we have no lack of them. It's men that we need: a hundred machines like mine will bring down an entire army. The reservations of kinship won't hold them back like imbeciles in the presence of others. Thus, my lady, your individual happiness, mine and that of our partisans will be assured forever. As for the Romans, Carthage will stand up to them again..."

The ladies scarcely heard the end of his speech. The madness of which he had just given proof in talking about his lunar army had given them time to recover their wits, and they ended up uttering a new burst of laughter, which did not finish. Politeness demanded, however, that they justify that spe-

44

cies of incivility. They gave him to understand that he ought not to interpret it as anything but the effect of a doubt, very pardonable in women whose knowledge was not as extensive as his. As it seemed necessary, at the same time, that they get rid of him, they flattered his hopes, pressing him to attempt the aerial voyage whose success was the only means of convincing them that it was his destiny to make his party dominant and drive the Romans out of Sicily.

The double temerity of Aristos blinded him too much for him to doubt the sincerity of Aglaonice's final words. He took his leave of her and went straight into the garden to rejoin his dear Cantabrian, whom he took to one side in order to tell him what had happened. Then he went to the machine, to give the order to make it ready to take off.

VI. The Tragic end of Aristos and the Cantabrian lord.

Aristos had not reached the bottom of the staircase when the Praetor appeared in the apartment with an expression as cheerful as usual, still gallant, and asked Aglaonice whether that equivalent of a private conversation had produced a good effect. The ladies did not know whether to laugh or adopt a serious attitude.

"You aren't saying anything!" said Cornelius. "Is that because your heart is already captured?"

"It's necessary to tell you," she replied, "and I can't hide it from you, that that lover, if he is one, is nothing but a monster that it's necessary to stifle immediately."

Cornelius secretly enjoying that sentiment of indignation, pretended to interpret it to Aglaonice's advantage.

"You're so charming," he said, "that it would be necessary to forgive a man who lost his head in your presence a good deal."

"It's not a matter of that," said Bazilide, excitedly. "Rather make sure of Aristos; he has formed a project to murder everyone in Ortygia, and your person is not safe from him."

"What! Is that all?" said Cornelius, smiling. "Oh, my ladies, you're accomplices. Why, Aglaonice is hiding it from me that she might have become Queen? However, she has every interest in my making her fortune; I even like her enough to assure her that a crown of flowers placed on her head by an honest citizen would honor her more than a diadem that she would receive from the hands of a new Agathocles."[30]

You can imagine the surprise of the two ladies at that observation by the Praetor; they looked at one another without saying a word.

Cornelius extracted them from their embarrassment by revealing the manner in which he had learned everything.

"Have no fear," he said to them. "There's more extravagance than reason in your Aristos' project. However, prudence requires that he presume that you have kept his confidence secret from me; otherwise, I shall be forced to take action, which would assuredly be futile. You'll see that within two hours, Aristos will have rid us of his presence.

Cornelius then went into the garden, as if he knew nothing about Aristos' perfidy, in order to see the preparations of the machine. It was a light chariot, to which to large wings had been fitted made of a fine linen fabric, supported by long struts of whalebone gathered together at the point where each wing was attached, and divergent that the opposite extremity. Those two wings took the place of wheels. They were deployed with the aid of hidden springs that were activated by means of a handle; then extended above the chariot, which they covered with their vast span, offering to the curious eye a motto that was not Aristos': *As the wind transports.*[31]

---

[30] Author's note: "The tyrant who caused Syracuse to lose the liberty rendered to it by Timoleon."

[31] The phrase *Autant en emporte le vent* [As the wind transports] subsequently became the French translation of the title of Margaret Mitchell's novel *Gone with the Wind* and the film based thereon. Nogaret doubtless derived it, as Mitchell did,

Time was pressing; they hastened to smear it, while waiting to be able to kill the author.

An awkwardness on Aristos' part had doubled the means. To the swingle-bar of the vehicle were hitched two large swans, which he had received as a present from a descendant of Cycnus, King of Liguria, and a relative of Phaeton.[32]

Aristos mounted his chariot. The springs continuing to move, the vast wings beat the air with so much force and speed that the vehicle and its conductor rose up more than six hundred feet, always diminishing in volume, to the extent of soon seeming to be nothing but an owl. It was remarked at the machine's departure that the swans would have sufficed,[33] or

---

from *Isaiah* 64:6: "our iniquities, like the wind, have taken us away." The "us" to which the Biblical verse refers are sinners.

[32] Cycnus of Liguria, who killed himself after Phaeton's fall, was probably his lover, so "relative" is euphemistic.

[33] Author's note: "Swans have been successfully employed for this purpose, it is said, by the Emperor Ki three thousand years before the Montgolfiers. See the *Memoirs on the present state of China* by Père le Comte, letter VI. A celebrated writer of our days believed it very sincerely, and I do too." The "celebrated writer" is Bernardin de Saint-Pierre, who commented at length in *Études de la nature* (1784) on Louis Le Comte's account in *Nouveau mémoire sur l'état present de la Chine* (1696), although he pointed out that other sources attributed the tale to the Emperor Tam, who reigned two thousand years after the (mythical) Kieu, or Ki.

The version of the story in *L'Antipode de Marmontel* adds a supplement to this note: "The Marquis de Vargas Machuca, it is said in a Naples gazette, possesses a manuscript printed in Bergamo in 1670 containing a long treatise on a "flying ship," which, with the aid of four copper balls, rose up to a certain height. The author explains the construction of those balls, and how the vessel can be steered with sails and oars. Another Italian writer, Bouilly, wrote the above in 1679, closely ap-

that they were surplus to requirements, because the machine carried them away vertically, while they were making an effort to fly straight ahead. A worse augury was, however, that one of them was singing; that was the trumpet of death.

Cornelius, then having no more to do than look up, had rejoined the ladies. A crowd of people had come from all directions to see the spectacle. The men, prompt to judge, said of Aristos that he had more genius than all the physicists of previous centuries, and that he would cause Icarus and the sun's bastard to be forgotten. One enthusiast even sustained that if the great Marcellus had been a witness to that prodigious ascension, he would be bound to agree that even Archimedes, a man so knowledgeable about statics that he called him a Briareus,[34] might not have imagined such a vehicle.

At the moment when the ecstasy reached its peak, however, a westerly wind plunged into the wings of the aristocratic machine and made it quit the vertical direction. The chariot, then drawn by the swans and pushed by the wind, followed a route parallel to the horizon, much more rapidly than the conductor would have wished.

---

proaching Montgolfier's idea. He thought of enabling us to swim in the air, as fish do in water 'with the aid of a bladder that will be filled with a fluid lighter than the atmospheric air.'" The first reference is to a hypothetical design for a flying ship published by Francesco Lana de Terzi. The subsequent reference to an Italian document of 1679 is enigmatic, and Bouilly is not an Italian name, although by 1800 Nogaret would have been familiar with the French writer and Revolutionary Jean-Nicolas Bouilly.

[34] Livy claims that Marcellus referred to Archimedes as a "geometrical Briareus" while complimenting him (posthumously) on his contributions to the defense of Syracuse, Briareus being a mythical giant with fifty heads and a hundred arms.

It was about to brush, at the entrance to the port of Trogile, the tip of the Timoleon beacon,[35] a famous obelisk two hundred feet high erected in memory of the liberty ren-

---

[35] Author's note: "This beacon, which I place at the entrance to the port of Trogile, and of which there is no other question in history, since there is only mention there of a tower, was probably constructed from the produce of the bronze statues that Timoleon had ignominiously cast down from their pedestals and sold at auction, after having put the tyrants figured therein on trial.

"Let us say in passing of that illustrious avenger of liberty that he had it published to the sound of trumpets that those who wanted to come with tools had only to set to work to demolish the fortress, and had tribunals erected in their place, in order that the ramparts would never be divined of the very prisons where the citizens had lost their liberty. Let us say that in that epoch he made tyranny and tyrants disappear not only in Syracuse but throughout Sicily, and that, far from having the pride to want to rule alone thereafter, he also forbade himself the insatiable thirst for riches and the perpetuity of honors. Syracuse became his fatherland. He spent the rest of his life as a simple individual, savoring the satisfaction of seeing so many cities and so many thousands of people owe the repose and felicity they enjoyed to him. So he was always respected, and consulted like an oracle. Plutarch even said that 'when he was old, the Syracusans introduced him into their assemblies mounted on his chariot, always as if in triumph and always to the sound of universal acclamations.'

"Frenchmen, you know in your hearts what passed in the soul of Timoleon. It is him who, sometimes at the tribune and sometimes on the battlefield, repeats to you incessantly: *Age, in manibus vestries libertatem, opem, spem futur temporis geritis.*" The quotation is improvised from a passage in Quintus Curtius' life of Alexander; the key section translates as "in your hands you now carry freedom, power and hope for the future."

dered to the city by the Corinthian captain, who defeated Denis and the Carthaginians. They thought that it was the end of Aristos, and that he was about to perish, hooked there. Let us leave him for a moment fluttering around the fatal luminary.

It is not possible, my dear reader, that you do not have some interest in his faithful Cantabrian and that you are not so much sorry as surprised not to see him here in the same cabriolet; I ought to tell you that, if he did not take his leave of the company too, it was because it had been agreed that he would remain behind for the benefit of service. His instructions included putting the world on the alert and also that, as a faithful observer of the voyage, he would be the first to publish an account of it. But it is necessary to show you the degree of elevation to which the zeal of his minister bore him. He dominated all the spectators; he was on the platform of the citadel; he perched higher still...

Imagine twenty vigorous men, lined up in a square, their backs bent, with both hands on their knees, in the guise of flying buttresses. On those strong arches pose twenty standing men, their arms extended, holding very firm. Above those men are placed others, each of whose feet is carried on the shoulders of the robust champions forming the first stage—and so on, always diminishing and varying the attitudes. Suppose, finally, a pyramid whose summit is terminated by four men, arms in the air, sustaining a shield, on which our faithful confidant is standing, his eyes turned toward the beacon where his friend is in great danger. One presumes that his head is spinning at that spectacle, and that he is about to fall backwards on to the parvis.

He does, in fact, fall, but the cause has not been divined. The need or the desire to sneeze grips a good plebeian who is there, a near neighbor in the pyramid, his elbows leaning on the parapet. With the effort that he makes to disengage his head, his body being bent double, his backside bumps into that of one of the curbed Atlases making the angle and base of the pyramid. Instantly, all of them tip over, all of them fall. The Cantabrian and twenty of his caryatids tumble pell-mell to the feet of the walls of the citadel, like the Gauls once precipitated from the Capitol; but misfortune determines that a part of the military band placed there to play a fanfare at the departure of the vehicle perishes with them.

Music-stands, instruments, players and spectators were scattered everywhere. As for the rest of the children of Bel Babel Belphegor, who had only collapsed on one another and the Paros marble paving the platform, the majority were only crippled. But the poor plebeian, on whose body three quarters of the mass had landed, was so maltreated that only one breath remained to him. He was to end like the terrible blind man who was crushed by the satraps, persecutors and tyrants of the Hebrews on whom he had wanted to take revenge. But the character of the dying man was not such as to be worthy of such noble comparisons. He had been cheerful all his life and he said, as he rendered his last sigh, that every cloud has a silver lining.

Let us now return our gaze to the winged machine and its conductor. A cry of dolor made itself heard on the part of a number of confederates placed here and there on the long chain of fortifications raised on the landward side and all along the coast. But the tragic end of Aristos would not have made enough noise if the Syracusans had been the only witnesses. The Gods wanted the death of that new Bellerophon to serve as an example to a large number of peoples.

A southerly wind, more impetuous than the first, carrying him away from the obelisk, caused him to traverse the Sicilian Sea and drove him in a straight line more than a hundred and twenty miles from Syracuse toward the northern entrance of the strait of Messina, a dangerous passage, where the gulf of Charybdis is located and the dogs of Scylla are heard barking incessantly. As he was completely lost to sight, it was necessary on either side to wait until the next day to discover what might have become of him.

Cavaliers dispatched by the Praetor, well mounted on Arab horses, set off for Messina at full tilt, and toward the evening of the following day, reported that the voyager, drawn down toward the sea, after having bobbed for a long time between the two reefs, had finally fallen on to the pointed rocks of Scylla, where laborers had even shown them the debris of the chariot, still suspended there. As for the individual, as no vestige of him had been found, the cavaliers added that the sea had surely engulfed him, along with all his great names.

That conjecture seemed as probable as it was satisfying to Cornelius and the ladies. However, those Syracusans who, not being fully informed, had only seen in the ascension of the machine a novelty in the success of which they were interested, were genuinely afflicted by the accident. As it was a discovery of which centuries to come would surely not fail to take advantage, however, and the invention would be attributed to them, their chagrin did not last long. On the part of the conspirators, it was mortal. All of them—with the exception of two, who threw the few drachms they had received in the faces of the others—departed for Messina, and engraved the following epitaph on a slab of marble they embedded in the rock:

It is noble, it is great, to fall from so high.

VII. The Flute-Player

"Another marriage failed," said Cornelius to Aglaonice, when the cavaliers had left his apartment. "It's a pity that I'm over sixty; no one could console me better than you for the annoyances of widowhood. A little vanity leads you to demand extraordinary things. If I read your heart correctly, your desires have the simultaneous objectives of youth, talent and fortune. If you were less pretty, you would not deserve to be pardoned for that excess of ambition. It would be necessary to diminish the extent of your pretentions, removing youth, for example, and the creative spirit so prejudicial to men who have too precipitate a confidence in their discoveries. Fortune is in my power; let it finally be sufficient for you, since you are now convinced that your mechanicians cannot succeed in contenting you."

"You would like me to limit myself to the advantages of fortune," Aglaonice replied. "Pardon me, my dear protector, but I am not sufficiently mistress of myself to stop there, and I believe you to be too generous to demand it of my gratitude. Let me tell you frankly that you have divined the secret of my heart. Yes, I do indeed aspire to everything that you have just explained in three words. But you despair of the accomplishment of my desires, while I have the greatest confidence in their fulfillment. The less one succeeds the more one strives to succeed. Self-esteem, and the desire to be talked about do indeed enter into it for two thirds, but you will allow me the small vainglory of attributing the rest to myself. Come on, agree that I merit grace on that article. You have said such flattering things to me so many times that it would cost me too much to think that you were deceiving me."

Aglaonice was not flattering herself without reason. Soon, two new competitors appeared on the scene, whose masterpieces would have caused hesitation over the choice if, when two things are equally admirable, the preference were not due to the one that brings a greater profit.

Of the two men in question, one, aged fifty, was an honest German, or rather a good Frank, a free man whose forefathers had lived on the banks of the Ister. One might have taken his talents and his politeness for Thamyris of Eritrea, a descendant of the celebrated Thamyris known as the rival of the muses. Our ancestors were not all as amiable.

As for his name, it resembled all the others, flaying the ears; it was Wak-wik-vauk-an-son-Frankestein. He excelled in the divine art of harmony, without ever having learned music, and furthermore, was a very skillful mechanician. His bearing and his physiognomy did not leave Cornelius without anxiety from the moment he appeared before Aglaonice, tall of stature, clad in a narrow surcoat that, not descending below the knees, showed off the entire framework of that handsome body.

His homage consisted of a laminated metal statue as tall as a man, dressed in the Sicilian fashion, seated in a rolling armchair and holding a flute in each of its hands, which he announced that it would play at will. The figure could play twenty-two tunes, a list of which Frankestein gave to Aglonice, saying to her: "You shall judge, my lady, whether there is a mortal that can refrain from falling at your feet. Command, and bronze itself will obey."

Aglaonice only convinced herself with difficulty that the automaton could fulfill such a fine promise, and Cornelius was even more incredulous, for he had never heard it said that a man had, so to speak, created his fellow. They both approached the statue, which bowed in their presence, and astonished them so much by that beginning, retaining the phenomenon of animal economy, that they took two steps back; they thought it organized by a divine hand, as if there had been something to fear in assuring themselves of the contrary by touch, they recovered their composure, and drew away from it to a certain distance.

Impatiently, Aglaonice ordered the statue to play one of the advertised twenty-two tunes, which she designated. That air slowly expressed the chagrins of a heart ulcerated by amour. The statue, putting the two flutes to its mouth, far surpassed Aglonice's expectations; she heard it extract the most varied sounds from the two instruments and execute the two parts marvelously. The prodigy caused her an emotion so keen that she almost fainted, her head leaning on Cornelius' bosom; he only brought her round by ordering the statue to play a livelier tune.

The author of that admirable invention had his share of modesty; he was flattered to have interested Aglaonce, but did not have the pride to believe that he would be her husband in consequence.

"I desire very keenly," he told her, "to have merited the possession of charms that would make the happiness of my life, but you are too amiable for me to be the last to have attempted prodigies in your favor. I saw, as I came in here, a man who is unknown to me, younger than me, covering with a veil the tribute he has brought you, and who, believing some regard to be due to the maturity of my age, demanded that I go ahead of him. If he is victorious over me, I shall be chagrined, but I shall not display any jealousy; I shall, on the contrary, see with pleasure that he has talents superior to mine; I shall believe that the gods have inspired him expressly to please you and I shall be more certain than ever that beauty can obtain the impossible."

It was not the ready-made jargon of an insipid gallantry that emerged from Frankestein's mouth; it was the expression of truth escaping a sensitive heart. Aglaonice resisted momentarily the invitation of that man, who was doubly interesting, by virtue of his talent and a modesty that increased its value. It is probable that she was composing herself, and secretly interrogating herself as to whether she might not give him her hand; but as the Praetor whispered in her ear that she should distrust her senses, and she reflected that music is only a delightful thing for people who have dined well, she said to him, honestly:

"Sir, you can dispense with making entreaties on behalf of the person you have announced to us; you must believe that you will not be surpassed by anyone. Your colleague, who is surely not your rival, will only enter if you request it; we shall see him with pleasure render further justice to your talents, and assure you a triumph too modest for such a sublime art."

Frankestein insisting, the order was given to introduce the young man in question.

VIII. Nictator. His masterpiece. The marriages of Alglaonice and Bazilide.

Nictator—that was his name—was a descendant of the shepherds of Chaldea, to whom the system of the heavens was known, almost as to the gods themselves. He had all the enlightenment of his ancestors, but in addition had devoted himself to mechanics, a science in which he had made progress that surpasses the conjectures of the human mind. He was also endowed with a perception that it was difficult for anything to escape, so that, after mature reflection, he had really been able to combine the agreeable and the useful.

Frankestein's flute-player had entered the apartment like an invalid who cannot make use of his legs; this time, as soon as the doors opened, a woman was seen to advance clad in the manner of vestals, walking without anyone's support. It was only when she had taken twenty paces that the handsome young man who was the father, taking her by the hand, presented her to the three individuals making up the company, raising his eyes to look at Aglaonice and lowering them immediately for fear of offending her.

Aglaonice perceived that, and blushed at the appearance of the new suitor. The nymph that he introduced to her deployed so much grace that she was obliged to suppose infinitely more of the person who had transmitted them. Without knowing what the statue was about to do, already vanquished by the seductive manner of its author, but taking a violent grip on herself in order to hide the sentiment he had made her experience, she said:

"Do you have enough confidence in yourself not to fear challenging an artist of whom Olympus might be jealous, as we are assured it once was of Prometheus? Still so young, do you suppose that you have talent enough to put your work in parallel with the most extraordinary that they have ever engendered? Listen and judge..."

Then, in spite of the entreaties of Frankestein, who refused, Aglaonice had the statue play several tunes. Nictator was delighted by it, but the imposing tone of Aglaonice, and that marked predilection for a statue from which such melodious sounds emerged, so powerful upon a woman's heart, intimidated him to the point that he thought he was dismissed.

"That masterpiece has a right to please you, beautiful Aglaonice," he replied. "I thought that an artist more skillful than me would succeed in gaining your heart, and that it was an advantage reserved for experience, the companion of maturity. Music has charms for you... I have reflected a great deal, but that means of pleasing you, which is not foreign to me, has escaped my foresight! If I had been fortunate enough to think of it, perhaps the love that inspired me would not have left me at an extreme distance from my rival; but since, in sum, that victorious idea did not present itself to my mind, forgive me; I leave confused, even making a kind of crime of the hope with which I flattered myself."

"Stay," exclaimed Frankestein, "stay, amiable young man. My lady, if the idea of charming you with sounds has not offered itself to his mind, mine lacked the thought of imitating the laws of nature. I have not given my statue, as he has, progressive moment so natural that it imposed itself on me at first sight, so that an inanimate body appeared to me to be a living being."

"Let us see," said Aglaonice, "what this statue can do..."

She represented Plenty. She was seen standing up, bearing lightly in her fingertips the orifice of a long horn, artistically sculpted, containing fruits of a ravishing beauty; the other hand supported the curled extremity of the horn; and the motionless statue awaited stimulation. Under her drapery, however, a young child was hidden, who, as if giving in to a surge of impatience, raised the flap of the long robe under which he was buried, and, drawing a little bow, sent forth an arrow, terminated, not by gilded iron but by a rose-bud. That dart, directed at Aglaonice's heart, did not miss the target at which the mischievous bowman had taken aim.

A hidden trigger, adroitly brought into play, had caused the arrow to depart; another lowered the drapery under which the child had the appearance of mischievously taking refuge. That entire maneuver had taken place without any jerkiness or mechanical sound—in sum, in a manner so true that Aglaonice saw Amour himself in the little automaton.

She sensed all the amiability of such a declaration and could not help freeing herself from the cold reserve under which she might still have enveloped herself in order not to respond to it. Nature was the stronger. Aglaonice turned her tender eyes toward Nictator, stood up, extended her arms to him, fell back on to her seat, and let slip a question that laid bare the hasty wishes of her heart:

"Nictator...will you love me?"

Nictator remained silent; the statue spoke, saying: "Yes."

"What have I heard?" said Aglaonice. "Am I mistaken? It's your work that replied to me? No, it's you...it's you...but you're so timid that you fear to put yourself forward. Do you believe, then, that you haven't yet done enough?"

The statue replied: "No." At the same time, she took a step forward and offered the beautiful fruits contained in her horn to Aglaonice.

Aglaonice, deceived by the appearance, broke one, which she thought she could share with the ecstatic old Praetor, but the two lobes, coming apart, let slip into her hand large diamonds and gems of every sort. A second fruit contained Oriental pearls of surprising dimensions.

The horn was inverted over Aglaonice's dress, and eventually covered it with more than a thousand gold coins; that river seemed inexhaustible. The beauty thought that she had been transported to a new world,

Then Nictator threw himself at her knees. "Forgive me," he said. "A thousand pardons, adorable Aglaonice, if, to the efforts that my art has attempted in order to please you, I have dared to join something more, but which you will agree is truly useful. Blind fortune has, it is said, forgotten you; I am only a shepherd, but if you judge me worthy of repairing a neglect so insulting, come with me to Chaldea."

"Go with him," said the Praetor. "I don't believe that you'll find such a handsome fellow, a man as rich and an artist as skillful in the entire world."

"Assuredly not," said Frankestein, in a enthusiastic manner, "and it is not difficult for me to admit it, as if I have told you. But my lady, since my statue was designed for you, deign to accept it, and that I shall at least carry away to my homeland that it has had the approval of a young man of whom, at my age, I would glory in becoming the pupil."

Aglaonice, incapable of taking aboard all that struck her eyes and ears at once, remained mute for some time. Finally, she said: "Dear Nictator, my desires are fulfilled beyond my hopes; I will go with you anywhere, I abandon myself to you; but since, by a stroke of fate above my merit, I find myself enjoying a happiness that a queen would envy, listen: I have a sister not as young as me; she is no longer pretty, but she is beautiful and worthy to make the happiness of an amiable man. If I had not given myself to you, Frankestein would have become my husband. I shall not offer him in exchange for his statue the magnificent gifts that I have just received from the hands of Plenty; give me the pleasure of enriching my sister with then, and that she should marry that gallant man. These jewels will be her dowry."

At these words, Frankestein, Nictator and the Praetor all began talking at the same time. The last abruptly gave orders for someone to fetch Aglaonice's sister, and for a magnificent feast to be prepared.

Frankestein was not unaware that the gravity of his fifty years was ill-fitting with the petulance of seventeen "Take back the jewels," he said, "and I'll accept."

"No," said Nictator, "no; and you don't have the right to refuse them, since it's not to you that they're offered. Do you want to wound the pure sentiment emanated by sensibility itself? Aglaonice does not want to be happy alone; she could not be. Be my friend, be my brother..."

"I shall be both," replied Frankestein, swiftly, with tears in his eyes, throwing his arms around him. "Young man, you have vanquished me today in everything."

Meanwhile, the tables were laid and Bazilide came in. I have no need to depict for you that new scene, in which the most tender sentiments succeeded surprise. The four individuals swore an eternal love in the presence of the Praetor.

Night was approaching; it was the perfect hour for celebration. Two thousand candles were lit around the palace, spreading a light that rivaled the light of day. In the middle of the island a flaming pyre was distinguished, composed of odorous wood, the symbolic blaze of which announced to the spouses that it was a law for them to maintain the household. The apartments were also embalmed by the perfumes of a hundred cassolettes, the voluptuous furniture of kings, which had never served such a beautiful occasion. The husbands supped with their wives that day, although it was not customary, but it will be remembered that the ladies were orphans, and could consequently do as they liked.

IX, the Last. The Supper

The supper was all the more agreeable because there were only five guests and everyone could make themselves heard. The conversation, in consequence, went on long into the night. Each of them talked about the customs of his homeland.

Aglaonice's little ship came back to mind—or, rather, she remembered a comparison of sorts that the Praetor had made on the subject of its disappearance.

"Sir," she said to Frankestein, "I have a question to ask you. I had an ivory miniature, a charming little ship, which fell prey to polypes in a vase where I had left it. The Praetor told me at the time that the great ship of Lutetia would not have suffered such a fate. I know that Lutetia is a city in the land where you reside; of the remainder I am very ignorant. Give me, I beg you, the key to that enigma."

"Madame," said Cornelius, anticipating Frankestein's response, "it would have taken me a fortnight to explain that remark to you, which I repented as soon as it had escaped me. If I kept silent thereafter, it was less an impoliteness than an attention on my part. The idea came to me that boredom might ensue; and that was not too poor an augury at the time, for remember that since then, Cyaxare did not amuse you when he came to talk politics with us. But since, at present, your happiness is assured, one can without displeasing you, entertain you with something other than the sole object that could interest you then. I shall join with you in asking Frankestein to satisfy your curiosity; he will acquit himself better than me in that task."

Bazilide also joined forces with her sister in testifying the same urgency.

"My ladies," said Frankestein, "you have heard the Praetor; he spoke of nothing less than a fortnight to leave nothing to your desire, and he was not deceiving you. Fourteen days, pass, but not nights, I beg you, or I shall think you have the malign project of abusing your rights. We have all the time we need to understand one another; permit me to abridge.

"Lutetia is the capital of Gaul and its inhabitants are one of the sixty-four peoples who make up that formidable republic. The coat-of-arms of that city represents a ship, a symbol of the worship it renders to the goddess Isis, who has enriched it with wheat and the fruits that are harvested there in abundance. Isis herself was the pilot of the ship that carried that precious cargo.

"You can appreciate that gratitude made it a duty to consecrate that floating house as an eternal monument to such a great benefit. But as the vessel had made a long journey, it was not possible to conserve it for very long. Another was constructed, similar in form but of much greater dimension, whose flanks were also more solid. That second vessel, the emblem of the first, has nevertheless been replaced ten times, and the Lutetians always give it more strength and volume every time they construct a new one.

"That edifice, once afloat, does not cast off its moorings; it is perpetually at anchor between a pastureland surrounded by the waters of the Seine, known as the Isle of Swans, and the muddy island on which the building of Lutetia commenced more than six hundred years ago, from the moment when I am speaking to you. The siege of Troy and the reign of Sesostris are the epochs of its foundation; Rome did not exist and we Germans had not yet penetrated into Gaul.

"The ship of Lutetia was well-guarded on the two banks by a good number of citizen soldiers. I have also seen it served by the Druids that live there and the nymphs of the Seine who serve them as wives—without, however, losing their quality as virgins."

"How is that?" asked all the guests, simultaneously

"Such is the effect of the communication of peoples, that along with the best things, the most prejudicial are introduced. Isis, at the same time as she gave the inhabitants of the Seine the what she had taken from the banks of the Nile, also brought them the execrable abuse of the most civilized, and hence the most corrupt, people on earth. There exists in Memphis a very great distinction between the 'children of the Gods,' or 'children of the Vessel,' and the 'children of Men.' Young women, after having given birth in the vessel to a few babies 'of the Gods,' emerge therefrom and are espoused as virgins by the 'children of man.' The reason is quite simple; there is such a vast inequality between the Almighty and humans that a young woman who has enjoyed the caresses of an Almighty is presumed to have gained by that celestial commerce and to be worth more for the earth than an entirely new young woman."[36]

---

[36] Author's note: "'It is doubtless the right owed to the Almighty of Egypt that gave birth in Europe to the rights of intercourse that did not diminish a young woman in public opinion.' The serfs became freedmen and all of that was abolished in France. 'In our day, however, the merchants of Negroes still enjoy the rights of the Almighty, and a young negress is presumed to be virginal in the eyes of the black man who receives her as a wife.' [*Recherches du tribun.*] Dion Cassius reports that senators opined in full Senate that Augustus had the right, at fifty-seven years of age, to lie with all the women that he wished. Montesquieu does not doubt that; Voltaire, less credulous, observes that Augustus could easily do that without authorization, but that the likes of Marcus Aurelius and the Julians dispensed with it." The internal reference is unclear, and I have not been able to trace it.

This is the last footnote to appear in the version of the story included in *L'Antipode de Martmontel* except for the mislead-

"Oh, what stupid credulity!" exclaimed Nicator. "And the inhabitants of Lutetia adopted that unworthy refinement of theocratic pride and lust?"

"What do you expect?" Frankestein continued. "It was not examined at first; people yield with heads bowed to superstition; devils appear to be celestial creatures; then evil pullulates like weeds, and it's the devil of a job to uproot it. For a long time, the Kings of Lutetia did all that they could, without success, to make the people lose confidence in the Druids, but the latter were dangerous, especially when they combined their ascendancy with the power of the nobles, or Iarles,[37] petty Regules that swarm in Gaul, and whose combined strength has more than once shaken the throne of the sovereign, to whom they give no other title that that of 'general of conquering soldiers.'

"'No one dared, for a long time, to resist the Druids, who took sole charge of the education of the young in order to inspire them early on and in an unalterable fashion with the most horrible opinions. Iarles have been seen to have the right of life and death over vassals whom they governed to their profit. Those two classes of citizens, one of which employed cunning and the other force to make itself feared, were balanced against one another, but they joined forces to tyrannize the people, whom they treated with sovereign scorn. I've seen that a man of the people could not succeed, among the Gauls, in fulfilling a public responsibility; it seemed that the nation was only made for the priests and the aristocrats. Instead of being

---

ing reference to *Études de la nature* (see note 36). All of the final diatribe, and the reprinted article on "massacres" are eliminated, having been deprived of their intended force in the intervening ten years.

[37] The Iarles are featured as contemporaries of the druids in Bernardin de Saint-Pierre's romance *L'Arcadie* (1781), which is set in a mythical ancient Gaul, from which the allegorical elements of this anti-clerical and anti-aristocratic tirade are taken.

consoled by the former and protected by the latter, as justice required, the Druids frightened in order that the Iarles could oppress.'[38] The Kings who were most successful were, however, those who overtly took up the defense of the weak."

"You speak of all that," said Aglaonice, "as something past."

"A considerable fraction of those abuses no longer exists, in fact," Frankestein replied. "The Nation itself has destroyed them; but not without difficulty. It was first necessary to make the truth known everywhere, leaving no doubt as to the rapacity of the Iarles, who, taking advantage of the facile generosity of the King, had themselves given under the title of recompense, the major part of the tax revenue, which reduced the people to languishing in opprobrium, only procuring their subsistence be serving in the manner most dishonorable to humanity. It was necessary to prove that the Druids had caused weak minds to give them so many arpents of the best-yielding land that they alone possessed a third of the wealth of the republic of Gaul, without, however, wanting it to be touched, without contributing, other than under the title of loans, to the settlement of the State's debts; and that their intolerance had occasioned massacres that, if they were renewed, might depopulate the land.[39] It was necessary to climb on to trestles to

---

[38] Author's reference: "*Études de la Nature*." *L'Arcadie* was reprinted in some editions of the later work, hence this slightly misleading reference.

[39] Author's note: "*Pax vobiscum omnibus*, etc., said Jesus Christ to his apostles. If peace does not reign among men, they are in consequence worse than ferocious beasts. Let us love our brothers whatever their religion is. If they are mistaken, so much the worse for them. All would have been lost if we had decreed that the Catholic religion would be the exclusive religion among us. 'The religion of the reformed,' said Mably, 'is no less appropriate than that of Catholics for making citizens useful and virtuous. Both have the right to enjoy the same advantages. It is only by that conduct that the Germans succeed-

ed in destroying fanaticism and affirming public tranquility in their homeland.... Tribunals composed of judges chosen from the two religions are sufficient there to repress certain abuses, and each party has protectors powerful enough to defend its rights and its liberty.... It would have been almost the same in France if the Estates-General, instead of being destroyed by the predecessors of Henri IV, had been solidly enough established to become a habitual and necessary mechanism of government. The closer they would have approached perfection, the more probable it is that the French would have ceased to tear themselves apart in civil wars that shed so much blood. It is natural that the people have more confidence in those assemblies, which are necessarily national maxims, than the counselors of a prince, who usually only consults shifting conveniences whose resolutions are too often the work of intrigue and mainly serve interests contrary to those of the public.'

Let us not lose sight of the useful comparisons drawn by another philosopher of this century; comparisons that prove without exaggeration that nine million seven hundred and eighteen thousand and eight hundred people have been butchered, drowned, burned or broken on the wheel 'for the love of God.' Read the article on 'Massacres' in the *Encyclopedia*. But I blush at my sloth. Why do I not take the trouble to make a copy of that depiction? Let us render a service to humanity. Let us take from the archives of philosophy a document more important than the Red Book. Learned reader, you know it, but the people do not know it, and it is them that it is necessary to enlighten. The man of the people that one hires and arms himself with a pike or a rifle for a loaf of bread, does not have the means to buy sixty volumes in order to read the twenty lines that would render him milder than two hundred sermons. Tear out of my book these useful pages, and give them to him; they ought not to cost him anything. Thus, you and I will have done well."

make the people hear that the king's counselors, charged with sending dispatches, abused his name, depriving honest citizens of their liberty in order to have their wives, and were no less predatory than the brigands stifled by Hercules. It was necessary to prove, in sum, that the plague was in the vessel.

"Weary of the miseries resulting from these tyrannical powers, the inhabitants of Lutetia then precipitated themselves with a kind of rage upon the mysterious ship; they devastated it with blows of the ax, after having let out the young women. The servants of the vessel and their friends the Iarles did not have a good time, but a short time afterwards calm succeeded the massacres and the burning. The same hands that destroyed the old poisoned ship have made a completely new one in which the children of men now replace the children of the gods. It is enormous in size and strong enough to endure for six thousand years and beyond.

"That is the key to the enigma. Furthermore, Isis has been banished; it is no longer her religious figurehead that is seen on the prow of the ship; it is that of the King of Lutetia, crowned with a civic branch, holding panthers on a leash in one hand and an olive branch in the other. At the top of the mainmast floats a large banner on which is written: *legum servi sumus, it liberi esse possimus*.[40] The gallery is ornamented with balustrades, from which emerges a lantern surmounted by a bonnet in the form of an epiroge."[41]

"Oh, you have charmed me," said Bazilide to her husband, embracing him in a bourgeois fashion, as was done in

---

The remainder of this footnote—which appears in the original text as an endnote—reproduces the said article on "Massacres." I have removed it to an appendix in order not to disrupt the main text too greatly.

[40] "We are slaves of the law in order that we might be free." (Cicero)

[41] An epiroge was a kind of cloak listed in many treatises on the French peerage as part of the ceremonial garb of the Greffier en Chef.

the times of Hector. "You talk about the change of fortune of the Lutetians with a kind of satisfaction that makes the greatest eulogy of your heart.[42] I cannot tell you all the tender sentiments that you make me feel."

"Is the King of Lutetia beloved, then?" asked Nicator.

"Greatly," said Frankestein, "and not only by the Lutetians, but all the people of Gaul. Look, I have in my pocket two medallions that can give you proof of it. The first, imagined by gratitude, was struck a few years after the King, at the time of his coronation, had handed back certain onerous rights due to the chief of the conquerors on his accession to the throne, in the temple of Mars. The Gauls then came to experience great calamities; the people lacked bread; touched by their misery, he reformed his expenditure; he had wheat imported from abroad at great expense, and distributed it first and foremost to the unfortunate cultivators. He is represented here in the emblem of the pelican, which bleeds itself to nourish its children."

"The idea isn't new," said Nicator."

"No," said Aglaonice, "but it has justice. Let us see the other."

"This one is very recent," said Frankestein. "It makes allusion to the reestablishment of the finances exhausted by depredations. The people are doing for their King here what he has done for them. You see the good city of Lutetia presenting her breasts to her father. Behind her is displayed the desire of all others to enjoy the same happiness as her."

"Oh," said Cornelius, "that trait of filial piety belongs to us, but the comparison is fortunate."

Aglaonice and Bazilide, indignant at the gluttony of the pontiffs serving the former vessel and the tyrannical spirit of

---

[42] At this point the text of the 1800 version deviates from the 1790 version, dropping all the text between this point and the paragraph in which Aglaonice and Bazilide express their indignation.

the Iarles, wanted to know what had become of both parties after such an upheaval.

"Let it suffice for you to know, ladies," said Frankestein, "that all distinctions have been abolished: that the great Druids, the servants of the god Tor-Tir,[43] the Druid sacrificers who lived on pure wheat steeped in human blood, are reduced at present to a fine broth of lupins and beech-nuts, all washed down with the milk of goats of the race that once nourished the father of men; for that posterity of Amaltheia was imported specially from Crete, on the grounds that such a mild aliment would surely bring about a complete change in their mores."

As he finished speaking, Frankestein put his arm around Bazilide amorously. Nicator leaned toward Aglaonice with a voluptuous expression; her eyes did not react badly to that attack. Cornelius, who was only serving as a witness, did not want to put a longer obstacle in the way of their impatience; he got up from the table and embraced all four of them, with tears in his eyes.

"One more word only," he said to them, "so that before I retire I shall know your projects."

Nicator had a father advanced in age, and could not renounce returning to him immediately

Frankestein made it a duty and a joy to introduce Bazilide to his family; he proposed then to take her to Aglaonice in the beautiful land of Sennaar, in order never to separate again from her and Nicator.

"My friends," said Cornelius, "At least wait until the end of my Praetorship. If you leave me so soon, I shall think that I am losing all my children at the same time..."

He was promised what he requested; they swore it. They embraced again, and then they went their separate ways.[44]

---

[43] Another name derived from *L'Arcadie*.

[44] The 1800 version of the text ends here.

Thus, in my gardens, where the mysterious Acacia is flowering—a partisan of sweet union, peace and equality—I take my pleasure in composing these stories, similar in their ensemble to those paintings that present one object seen at a distance, but change and become something else as one draws closer, glad to think they might perhaps make some contribution to preventing my brothers from butchering one another...

Meanwhile, a new Erostratus, the furious Bergasse,[45] too eager to render his name celebrated, spreads in profusion throughout France the new fruits of his incendiary pen, and avarice trembles to open its coffers...

Recalcitrant to the voice of wisdom, which invites tolerance, the inhabitant of the countryside blindly obeys the seditious declamations of a host of false prophets; blood is flowing again; the sky is darkening, obscured by a thick cloud of unclean spirits that Hell has vomited forth, and which are breathing hatred, fanaticism, vengeance and discord everywhere. Vile ogre with eight hundred farms!

O Aristos! I would like to think that you are mistaken if you believe you see the armed plebeians exterminating one another like the soldiers born from the teeth of Cadmus' serpent, or of you flatter yourself by seeing them at your feet demanding shackles once again, while you, prideful despot, continue to live on their substance. Your unworthy heart is for me the image of Tartarus.

> Deadly partisan of a detested power
> Monster jealous of the air that human breathe;
> Succumb; die in the end of the infected sting
> Of black serpents that tear you apart.
> In his simple redoubt, let the humble pauper.

---

[45] The revolutionary Nicolas Bergasse is here likened by Nogaret to the Greek Erostratus, who set fire to the temple of Diana at Ephesus in order that his name would become immortal in history. The Ephesians banned its pronunciation, but (evidently) failed to prevent the achievement of the ambition.

Sure of the little wealth that enables him to live
Subsist, blessing a King that freed him
From the deadly effects of your voracity.

APPENDIX

Massacres

An Englishman[46] has compiled a summary of all the
massacres perpetrated for the cause of religion, since the first
century of our vulgar era. This is a translation of it.

Christians had already excited some troubles in Rome
when, in the year 251 of out vulgar era, the priest Novatien
disputed what we call the seat of Rome, the papacy of Cor-
neille, for it was already an important position that was worth
a great deal of money. And at exactly the same time, the seat
of Carthage was similarly disputed by Cyprian and another
priest named Novat, who had killed his wife by kicking her in
the stomach. Those two schisms occasioned a great many
murders in Carthage and in Rome. The emperor Decius was
obliged to repress those furies with a few executions, which
became known as the "great" or the "terrible" persecution of
Decius. We shall not talk about that here; we shall limit ourselves to the murders of Christians committed by other Christians. If we estimate at two hundred the number of individuals
killed or grievously wounded in those first two schisms, which
were the model for so many others, we believe that that item
will not be overly exaggerated. Let us therefore say:

200.

As soon as the Christians could deliver themselves with
impunity to their vengeances under Constantine, they assassi-
nated the young Candidian, son of the emperor Galerus, the
hope of the empire, who was compared to Marcellus; a child

---

[46] John Trenchard, in *Cato's Letters; or Essays on Liberty,
Civil and Religious* (1724). The adaptation for the
Encyclopédie was done by Voltaire; hence Nogaret's final
comment.

of eight, the son of the emperor Maximin; and a daughter of the same emperor aged seven. The empress, their mother, was dragged out of her palace with her women into the streets of Antioch and they were thrown into the Oronte. The Empress Valerie, widow of Galere and daughter of Diocletian, was killed in Thessalonika in 315 and had the sea for a sepulcher.

It is true that a few authors do not accuse the Christians of that murder and impute it to Licinius, but let us reduce the number of those that the Christians butchered on that occasion to two hundred; that is not too many. So:

200.

In the schism of the Donatists in Africa, one can hardly count less than four hundred people killed by blows of clubs, for the bishops did not want anyone to fight with swords. Put: 400.

It is well-known of what horrors and how many civil wars the mere word "consubstantial" was the origin and the pretext. That conflagration set the entire empire ablaze several times and was reignited in all the provinces devastated by the Goths, the Burgundians and the Vandals for nearly four hundred years.

If we only include the three hundred thousand Christians butchered by Christians for that quarrel, without counting the errant families reduced to mendicity, we cannot be reproached for having inflated our count. So:

300,000.

The quarrel of the iconoclasts and the iconoclaters certainly cost no less than sixty thousand lives.

60,000.

We must not pass over in silence the hundred thousand Manicheans that the empress Theodora, widow of Theophilus, had butchered in the Greek empire in 845. It was a penitence that her confessor had ordered, because until that epoch no more than twenty thousand had been hanged, impaled and garroted. Those people merited all being killed, in order to teach them that there is only one good principle and no bad one. The total amounted to a hundred and twenty thousand at least. So:

120,000.

Let us only count twenty thousand in the seditions excited by the priests who disputed all the Episcopal seats; it is necessary to exercise extreme discretion.

20,000.

It has been supposed that the horrible folly of the holy crusades cost the lives of two million Christians, but I would like, by the greatest reduction that has ever been made, to reduce them to one million. So:

1,000,000.

The crusade of the sword-wielding religious knights that devastated so honestly and in such saintly fashion all the shores of the Baltic Sea must have left at least a hundred thousand dead. So:

100,000.

As many for the crusade against the Languedoc, where one saw nothing for a long time but the ashes of pyres and the bones of the dead devoured by wolves in the country. So:

100,000.

The devotion with which the priests Jan Huss and Jerome of Prague were burned in the city of Constance at the end of the great schism did great honor to the emperor Sigismund and the council, but it caused, I know not how, the war of the Hussites, in which we can boldly count a hundred and fifty thousand dead. Hence:

150,000.

After those great butcheries, we admit that the massacres of Merindol and Cabrieres were very minor affairs. It is only a matter of twenty-two large towns reduced o ashes, eighteen thousand innocents slaughtered and burned, infants at the teat thrown into the flames, young women raped and then cut into quarters, old women who were no longer good for anything made to leap into the air by forcing cartridges charged with powder into their two orifices. But as that execution was done juridically, with all the formalities of the law, by men in robes, it is necessary not to omit that part of French law. So put:

18,000.

Now we reach the holiest and most glorious epoch of Christianity, which a few people wanted to reform without consent at the beginning of the sixteenth century. The saintly popes, the saintly bishops and the saintly priests having refused to mend their ways, the two parties marched over the bodies of the dead for two entire centuries, with only a few intervals of peace.

If the amicable reader wishes to take the trouble to add up all the murders committed between the reigns of the saintly Pope Leo X and the saintly Pope Clement IX, whether juridical or non-juridical, the heads of the priests, secular individuals and princes felled by the executioner, the wood whose price was driven upwards in several provinces by the multitude of pyres lit, the blood spilled from one end of Europe to the other, the executioners worn out in Flanders, Germany, Holland, France and even England; thirty civil wars for transubstantiation, predestination, the surplice and holy water, the massacres of Saint Bartholomew's Eve, the massacres in Ireland, the massacres in the Vaudois, the massacres in the Cévennes, etc. etc. etc, one would doubtless find more than two million bloody deaths, with more than three million unfortunate families plunged into a misery perhaps worse than death. But as it is only a matter of deaths here, let is quickly pass with horror over two million.

2,000,000.

Let us not be unjust and impute more crimes to the Inquisition than it actually committed in surplice and in stole; let us not exaggerate anything and reduce to two hundred thousand the number of souls it sent to Heaven or Hell. So:

200,000.

Let us even reduce to five millions the twelve million humans that Bishop Las Casas claimed to have immolated to the Christian religion in America, and let us, above all, make

73

the consoling reflection that they were not human, since they were not Christians.[47] Hence:

5,000,000.

Let us reduce with the same economy the four hundred thousand humans who perished in the civil war in Japan excited by the Reverend Father Jesuits, and only raise our count by three hundred thousand:

<u>300,000</u>.

TOTAL: 9,718, 800

Whoever you might be, reader, if you conserve the archives of your family, consult them, and you will see that you have had more than one ancestor immolated on the pretext of religion, or at least cruelly persecuted, or who was a persecutor, which is even worse, etc. Whatever your calculation might be, you descend from murderers or the murdered; choose and tremble. But you, prelate of my country, rejoice; our blood is worth an income of five thousand guineas to you.

I have been strongly tempted to write against that English author, but, his memoir not seeming to me to have been inflated, I have refrained. At any rate, I hope that there will be no more such calculations to be made—but to whom will we have the obligation?

It is to you, Voltaire, as is evident, albeit with the precautions of sometimes putting on mittens; it is to Jean-Jacques, of whom you were jealous; it is to Mably, whose name you have malevolently mounted in your overly pompous verses; to the example of Boileau, whom you scolded on that article, but

---

[47] Author's note: "Let us not forget that they were in part exterminated by dogs, to which pensions were awarded from the public treasury. Let us not forget that the Spaniard converters who had Kings burned on small fires under the pretext of the salvation of their souls, were only thinking of despoiling them of their wealth."

who merits inclusion here since he mocked the stupid martyrs of a diphthong.[48]

Immortal philosophers! You have all been in accord; you have all said: "Humans are born to help one another and to love one another." Would that our honest rural curés might say as much! Would that they read from the pulpit that summary of our stupidity to the hundred thousand peasants that they reproach for not being able to read. Thus the Bishop of Ypres and the Eponymous Archonte, leader of the gribourdonique[49] Sabbat would lose the fruits for which they hope from their bloodthirsty preaching.

---

[48] Author's note: "Oi. The Arians wanted to say, in speaking of the Word, *om-oi-oufios*: "of a substance similar to that of the father." The Christians claimed that it was necessary to say *omooufios*, "of the same substance" and they staked their heads on it.

[49] This adjective is improvised from the name of the notional author of Jean-Baptiste de Junquières' *Epître du père Gribourdon, date de l'Enfer à l'auteur de la Pucelle* (1756), a satirical attack on Voltaire. *L'archonte éponyme* [Eponymous Archonte] was the supreme magistrate in ancient Athens; the Bishop of Ypres was Cornelius Jansen (1585-1638), the founder of Jansenism.

Jean Rameau : *Future Mores*
(1887)

Prologue

Until now, writers have generally had the bad habit of recounting things that have already passed. It is time to break with that deplorable mania and set about recounting events that will occur in the future.

Here, therefore, is a story that will be realized faithfully, believe us, in the first half of the twenty-third century.

I.

Characters: Monsieur 517,383, series L, section R; and Madame 491,536, series M, section K.

(The reader has divined that in the twenty-third century there are no more of those absurd names and surnames, causes of so much equivocation, and the people simply have a registration number, which renders any error impossible.)

So, Monsieur 517,383, who had married the young and charming Mademoiselle 491,536, suddenly conceived, three weeks after his marriage, violent doubts regarding the fidelity of his wife and, penetrating unexpectedly into the apartment reserved for the said 491,536, found her, or thought he found her, in criminal conversation with an individual of the masculine gender.

The unfortunate husband, who had an excessively sanguine temperament, fell upon the unknown man.

"Who are you?" he demanded, his eyes injected with blood.

"I'm number 87,329, series B, section F," replied the stranger, calmly.

"Wretch!" roared the husband—and he discharged at the individual in question his pocket electric machine-gun, the revolver having had its day.

II.

"Monsieur," said number 87,329 to the husband, when he had got to his feet and had his wounds patched up, "you have lodged two bullets in my back because you believed that your wife was deceiving you with me?"

"Yes, Monsieur."

"Is she had been deceiving you, you would, indeed, have had the right to kill me, in accordance with existing laws; but that is not the case."

"What are you saying?" demanded the husband, going pale.

"I'm saying that I'm Madame's corset-maker, that I came to take measurements for a corset, and that you have not been dishonored in the slightest. I shall prove it to you..."

And he did, in fact, prove it.

"But in that case…!" cried the husband, nonplussed.

"In that case, Monsieur, you will be arrested and condemned to a few years in prison and a few tens of thousands of francs damages and compensation. That's inevitable."

"The husband turned poppy-red, green, yellow, violet, peony-red...

"Damn! How am I going to get out of this!" he exclaimed, putting his head in his hands.

"There's only one means, Monsieur," said the corset-maker, after having reflected momentarily. "Give me an entitlement conferring the right to take the thing for which I have been wounded, and we'll be quits."

The husband went peony-red, violet, yellow, green and poppy-red again, reflected on the scandal of the assize court, prison, damages and compensation, the dishonor of his entire family...

"Well, yes!" he sighed. "There's no alternative."

And he handed over the entitlement demanded.

III.

Three weeks later, the same husband, having the same violent suspicions, entered his wife's apartment armed with the same pocket electric machine-gun.

He found his other half in the arms of a man he had never seen before.

"Blood and thunder!" he howled—that sanguine temperament again—"what are you doing, Monsieur?"

"Monsieur, I'm making love to your wife."

"You admit it? You both admit it?"

"Indeed."

Bang! Bang! The electric machine-gun is discharged in the blink of an eye, and the new stranger falls to the ground.

"Monsieur," he says to the husband, with his dying breath, "you'll be condemned to death."

"What!" says the husband.

"I had a perfect right to make love to your wife; I have an entitlement to her, signed by you. Here it is."

The husband ran forward, his eyes bulging.

"An entitlement?"

"Endorsed by Monsieur 87,329 in my favor. Here's the endorsement."

The husband uttered a cry of despair.

"All is lost!" he said.

And he threw himself upon his machine-gun, reloaded it and put the barrel to his temple in order to blow his brains out."

IV.

"Stop!" cried his panic-stricken wife, snatching the weapon from his hand.

"All is lost, I tell you!"

"No! All is saved!"

"What are you saying?"

"That document," said the young woman, blushing slightly, "has no value; the negotiator had nothing more to take."

"Can it be?" said the husband, to himself, hope returning.

"Yes, my love."

And, rummaging in a drawer labeled *Miscellaneous*, she took out a piece of paper duly signed and stamped.

"Here's the receipt...*paid in full*," she added, in a low voice, turning her head away slightly.

"Angel!" cried the husband.

And, his eyes inundated with tender tears, he threw himself at the feet of Madame 491,536, series M, section K, and embraced her effusively.

Epilogue

And after that, having taken the trouble to put a little more order in their accounts, they were very happy and had lots of children.

Jean Rameau: *The Transportation of Forces* (1887)

I.

In those days—1987 years after Jesus Christ, 63 years after Blagheston, the immortal scientist whose apparatus for transmitting and storing forces, an apparatus applicable to all things and permitting the usage of the slightest wasted movements, revolutionized the world—Monsieur and Madame Arthur Brack learned that their refinery was no longer functioning, because of the exhaustion of motive forces.

"We need to see about that!" sad the spouses, with a common accord.

And they sent out a thousand invitations to a grand fancy dress ball, to be held at their home, in their vast fourteenth-floor apartment in the Boulevard Gamehut.

II.

The dancers of both sexes arrived in a crowd.

"Let the party begin!" ordered Arthur Brack, at precisely half past eleven.

And immediately, the couples started trampling the carpet with a rare verve.

Two hours later, Monsieur Brack, who had had the fine inspiration of placing Balagheston transmotors under the parquet, observed with pleasure that each dancer had produced an average force of three and a half horsepower, which, for the entire company, was 2,534 horse-power.

"By dawn, I'll have enough to enable my refinery to function gratuitously for a week!" he said, rubbing his hands.

III.

Suddenly, as he was about to go and slake the thirst of such conscientious guests, Brack perceived a bald man who was inactive in a corner.

"Monsieur isn't dancing?" he asked.

"No, Monsieur."

"Would you like me to inscribe you for a waltz with my wife?"

"All my regrets, Monsieur. I'm a poet."

"A poet? Bah!" exclaimed Brak, who had a sudden idea. "Would you care to recite some verses for me?"

"Gladly, Monsieur."

And the poet recited.

IV.

Louder. I beg you, and a few more gestures!" begged Brack.

But he placed transmotors in all directions around the poet in vain; the latter's vocal outbursts and deep breaths only produced an insignificant force: a twelfth of a horse-power at the most.

"Ha ha! Not famous, your verses, not famous!" Brack concluded.

"I can dedicate them to you, Monsieur, then!" the poet riposted.

Clack!

Brack could not retain himself; he gave the insolent individual an enormous slap.

The poet did not say anything. He merely took a transmotor, which he had rapidly placed on his cheek when he saw the slap coming, and consulted it with a certain satisfaction.

"Ha! Enough to grind my coffee for three weeks!" he reflected.

And he went out, with dignity.

V.

But Brack's mother-in-law had seen everything.

"That's shameful, Monsieur!" she said to her son-in-law, coming in like a thunderclap. "One doesn't treat a poet like that!"

"But Madame..."

"The force expended on his cheek, applied to one of our transmotors, Monsieur, would have been sufficient to operate the turnspit for six months. Oh, men! Oh! Oh…!"

But the mother-in-law went pale.

She perceived that, while she was uttering her exclamations, her son-in-law had shut her in a special chamber whose walls were covered in transmotors, and that it was her who had been powering the house elevator with her sighs for three years.

Hideous!

And the mother-in-law fainted.

VI.

Meanwhile, Arthur Brack, quite enervated by those two successive scenes, was walking feverishly through the ball-rooms.

He soon remarked that his wife, an inconsiderable person of 112 kilograms (net weight) was not visible among the dancers.

"That's a very regrettable loss of force," Arthur said to himself, frowning.

And he set out in search of his wife.

VII.

He did not find her. He ran through all the drawing rooms, all the bedrooms, all the corridors. Nothing.

"What does this mean?" Brack muttered, anxiously.

Suddenly, he uttered a cry.

There...behind a screen...that woman allowing herself to be embraced...her!

"Unworthy creature!" the deceived husband vociferated.

And he rushed upon his wife—because he loved her, the poor fool!

VIII.

The beautiful Madame Brack did not try to deny it. Terrified, she fled, her hair in the wind.

Brack set out in pursuit of her.

"Unworthy creature!" he was still howling.

Madame Brack ran through the bedrooms, the drawing rooms and the corridors, opened a window, took refuge on a balcony and then, seeing that she was still being tracked by her husband, uttered a terrible cry and hurled herself into the void.

The husband shuddered. He saw the 112-kilogram body fall from a height of fourteen stories!

"Concierge!" he cried, at the top of his voice. "A transmotor on the sidewalk! Quickly!"

Too late. Madame Brack arrived at her destination before the apparatus was in place.

"Wretch that I am!" exclaimed the unfortunate husband.

And he lost consciousness, exhausted by so many emotions.

IX.

Arthur Brack did not get up again.

He died four days later, prey to a frightful delirium in which he talked of nothing but dishonor, alexandrines and mothers-in-law.

However, he calmed down toward the end of the fourth day, and, sensing that death was coming, he said to his son in a faint voice: "John, it's necessary not to waste anything. A transmotor, quickly!"

"Here you are, Papa!" replied the son, his eyes full of tears.

X.

And with his father's last sigh, piously collected, John had enough to beat an omelet for his lunch.

Jean Rameau: *A Poisoning in the Twenty-First Century*
(1887)

I.

It was in the year 1934 that the French, slowly poisoned by their suppliers of comestibles and the sickening odors that, after having infected Paris, spread rapidly over the whole of France, perceived that their nature and their needs had completely changed, and that, new Mithridates, they were not only armed against the poison but also had the need to absorb it three times a day, or die of starvation.

That state of things, thanks to the progress of adulterators, could only get worse, and in the year 2056, they were obliged to build villas and cottages in the sewers of Paris, for the use of socialites of both sexes, who, abandoning the spas and the unhealthy countryside, experienced the need to steep themselves, for a few weeks, in the beneficial effluvia of the great collector.

II.

In June 2083, the epoch in which this story is set, foreigners and tourists were very numerous in the Paris sewers. All the villas were occupied, and the rent on a simple cottage in the vicinity of the Saint-Denis fecal depository was crazy.

Let us enter into one of those villas—Microbe Villa, situated in the Avenue Lesage—and witness the magnificent dinner that two young newlyweds, who had hastened to the sewers in order to spend their honeymoon there, were offering to the whole of elegant high-class Parisian society.

III.

The table of the splendid dining room is regally garnished. And everywhere there is light, crystal and flowers: rare and distinguished flowers, artificial flowers exhaling the healthiest and most recommended perfumes, in which asafetida and valerian are dominant.

Suddenly, a loud cry.

The young husband falls under the table.

"Heavens!" clamor a hundred voices.

People hasten, take a look, and observe that the young husband's face has taken on a violet hue, like certain cadavers of old that had absorbed certain venomous juices.

"Oh! My husband has been poisoned!" cried the unfortunate wife.

And she fell in a faint.

IV.

He had, indeed, been poisoned.

A woman's vengeance!

But poisoned by what? With the aid of what redoubtable substance? That was what the investigation could not establish immediately.

"Examine all the aliments, all the beverages!" instructed the inconsolable widow as soon as she recovered consciousness.

And her instructions were carried out.

The wine was taken to the municipal laboratory.

The municipal laboratory replied:

"Wine finest quality. Composition: 23 parts Seine water, 57 parts vitriol, 17 parts decoction of old leather gloves, 3 parts essence of turpentine; the whole constituting an excellent Château Léoville, 2046."

"Analyze the vinegar, the oil, the vegetables!" ordered the widow, intent on knowing how her husband had died.

But all those products were found to be irreproachable.

86

The green peas came from one of the best factories in Grenelle and contained 49% copper acetate.

The pepper was furnished by an entrepreneur of demolitions and contained nothing but extra-pulverized brick.

The vinegar was rich in ammonia and *eau de javelle*.[50] As for the oil, the Compagnie d'Orléans had only ever employed the best to grease its machines.

"What poison, then, has killed my poor husband?" the tearful widow asked herself.

V.

"Ah!" she exclaimed, suddenly. "That half-full glass from which the dead man drank—what is that?" She presented the glass to the experts.

The latter had no sooner cast their eyes upon the beverage than they went pale with fear.

"Get back, Madame!" they proclaimed, their minds traversed by a terrible suspicion.

And, having covered their hands with impermeable gloves and their faces with glass masks, they set about analyzing the mysterious beverage. They had guessed right.

"Oh, Madame," they said to the desperate widow, who was getting thinner by the day, "what an abominable crime!"

"It's a frightful poison?"

"A deadly poison."

"Which?"

"Pure water."

And the servants who overheard that fled in terror, their teeth chattering.

VI.

But the unfortunate widow did not flee.

---

[50] An oxydizing liquid whose active component was sodium hypochlorite, used as a disinfectant and bleach.

Sublime, she approached the chemist.

"Give me the rest of the poison," she said.

"Why, Madame?"

Then, adorable in her grace and affliction, she said: "I've sworn to die the same death as my husband."

But the chemists refused. They had a deep hole dug and threw the redoubtable liquid into it.

"Curse you!" cried the poor young woman.

And, maddened, she started running through the streets of Paris, in search of someone who would give her the alms of a few drops of pure water.

VII.

She did not find any.

She went to a pharmacist.

"Two grams of pure water, Monsieur," she begged.

"Do you have a prescription?" demanded the disciple of Galen.

The desperate widow visited every pharmacist in the capital, offering them pieces of gold.

All of them were unshakable.

Then, crazed, she quit Paris and started roaming the countryside.

"Ah, rain!" she said to herself. "That's pure water! I'll wait until it rains!"

Having considered the sky attentively, however, she saw—as she had suspected, alas—that as a public safety measure, the State had installed a kind of glass roof over the countryside, in order that the water of the heavens should never fall upon human mucus.

"A river!" she said, then. "A stream! A spring!"

But there were no longer any springs, streams or rivers in France. Sagely, the State had captured all the pure watercourses, for fear that the inhabitants of rural areas might poison themselves, and only the Seine flowed in the open, triumphantly, because of its wealth of microbes, which were so large and so invariably prosperous, that one could fish for them with a line all the way from Paris to Le Havre.

VIII.

And after a week of vain running around, the poor widow collapsed, exhausted, in a desert plain. Heartbroken to be unable to die like her husband, she awaited death with resignation.

But then the Creator took pity on her.

The zenith suddenly darkened, and, at the moment when the disconsolate widow stammered the name of her spouse, she expired gloriously, poisoned as her husband had been.

With enormous hailstones, Heaven had smashed the bell-jar under which the French were ripening, and, mercifully, having perceiving that the widow had an upturned nose, had deigned to rain inside.

Jean Rameau: *Future Art*
(1887)

I.

In those days, Raphael Larifla, a young painter of great talent who had the fantastic ambition of living on the produce of his work, presented himself at the establishment of an art dealer at the same time as a heavy truck carrying a pictorial masterpiece of 84 square meters (seven by twelve).

"Monsieur," he said to the dealer, "I offer you *Vercingetorix Before Caesar*, a painting that attracted a great deal of attention at the Chicago Exposition last year, where it prevented the air currents from getting into the Hall of Fine Arts.

And Raphael had his work unwrapped.

"Monsieur," the painter went on, "I know the taste of buyers, so I have taken my precautions to ensure the painting's sale. Notice that one would only have to stick a newspaper on the head of my Vercingetorix for the celebrated Gaul to resemble Monsieur Ohnet, and that Caesar, rigorously speaking, could pass for Monsieur Paulus."[51]

The art dealer seemed cold.

"Remark in addition, Monsieur," Larifla continued, "that my paining is conceived in accordance with the principles of the new school; that my Vercingetorix is sufficiently imprecise for one to be able to see, by blinking one's eyes, entire scholarly battalions filing past; by turning the frame upside

---

[51] Georges Ohnet (1848-918) was a prolific novelist reputed to be an expert judge of popular taste. Paulus was the stage-name of the singer Jean Paul Habans (1845-1908), a star of the café concert circuit.

down, a steamship or something approximating thereto; by leaning to the left, Monsieur de Lesseps and his family; by leaning to the right, a unset over Constantinople, or perhaps an equestrian portrait of Sarah Bernhard—look for Damala."[52]

The merchant made a gesture of impatience.

"Well, Monsieur, if it's necessary to tell you everything," Raphael sighed, desperately, "the canvas is impermeable, and I don't doubt that you'll be able to place it with a packer who…"

"Monsieur," said the dealer, "I like your painting very much, but unfortunately, America sends us articles wrapped in gutta-percha…"

"Raphael did not wait to hear any more. He went out like a gust of wind.

"Bourgeois!" he shouted. "Make works of art yourself, then!"

And he broke his brushes.

II.

Ten years later, Larifla, still an artist and still fantastically ambitious, went into the establishment of another dealer.

Disgusted with painting, he had taken up sculpture and had come to offer a group: *Vercingetorix Before Caesar* (again!), which Pugin would not have disavowed.

"Monsieur," said Raphael, "I'll let you have this work of art at a good prince: sixty francs. Notice, I beg you, that Vercingetorix has, around the waist, twenty-four rings for umbrellas, and that on Caesar's head, I've stuck a few pegs on which hats and overcoats can be hung. I hope, therefore, that for a vestibule…"

---

[52] Jacques Damala was the stage-name of Aristide Damalas (1855-1889), who married Sarah Bernhardt in 1881; he was an utter swine, and no one else could understand why she was briefly infatuated with him; the spouses soon separated but never divorced.

"All my regrets, Monsieur," the dealer interrupted. "For nineteen francs ninety-five I already have one far more advantageous, sculpted by the celebrated Balaruc himself."

And he showed Raphael a superb Apollo, metamorphosing successively, into a billiard cue, a telescope, a rod for angling and bootjacks, which had won the medal of honor at the previous Salon.

Larifla went away, tearing out his hair.

III.

Fifteen years later, the impenitent artist, who called himself Raphael, went into a publisher's office. Seeing that he had not been able to achieve anything with painting and sculpture, he had devoted himself to poetry.

"Monsieur," he said, "I've brought you *Vercingetorix Before Caesar*, an epic in verse, which I shall have printed at my own expense. I only ask you to put the name of your house on the cover."

The editor started.

"Oh, have no fear," said Raphael, "it's poetry written in the modern fashion. I say that two and two make five at the beginning of every chapter, I mention a young mother who eats her baby with asparagus tips and, half the time, I write things I can't even comprehend myself. So..."

"Monsieur..."

"That's not all. The work will be printed on emery paper, so that the buyers of my books can always use it for scouring their saucepans."

"Monsieur," replied the editor, with dignity, "here, we only publish works in verse whose paper can serve as flypaper."

Raphael became livid, put his hands to his neck, and vanished.

IV.

What became of him? No one knows. Friends found him in a hospital a few weeks later. Then, well-informed people affirmed that Raphael was living locked away in his studio with his three masterpieces, at which he gazed successively, while making broad gestures madly, and anointing them with bizarre drugs.

V.

Fifteen years later, the dealers in paintings, statues and books of verse saw a thin old man arrive who presented himself to them under the appearance of an escapee from a lunatic asylum.

It was Raphael Larifla.

"I've found it, you know!" he cried. "I've found it!"

"What?"

"The means of disposing of my works. Do you want to see?"

They went to see.

On the way, Larifla picked up art critics, reporters, grocers and all the luminaries of the artistic world.

"You'll see! You'll see!" Raphael was still shouting—and his voice had vibrations of triumph..

"There they are!" he said, taking his hat off before his works.

They saw the immense painting, the immense group and the immense poem.

"Is anyone here bald?" asked Raphael.

They looked at one another in bewilderment.

"Does anyone here have a headache?"

He had decidedly become an idiot.

"Is anyone here hungry?"

More than an idiot, a madman.

"Here, appreciate this work of art for me," said Larifla, cutting the hand off his Vercingetorix and offering it to the critics.

A shiver ran through the audience. They threw themselves upon the group, upon the poem, upon the painting...

"Long live Larifla!" the cried, in formidable unison.

And Larifla fell down, stone dead, killed by the unexpected but legitimate triumph.

In fact:

His group was made of spiced bread.

His poem was written on mustard-plaster paper.

And his painting, exceptionally fatty and divisible into little pieces, was a sovereign remedy against hair loss.

VI.

There was a rush to acquire the Master's works.

It was the city of Paris, let us say in his honor, that put in the highest bids.

The *Vercingetorix* (group in the manner of the Foire du Trône) was erected in the courtyard of a communal school.

The *Vercingetorix* (poem imitative of Rigollot)[53] was placed in the Salpêtrière.

And finally, the *Vercingetorix* (painting for the hairy scalp) was placed worthily in a hospice for the aged blind.

Everything comes to he who waits.

---

[53] Paul-Jean Rigollot (1810-1873) was the pharmacist who invented "Rigollot paper," a poultice made from black mustard, intended to facilitate breathing during respiratory distress.

Jean Rameau: *The Mannequin-Man*
(1887)

I.

That day—one day next year, no doubt—was the birth-day of the great, the illustrious, the enormously popular Cabalistras.

Since the morning, delegations of all sorts—musical so-cieties, hairdressing academies, orthopedic institutes—had filed under the windows of the Master, who, intent on nurtur-ing his celebrity, was obliged to appear on his balcony three hundred and forty-seven times and kiss queues of young women clad in white, who offered him tricolor bouquets.

II.

"Oof! I'm exhausted!" cried the great man, at about three o'clock in the afternoon.

And, his spine exhausted by little bows, his head disequilibrated by accolades, and his hands swollen by ap-plauding fanfares, he collapsed on a sofa.

"Master!" cried one of the most fervent disciples of Cabalistras, at that moment. "Here comes the delegation of Colossal Women; it's indispensable that you appear and ad-dress a few heartfelt words to the crowd."

"Send for the mannequin," sighed the great man. "I can't do any more."

And, in accordance with his orders, they sent for the mannequin.

III.

The mannequin was a Cabalistras in wax, articulated and able to talk, which the real Cabalistras, who liked to see his name in print in the newspapers as often as possible, sent in his stead to premières, inaugurations of statues and various official solemnities in which it was sufficient to put in an appearance, when he did not have time to go there himself. A fine invention, that mannequin.

The Cabalistras in wax, moreover, represented the Cabalistras of flesh and blood very worthily, and the reporters never had to point out anything that was incorrect in his behavior.

Two of the Master's disciples, therefore, opened a cupboard and brought out a gentleman in a black suit, loaded a roll into his belly—the accolades and ovations roll—switched on a mechanism hidden in the back...*vroom! vroom! vroom!*...and shoved the mannequin toward the balcony.

"Long live Cabalistras!" cried ten thousand throats.

The mannequin bowed, and in a perfectly imitated voice, said "Flattered. Very flattered...!"

Then, at brief intervals, while bouquets, palms and crowns were thrown to him: "Thank...you! Thank...you! This great day...ineradicable memory in my heart...Thank...you... Very flattered!"

And finally, as the choir-master of the Midwives of Montmartre intoned a "Hymn to Cabalistras" composed for the occasion:

"Bra-vo! Bra-vo! Bra-vo!" said the mannequin, applauding with his hands, correctly.

And he went back in, saying several times to the delirious crowd:

"Bless you! Bless you"

IV.

Now Cabalistras—the real one—who, in order to be better shielded from importunity, had retired to the apartment reserved for his wife, was sleeping peaceful on a sofa when he was woken up with a start by the sound of resounding kisses, coming from the next room.

"Can't they go and kiss one another further away?" he muttered.

Intrigued, he took a few silent steps in order to see where the unusual noise was coming from.

He suddenly recoiled.

"Heavens! My wife with one of my admirers!" he exclaimed.

After reflecting for a second, he added: "As long as they don't know that I've seen them!"

And he went away discreetly, on tiptoe.

V.

He went into another room, and then into a second, and then a third—but by a sinister fatality, his wife and his admirer came in after him.

"Oh! No other way out!" he observed, with terror, on arriving in his wife's bedroom.

He tried to hide behind the door, but a mirror betrayed his presence. He tried to slide behind a sideboard, but rheumatism prevented him from doing so.

"Damn! They're going to catch me!" said Cabalistras to himself, shivering. "Oh, it's terrible! Doomed! Dishonored! Obliged to fight a duel! Criminal that I am! That'll teach me!"

And, his legs trembling, he stopped.

VI.

"Heavens! My husband!" said Madame Cabalistras, with a stifled scream.

"Where?" asked the Master's admirer.

"There, in that corner! We're doomed!"

And they remained nailed to the pot.

But Cabalistras also remained motionless...

And a sudden burst of laughter suddenly resounded.

"He's not moving! It's his mannequin!" the lovers said to one another.

And they entered without fear.

My mannequin! reflected the illustrious husband. *What an idea! Yes, everything's saved! Thank you, God!*

VII.

"Flatt-ered! Very flatt-ered!" said Cabalistras, bowing to the two lovers.

There laughter was redoubled.

"Ah! Good—it's the accolades and ovations roll. This will be funny."

And they locked the door.

"Oh, my angel!" exclaimed the admirer. "Oh, my Suzanne…!"

"Very flatt-ered, Thank...you!" the husband continued, his fists clenched.

And he gazed imperturbably at his disciple, who kissed Madame Cabalistras on both cheeks.

"Wait! He's no longer talking!" said Suzanne, suddenly, blushing slightly. "Is it..."

Cabalistras rolled his eyes ferociously.

"This fine day... Thank...you! Thank...you!" he said, clicking his teeth.

"What if we put him in a cupboard?" risked the admirer.

"Oh, no, André! It's too amusing. Listen to him!"

And she put her arms around her lover's neck.

Cabalistras thought he was going to explode with rage. What an ordeal, Lord!

"I'll go and wind him up," said his wife. "The roll must have run out."

She offered her neck for a kiss.

"Bra-vo! Bra-vo! Bra-vo!" roared Cabalistras, whose eyes took on a gleam of madness.

And that was said in a voice so forceful, so desperate and so strange that the two lovers looked at one another, bewildered, and started to tremble...

VIII.

Several seconds passed like that, perhaps several minutes, during which no one moved, no one spoke, and everyone's teeth were chattering. A tragic situation.

And the mannequin's hair was seen to stand up on his head.

They drew nearer.

"He's sweating huge drops!" exclaimed Suzanne. "If that isn't..."

The lovers drew nearer, coming to look the mannequin in the face.

"I bless you! I bless you!" gasped Cabalistras.

And, to their great amazement, he ran for the door.

"God!" cried the guilty pair, chilled by fear.

And they fainted.

IX.

And Cabalistras continued fleeing, recklessly, along corridors, along galleries, up and down staircases

"Long live Cabalistras!" he suddenly heard.

It was the crowd, a hundred thousand admirers acclaiming him.

He stopped, and looked around fearfully.

"Eh? What! I'm...but yes, the mannequin! Flatt-ered! Very flatt-ered!" he declaimed.

And, no longer knowing whether he was a man or a mannequin, he ran to the balcony.

"Long live Cabalistras!" shouted the crowd.

Cabalistras took a revolver from his pocket.

Bang! Bang! Bang!

Three detonations rang out. And the mannequin, who was saluting the crowd, fell to the ground, its cardboard head traversed by three bullets.

"Well, what?" howled Cabalistras—the real one. "He's dishonored, that man! He has a right to kill himself!"

And imagining that he had killed himself, he fell down on the parquet, insane."

X.

"Damn! Damn!" exclaimed the director of the lunatic asylum to whom Cabalistras was handed over, a short while later. "Here's one who must have passed through terrible anguish!"

And it was remarked, in fact, that the eminent husband's hair had turned instantaneously white—with a hint of yellow.[54]

Horrible!

---

[54] In France, yellow, rather than green, is the color emblematic of jealousy.

Jean Rameau: *Electric Life*
(1887)

This story will happen before long.

I.

One morning, a child came into the world.

"What shall we call him?" said the father.

"To," replied the mother.

"Right! To: a short name. We won't waste as much time pronouncing it."

And the child was called To.

II.

The day after his birth. To was placed by his parents in an apparatus for maturing babies. It was a recent invention: an apparatus that, in seven months, rendered an infant seven years old, physically and intellectually—which made a saving of six years.

III.

"My son," said To's father, at the end of the seventh month, "you're now ready to study and undertake your apprenticeship in life. Study and learn! Remember that time is money and that the future belongs to the man who knows how to use all the minutes of his life. Go, my son; I'll cuddle you tomorrow if my rheumatism prevents me from going to the Bourse.

IV.

And To studied, learning frenetically, devouring books night and day, only eating condensed aliments in order to waste less time on meals, and teaching himself to squint, in accordance with the method of a famous physician, in order to be able to read two books are the same time.

At twenty-five, To was already the most energetic man of his century

V.

One day, when he was dictating five dispatches simultaneously—pardon, shade of Caesar!—riffling through a directory with his left hand and an atlas with his right, while one of his ears was listening over the telephone to a speech made in the Senate and the other to the song of a nightingale, To perceived with his left eye, in the street, an adorable young woman passing by.

Thunderbolt!

She was beautiful…etc, etc.

In brief, he made enquiries, found her address, presented himself and was admitted to pay court to her.

VI.

Oh, their hearts were both beating rapidly!

"My name's To," he said. "And you, Mademoiselle?"

"Zi!"

"I have a fortune of a million. And you, Mademoiselle?

"A million and a half."

"Good. I love you. And you, Mademoiselle?"

"I love you too."

And no sooner said, than they were married.

Hup!

VII.

Were happy.
Had few children. No time.
Only two twins.
And To made fabulous sums.
Zi too.
To founded, on average, a bank a day, in Paris, Berlin, Constantinople or Santa-Fe-Bogota.
On average too, he created at least one bankruptcy.
Colossally rich.

VIII.

He dug canals, discovered mines, dried up seas, reconnected pierced isthmuses, reignited extinct volcanoes and amazed his contemporaries with his exploits.

One evening, busy transforming Etna into a vast central-heating boiler to warm the whole of Sicily with the aid of subterranean conduits radiating from the volcano, he learned by telegram of his father's death.

To was worthy.

"I'll weep for you," he said, in a tone penetrated with tenderness, "when I have time, in my old age."

He inscribed in his account book:

Owed to Papa: tears and eternal regrets.

IX.

Returning home unexpectedly one evening, he found a man in his wife's boudoir.

"Huh! Ought to know, Monsieur," To grunted, "not too much free time at the moment..."

He interrupted himself. A second individual was hiding under the table.

"Eh! But...! What the...?"

A third appeared behind a screen.

"But...!"

"Pardon, my love! Am very guilty!" sobbed Zi, who appeared in the company of a fourth lover. "But to save time, I thought..."

"That's fine!" exclaimed To.

And, putting his wife's lovers side by side the middle of the room: "No time to kill you one by one," he announced. "Going to avenge my honor *en bloc*. Don't move!"

And he aimed a newly-invented device at the platoon: the household machine-gun.

X.

The lovers tried to flee, each in a different direction.

"Monsters!" roared To. "You'll pay me, then!"

And, having closed the doors, he took a dagger in each hand and, frantic and terrible, desperate in thinking about the time he was about to waste avenging his honor piecemeal, he charged the platoon

Screams. Blood. Death-rattles.

XI.

He used feet and fists. It was horrible. It took him half an hour to kill them all. And when he had laid all four rivals on the floor, To's teeth stated chattering.

He could not stop the convulsive movements of his arms, his legs, his head and his body. He had himself tied up, garroted, bound to a plank.

In vain.

The puppet, overtaxed by frenetic roil, had broken down. He had St Vitus' Dance.

"That's fine!" he said. "Will be able to amuse myself cultivating the arts now."

And, seeing the disordered twitches that his hands were making, he sat down at the piano.

XII.

A few minutes later he fell over, paralyzed on the right side.

"Papa," one of his sons said to him. "Have consulted medic on your case."

"Well?" asked To, anxiously.

"As going to Père-Lach, would you like me to light oven for your cremat?"

"Go light my inf!" cried To, flattered to have a son so energetic and so hurried.

And he expired.

XIII.

"Mama!" said the two twins, then. "Pap's dead, never having had time to kiss us."

"That's true," reflected the mother. "Nor me."

Rapidly, they approached the dear departed, provoked a stirring of his lips with the aid of an electric current, and then, piously, all three of them advanced their faces and were given a posthumous kiss.

Régis Vombal: *The Immortal* (1908)

I. In which there is question of an astonishing discovery and some sensational amputations

Midnight was chiming at Saint-Jacques-du-Haut-Pas when Doctor Jacobus van Brucktel raised toward his lamp the test-tube, full to the brim with a liquid, that he had been watching over for an hour. The old scientist had just discovered, quite simply, the elixir of life: the divine liquor that assured anyone who took a few drops of it of immortality.

He remained pensive for a moment.

That phial of violet liquid could upset the world, which had no suspicion of anything.

Death was henceforth a word devoid of meaning; the natural order was destroyed; and yet, at that moment, physicians' bells were ringing; sons at bedsides were receiving their mother's last breath; people everywhere were suffering, weeping and dying.

Everything was changed completely; humans would no longer be human. And he, Jacobus van Brucktel, had just carried out a theft from God similar to the one for which the Titan Prometheus, millennia ago, had been subjected to the agonizing outrage of the vulture that devoured his liver.

Yes, like him, but less fortunate, Prometheus had once stolen the sacred fire of the Master of gods and men, the redoubtable thunderous Zeus, who, having had him chained to a rock, sent a bird of prey that plunged its hooked, bloody, horny beak into his renascent entrails every day.

In the street, long silent, students who were coming out of the brasserie and returning to their lodgings went by, laughing; a young woman was singing, and the light couplets rose up to the scientist's window, celebrating in the peace of the spring night, the card games at Robinson's, the swings in the gardens, the intimate suppers under arbors garlanded with convolvulus, and the melancholy of all the human things of which people would weary, and which would end after a few seasons.

The old man smiled strangely and gazed ardently at the crystal phial in which the clear violet liquid was sparkling.

He was only thinking about himself. Since he had discovered the remedy for death, he was about to be the first to test it. He was old, to be sure, but robust, and without any of the infirmities that make old age an interminable agony; he was about to drink, to become immortal.

He went to fetch a small glass from the kitchen, poured the contents of the test-tube into it and raised the glass toward the lamp.

It was of Prometheus that he was still thinking, and it was him that he saluted with a slightly puerile bombast, offering to that torture-victim of mythological legend a radiant toast with the most precious of liqueurs.

"Salut, O Prometheus," he said, "distant ancestor, precursor, forefather of all those who have wanted to steal the fire and unveil the great secrets! Salut, admirable thief, for it is in honor of your memory that I am about to drink this elixir, which you foresaw at the dawn of the centuries, O thunderstruck!"

In a single draught, he swallowed the warm liquid. Then he remained alone in the silence of the night, listening to the rumble of carriages, the laughter of the students and the young woman's song die away in the depths of the Rue Gay-Lussac.

When he woke up the next day, the May sunlight came into his bedroom, the shutters of which he had forgotten to close, and he recalled his discovery of the previous day in a flash. He got out of bed delightedly. As soon as he was dressed and his housekeeper had served his chocolate, he went out, having to buy a few drugs from a pharmacist that he needed for his experiments.

It is futile to explain what happened as he came out of the shop; such things have no explanation. Doubtless distracted, he could not get out of the way in time, and an enormous autobus laden with passengers ran over him. He was carried home, and one of his friends amputated both his legs.

It is necessary to admit that the elixir he had discovered did not render the body any younger, nor invulnerable, but only ensured that the soul, the principle of life, withdrew from the mutilated parts, able to animate the smallest parcel, the most humble organism, that remained intact.

Furthermore, the liquor embalmed, in a sense, the entire being, and there was no further need for nourishment once it had been absorbed.

The shock of the amputation, however, had had an effect on the scientist that has often been observed. A curious amnesia followed the operation, and Jacobus van Brucktel could no longer remember the miraculous formula.

Cases of amnesia are more frequent than is believed, and often rather bizarre.

There is the well-known story of the banker who was carrying half a million in a valise, and was the victim of a derailment on the railway; there were no papers in his bag and no card in his wallet. He was cared for in a small station in the Midi, where he settled and lived for five years. He had forgotten his name, his wife and his children, and was about to get married when he read on a café concert poster: *Debut of Madame Georgette Stella.*

He was like a man walking through a dark stormy night who sees, in a flash of lightning, an entire red-tinted horizon, chalky and yet quite clear, with the crenellations of rocks on the mountain, and trees exactly delineated by the abrupt light. From the utmost depths of his torpid memory, a name—his forgotten name—rose up slowly; he sensed it, like a little bright bubble that is only waiting for the open air to burst. Frightened, he followed its dolorous ascent, full of hope, fearful of the dark, for the interval of a quarter of a second, and suddenly the words he sought sang in his brain like the clang of a bell, hummed in his joyful heart and filled his mouth: Georges Estel! His name was Georges Estel!

Dr. Jacobus had only forgotten his formula.

The physician, who did not expect him to pull through, because of his advanced age, was astonished to see him, after a week, not on his feet, since he no longer had any, but as hearty as in the times when, shod in sturdy American boots, he had taken his regular after-dinner walk in the Luxembourg.

Jacobus van Brucktel was rich. He hired a valet, bought the most advanced carriage, and did not sacrifice any of his habits.

Nor did he abandon either his work or his scientific research, and he was in the process of inventing a new powder when his retort exploded, this time ripping apart his arms, in such a fashion that they had to be amputated at the shoulder.

He recovered.

His valet picked him up like a parcel, put him on the seat of an automobile and took him for an excursion in the Bois every afternoon.

The sleeves of his jacket dissimulated the absent limbs quite well, but among the strollers and the masters of elegant carriages that the doctor's machine went past, no one would have thought that that human trunk had once known the secret of life.

He was even-tempered; the experience amused him prodigiously, and what infirm individual does not, over time, become accustomed to his condition?

The days went by, and the years.

Scientists came from all over to see what remained of Dr. Jacobus van Brucktel. He had followed in his vehicle the funeral processions of all his friends, the sons, the daughters and the grandsons of his friends, and he alone remained of an epoch whose houses were already beginning to be demolished.

People came to consult him about everything; historians laid siege to his door, for his journal, written day after day by his secretaries, was the most complete of the records of history.

He was for the generations of the year 2300 what an old man who had known Louis XIV would have been for our time, and who could say: "I saw the king on the evening of the day of the death of Charles le Téméraire; he had toothache, and his jaw was swollen, but he was laughing..."

One day, he confessed to a journalist that he repented of having drunk a toast to Prometheus when he had drunk the elixir, still warm, that he had discovered. He believed that God had struck him as Jupiter had struck the Titan.

He endured, he still endured, and that appeared to him to be a supreme irony; he, of whom hardly anything remained, witnessed the deaths of all those robust individuals; he saw the young women depart who passed beneath his windows, drunk on youth and spring, saw generations extinguished, governments succeed one another, the centuries file past before him, an imperishable human milestone, like the images of the god Terminus that had witnessed in their stone sheath the festivals of ancient Rome, the invasion of the Barbarians, the devastations of several thousand years, and which remained, in spite of everything, in spite of the days of murderous time.

He had rented a country house in a pleasant setting on the banks of the Marne, and gave orders, one July evening, for the departure. The following morning, the automobile was humming outside his door like a huge insect of vermilion-painted steel, and his valet took him down to the vehicle.

The light machine carried him to what had been in our day the Gare de l'Est, through avenues two hundred meters wide bordered by fifty-story houses.

None of the heavy vehicles we know encumbered the streets with their slowness and their noise; only a few rapid automobiles, silent and infinitely improved, furrowed the gigantic boulevards—but in the air, the spectacle was prodigious!

Aerial trains and vast airplanes transported hosts of passengers a thousand feet up in the azure. Aerostatics no longer had any secrets for that epoch, and squadrons of balloons were moving through the open sky.

They were of all forms and dimensions. The largest were elongated, like ships, others were similar to fish, baskets or birds, and they were all crossing paths, flying, soaring in the blue sky with their flags, the fabric ornamenting their nacelles, and women's veils floating in the wind.

Dr. Jacobus van Brucktel's automobile was speeding along the immense avenue beneath the splendid airship when a dog that the driver had not perceived was run over, and caused the machine to swerve fatally. The man let go of the steering-wheel and the vehicle crashed into a wall.

II. In which nothing but a head can any longer be seen, but in which an issue of the Petit Parisien *can be read 405 years in advance.*

When Dr. Jacobus van Brucktel was brought out, there was great alarm: on the crushed torso, the head alone was alive.

At the hospital to which he was immediately transported, he asked to see the surgeon. He explained to him that so long as a piece of him remained intact, he would not perish; they could cut off and remove anything they wanted.

He was relieved of his pulped torso. He was reduced to his simplest expression, conserving nothing but his head. On the evening of the accident, all the newspapers carried banner headlines in which one could read:

DOCTOR JACOBUS, THE IMMORTAL,
VICTIM OF AN ACCIDENT
ONLY HIS HEAD SPARED: STILL ALIVE.

And great luminous transparencies displayed in the open sky, all night long, in all the cities, the illustrious head on the hospital bed: the serene, clean-shaven head with the soft smile on its lips.

When the bloody section had scarred over, the doctor who had carried out the operation picked up the head and carried it away. In the same voice, Jacobus van Brucktel greeted his domestics, joking as he entered, and, not wanting to remain on the table where he had been placed like a melon, had a kind of pedestal constructed by a workman, as tall as a man: a padded stele on which he lived henceforth.

He seemed thus, alongside his bookshelves, to be a living piece of sculpture. He stayed there until dusk. He read, his maid turning the pages of the book she held in front of him. Sometimes, the pedestal was taken to the window, and the doctor's head watched the bustle of the street, recognized passers-by, always interested in life.

Time passed, but his symbolic scythe would have blunted itself in vain on the threshold of Dr. Jacobus van Brucktel.

Like the Roman images of the god Terminus to which we have already compared him, he witnessed all the evolutions impassively.

In any case, nothing very sensational occurred after the year 1989. When we say "nothing very sensational," we obviously do not mean that literally, but nothing caused any abrupt upheaval in the world. The sure scientific conquests, linked to one another, the progress that we cannot even suspect, seemed natural and inevitable things, arriving in their time with a mathematical precision. People scarcely remembered the great shock of 1989.

After muted agitations, discontentments, and an abominable war that had scythed down several generations, the antique social framework had simply cracked, like something too old, too worn out, and a new order had triumphed. Life was enlarged, powerful machines reduced the part of labor and drudgery to negligibility; peaceful humanity relaxed.

For the cost of a lunch in an airship restaurant one could go to Venice or Moscow.

Distance no longer existed.

The most sedentary, most home-loving people had seen the marine solitudes of oceans, deserts, high African plateaux, the icy peaks of Cordilleras, mysterious islands and unexplored wildernesses flee beneath their feet, from nacelles decked with oriflammes.

Newlyweds made their honeymoon voyages to Tahiti or Ispahan amid fields of roses or garden of jasmine. All the maladies that decimate us scarcely existed; powerful serums preserved people from them. It also seemed that the old wines had lost all their force, and that Evil, weary of being Evil, had been vanquished.

Only Death had not been disarmed. It was, as it is today, on the horizon of all hopes, al joys and all lies, like a great mysterious black hole. The human mind had only conquered the earth, but that it had conquered completely; it was no longer a vale of tears, a dolorous halt, a poor inn full of moans and resentment; humans disposed of it at their whim, while awaiting peace there.

One morning in May 2313, Dr. Jacobus van Brucktel's head, posed on his stele, some distance from the window, was gazing at the light sky, in which innumerable airships were floating, when Clarisse, his maid, knocked on the door and came in.

She was holding a newspaper in her hand; it was the *Petit Parisien*, the only title that had lasted until then.

Clarisse was not dressed like the women of today, but in a kind of pink tunic, and veils draped in the Greek manner, for in that era, loose, comfortable and brightly-colored garments had replaced the sheaths that confine our bodies narrowly.

The sports that almost everyone practiced made limbs more robust and supple, and Clarisse displayed two bare, round, muscular arms: the adorable arms of a young female wrestler. Her feet were also bare, in sandals attached at her ankles by an apple-green ribbon. A blue headband gathered her beautiful blonde hair.

She moved the doctor's head to one side, into the frame of the window, and the light sunlight of the nascent spring played in her gilded curls, as immaterial as smoke.

Although it was prohibited for balloons to pass between the houses, Clarisse's fiancé, a mechanic with a short brown moustache, caused the two-seater dirigible that he was piloting to execute a savant swoop, stopped momentarily outside the window, and blew the blushing young woman a kiss.

"Amour is ever imprudent," murmured Dr. Jacobus, with his centuries-old lips. "Ever imprudent, and ever joyful."

Clarisse's face was still tinted pink when she came to sit on a divan upholstered in colors that would astonish us a great deal, and unfolded the newspaper that she was responsible for reading to her master.

She had the trained diction of an associate of the Comédie-Française and the learning of a Faculty professor, like all the young women of the day.

She began:

"The Yellow Peril. Finally, the anxiety in which we were living has dissipated. The Asiatic fleet has been annihilated at sea in the Pacific Ocean.

"The yellow coalition would certainly never have been able to disembark its forces in European ports, but such a prompt annihilation was unexpected.

"A few Japanese battleships were able to escape the disaster, but the heavy Chinese transport ships have all sunk.

"The international squadron of military airships had arrived at daybreak, with all lights extinct, over the immense Asiatic fleet, like s sudden flock of mighty birds of prey. The spectacle was prodigious. A centuries-old quarrel was about to be settled. Europe, redoubtable, knowledgeable old Europe, having conquered all, was floating above the menacing forces of Asia.

"Beneath the armored nacelles, the solitudes of the Pacific extended infinitely, like turbulent plains. Thousands of ships formed a kind of moving city in that marine desert. It was four o'clock in the morning when the chief engineer, the Frenchman Jacques Desaix, gave the signal to attack.

"The valves opened, the terrible rain, the rain of iron and fire of immense bombs, fell, while the aircraft climbed out of range of the fleet's cannons, which scarcely responded. Beneath the torpedoes and explosives, beneath the great tubes charged with our frightful blue powder, the sea and the air reared up toward us, and then gulfs opened, swallowing the broken, burning, smashed ships.

"The enormous cannons of the vessels coughed lugubriously and sank into the sea. The disaster is complete, and we shall be tranquil for a century."

The immortal head of Dr. Jacobus smiled. He remembered the year 1905, European battleships blown up in Japanese bays, Russian armies vanquished in the bare and torrid plains of Manchuria!

"Continue, I beg you, Clarisse," he requested—and the young maidservant finished the sensational article.

"The dirigibles are to return this evening, in the course of the celebrations that Europe entire will hold for those formidable iron birds, emerged from their hangars and moving through the sunlit sky...

"Latest news. The Council of the Just decreed this morning that the gold and silver coins withdrawn from circulation will be made into crowns for young women who already have two children.

"The death has been announced in Saint Petersburg of the President of the Russian Republic, Dr. Yvan Sianeski, the grandson of the scientist who discovered the cancer microbe and found the serum against the terrible malady that ravaged the twentieth century.

"The death has also been announced of the celebrated cantatrice Bianca Dantellina. She was eighteen years of age. A national funeral will be held in Rome.

"The Ancients have organized the spring festivals. Balloons will sprinkle flower petals over cities all night and all day."

III. Which might be entitled: Memories and Tears...

After Dr. Jacobus van Brucktel's last accident, which had reduced him to his simplest expression, since nothing more remained of him than his head, the government of the epoch, the Council of the Just, decreed special measures whenever the extraordinary head undertook an excursion in his automobile or his balloon.

Vehicles had to travel when he passed by at a speed of fifteen kilometers an hour, and his two-seater airship had permission to fly between the walls of houses in the city, or, at high altitude, in zones of the sky in which other balloons never traveled.

On day in May 2450, the doctor's head expressed the desire to visit the Louvre, the rooms of which conserved the costumes, furniture and everything that remained of our century.

He had never made that pilgrimage to the relics of a distant past, which he nevertheless remembered as if it were yesterday.

The appearance of the old and somber Louvre, massive and solid, had hardly changed.

The curator of the Palace came to meet his machine and took the doctor's head in his own hands in order to take him in and take him up the broad marble stairs.

The galleries of paintings presented a lamentable sight. The bitumen of the canvases had risen to the surface and almost nothing remained of the masterpieces that we admire. Leonardo da Vinci's *Gioconda*, the pure face with the troubling smile, was a black patch in which a few features could barely be divined.

Only the old paintings made on wood, with pigments prepared by conscientious and savant artists, still survived. Of the moderns who had simply bought their tubes of paint from merchants, nothing at all remained.

Immediately, the head of Dr. Jacobus asked to be taken to the nineteenth century galleries. In the display cases, one could see costumes similar to the ones we wear. All the uniforms of our soldiers, along with weapons, short-range rifles, primitive and barbaric sabers, were assembled and labeled, like the short swords and rusty broken helmets of Roman soldiers, and the bucklers and pikes that we see in visiting he displays of antiques in our museums.

Before those costumes, and all the centuries-old garments, Dr. Jacobus van Brucktel remembered exactly. He had worn a uniform similar to that one more than five hundred years ago, when he had done his military service in a small town in the south of France.

He asked the curator who was listening to him speak if he could remain alone in the room for an hour, and when the functionary has placed the head on an armchair and had closed the door. Dr. Jacobus van Brucktel abandoned himself to his memories. They emerged from all those items of furniture, those costumes, those objects that were no longer used; they surrounded him, those memories, like a tide, and for the head that had triumphed over the murderous years, the emotion was infinitely powerful and sweet.

His youth rose up…he saw once again the serious and delicate face of his mother, in the little apartment in which they lived, near the Jardin des Plantes; the meals eaten on fine summer evenings next to the window open to a sea of foliage, while a young woman with whom he had been in love played the piano on the floor below. He distinctly heard the music, after centuries, slightly muffled by the floor. It began with a waltz by a celebrated composer of the epoch, whose name was no longer remembered; afterwards, the young woman played a sequence of popular songs, slow, sad and tearfully sentimental; and in the solemn silence of the room he murmured:

"Remember that, remember that!"

Yes, it was that tune she had played before closing her piano, on summer evenings, in the Rue de Buffon! And that was centuries—my God, centuries!—ago…

What moved him most of all were the dresses of the women of the nineteenth century. Elegant wax mannequins wore narrow dresses that molded them like sheaths. One

117

young woman with blonde hair hanging down over her fore-head, tucking up her skirt, still seemed to be alive and smiling. A long lace jacket floated over the summer dress; between her white ankle-boots and her bright skirt walnut-colored sticking were rounded, with silver flecks, and beneath an umbrella of cerise silk, her immense straw hat set a nimbus around her lovely face, like that of a tall, pert child.

Then the creamy white of an embroidered satin dress attracted his gaze, and he thought about his wedding.

His wedding! It was in 1865. Valentine had been twenty-five, and he had been twenty-six. He had just completed his studies, and a small fortune permitted him to envisage the future without dread.

What a day! It had been May, he remembered, and the sky had never been so blue. Washed by the previous day's rain, it had the appearance of an immense opal. The Église Saint-Etienne-du-Mont, near the Panthéon, was embalmed with incense, and when the ceremony was over, as they left, he had bumped into a red-haired girl who was selling white roses. He had bought the whole basket, and had covered Valentine's knees in flowers in the coupé cushioned in white velvet. Pigeons had been flying over the roof of the Bibliothèque Sainte-Geneviève; it was the time when the students were coming out of the schools in noisy bands. Their youth smiled at the nuptial cortege, and in the carriage that was carrying them away, he breathed in the odor of fresh roses, mingled with the perfume of new fabric rising from the dress of his blonde bride. Was she blonde! Was she pretty, Lord! Beneath the light crown of orange-blossom garlanding her hair, with its rebellious curls, and her cornflower-blue eyes...

Oh, what a life...what a dream, rather. If only he had discovered his elixir then, if only he had been able to immortalize his young wife, so that both of them could live with their bodies eternal!

But like a large bloodstain, in a nearby display-case, the madder-red trousers of a soldier of the line burst forth, and

Jacobus van Brucktel immediately relived the terrible year: 1870!

He had left his young wife with his mother and resumed service as a military physician, following the army, for in spite of his Dutch name, his family had been French for several generations. He had been wounded at Beaune-la-Rolande, and decorated by Gambetta's own hand. He had been part of General Crouzat's twentieth corps, and had fought against the troops of Grand Duke Mecklembourg.

Something else that was far away! And yet, no detail of it escaped him, for that year and the one that followed had been frightful for him, as they had been disastrous for France.

He saw it all again: the muddy, soaked roads where men and cannons were entangled; long, bleak, uncertain columns, marching with bowed heads, while along the flanks of the brigades, couriers and generals and staff-officers galloped past, hastening toward hills crowned at every moment with plumes of smoke, while the patient Prussians, like innumerable cockroaches, tightened their circle of iron every day. He had supported fatigue, hunger and cold, and when, after the war, he had returned to Paris, his mother had been waiting for him, dressed in black.

He had understood immediately. Valentine had died during the siege, and the letter had never reached him across the disorganized fatherland; he had not known.

The blow had been hard; then the days had passed, and he undertaken, in order to forget, studies that had absorbed him completely

He had reignited the extinct furnaces of the of alchemists, madmen, seekers that the Church had burned in the Middle Ages, prodigious occult scientists—and in the twilight of his life, when he no longer hoped for anything, he had seen the miracle produced and the marvelous liqueur fall in violent droplets, like liquid amethysts, into his retort...

When the curator of the Louvre opened the door, the hour having elapsed, the doctor's head, on the red damask armchair, was weeping.

IV. In which is witnessed a great celebration and a...

More large intervals of time went by. The generations succeeded one another, each bringing its discovery, and the immortal head of Dr. Jacobus van Brucktel witnessed those passages and those victories of humans over natural forces and old mysteries. The scientific conquests extended logically, like a long sequence of theorems, flowing mathematically one after another, and there was only one crime of savant madness to deplore. The scandal was enormous, but it would take us too far astray too recount that terrifying history, for which the entire twenty-sixth century retained an insurmountable horror.

Fortunately, toward the end of the same century, an astronomer discovered an apparatus that permitted life on the planet Mars to be seen. It vaguely resembled today's cinematographs. On great screens the appearances were imprinted of a world hitherto unknown. Theaters no longer existed, people having wearied of old worn-out and decrepit dramas, and the crowds of the year 2600 were surprised, in the luminous transparences, by the agitations of the beings that inhabited a heavenly body millions of leagues from the Earth.

The immortal doctor enjoyed an immense popularity, and every evening, the powerful luminous projections outlined his illustrious head in the clouds. It was during that year, 2600, that the government decided solemnly to celebrate Jacob van Brucktel's seven hundredth anniversary. The President of the Council of the Just disembarked from his airship, at the hour fixed for the ceremony, on to the balcony of the house where Dr. Jacobus lived. He was introduced into the room, where he made a speech; then, personally taking the celebrated head in his hands, he carried it to the nacelle ad placed it in the midst of the members of the government, on a mechanical pedestal admirably ornamented with foliage.

The machine rose into the sky above the colossal city.

It was floated alone in the blue solitudes of the sky when, at a given signal, balloons rose up from everywhere.

Aboard every nacelle, a young woman dressed in incredible silks threw flowers toward the machine in which the members of the government were, presided over by the doctor's had.

The people of Paris soared over the deserted city.

In an immense dirigible painted blue and entirely garlanded with branches that formed porches of verdure and charming triumphal arches, a choir of women, chosen from among the most beautiful, sang a hymn, and beneath the sparks of rockets that were bursting at vertiginous heights, the sky released a rain of iridescent pearls, vermilion fires, and clusters of bright stars.

Gradually, however, the sky cleared, and by midday, nothing remained in the open air but the government dirigible.

Then, the dull rumble of thunder was heard on the horizons, and war balloons—the entire international squadron—arrived, like a monstrous whirlwind. They stopped a hundred meters from the flowery nacelle, immobilized, forming an immense circle, lined up as if for a review.

The airship contained the head moved, passing slowly before them, like a delicate basket of flowers before a population of whales.

The crews applauded; vast red banners floated from the rigging, bearing inscriptions in white letters celebrating the glory of the doctor.

The President of the United States of America left his vessel and came to place a crown of laurels on the snowy hair of the immortal head.

After the popular rejoicing, which lasted all day, there was a great banquet that evening at the French presidency.

Although not eating, the doctor's head watched from the best place, on a flowery pedestal, wearing the crown offered by the United States.

When the meal was over, the guests went into the reception rooms of the Palace, where Dr. Jacobus van Brucktel met then; the interminable file-past lasted until midnight.

In a matter of hours people were able to come from Germany, Greece, Vienna or Constantinople, and the air was furrowed all night long by moving lights, which were the searchlights of dirigibles bringing all the dignitaries of Europe to the doctor's reception. On his decorated stele, with a word for everyone, he greeted those bowing passers-by and beautiful ephemera from the height of his immortality. He was, undoubtedly, only a head, and everything save for the pleasure of his eyes was forbidden to him, but at least he was alive, he could think, and his sensations were as fresh as in the days when, young and possessed of all his robust limbs, he had trod the paving-tones of a vanished Paris with his solid heels.

Those who filed past his living ruin certainly enchanted him with their beauty, and the complete harmony of their bodies. Wine delighted them, they could walk under the trees, over carpets of moss and grass, huddle together and embrace one another, but what did all that matter, since they would end, since each of them had a skeleton within, like a livid hidden monster, lying in wait, sly waiting for the moment of death to show the chalky whiteness of its bones.

He was philosophizing thus when a fresh young voice spoke behind him.

"Master, can you spare me a few moments?"

It was the daughter of the President of the Council of the Just, a tall child of twenty. She leaned on the flowery pedestal on which the laurelled head rested, near a window open to the delicious spring night, similar to the one on which Jacobus van Brucktel had found the secret of life.

From the fortieth floor of the palace, built on an artificial hill in the middle of parks, Paris extended, dotted with stars, which were lamps at windows.

The young woman spoke to the head, who replied now, in a different voice: "Yes, Mademoiselle, it's to you, it's to you above all that I ought to give the formula of my elixir. Don't hold anything against me; people have thought for a long time that I wouldn't surrender the recipe of my discovery out of jealousy of all those robust and healthy people. That isn't true...

"I shall try everything. Come and see my tomorrow; perhaps you'll discover among my papers, which you'll show to me, a clue, a sign, that will put me on the right track. I doubt it, but I'd like to do what I can for you.

"I'd like to conserve for you, firstly, that youth and that charming purity, but I'd like it, above all, because you remind me of the most cherished memories.

"More than seven hundred years ago, my dear child, I led to the altar of a church of which nothing much remains today a young woman who resembled you.

"Forgive my emotion, your eyes are the same violet color, your lips have the same shape.

"Look, would you like to accord me a favor, would you care to give me a kiss?"

The young woman's beautiful lips were near the doctor's mouth.

She leaned forward, but the head balanced on the flowery cushion titled backwards at the impact of the pure carcass, and, the window being open, the head fell from the fortieth floor into the street.

There were terrible cries, and everyone rushed forward. The young woman recounted what had happened.

When the head was found, it no longer had any form. Only one eye was still alive, as clear and lucid as that of a child. The soul of Jacobus van Brucktel had taken refuge there. He was not yet dead.

The Council sentenced the young woman to carry the living eye, set in a golden bracelet and protected by a thin sheet of crystal—a crystal chemically prepared, which nothing could dent or break.

And when nothing else remains of the world, when monuments of granite are nothing more than sections of crumbled walls, after centuries and centuries, at the end of everything, in the twilight of everything, in a clump of grass, only that strange pupil will continue to live, in the tarnished gold of the bracelet, and to remember.

Georges de La Fouchardière: *The Galloping Machine*
(1910)

Foreword

Even today, old sportsmen still cannot think without a sentiment of anguished curiosity about the mysterious events that unfolded on the turf twenty years ago and ended in the simultaneous and inexplicable disappearance of the trainer T. Griffith, senior, his crack horse Peau-de-Balle[55] and Baron Isaac de l'Échelle-Jacob.

With their vain investigations, seekers of enigmas have exceeded the patience of Comte Jérôme Thomas and the infinite forbearance of Monseigneur Bénin-Despalmes, the archbishop of Caudebec-en-Caux. Those honorable witnesses could provide no enlightenment, because they did not know anything, and had not seen anything or heard anything. Their role, although they had apparently been in the foreground, had been passive and unconscious.

I want to attempt to provide here a scientific explanation of that strange story; my task is facilitated by discreet and recent revelations.

I apologize to the readers of *Paris Sport* for fulfilling that office too simply, without literary effort and without employing the effort of preparation. I shall neglect the traditions of

---

[55] Peau-de-Balle has more than one colloquial meaning, the most innocent of which refers to the husk of a grain, and hence, metaphorically, to the uninteresting exterior of any precious or useful content. In one specialized instance of that formula, deriving from the fact that *balle* can mean testicle, the expression refers to the scrotum.

modern feuilleton fiction, whose formula is not dissimilar to that of a horse race: all the characters in the story start in a line; if one of them is detached at the beginning it is a deceptive sham; it is only a hundred meters before the finish—I mean the last hundred lines of the feuilleton—that one sees the outsider surge forth, the important and unexpected character, the one who has murdered the old lady or who will marry the general's daughter.

My method will be quite different; I shall represent the events in the order in which they happened, and immediately put in the light the principal facts and individuals. Readers will perhaps be grateful to me for not having decorated the narrative with any love story, however slight, in order not to hinder the rapidity of the action.

Finally, it is necessary, in order to avoid any malevolent supposition with regard individuals presently in view, not to lose sight of the fact that the affair happened not long after the Exposition of 1889—which is to say, in an epoch when jockeys still placed their backsides on their saddles, when trainers watched their colts gallop instead of watching the needle of a stop-watch turn, and when, finally, horses did not know the charms of the starting gate and only remained at the starting-post when they wanted to.

PART ONE: MADAME TAFOIREAU'S CRACK

I. In which the trainer Griffith receives strange visitors.

As all the sporting papers did not fail to report the following day, with touching unanimity, that the 26 April race meeting at Maisons-Lafitte was marked by two circumstances that had tended to become habitual since the beginning of the season: firstly, a diluvian rain that would have put out a Krakatoa—which deplorable weather, the reporters added, judiciously, using a formula that had never served any purpose, had had an unfortunate repercussion on the entrance receipts and the elegance of the paddock—and, secondly, the persistent bad luck, to the point of becoming proverbial, of the trainer T. Griffith senior.

In the course of the day, the stable had put five representatives in the starting line, three of which wore the striking colors of Madame Tafoireau and the other two the discreet silks of Comte Jérôme Thomas. All of them had met the same fate and had finished last, completely exhausted. The jockey, Blight, had the reputation, in fact, of not sparing either his whip or his spurs and striping the horses he rode even when all was lost, for honor's sake; he was a jockey of the old school.

T. Griffith senior, therefore, on returning home, had five good reasons for being in a filthy mood. He shut himself in his smoking room and, as it was necessary to expect, by eight o'clock in the evening he was the most perfectly drunk man in all Chantilly—which, in that epoch, supposed a veritable *tour de force*.

That was his fashion of consoling himself. In ordinary times he was very sober, and agreeable company; his intelligence and his culture put his professional qualities in relief; but in periods of bad luck, his capacities as a trainer gave way to a unique, exceptional quality as a recipient of alcohol. And, as the run of bad luck surpassed all measure this time, as much in intensity as duration, he beat his own consumption record every evening—which did not help at all, and gave no supplementary value to the next day's training.

Griffith had invented extraordinary mixtures in which champagne, pale ale and whisky, confusing their floods, were additionally seasoned by pimento and Cayenne pepper.

That evening, he was on his fifteenth glass when someone rang his doorbell.

"Eh! Joe, you damned blockhead! Go and open the door if you value your accursed jaw!"

Joe was Griffith's domestic. He had once been a jockey, but age, weight and, above all, a progressive stupidity had forced him to renounce his métier. Toward the end of his career he had not run a single race without taking the wrong course if it was not a straight line, and in that circumstance he mistook the finishing post.

Griffith had immediately taken him into his personal service. As a domestic, Joe had two precious qualities; firstly, he bore with a smile the volleys of blows administered to him by his employer; and secondly, when the trainer got drunk, he rapidly caught up with him. Certainly, in that special sport, Joe did not have the same expertise, or the same impressive style—the same class, in a word—but he was a good handicapper; he carried weight well.

Without staggering, Joe went as far as the entrance gate; he saw on the other side two people that he did not know. He decided, judiciously, that it must have been them who had rung the bell and examined them. One of them was enormous in every sense; the other, in Joe's intuitive opinion, could not have put up fifty-two kilos.

"Is Monsieur Griffith at home?" asked the big one, in French.

"He's in his *fumier*,[56] Monsieur," replied Joe, who could only speak English correctly.

"Well, go find him in his smoking-room and tell him that two gentlemen desire to talk to him about an urgent matter."

The gentlemen followed Joe as far as a tiled parlor abundantly decorated with portraits of horses.

A moment later, Griffith appeared. With a dazed expression he inspected the visitors from head to toe, as one looks at something one wishes to buy. A baroque association of ideas formed in his brain, and he suddenly burst out laughing.

"Why, it's the band!" he said

The fact is that the smaller of the strangers, with his clean-shaven, impassive face and his long gray hair carefully combed and swept backwards, really did look like a violinist, and the giant, with his curly beard and bald cranium, on which

---

[56] Were he able to speak French correctly, Joe would have said *fumoir* [smoking room]; a *fumier* is a dung-heap.

a russet patch looked more like mildew than a sprinkling of hair, irresistibly evoked the image of a trombone-player.

The two of them exchanged a glance and a shrug of the shoulders, the significance of which was obvious.

He's in a fine state! indicated the first.

It's to be expected—we were warned! suggested the second.

After which, they addressed gracious smiles to the trainer, which uncovered two rich sets of teeth, in the sense the gold played a large role therein.

At that sight, Griffith's ideas changed direction. *Yankees!* This time, his perspicacity was not in doubt.

The bearded giant, who seemed to want to take the lead, said: "Yes, Monsieur Griffith, we've come from Chicago. We've come especially, to talk to you about serious and confidential matters, and that's why we permitted ourselves to present ourselves at your home at this undue hour."

He waited for a polite protestation, but Griffiths attitude was not at all encouraging. He was thinking: *If these fellows have come to ask me for tips, or if they bring out a subscription list for the flood victims of Arkansas, or if they've come to disturb me in order to stick me with shares in Atkinson-Topeka Gold Mining, I'll bring my lads down and we'll escort these clients back to the railway station with the aid of pitchforks.*

The bearded Yankee continued: "I know, Monsieur Griffith, that in spite of your well-known skill, chance isn't smiling upon you at the moment. Your horses are having difficulty finding their form…and you also have other troubles…"

What's it got to do with him? wondered the trainer.

"So, Fred and I—my name's Tod—have crossed the herring-pond to say to you: Monsieur Griffith, would you like to win races again—lots of races? Would you like to make an excellent deal with us?"

No longer able to contain himself, Griffith howled: "So you've come, have you, to propose some new method of doping to me, some new drug? A scam, eh? I know your type. Either that or you want to sell me a new kind of horseshoe, a shoe that will make nags win, a shoe for galloping in heavy ground, with an excellent modification for hard going?"

He advanced menacingly. "Would you like to get out of here? Or you'll see that I can fix things too—would you like to bet that I can fix you a swing in the stomach?"

And the excellent man would have done as he said if Tod, the bearded Yankee, had not, with a simple parry, sent him rolling on the tiles of the parlor.

Fred, the little clean-shaven man, watched the scene with a remarkable indifference, as if absent-mindedly.

Griffith got up, astonishingly calmed down, and suddenly seemed to have returned to a more exact sentiment of the duties of hospitality.

"In sum, Messieurs, tell me what you want...sit down, I beg you."

Tod continued, tranquilly: "Monsieur Griffith, we want to sell you a horse of the highest quality: a unique opportunity; one can't do better, I assure you..."

That fashion of offering a horse like a set of binoculars or an Oriental carpet returned Griffith's hilarity.

"A horse? But I have more than enough of them here!"

"Which don't win, Monsieur Griffith, which no longer win! Ours, on the contrary, will win all the races you could wish."

"Oho!" said the trainer, who seemed to have decided to take the joke in good part. "That's lucky! I was just looking for a good horse, not too shabby, to prepare for the Cup. Who's he by, your horse?"

"By?"

"Yes...his breeding. His sire and dam. And how old is he?"

Tod turned indecisively to Fred, who emerged from his mutism to say, with a gesture of indifference: "We don't know. It's of no interest..."

"It's of no interest—understood. But your horse has papers?"

"Oh yes, certainly, he has papers...they must be in the trunk, mustn't they, Tod? But we haven't looked at them. We're trainers, and horses' family affairs, you know..."

"Yes, you're not curious."

Tod darted a glance at Fred, as if to say to him: *This isn't starting well*; then, abruptly making a decision, he took an immense wallet out of his pocket.

"Look, Monsieur Griffith, there are things we'll tell you later. But it's necessary to understand right away that we're not jokers. Here's five thousand francs; that's all we possess. We want to treat this affair squarely, as we would at home, in America. I'll put our five thousand-franc bills on your table and I'll leave them there. Good. Tomorrow morning, at six o'clock, you'll come to your training track—it's the Allée des Éléphants, I believe—with your horses, with any horses you like, the best you have, and we'll bring our horse for sale, and we'll try him out against yours: two races, three, as many as you like. If our champion doesn't win every one, and easily, our five thousand francs are yours. Take note that we're not asking for anything in exchange. You're not risking anything, you're not promising anything, and you'll be free, afterwards as before, to accept, to refuse or to discuss the deal."

Griffith could not help being, if not seduced, at least greatly intrigued. He looked carefully at the banknotes, and then at his visitors.

A thought occurred to him. *If they're crooks and they've stolen the horse in question, I can always do useful work in having them pinched tomorrow.*

"It's agreed, Messieurs," he said. "Until tomorrow morning. Oh, take back your bills, I beg you. I trust you, I trust you..."

When he had shown the strangers out and closed the door behind them, he added: "That's annoying; I would have liked to finish that bottle of whisky, but if I drink it, I won't get up tomorrow morning... Yes, but if it stays there within arm's reach, I'll certainly drink it..."

He called Joe. "Joe, drink this bottle for me right away. If a single drop remains in five minutes, I'll clip your damned old ears!"

II. In which Griffith discovers that he is not completely blasé regarding the surprises of the Turf.

Although he was rather skeptical about the matter of the proposed trial, Griffith took with him to the Terrain des Éléphants two old horses of a rather high class, which could give him a serious line. The first, Cauchemar II, was a very reliable miler, which, in spite of the general poor form of the stable, had figured honorably under a big weight in the first handicaps of the year. The second, Salsifis, was endowed with a remarkable stamina, and could make the best gallop, especially on heavy ground, over long distances.

On arriving at the rendezvous, Griffith perceived a group consisting of the two Americans of the previous evening and a superb negro, who was holding by the bridle a horse of which not much could be seen; the animal's head was hooded, its back covered by a sort of blanket, and its limbs bandaged with flannel.

Where did they find that? the trainer wondered.

He increased the pace of his cob, however, and advanced toward his visitors, smiling. He was in a good mood, having slept well and recovered his equilibrium.

"Aha! There's the crack. We'll examine him, if you'd care to undress him."

The Yankees manifested a sharp anxiety. "No, no, if you please! It's understood that before anything else, we'll hold the trial. Try him—we'll chat later."

Evidently, the horse is stolen, the trainer thought. *They're afraid I'll recognize him.* But he replied: "As you wish. Over what distance shall we gallop? What are his aptitudes?"

"He has all aptitudes," pronounced the huge Tod, forcefully.

"That's admirable. Then, with your permission, I'll match him first against Cauchemar over sixteen hundred meters, and then against Salsifis over three thousand."

The Americans did not flinch. They didn't know the first thing about horses, that was becoming evident—and Griffith began to be amused.

"But who's going to ride your beast? I warn you that there's a forty-kilo lad on Cauchemar II."

"Fred will begin. He's a little heavier than your man, I think he weighs fifty-five—but that's nothing.

The negro briskly removed the blanket, under which appeared, ready-saddled, a thoroughbred that Griffith judged to be ordinary. The little Yankee with the violinist's head hoisted himself awkwardly on to the beast, with his friend's help. He was in city clothes, and his trousers immediately rode up ridiculously to his knees, uncovering bright-red long johns. As soon as he was in the saddle he took hold resolutely of his mount's mane.

It was becoming grotesque, but the trainer, in a cheerful frame of mind, was delighted, as if by the entrance of a clown at the circus.

"Hey, Charley!" he shouted to the lad who was in the saddle on Cauchemar II, "go line up with the gentleman in the red socks. Damn it, Monsieur, he looks as if his joints are rather stiff, your horse. I'll be curious to see him at the gallop. Pay attention! I'm going to take out my handkerchief and raise my arm; when I lower it, you're off. The finishing-line is way over there, at the big oak overhanging the edge of the track. It's not exactly sixteen hundred meters, but these gentlemen are very accommodating..."

Griffith went to post himself a hundred meters in advance, and gave the agreed signal.

Cauchemar II, whose aptitude for acceleration was remarkable, immediately took a lead of five or six lengths. The unknown horse, whose rider had not budged—Griffith was absolutely sure of that; he had not taken his eyes off him; Fred's arms and legs had remained motionless, not to say in-

133

ert—then started moving, and, to the trainer's great surprise, soon drew level with Cauchemar II.

Charley's amusing himself, Griffith thought, giving the circumstance the only possible explanation.

However, as he went past him, Charley began to shake up his horse, of which the other was progressively pulling ahead.

That's a bit much!

And Griffith immediately put his cob to the gallop, in order to keep track of the match for longer. But the match was over. Cauchemar II folded up, completely exhausted, against a superior mechanism, and his rider wisely gave up the contest.

As the little American came back at a walk, Griffith conceded, with a very ill grace: "Yes, your horse has a nice burst of speed...either that or mine is indisposed."

Fred, out of breath after a ride to which he was evidently not habituated, stopped his mount and let himself slide to the ground, rather awkwardly.

But the huge Tod said tranquilly: "Would you like to race over three thousand meters now? I'll ride our champion."

"You! But you weigh..."

"I only weigh ninety-six kilos, Monsieur. That won't inconvenience the horse."

"That's a bit stiff, though! Harry, come over here!"

The small apprentice who was riding Salsifis advanced to order. The bearded giant bestrode his thoroughbred, deploying much more strength but no more ease than his friend had shown; that exploit accomplished, he showed exactly the same elegance as a rider, with the exception that his long-johns were mauve.

This time, Griffith neglected the ceremony of the handkerchief and explained to the competitors that there were going to go around the circular path at the end of the track and then come back to the point of departure in order to complete the distance of three thousand meters.

The unknown horse, without Tod having budged any more than Fred had done, set off at exactly the same speed.

Harry, in putting Salsifis into his stride, darted a smile at his employer that signified: *That's extravagant! He won't go far at that speed!*

That was Griffith's opinion too. But the American had taken a lead of five lengths, and then ten; he was a good fifty meters ahead when they arrived at the circular path.

"Ah! I thought as much!" exclaimed the trainer, triumphantly, having taken out is binoculars to see it.

Tod's horse had just stopped abruptly, and accomplished its turn at a walk, while Salsifis caught up with it.

"He's exhausted, of course!"

However, when the turn was complete, the strange animal set off again, resumed a five length lead, and then ten, and was finally fifty meters ahead when they arrived in front of Griffith, who was representing the winning post himself, and, for an observer, the equestrian statue of Amazement.

"You understand," explained the huge Tod, getting down, "that I'm not a jockey, and don't even know how to mount a horse, so I didn't want to break any bones, and went around the bend at a walk."

Griffith, in whom amazement had given way to a state of extraordinary excitement, seized the American by the cravat and started shaking him unsparingly.

"Oh! But...but...you're going to tell me what that horse is, and you're going to tell me right now!"

Tod disengaged himself effortlessly, and asked Fred, smiling: "Should we tell him, Fred?"

Fred gestured indifferently; he seemed to be thinking about something else.

Meanwhile, Griffith's gaze had fallen upon the mysterious horse. Again he was petrified, his mouth open. Not only was the beast's coat not moist with sweat, but, inconceivably, it could not be seen to be panting—or even breathing.

Tod placed his hand on the trainer's shoulder and said: "Look...look closely. You don't see that every day. That horse, Monsieur Griffith, is a mechanical horse!"

III. The Origin of Peau-de-Balle.

The thing was so enormous, so unexpected, that Griffith did not understand at first.

"A mec..."

"Oh, I beg you, Monsieur, don't shout it to the treetops. We're counting on your discretion. First of all, send away your people and your animals...

"Good...

"I was, saying, then, that our horse is an automaton, a horse that we've fabricated completely...at least, Fred has fabricated it. Fred's a first-rate engineer, who knows how to work; there's already some talk about him in the United States. Take account, Monsieur—pass your hand over the face of our thoroughbred."

Griffith obeyed mechanically and passed his hand over the nostrils. Instead of touching the quivering flesh of a living animal, he had the sensation of palpating leather. Not without repugnance, he placed a finger on one of the eyes. There was no possible error; it was made of glass.

"What a diabolical invention!" he murmured.

"Don't worry," Tod replied, laughing. "We'll give you all the desirable tips. But take a look first."

He lifted the mane, and showed Griffith three minuscule nickel-plated levers, scarcely projecting from the neck.

"These are the levers that control the three essential movements: walk, gallop, stop. The rider doesn't need to know any more. The delicate pieces of the mechanism are inside, along with the accumulators furnishing the energy necessary to activate the articulated steel legs. Those organs are hidden, like the phantom of the body, under a very clever imitation skin. Caress that silky coat, and admire the padding that completes the framework and gives the illusion of a powerful musculature. It's almost life, that! Certainly, one could desire a few improvements in certain matters of detail; for instance, it would be preferable to get rid of the little click, perceptible for a keen ear, that's produced when it's set in motion. It would be better, too, if the gait of the automaton at the walk were more supple, smoother, and didn't present that displeasing stiffness, the jerky style that you noticed. In a few years' time, when Fred has constructed another equine automaton, he'll give it, in addition to the two speeds this one has, a trot and a canter, and he'll endow it with a mechanism of respiration, and one of transpiration..."

Griffith, motionless and bewildered, seemed much less alive than the strange horse.

"Anyway, such as it is," Tod said, "this one is adequate to create an illusion, even in the eyes of a connoisseur in equine matters. You've seen that for yourself, now? Good. We have a story to tell you, and above all, a deal to strike with you. We can't do that here; this training-ground is beginning to be a little too populated for our taste. You must know a tranquil tavern in Chantilly where one can chat without being disturbed."

Griffith acquiesced; he no longer had any will to resist. Tod gave orders to his negro, who started the equine automaton walking and led it away.

The trained watched the man and the beast draw away. A new suspicion occurred to him. "But what about him? He's alive? He's a natural person?"

"Who?"

"The negro. He's not an automaton too, I assume?"

"No, no," Tod replied, laughing. "He really is a natural negro, a good fellow. As a mechanism, he's infinitely less complicated than our horse..."

A few minutes later, the trainer and his companions were at a table in a bar that bore the classic sign: *The English Stables*, and was deserted at this hour, the work of training being in full swing. They ordered a bottle of soda water from the astonished barman; the Americans were very sober and Griffith, as a matter of principle, only drank soda water when his ideas were in disorder.

As usual, Tod acted as spokesman while Fred, his eyes on the ceiling, followed his interior reverie.

"You're wondering in what capacity I'm putting myself forward and discussing interests that ought not to be mine, since I haven't invented anything, personally, and the mechanical horse belongs, in sum, to Fred, who created it lock, stock and barrel. It's because Fred, you see, is a genius as an inventor, as a machine-maker, but in life, he's an utter child, who needs leading by the hand, otherwise he'd be run over by a handcart or drowned in a puddle. Look at him now—he has the expression of an oyster. He's thinking about something, seeking something extraordinary, which he'll fabricate when we return to Chicago. If he talked, that would distract him, it would be time wasted, and Fred's time is valuable. So, he needs me to talk for him. That's why I became his manager, and that doesn't date from yesterday.

"He was like this when we were in school. At the age of fifteen, he invented machines to compose Latin verses, machines to do all the things that are so bothersome for schoolboys. It was truly extraordinary; it was me who got the value out of his inventions; we got our little comrades to pay a penny a line. But once a machine has been invented, Fred isn't interested in it any more, he goes in search of another on which to work, with the result that he's always come off badly."

Tod darted an indulgent pitying glance at his friend, and went on: "Later, Fred got himself talked about in the press, but without making a fortune. You know the artificial pig that played the hunting horn at the Cincinnati Exhibition? He invented that; at that time he was also making ducks that swam on the water, and was taking around a little greyhound on a leash so lifelike that all the dogs in the neighborhood followed her in a pack, paying their habitual polite attentions to the mechanical bitch. But all that was child's play.

"He had, after that, ambitions that did him more than one bad turn, because they consisted of realizing poetic ideas. It's necessary to be practical when one's a mechanical engineer. It was then that he fabricated humans. Oh, don't protest! Just now you thought my negro was artificial. Then again, a hundred years ago, a French inventor by the name of Vaucanson fabricated an automaton that played chess.[57] Edgar Poe wrote a study in which he went to a great deal of trouble to explain it, without succeeding in doing so, I believe,

"So, Fred created humans. First he constructed a worldly young gentleman, who did what all worldly young gentlemen do: he bowed, waltzed, and said, thanks to a phonograph placed in his stomach, 'You're charming, Mademoiselle.' Then he sang a ballad by Tagliafico. Can you imagine that a young miss from Boston fell madly in love with that doll and talked about killing herself over him? In truth, she could well have married him. He had, in sum, all the qualities of distinction and elegance that constitute those fellows, and just as much conversation; he only lacked the faults and vices with which they're abundantly supplied.

"It was whimsy, in sum. Fred had taken a false path in fabricating, in a supplementary and superfluous fashion, a specimen of whom there are hundreds of thousands in the drawing rooms of the old and new worlds. When human genius gets mixed up in creating, it ought to do better than nature, not repeat, once again, a model whose examples she's distributed in regrettable profusion. Then again, from the commercial point of view, who wants to make the acquisition of a young fop? It really was a waste of time and money.

"I had given my friend the idea, rapidly put into execution, of fabricating an orator for a political party that lacked a leader. At first, the success appeared dazzling. Our automaton made speeches with an admirable eloquence and confidence. Unfortunately, his phonograph was fitted with rolls once and for all; his opinions, like his harangues, remained immutable.

---

[57] In fact, it was Wolfgang von Kempelen (1734-1804) who constructed the chess-playing automaton known as the Turk in 1770, which was subsequently exhibited by Johann Mälzel before bring exposed as a hoax. Edgar Poe wrote a story based on it after the machine was purchased by his doctor, explaining how the hoax was contrived.

While he was repeating himself, the ideas and votes of his political group evolved to the point of changing radically. You can understand that the orator became embarrassing. They had promised to pay us when their party was in power; the account is still unsettled.

"It costs a lot to fabricate those machines! So, we were soon reduced to our last banknotes, Fred and me. At that moment, I fell upon the true seam, I had a real inspiration. I said to Fred: 'We're going to fabricate a racehorse, an unbeatable crack. On that terrain, we're sure of doing better than nature, aren't we, the electric motor having an incontestable advantage over the oat-fueled motor? It will even be necessary to regulate its power, in such a manner that it doesn't go too quickly and that it's speed in plausible. Then, when it's ready, we'll sell it to an intelligent man who wants to make a fortune...'"

When Tod, having reached that point, paused in order to let him get a word in, Griffith remained silent, seemingly as absent mentally as little Fred. The latter was humming a little tune, nasal and irritating.

Tod continued: "I'm sure that you're thinking about the papers. We've thought about that too. We knew that a thoroughbred has no market value unless it has papers, and can scarcely build a good racing career other than in its country of origin. Then I came here to Chantilly and I bought from Ely Pauwels—your neighbor, I believe—a colt then aged three: Peau-de-Balle, by Toenia out of Polaire VI. That thoroughbred, a reject from Baron Isaac's stable, had never appeared on the track. He was useless from the viewpoint of racing, and Pauwels had a good laugh in sticking him, along with his entries, on a Yankee sucker for a hundred louis. But he's been extremely useful to us. First of all, he served as a model to fabricate our automaton in his image and his resemblance before sending him to the abattoir—I ought to warn you, in fact, that the real Peau-de-Balle has been distributed, in assorted fragments, in various tins produced in a canning factory in

Chicago. Secondly, and more importantly, we needed his papers, and we still have them.

"In consequence, our automaton is perfectly in accordance with the stud-book; his name is Peau-de-Balle and he has received in heritage from the deceased, as well as his name, his entries in all the major races to which four-year-olds are admitted this year; we've refrained, of course, from declaring any forfeit.

"It remained for us to resolve a delicate problem concerning the sale of the horse: where to find a buyer? It was necessary to tread carefully, fur unfruitful negotiations would have burned us definitively. We had a correspondent in England, but in England, the lovers of the equine race have a habit of looking very closely at thoroughbreds, and the trick would have been discovered.

"The best thing to do was to find a trainer in France who was...how shall I put it? I don't want to offend you, Monsieur Griffith...in circumstances such that our proposition would appear to him to be not only an advantageous business deal but...a unique means of salvation. We thought of you."

"You're too kind," said Griffith, with a pinched expression.

"We thought of you because you're presently in a very difficult situation. Oh, we did our research before coming... I don't want to talk about your lack of success on the turf, which doesn't detract, in sum, from your professional reputation, but you're a gambler, and you've gambled too much...and you owe a great deal of money to Sem Lévy, the bookmaker. Yesterday, you asked him for more time to settle your losses. I can only see one means for you to get out of trouble...

"Peau-de-Balle is the only possible savior. In one season, Peau-de-Balle can make you a fortune. Not only will you pocket ten per cent of the prizes he wins—and he'll win all the prizes you wish—but you'll be able to bet on him as a sure thing. You'll even get a good price for his first win. With Peau-de-Balle, you need have no fear of ailments, loss of form, meteorological circumstances, or anything else. He'll always be there, in all weathers, on any ground, at any distance..."

Griffith was evidently seduced, and even conquered. Independently of the fact that his situation, even more difficult than the Yankee supposed, could become desperate if he did not find a means to lay his hands on a large sum of money before the end of the month, the possession of a miraculous crack tempted his ever-alert ambition. His self-esteem, rudely afflicted following the recent defeats of his horses, blossomed at the idea of the revenges that he might obtain against his neighbors in Chantilly and his rivals at Maisons-Lafitte, so proud of the present good form of their stables.

And then, in addition to any idea of lucre, the idea of a colossal hoax tempted his adventurous Anglo-Saxon spirit. English fantasists—and there are more of them than is generally believed—are great lovers of enormous straight-faced practical jokes that bear upon the most serious matters; that fact can readily be observed in colonial, diplomatic and political affairs.

The project of taking the entire racing world for a ride, including Comte Jérôme Thomas and Madame Tafoireau, for whom he trained, delighted him.

"How much do you want to sell your horse for?" he asked.

"He cost us thirty thousand dollars to manufacture. He's a unique specimen. We won't let him go or less than a million francs."

"A million! Where the devil do think I can get that?"

"Don't ask ridiculous questions, I beg you. Recognize, first, that the price isn't too high, with regard to the races that the automaton can win; in six months, you'll have got the money back. And then, it's not you who'll be laying out the funds. We chose you because you train for an owner who throws money out of the windows. Come on, between ourselves, what do you think of Madame Tafoireau?"

"Oh, she's a halfwit!" Griffith replied, without hesitation.

"Very good. But Comte Jérôme Thomas is doubtless not as limited in his scope, as you connoisseurs put it?"

"Certainly not," affirmed Griffith, with remarkable energy. "He's four times as bad. Comte Jérôme Thomas is a perfect imbecile."

"We couldn't hope for better. Those are precious qualities: rich, generous owners, who know nothing about horses, and whom it's easy to persuade that a sparrow is an eagle, or that an automaton is a thoroughbred. Furthermore, an honorability universally recognized on the Turf: their silks will be the flag that covers the merchandise. Then it's a done deal, my dear Griffith...yes? Yes! You'll need forty-eight hours to persuade your owners to make the purchase. As for payment of the sum, we'll be very accommodating...as accommodating as your Monsieur Deschanel...yes, yes, I mean Monsieur Dufayel,[58] anyway, the man who sells things on the installment plan...

"You'll send me a first check for a hundred thousand francs after Peau-de-Balle's first victory, and a second check for the same sum after the second, and so on until the payment of the million is complete. If he's beaten once, one single time, you can stop the payments. We're generous...

"The horse will be brought to you in an hour. You have a little isolated pavilion that's entirely appropriate to lodge him. In the evening, Fred will come to explain the mechanism to

---

[58] Paul Deschanel (1855-1922) was a prominent right-wing French statesman, very prominent in the Chambre at the time the story was written; La Fouchardière was not to know that he would go on to be elected President of the Republic and then forced to resign on mental health grounds. Georges Dufayel (1855-1916) was a retailer who popularized and vastly expanded the practice of selling goods on credit with the aid of installment plans; his vast department store was one of the landmarks of Paris when the story was written.

you in detail. He'll show you where the accumulators are, which it's necessary to charge fully before every race, because there's a great expenditure of electric energy...

"*Au revoir*, Monsieur Griffith; you'll be kind enough to settle the bill for the soda water. Hey, Fred, old man, it's time to go. You can sleep on the train..."

Left alone, Griffith shook his head, thoughtfully, and then sniggered.

"It's quite simple now...I only have a couple of small steps to take: firstly, to persuade Madame Tafoireau or Comte Jérôme—I have a choice—that the purchase of Peau-de-Balle is necessary, and that the horse is a steal at a million; and secondly, to find a jockey for the machine."

IV. In which the reader makes the acquaintance of Madame Tafoireau and Comte Jérôme Thomas.

Griffith had defined Comte Jérôme Thomas very accurately, from the intellectual point of view. From the viewpoint of social status, the aristocrat in question, whose nobility went back all the way to Pope Leo XIII,[59] possessed one of the largest fortunes in Paris, and even in the Champs-Élysées quarter. He had not made that fortune himself, firstly because he was incapable of "setting a river on fire," as his trainer put it and secondly because he would not have had the time. He was only twenty-three years old and, since leaving school, had only given evidence of his existence by the sole means that was within his range—which is to say, by spending money. "I spend, therefore I am," was the motto that malicious friends had composed for him, to combine with an appropriate heraldic arms: a pump on a red field.

In fact, the millions of which the Comte disposed with such casual charm had been amassed by his father, Monsieur

---

[59] Pope Leo XIII reigned from 1878-1903. French "aristocrats" whose ancestors had bought their titles in Italy were commonly known as "papal barons."

Jules Thomas, who was known as the Pump King. Understand what I mean: Monsieur Jules Thomas was not in the funeral business, nor did he sell fire-pumps. His specialty was a perfume of the most excessive Parisianism.[60] He liquidated his funds, fortunately for him, before the law requiring the exclusive use of sewers had been imposed on property-owners by the municipality. As indicated, it had brought him luck.

From that moment on, he preoccupied himself, above all, with giving the heir to his name a distinguished education, and he applied himself personally to making him the beneficiary of a culture that he had acquired himself very belatedly and in an incomplete fashion. When the young Jérôme, at the sage of six, committed a grammatical infelicity by saying to his father "You're an imbecile," Jules Thomas had taken his offspring severely to task. "My son, one ought not to talk like that. It's necessary to say 'You *is* an imbecile.' Come on, repeat it..."

Jérôme repeated, meekly: "You is an imbecile," and Thomas senior, very proud, predicted that something would be made of that boy.

Jérôme reached his twentieth year without having been able to pass any baccalaureate, even restricted, and then his twenty-first without having conquered the rank of corporal in the infantry regiment where he had copiously wined and dined his superiors for a year. His father, thanks to good connections in the diplomatic world, enabled him to enter the Ministry of Foreign Affairs in the quality of cabinet attaché, but there,

---

[60] The French *pompe* [pump] also means pomp, in the context of funeral ceremonies; hence the first pun. French firemen were known as *pompiers* because of the pumps they used to supply their hoses with water. M. Thomas' pumps however, were those used by the cesspool-emptiers whose métier was a lucrative business in Paris before and during the installation of the still-famous system of sewers, against which they fought tooth-and-nail for decades, eventually requiring stern legislation for their suppression.

even though his tailor was excellent, his colleagues soon perceived his irremediable cretinism.

It was then that he found his path: he would be, exclusively, a man of the world. He had everything necessary to succeed in that career. He got into the most select gambling clubs and was soon up to date with the routines. He punted like Mithridates, King of Pontus, in person.[61]

In that epoch, Jules Thomas learned that, in return for a slight sacrifice of ten thousand francs, which one caused to reach the Roman curia discreetly, his son could receive the title of Comte de Saint-Siège. That title, moreover, if one thinks about it, was marvelously adapted to the profession that had enriched the former Pump King. It was nevertheless necessary to legitimate, in the eyes of France, the privilege of that distinction, by exceptional services rendered to Christianity. Jules Thomas therefore founded, in his son's name, a Catholic club destined to moralize the dominical leisure of the workers who, by night, operated the famous pumps. He had thought of baptizing the club with his own patronymic—the Cercle Thomas—which sounded good, but the ambition seemed excessive. He used instead a distinguished euphemism whose synonymy seemed striking to him, and called the club the Cercle Bourdaloue.[62] That good work cost him twenty thousand francs; with the ten thousand to the curia that made the Comte.

---

[61] The pun does not translate, in spite of the similarity between the English punt (in the sense of laying a bet) and Pontus, and their French equivalents *pont* and *Pont*, all the more so because *pont*, which also means "bridge," was adapted in French to a crude cheating technique involving bending cards, and thus came to imply cheating at cards in general.

[62] Louis Bourdaloue was a seventeenth century French Jesuit, but the word's other connotations are aptly summed up by the fact that chamber pots are still called "bordaloos" by posy antique dealers. "Thomas" is also French argot for chamber pot, hence the synonymy.

It was then that, departing from the principle that *noblesse oblige*, and for the first time in his life, Jérôme had an idea: he wanted a racing stable.

He did not, of course, lower himself to "doing the nags," as he put it and go to Tattersall's to bid for horses at public auction. He employed an infinitely more chic procedure: he bought the entire stable, including the stud-farm, of the Marquis de Latour-Prangarde, who had had enough of breeding and was only waiting to encounter a sympathetic head to liquidate his entire bazaar at a "friend's price." By the same token, he ceded his trainer, Griffith.

Strangely enough, the colors of Comte Jérôme Thomas, when they first appeared on the turf, had a run of unexpected successes, explicable only by the fact that the new owner entered runners out of pure snobbery, uniquely so that his silks could rub shoulders with illustrious colors, without having the slightest desire to win a race. In fact, nothing is more disastrous for an owner than the ardent desire to win, and also the pretention of knowing how to do it; the result of the combination of those two factors is entries made without rhyme or reason, savant and fatal instructions given to jockeys, and finally, the dangerous enervation of the trainer, who always finds the irritating horse-fly buzzing around him.

Jérôme Thomas, on the contrary, had at least the virtue of knowing perfectly well that he knew nothing at all, and left, if one might put it thus, the bridle on his trainer's back. Griffith knew his métier, did his own thing, and won races.

Things became slightly complicated when Jérôme made the acquaintance in the theatrical wings, of Madame Mag Iris, alias Caroline Tafoireau. It was at the Boîte-à-Clous, a café concert founded by a deadpan impresario who had announced to one and all the renovation of the café concert by virtue of his involvement. Mag Iris, the star of the troupe, sang songs there that, according to the posters, were very witty and in good taste,

Her repertoire included the delightful Bacchic refrain:

Oh, he gets out of line
When he's had a drop of wine!
Augustine! Augustine!

And also this one, with a fine Gallic savor:

Where are you going, Mam'zelle?
Monsieur, I'm going to Celle...
Where is it you're going to?
I'm going to Celle-Saint-Cloud![63]

She also sang these verses, as richly rhymed as moralizing in their tendency:

Arthur, Arthur
I implore you,
Don't drink so much wine
It gives your sister pain.
If you don't control yourself,
You'll ruin your health.
(Repeat.)

The delightful artiste was no longer in the first flush of youth. The most loyal of her friends even claimed that she had a son who was a sergeant-major in the territorial army.

At any rate, she had, for a long time, made the happiness of the Marquis de Latour-Prangarde. The latter, in liquidating his situation, formed the project, crowned with a dazzling suc-

_____

[63] The vein of toilet humor is continued here, as the end of second line is phonetically identical to "la selle," which, in argot would make the line mean "I'm going to take a shit," rather than taking the suburban railway line from Paris to Celle-Saint-Cloud, as the final line explains. My translations of the "songs" are a trifle free but attempt to capture the spirit while substituting English rhymes (including deliberately faulty ones in the last case) for French ones.

cess, of similarly ceding the lady to the acquirer of the sable. Comte Jérôme Thomas had an ambition—he was at that age, after all—to entertain an actress at a subsided theater, but he resigned himself with good grace to accepting the flattering succession of a notorious gentleman. Besides which, he had an infinite appreciation for the talent of Mag Iris, who, according to him, performed with an incomparable finesse literary productions more accessible to his comprehension than the songs of Xavier Privas or Dominique Bonnaud.[64] Then again, she was a well-educated woman; she could play you the "Virgin's Prayer" on the piano and talk to you about Paul Bourget as if she had slept with him.

From the first day of their liaison, Mag Iris undertook the facile task of turning Comte Jérôme into a complete blockhead. When her lover had paid her, with a smile, everything that a man can pay a woman who is not his own, she had a remarkable idea. It was one evening, on coming back from Longchamp, to which she went regularly, not because she liked it, but because she thought she had noticed that it tickled Jérôme to take her there. In the tone in which she spoke about a new hat, she announced, tranquilly:

"You know, I'm going to need a racing stable."

Jérôme opened his stupid eyes wide. "But my dear child"—the dear child was much the older of the two—"I have a racing stable. You see my horses; you can talk to them. Griffith even tells us sometimes when they're going to win, when he's in a good mood."

"No, no, you don't understand. I want my own horses, my own silks, Nelly Caroubier and Diane de Vaucresson have their own stables. I'm worth just as much as those whores!"

Before that peremptory argument, whose value was incontestable, the gallant man could only incline. Mag Iris then

---

[64] Xavier Privas and Dominique Bonnaud were among the co-founders of the Cabaret des Arts and sang in many other establishments a substantial cut above the vulgar café concert circuit.

ran to do the most urgent and most important thing—which is to say that she embarked on a long series of conferences with the costume designer at the Boîte-à-Clous, with the aim of planning the most harmonious hues that could make up her racing colors. In the absence of the director of the music hall, and with the complicity of the stage-manager, all the bit-part players were made to file past, dressed in the whole spectrum of multicolored fabrics, between which it was necessary to choose. Mag Iris decided on silks hooped in cerise and jonquil and an azure cap. Jérôme agreed that they were in exquisite taste.

A slight disillusionment irritated the new owner against the members of the Societé d'Encouragement. Had they not insisted, in the most polite fashion in the world, on the article of the racecourse Code that forbids entering runners under a pseudonym? And they had treated as such the name Mag Iris, even though it was the stage-name of an artiste acclaimed by the crowds and saluted by all the newspaper gossip columnists:

"Let us note, among the elegant ladies in the paddock, the delightful Mag Iris, in robe x, with trimmings y, the creation of the great designer Z , the Napoléon of couture; people estasized over her shoes, from the maison Z***, and her hat, signed by the milliner of genius Z***, etc." They barely refrained from citing the manufacturers who had furnished her hair and teeth.

But the commissars of the courses had been implacable, even though Comte Jérôme Thomas had threatened to complain about them to his father, and then to refer the matter to the pope, under the lofty protection of whom he had been placed once and for all, in return for a determined sum.

It had therefore been necessary for the charming artiste to resign herself to entering runners under the name of Caroline Tafoireau. It was, in any case, the name on her birth certificate; it had been given to her a certain number of years before—she did not care to be precise—by a poor but honest couple to whom she also owed the light of day, and who had maintained a sufficiently prosperous commerce in fried potato chips on the Montagne-Sainte-Geneviève.

Once those petty difficulties were resolved, Madame Tafoireau—that is the name that official programs employed, and also the one under which she will be designated here henceforth—occupied herself with forming a string of horses. That was rapidly done, and, in that epoch, Griffith's equine personnel increased beyond plausible limits.

In fact, every time Madame Tafoireau arrived at the paddock in time to witness the prize-giving, she had Comte Jérôme Thomas buy her the winner.

"Oh, how beautiful he is, that horse! Did you see how he won? I'm sure that Griffith can do something with him. Go put in a bid for me; round out the sum to be sure of getting him."

That was so much profit for the treasury of the Societé. Madame Tafoireau soon had such a large quantity of horses that she started winning races. On those days of victory, she said to Jérôme: "I intend to direct my stable myself."

It also happened, sometimes, that the luck turned; the cerise and jonquil silks were unfortunate, while Jérôme Thomas' colors passed the winning post victoriously. Then the charming owner made a terrible scene with her consort, claimed that she had been wronged, and sustained the contestable thesis that such luck should only befall deceived men when they are deceived by their legitimate wives—which was not exactly the case. Jérôme understood what he had to do, and the following day, the specialist newspapers reported:

Madame Tafoireau has just acquired Ménélas, the horse that won the Prix Bétheny yesterday in the colors of Comte Jérôme Thomas.

At that little game, the son of the Pump King soon no longer conserved any but the nags in his stable, and still feared seeing them win, knowing that his mistress, in the case of victory, would immediately annex them.

"The winning post came just in time!" he cried in relief, one day when his representative had been beaten by the shortest of short heads for having come too late. The reflection might have caused ill-informed people to think that Comte Jérôme Thomas was having his horses pulled, but everyone was well-informed; they knew he was too stupid for that.

In the enclosure, it was said that Madame Tafoireau's horses and those of her lover ought to be coupled, as the owners were.[65]

When the trainer Griffith, after a brilliant period of success, had known bad days, Madame Tafoireau had urged Jérôme in vain to be more energetic.

"He's our trainer, after all. You ought to make him understand—demand, if necessary—that he wins us races."

But Griffith interrupted the stammering speeches of the young man by raising his arms to the heavens.

"It's not to me, Monsieur le Comte, that you need to explain that, it's to your horses. What do you expect? The stable is poisoned!"

At the moment when the equine automaton as about to make its first appearance on the French turf, the newspaper *La Veine* announced that the trainer Griffith had had forty-nine consecutive losers, and refrained from mentioning him among the trainers in form.

V. The Diplomacy of T. Griffith

Madame Tafoireau was still in bed at eleven o'clock in the morning when her trainer was announced. She did not get up to receive him; she had seen many others there, and vice versa. Of that fact, Griffith had just had the proof, on encountering his jockey Blight on the staircase, who had saluted him with a mocking smile. The charming owner made it a duty to deceive her noble lover with all the jockeys in view—successively, of course—whatever their weight and physique. The jockeys did not find an enormous pleasure in the accom-

---

[65] On the French *parimutuel* horses in the same ownership are "coupled" for betting purposes.

152

plishment of that performance, but they thought it flattering to cuckold Comte Jérôme Thomas, in the same way that Comte Jérôme Thomas had thought himself flattered to have succeeded, in Mag Iris' good graces, the Comte de Latour-Prangarde.

On penetrating into the overly perfumed bedroom, and in spite of the evocation of overly precise memories, Griffith was untroubled. He was a gambler and, contrary to admitted prejudice, true gamblers, like true drinkers are generally almost asexual beings. Besides which, he had other things on his mind, which preoccupied him exclusively.

"Oh, there you are!" exclaimed Madame Tafoireau, whose nerves, it appeared, had not been sufficiently calmed. "You've probably come to tell me that my horses can't go in the mud? Last week, the going was too hard. It's very amusing, you know. Before the race, my horses are always well, according to you. I give the tip to all my friends; and I end up in the doghouse. Do you know what they're saying in the enclosure? They're making delightful jokes; no one's talking about anything but Madame Tafoireau's losers. Baron Isaac de l'Échelle-Jacob, who's got it in for me because I didn't want to do it with him, made a witty Biblical allusion the other day to the parable of the fat cows and the thin cows. That's charming!"

Griffith did not flinch. He knew that with women, it is necessary to let the sheep pass by, even if they seem rabid.

"Madame," he eventually said, "this month, you're going to win the Biennal des Quatre Ans at Longchamp, the Prix Lutin, the Cup, the Biennal des Maisons and the Prix du Cadran…for starters. Afterwards, we'll see…"

"With what?"

In those days, one didn't yet say: "On what?"

"With a new horse that Monsieur le Comte will buy for you."

"Oh, thanks! A horse that won't be able to put one foot in front of another once it's with you. The Comte is a mug, but I'd rather he gave me another pearl necklace."

Griffith became solemn and brought out the grandiose phrases that always have their effect, even on a former actress.

"Madame, on my honor as a trainer, I swear to you that never—never—have I seen a horse like the one I'm advising you to buy. It's a veritable phenomenon that two Americans have brought me. I tried it out yesterday morning against my horses, which were left flat in receipt of enormous amounts of weight; there isn't a single beast in Chantilly that could have kept up that pace. If you buy it, and it's beaten one single time, by no matter what horse, I give you my most sacred word that I'll abandon my training establishment to go muck out stables for Ely Pauwels for forty sous a day."

Madame Tafoireau had lit a cigarette, and was expelling the smoke from the corner of her mouth, as she had seen Blight do. She did not spit on the floor, like the gentleman in question, but she raised her eyebrows in a bored and indecisive fashion.

Griffith then had one of those flashes of genius that decide the outcome of battles. He understood that there were two things he had to say, and he said them both at the same time.

"In any case, Madame, if you fear imposing too heavy a sacrifice on Comte Jérôme Thomas, or anticipate a refusal on his part, it's easy for me to break my engagement with the two Americans. They'll have no trouble selling their horse, and if you don't want it, you'll see it running imminently in the colors of Madame Diane de Vaucresson, who has the intention of making a deal with those gentlemen—if you don't, of course."

Griffith sensed that he had won the race merely by the weary tone in which Madame Tafoireau replied to him.

"Oh, you're annoying with your horse. I'll talk to the Comte about it, all the same, if I remember. In that case, you'll be notified. Go on, get out and let me get dressed. It's nearly noon; I need to get up early today."

Griffith noticed in that speech a few imperceptible intonations familiar to Norman horse-dealers who really desire to buy what has been offered to them but mask that desire with scornful remarks. He left full of hope.

On arriving at Chantilly he was not at all surprised to receive a telegram thus conceived: *Buy horse soonest. Jérôme Thomas.*

That had not taken long. Contrary to what the trainer had feared, the question of price, which might have led to great difficulties, had not even been raised. It would be very easy to defer, given the mode of settlement proposed by the sellers, and the sums demanded would not appear excessive when the horse had been seen winning.

For the moment, there was nothing astonishing in the fact that that pecuniary question had not preoccupied Madame Tafoireau. For what it cost her, in real terms, she could proceed without haggling.

As for Comte Jérôme Thomas, Madame Tafoireau led him literally by the bridle, and even better: it was free dressage, fine work of the highest school.

VI. How Peau-de-Balle found a jockey.

The equine automaton, brought discreetly to Griffith's establishment by the Yankees' negro, had been immediately lodged in the isolated pavilion that Fred had noticed. The trainer had put the key in his pocket, and had strictly forbidden his lads to go near it. As a supplementary measure of security, he had even ostentatiously removed a barrel of whisky he had found there, which might have attracted his domestic Joe to the place.

The strange machine impressed Griffith to the point that, in spite of his curiosity, he had not dared to visit it in the first few days. He had familiarized himself with it somewhat since Tod, in accordance with his promise, had come to give him a lesson in applied mechanics and had explained to him in detail the anatomy and functioning of Peau-de-Balle.

The Yankee had taken his leave of him definitively by giving him these final instructions, inspired by Mark Twain:

"There isn't the trouble of giving him something to eat and changing his litter every day, but it'll be necessary to dust him down from time to time. Don't wash him, of course; there are a few little things that might come unstuck. I've shown you how to open the belly; the most practical way to clean him up and replace his accumulators is to stand him on a pedestal—the dining room table, for instance."

There was one important and delicate problem to be resolved; Peau-de-Balle required a jockey. And the difficulty consisted in the fact that he needed someone who was not a jockey. The trainer was certain that the act of confiding a secret to any professional in Chantilly, especially John Blight, who was the stable's first jockey, was exactly equivalent to shouting it from the rooftops. In addition, he needed a man who had some notion of mechanics, at the same time as a certain aptitude for the métier of acrobat.

It was not that the manipulation of the little levers was extremely complicated, but there was a question of touch and composure; and the mechanical horse was very difficult to turn at top speed. It was necessary to take corners almost as with a child's mechanical horse, the neck being articulated in such a fashion that its stem, encased in the axis of forward motion, commanded the direction. That scarcely resembled the handling of a horse of flesh and blood, which, by virtue of its animal flexibility as well as its instinct, is to some extent the collaborator of its rider. Peau-de-Balle was obliged to take his turns very wide, and, by virtue of his constitution, was unutilizable at Colombes or the tight track at Longchamp.

Finally it was preferable that the automaton's eventual rider did not speak English, and desirable that he was very sober, those two conditions being necessary and sufficient to avoid any contact with the world of professionals.

Griffith, absorbed by the search for that unknown individual, was spending an evening near the château when he heard the noise of something falling into the pond. He hastened his steps in that direction and perceived a young man of about fifteen who was struggling in the water, which was fortunately not very deep, in the company of a remarkable assemblage of metalwork and sail-canvas.

"It's that bird again!" exclaimed Griffith, despairingly. More sensible than La Fontaine's schoolmaster, however, be began by fishing him out.

The word "bird" was, in sum, just. The young man's name was Gustave Louffe. The son of a former forest warden who, on observing his precocious aptitude for mechanics, had dreamed of making him an employee of the railway company, the boy had disconcerted those parental ambitions by adopting a much more specialized vocation, which, in that era appeared to be the most ridiculous thing in the world. He wanted to succeed in imitating the flight of birds and had, with that aim in mind, invented an apparatus that was both complicated and rudimentary. He had procured and old bicycle, whose movement he had modified—bicycles in those days, weighed about twenty-five kilos—and to which he had fitted canvas wings, stolen, in the form of drapes, from the maternal cupboard.

His experiments generally commenced on the lawn of the racecourse, but invariable terminated in the pond. The stable-lads of Chantilly, who have positive minds, and to whom that vain agitation and obstinacy in failure appeared utterly unreasonable, considered the young man as slightly cracked, and naturally called him the Louffe.[66]

Griffith had already reproached him several times in the same place, but at times when the temperature was warmer and a plunge into water more agreeable. That April evening, after having hauled him back on to the bank, he was about to administer a solid correction in order to warm him up when an inspiration lit up in his brain.

If he had known Greek, he would certainly have cried "Eureka!" as Archimedes had, on emerging from another bath, when he too had had an excellent idea.

Young Gustave, who was already extending his back stoically, and thinking that an ill-acquired bath never brings prof-

---

[66] The French *loufoque* means crazy, *louffe* was used as an abbreviation, although it was most common in *fin-de-siècle* Paris as an argot term for "pet."

it, had the surprise of only receiving an amicable slap, accompanied by the kind words: "My little Louffe, would you like to earn a thousand francs a month?"

"Doin' what?" asked Louffe, who had neglected school in favor of his studies in aviation.

"You'll find out. In the meantime, it's necessary to renounce your little experiments. If five or six years, you'll be rich, I'll return your liberty, and you can break your bones, if you insist. Let's go."

"But my gear's in the drink!" said Louffe, who wanted to profit from the good dispositions of the trainer and vaguely hoped that Griffith might go back into the water to fetch his machine.

"You're going to leave it there and come and have a hot toddy. My backside is freezing!"

An hour later, Gustave Louffe, after being dried off, was installed in the little pavilion with Peau-de-Balle. After a long conversation with the trainer, he applied to the Societé d'Encouragement the following day for his jockey's license.

His father, the former forest warden, took it very well.

"At least it's a métier—and then, if you break anything, you've got a boss to pay you compensation."

VII. Peau-de-Balle loses his maiden status.

Seven horses remained engaged in the Biennal de Quatre Ans, which was run on 26 April at Longchamp, and the list of runners and probable riders published by the newspapers was composed as follows:

```
Agamemnon...............Barleu
Montargis...............T. Lane
Givelin.................Bowen
Pruneau II..............E. Watkins
Tringlot................W. Pratt
Gazomètre...............Dodge
```

Doubtful starter:
Peau-de-Balle...........X

The probable favorite was Agamemnon "whose fine action and powerful mechanism ought to accommodate marvelously to the wide course and the distance of three thousand meters," as the sporting writers put it, although the veritable factor in his favor, fundamentally, consisted in the fact that he wore the colors of Stéphane Weiss, and a horse owned by Stéphane Weiss had to be favorite, for reasons that reason knows not.

A good chance was also accorded to Montargis, who might be dangerous to Monsieur Weiss's horse "if he succeeds in making use, at the end of a severe test, of his irresistible burst of speed," as the same authors remarked.

The rest of the field had no obvious chance, although Gibelin "thanks to his courage and aptitude in heavy ground might claim a place if sagely held up during the race."

As for Peau-de-Balle, the unknown horse that remained among the entries, the prognosticators contented themselves disdainfully with declaring that he had been forgotten at the forfeit stage. One of the gentlemen, however added gallantly: "Peau-de-Balle, if he starts, has no other pretention than allowing the silks of his gracious owner to get a little air."

That did not prevent a reporter for *Le Tuyau*, who suspected nothing, from announcing that Peau-de-Balle had been galloped that morning for two thousand meters over the Aigles.

As can be seen from the abovementioned list, all the renowned jockeys of the epoch were up in the race: the energetic Watkins, "the crocodile"; the savant Barleu, a specialist in the Grands Prix; Willy Pratt, whose finesse and touch were legendary; Tom Lane, the great tactician who employed the ruses of an apache to put his colleagues in his pocket; Dodge, the Cunctator of the Turf; and finally, the excellent Bowen, who was—no one knows why—the bête noire of the journalists of the time, who was never permitted to lose, or even win, a race tranquilly.

The day of the Biennal arrived. When the bell sounded for the posting of the runners for the big test, and the seven advertised participants appeared with the anticipated jockeys, a slight surprise was manifest among the public on observing that the list was not immediately posted. After a few moments, the number 5 was seen to appear in its frame, which was that of Peau-de-Balle, and then, opposite, on a hand-written board, the name of Gustave Louffe.

There was a murmur of coarse hilarity in the crowd. "Louffe! Oh la la! Loufuque, Loufetinge! It's another gigolo that Môme Tafoireau has sent!"

In those days, Aristide Bruant being infinitely better known than Aristide Briand—the one who subsequently became President of the Council of Ministers by virtue of a combination of circumstances independent of my will—the expressions "môme" and "gigolo" were in fashion. By coupling them together on the day of the Biennal, the crowd was proving that the reputation of Mag Iris had extended beyond the walls of the Boîte-à-Clous.[67]

At the weigh-in, too, there were smiles among the ladies surrounding Madame Tafoireau, who did not know, the excel-

---

[67] The singer and comedian Aristide Bruant (1851-1925), still familiar as the man in the red scarf in an oft-reproduced poster by his friend Toulouse-Lautrec, was the owner and star of the Montmartre cabaret Le Mirliton throughout the 1890s, and his comedy routines made a specialty of insulting the upper-class clients who went slumming there, in a supposedly jocular fashion, frequently referring to female socialites as "*mômes*" [kids, when used innocuously, but routinely applied to prostitutes] and their cavaliers as "gigolos." The socialist statesman Aristide Briand, later to win the Nobel Peace Prize for his pacifist endeavors, was still at the beginning of his glittering career when the present story was written, but had begun the first of his six terms as Prime Minister in July 1909.

lent woman, what her trainer had certainly wanted to tell her, as she had got up to late to go and see her horses taking their exercise gallop—or, rather, the horses had gallop too early for her to get up—but thought she ought to inform her good friends anyway.

"My dear, it's an extraordinary horse that Griffith has discovered and Jérôme has bought for me. He'll certainly win, but keep that to yourselves, because we're laying very big bets."

The good friends, secretly, were greatly amused; they had been able to observe many a time that Madame Tafoireau always had unbeatable horses, whose chance was as certain as it was mysterious, and that her horses never won. But the person who was the most amused was Ely Pauwels, the trainer who had sold Peau-de-Balle the previous year for export to America.

"Where did Griffith fish up that damned nag?" he said to his employer, Baron Isaac. "La Tafoireau is well served. In any case, he's got a cheek sending it out in the Biennal."

The bookmakers, as a joke, put up Beau-de-Balle at 66-1. They were not thought generous.

The horses circled in the paddock, under the severe and competent eyes of the connoisseurs. Peau-de-Balle was not there; his trainer had good reasons for leading him straight on to the track.

Gustave Louffe had put on the cerise and jonquil silks of Madame Tafoireau; to his great surprise, Griffith had furnished him with a whip and attached spurs to his bots.

"Why do that?" he asked.

"It's part of the décor," the trainer replied.

The exit bell sounded. At that moment, an unexpected phenomenon occurred in the bookmakers' ring. Jérôme Thomas went in there like a tamer into a cage full of lions, and threw a few numbers right and left. When he came out again, Peau-de-Balle was no more than 8-1.

"He's gone completely crazy," said a big gambler.

"He has to do something with his money," replied another. "It embarrasses him."

In passing, Comte Thomas said to Griffith: "I've put a hundred louis on for you at a good price, but are you sure that the horse is a good thing?"

"Don't worry, Monsieur le Comte."

"Would you like me to give the jockey his orders myself? I'll explain the tactics to him."

"No, no, I beg you!" Griffith exclaimed.

The horses went out on to the track. Peau-de-Valle's six competitors took to the canter, while the automaton walked to the start, with a jerky gait as displeasing as could be.

"What's that!" someone in the crowd shouted. "As if that could ever make three thousand meters!"

Gustave Louffe was rather emotional, not such much because he was making his debut as a jockey as by raison of the unique and paradoxical situation in which he found himself. Once arrived opposite the podium at the three thousand meter start he turned the mechanical horse awkwardly, and the track was not wide enough for that maneuver. Then, pressing the stop lever, he waited, under the gibes of the crowd, for the other horses to line up.

Having seized the moment, the starter lowered his flag. Six competitors departed in a line but Gustave, taken by surprise, fumbled momentarily in the mane before finding the gallop lever. Peau-de-Balle then set off ten lengths behind. Jeers went up.

In the jockeys' stand, John Blight, who usually rode for the trainer Griffith, gave explanations: "They didn't even dare to ask me to pilot that beast. I would have been truly ashamed!"

Meanwhile, Peau-de-Balle, galloping down the center of the track, had caught up with and passed the group massed against the rail. For the moment, no one was astonished; the pace was, in fact, very slow; all those excellent jockeys belonged to the old school, according to which the most cunning rider was the man who waited as long as possible behind the others. The arrival of that willing pacemaker seemed to them to be fortunate, and they slowed their pace even further.

"Oh! The bend!"

Peau-de-Balle had, in fact, gone very wide, but had nevertheless increased his lead. He went past the windmill with fifteen lengths on his competitors, who were nevertheless pulling hard, while he appeared to be cruising.

"The child has no idea what a race is," said John Blight in the stand.

"Bah!" said Ely Pauwels. "I'd never have thought that beast capable of doing as much. In sum, it's flattering to make a show in the Biennal, and that's all that one could ask of him."

Griffith said nothing, but he had a desire to howl; that is the fashion in which the English relax their nerves on big occasions. And he thought: *As long as he doesn't break down before the end of the race! Do the accumulators have enough charge?*

In the owners' stand, Madame Tafoireau squeezed the arm of Comte Jérôme Thomas, who had stuck the pommel of his cane in his mouth by way of a gag.

"That Louffe rides very badly," she said. "He's going to get my horse beaten. Why hasn't Griffith put Blight up?"

"But my darling…," Jérôme tried to explain.

His darling, irritated, drove the improvised gag back into his mouth so hard that tears came to his eyes.

The horses had just gone behind the little wood, and Peau-de-Balle reappeared with a lead of a good twenty lengths. The jockeys on his rivals had ended up becoming anxious, and giving their animals their head. Edward Watkins had even launched Pruneau II vigorously in pursuit of the leader.

But Peau-de-Balle, without losing an inch of ground, went down the Boulogne hill at great speed.

In the Press stand, decisive words were already being heard that consecrated the conclusions:

163

"He's already finished. He's not getting any further ahead."

"Look, the others are getting on top."

"All the same, he's falsified the race with his damned impetuosity," added a third arbiter, with the utmost seriousness.

These judgments of last resort did not prevent Peau-de-Balle, who was still taking the bends with a generous margin, from entering the straight on his own. Then Gustave Louffe, remembering Griffith's recommendation, started waving his whip desperately.

Behind him, there was a frantic thrashing; the likes of Lane, Dodge and Barleu, who made it a principle not to massacre their horses when they were beaten, could not believe that that was going to happen. They were convinced that Peau-de-Balle was going to blow up, that they would have a contest, and that, finally, the god of racing would not permit such a sacrilege.

All the same, Peau-de-Balle passed the post first, winning by a hundred meters under the nose of the bewildered judge, who looked at his program twice before putting up the number, even though he knew Madame Tafoireau's colors perfectly well.

As soon as he had taken account of his victory, Gustave Louffe applied the stop lever a trifle abruptly, with the result that he lurched over the automaton's head; then he brought him back at a walk.

For the record, Pruneau II was place second and Gazomètre third. Agamemnon, naturally, came last.

Numerous sportsmen raced to the weighing-room enclosure to watch Peau-de-Balle come in, but the horse was swiftly taken away by Griffoth, who wrapped him up carefully and immediately loaded him into a van, into which indiscreet gazes could not penetrate.

As soon as he had weighed in, Gustave Louffe rejoined him, without waiting for the owner's congratulations. He had understood, once and for all, that he ought never to leave the automaton by day or night.

In the crowd, meanwhile, the surprise had affected a form both mocking and admiring.

"Well, well! Would you believe that he's put one over on us? They put Louffe up to get the odds, you understand? What's that going to do on the Mutuel? No one's bet on it at the little windows."

But the surprise reached its peak when the Mutuel return was announced: fourteen francs fifty (a packet of tobacco!) for a hundred sous.

"Oh la la! It's La Tafoireau! It's Jules Thomas' son who's played that, and how! They'll have a feast, the brethren! They could be sure of their coup! When I think that my hairdresser gave me the tip this morning and I didn't back it!"

The gossips were mistaken about the reason for that derisory return. Tod and Fred, the constructors of the automaton, had come to take a little stroll round the lawn, and as, out of courtesy, Griffith had invited them to come that morning in order to make the first payment on account of the sale, they had found themselves in a position to risk something on their thoroughbred. They had done so squarely. It isn't every day, Messieurs, that one has the opportunity to bet on a veritable certainty, a race in the bag, a father of a family's placement.

VIII. The Sport and the Papers.

The day after the Biennal, Griffith and Gustave Louffe made themselves a good pint of blood as they savored the accounts rendered in the specialist newspapers. They were installed in the trainer's little pavilion. Griffith was reading aloud, with his slight English accent, which gave a particular flavor to the prose of the sporting reporters. Gustave Louffe, lying in a rocking chair, was smoking a cigarette and underlining the interesting passages by waving his feet frenetically above his head as a sign of delight. As for Peau-de-Balle, he was calmly—very calmly—playing the role of a mute but attentive character.

First the trainer unfolded *Le Sport Légitime*, in which Brobdignac waxed lyrical, within the rules of syntax, with his accustomed competence and his usual stylistic elegance. Under his signature, the following lines could be read, word for word:

"The result of the Biennial has certainly been falsified, if not by lack of skill, at least by a tactical error that would have been, all things considered, excusable on the part of apprentices, but which becomes incomprehensible on the part of the fine whips grown old in harness who rode in the great test, which renders the result particularly subject to caution. They allowed an unraced horse to escape completely, which bore the name of Peau-de-Balle and the colors, which one has grown used to seeing over a period of time, of Madame Tafoireau. The unfortunate Bowen, naturally, was particular uninspired in only giving Gibelin his head after having lost his own, along with the battle. There was no chance, at that point of catching the leader, who had taken an unassailable lead at the start, with the result that Peau-de-Balle, although visibly on his last legs, and in spite of having lost an incalculable number of lengths on the bends, passed the winning post with ridiculous ease.

"What I like about Brobdignac," Griffith remarked, "is that his articles are both documented and well-written—but you need plenty of breath to get to the end of his sentences."

Then he started on the appreciations of Beni-Mora, who, in *La Cravache*, displayed both the most brilliant hippic science and an extraordinary nerve.

"At the examination in the paddock the most pleasing of the lot was incontrovertibly the one that was to furnish the winner: Peau-de-Balle, a superb product of Toenia, solidly built on the paternal model, with quite remarkable points of strength, an emergence on to the course of striking distinction, and a stride like a greyhound; perhaps he might be reproached for an excessive saddle, but that fault will pass with

166

age. Griffith had brought him, for the great test, to a marvel-ous state of preparation, and his calmness, his supple and graceful walk on the track and his satiny coat contrasted with the dancing allure of Agamemnon, the enervation of Montargis and the languid gait of Pruneau II.

"In any case, he won like a good horse, regulating his pace himself and responding courageously to the solicitations of his jockey when one might have thought that he was fin-ished. Let us hope that this success of sympathetic and too long unlucky colors is only the prelude to numerous and im-portant victories."

"Now you're talking!" remarked Gustave Louffe. "And what does *Le Tuyau* say, now?"

For *Le Tuyau*, Peau-de-Balle owed his victory exclusive-ly to the coolness and energy of which his jockey had given proof.

"G. Louffe will certainly generate talk. He rode the course very adroitly, immediately allowing his horse to settle into its action at the start, but without bustling him, effortless-ly taking the lead, while the favorite fought against his jock-ey's hands. At the top of the hill, he wisely took hold of Peau-de-Balle, allowing him to take a breather for a hundred me-ters..."

Griffith, in a fit of jubilation, interrupted himself to slap his thigh, laughing until the tears flowed.

"Do you hear that, Gustave? You took hold of the horse on the hill, and you let him take a breather. That's very good, that, my lad. *Le Tuyau* congratulates you, and your trainer is proud of you. I'll go on...

"...for a hundred meters, and then, without waiting to be caught up, abruptly set off again, and put himself definitively out of reach on the last bend, in order to reach the winning post in the most common of canters. The superiority of the beaten horses—I will even say their intrinsic superiority—was incontestable, particularly that of Agamemnon, the favorite, who finished like a horse caught for speed but not broken

down. In sum, the race was stolen by surprise, thanks to Gustave Louffe's savant policy of waiting in front.

"A waiting ride—I don't think so," said Griffith. "But as for front-running, that was front-running. I'm sure that the bouquet will be found in the *Winning Post*. Listen to this:

"The running of our favorite Agamemnon in the Biennal was too bad to be true. The prize was claimed by Peau-de-Balle, a reject from the Pauwels stable. We would be astonished if the result was true, even though heavy betting on the mutuel by the victor's entourage lowered the price, and if the latter surpasses, in class and quality, the average of claiming races. In any case, if his victory is disputable, his bad character appears certain; he has, indisputably, the same fault as his mother Polaire VII, who was the most peevish mare we have ever seen on the Turf.

"Did you know Polaire VII, Gustave? Personally, I didn't have the honor. These sporting reporters have a marvelous memory. I'll go on...

"The horse sketched an attempt at running out, and finished like an animal completely exhausted. He will certainly conserve a bad memory of this first and excessively lucky attempt...

"At any rate, if he doesn't say very much, he doesn't give the impression of thinking anymore," Griffith concluded, darting a glance at the automaton.

IX. Peau-de-Balle receives a few visits.

At that moment, the voice of a lad hailed Griffith from the courtyard.

Madame Tafoireau had come to visit her trainer; she had even brought Comte Jérôme Thomas, who allowed himself to be taken everywhere with an exemplary docility.

"Oh, Monsieur Griffith, we don't often come to Chantilly, but it's our duty to bring you our congratulations. At the same time, I'd like to say a little bonjour to my Peau-de-Balle.

I've even instructed Jérôme to bring the poor dada a sugar-lump—he's certainly earned it."

When she was being childish, Madame Tafoireau was rather touching—but less so than Comte Jérôme, who plunged his gloved hands into his jacket pockets and pulled out two handfuls of sugar-lumps, laughing stupidly.

Good—that's all we need, thought Griffith.

Gustave Louffe came to his aid.

"No, no—no sugar! It's very bad for his stomach. You must never give horses sugar between races."

"I'll go caress him in his box, then," said Madame Tafoireau.

"If you wish, Madame," said Griffith, who had got a grip on himself, "but be very prudent—the horse isn't in a good mood. This morning, he demolished two lads, one with a bite and the other with a kick."

"There! What did I say! cried Madame Tafoireau, furiously, turning on her unfortunate lover, who had not opened his mouth. "You always have ideas like that. So, you were going to make me go into the stall of an enraged horse? You'd be well advanced when I'd had an accident! You won't find another one like me! Perhaps you want to get rid of me?"

These grievances did not accord well with one another, let alone with logic, but Comte Jérôme was incapable of perceiving that.

Griffith then had the idea of occupying his owners by steering them toward the box of the placid Salsifis. The Comte was able to liquidate his sugar-lumps by paying homage to the trainer's cob.

It was at that precise moment that John Blight, passably lit up, irrupted into Griffith's yard. He did not salute either Jérôme Thomas, who did not exist for anyone, or Madame Tafoireau, toward whom he might have believed that he was liberated from any duty of politeness. In order to be understood by everyone, however, he started talking in French, and very loudly.[68]

"Monsieur Griffith, I have something to say to you. Monsieur Griffith, I am, yes or no, the first jockey of these Messieurs-Dames? I ask Monsieur le Comte Thomas, who is here, and Madame Tafoireau, who is here presently?"

"But no one is telling you anything different. What are you complaining about?"

"Why, then, was it not me that I mounted Peau-de-Balle on Sunday? If the horse was not to win, I understand, but a horse that is going to win sure, one lets the first jockey of the stable set foot.... It's stupid, that's all."

"Don't get upset, Blight, I'll explain it to you. Peau-de-Balle is a horse of a rather difficult character, a bit of a lunatic. He undoubtedly wouldn't accommodate an energetic rider, but he has a good understanding with the apprentice."

"Then, the apprentice, he rides him well, and me, I couldn't? It's silly, that! I'd like to see, if Madame Tafoireau permits. Do you want me to try for the Cup?"

"Well, damn it, try right away!" cried Griffith, whom these pretentions were beginning to irritate, and who saw that he would be obliged to go all in. "Listen, Blight: we'll bring you Peau-de-Balle ready saddled. If you succeed in making him circle the yard, at a walk, a trot or a gallop, no one but you will ever ride him, and I'll immediately have two bottles of champagne brought up from the cellar for you, into the bargain."

He made a sign to Gustave Louffe, who immediately disappeared, and came back almost immediately with the automaton.

"But...you said he was bad-tempered?" remarked Madame Tafoireau.

---

[68] As an Englishman, Blight naturally speaks French very badly—an impression difficult to convey in English translation. I have done my best.

"Come with Monsieur le Comte. I'll put you at a first floor window. You'll have nothing to fear, and you'll witness a jolly session of dressage."

Gustave Louffe had stopped the automaton. With an ironic smile, Blight leapt into the saddle.

"Let go now!"

But Peau-de-Balle did not obey either a light tap of the heels, nor an appeal of the arms, nor even a click of the tongue. Blight, surprised to the highest degree, but not wanting to appear so, turned to the trainer.

"If I had a crop, you'd see something!"

Griffith held out his own, which he had picked up in anticipation of that request. They then had the strange spectacle of an agitated ride on a motionless horse. But it was in vain that Blight belabored Peau-de-Balle, in vain that he called him an accursed pig, while daring furious glances at Gustave Louffe, who was writhing with laughter.

"Now," said Griffith, when his first jockey was out of breath, "take a rest for a moment. Oh, how hot you are! I'll make you another bet. The young man here present will make the horse depart at a walk, very gently. If you succeed in stopping him by the means you have to hand, I'll have four bottles of champagne brought up for you"

Gustave Louffe passed his hand over Peau-de-Bale's neck, who started to walk. Blight, tipped backwards, applied a violent traction to the reins.

"He's got a mouth as hard as the devil's horns!" he cried.

"No, no," said Griffith, mildly. "The young man will stop you without any effort."

Peau-de-Balle was still walking. Gustave Louffe who was accompanying him, appeared to caress him again. The automaton stopped dead.

"You can see that he's a funny beast," Griffith concluded. "He doesn't obey everyone."

He called his domestic, who was passing by. "Joe, bring us up six bottles of champagne. In truth, Master Blight, you've earned them anyway!"

X. Baron Isaac's little schemes.

Among the notable competitors that Peau-de-Balle was due to met in the Cup, where this time he was announced as a certain starter with Gustave Louffe aboard, we ought to mention especially Huit-Pour-Cent, a four-year-old trained by Ely Pauwels and belonging to Baron Isaac de l'Échelle-Jacob.

Baron Isaac de l'Échelle-Jacob was one of our most popular owners, one of our most eminent financiers, one of our most well-known clubmen, and one of our most generous Maecenases, who had shares in great and small theaters.

And along with all that, an utter scoundrel.

If the good God saw everything, as certain parties interested in putting that rumor about contend, the place of Baron Isaac would have been clearly marked in some central house for the fabrication of cheap footwear.

Physically, he had the appearance of a beast of prey, or more exactly, a captive carnivorous bird; one wondered in what cage in the Jardin d'Acclimation one had seen him before. Sem[69] would have designed his silhouette in a few stokes: a arched back, a neckless head trying in vain to retreat completely into the shoulders, a gray beard made with poor-quality horsehair from which a hooked beak emerged, and then, under bushy eyebrows, two little black eyes, mobile and anxious, studying an adversary or on the lookout for prey.

Baron Isaac claimed descent from the patriarch Jacob, of Jacob's ladder fame. Without going back so far, everyone had known his father, who sold opera-glasses at the Hippodrome de la Marche. Personally, he had made a vast fortune on the Bourse, in a very short time, by launching a magnificent industrial and colonial affair. It was a matter of a company exploiting the sugar plantations of Puerto Rico, shares in which he had sold at truly remunerative prices, all the more remuner-

---

[69] The signature of the caricaturist Georges Goursat (1863-1934), a great lover of the Turf.

ative because they only cost him the price of the paper and printing. It had been perceived subsequently that the sugar plantations did not exist and that the island of Puerto Rico was a geographical expression of no great significance, except to the Bureau of Longitudes.

Baron Isaac de l'Échelle-Jacob had then been much admired, and he had continued his strolls under the colonnades of the Bourse, with his hands in pockets-other people's pockets, of course. Siegmund Wolf, one of the kings of finance, had conceived a particular esteem for him, which went as far as letting him marry his mistress. Around the following fourteenth of July, his buttonhole had suddenly sprouted a red ribbon; the "Setting Sun" lodge, of which he was one of the principal dignitaries, had certified his titles—at that moment well above par—with regard to the Minister of the Colonies; the Croix des Braves had recognized services rendered to the national expansion in the Antilles and French savings in the metropolis.

Baron Isaac, whose activity was devouring in the broadest sense of the word, had then sought a new field of action— no longer a matter of those in Puerto Rico[70]—for his financial capabilities. He had discovered that racecourses lend themselves marvelously to intelligent and reasoned speculation. There was no need to know anything about horses; it was sufficient, as on the Bourse, to be well-informed and to depreciate the item that one wants to buy and boost that of the item of which one wants to rid oneself. Isaac had therefore bought a few thoroughbreds and had confided them to Ely Pauwels. The latter was just the man he needed, and the two sly rogues had understood one another immediately.

It was not a matter of winning many races. Two conditions were necessary and sufficient: firstly, to know when one will win; and secondly, to be the only ones who know it.

---

[70] An untranslatable pun—the French *action* also signifies a share.

That is why the victories of the Échelle-Jacob stable were often unexpected and always coolly welcomed. Thus, after the Biennal, it had been observed with amusement that the winner, Peau-de-Balle, was a reject of that unpopular establishment, and that the wily speculator had let him go for a few louis.

Baron Isaac and Ely Pauwels had had their eyes of the Cup for a long time. As much as possible, they sought out the big races, certainly not for reasons of self-respect, not even that of allocation, but because the betting market is larger and it is easier to bring off a discreet and remunerative coup.

Huit-Pour-Cent had been prepared for a long time, which is to say that he had carried Baron Isaac's sky blue silks around all the hippodromes for two months, always running over distances too short for him, On every occasion, the Baron had had told his best friends: "The horse only has one burst of speed."[71]

However, the financier possessed form lines precise enough to be sure that with his weight and over three thousand meters, Huit-Pour-Cent had the beating of all his competitors, even though, on paper, those did not appear negligible.

There was, naturally, Agamemnon, who, to all evidence, ought to be the favorite again. He might have finished last, but that was of no account. Stéphane Weiss's horse could not be anything but a crack.

There were also Monocle and Scaferlati, two three-year-olds who had shown stamina and a certain quality.

Finally, and above all, there was the Tafoireau stable. For Griffith, partly by way of diplomacy and more particularly to soothe the wounded self-esteem of his first jockey, had added to Peau-de-Balle his stable-companion Salsifis, in the same colors, ridden by John Blight.

---

[71] The Baron's speech is rendered in an atrocious eye-dialect supposedly reflective of his ethnic origin, of which I have not attempted to reproduce an English equivalent; it is of no significance to the story.

In the general opinion, Salsifis was the veritable champion of the stable, the preceding performance of Peau-de-Balle being considered as deceptive, a pure fluke.

From the viewpoint of Baron Isaac, Huit-Pour-Cent had the beating of Salsifis; in a handicap run recently at Maisons-Lafitte, he had felt out that competitor at the end of the race. The impression of the Pauwels stable jockey was that he would have reckoned with him that day if he had tried; they had been at level weights on that occasion, and in the Cup, Huit-Pour-Cent was getting six kilos from Salsifis.

Baron Isaac de l'Échelle-Jacob, who never left anything to chance, disposed his batteries on the day of the race with the remarkable strategic art that ensures victory on all the battlefields where intelligence takes precedence over brute force.

At the weigh-in he was seen running from group to group, affirming that his horse had no chance.

"I'm letting him go to give him a good gallop with class horses; he's going over the sticks next month; he's already being trained for that."

And he was seen heading for the pari-mutuel windows, where he ostentatiously bet ten francs on Agamemnon.

Meanwhile, he had small sums put on at good prices on Huit-Pour-Cent with the bookmakers in the ring. In addition, his agents on the Bourse, whom he used at the racecourses n Sundays, discreetly collected tickets at the windows in the cheap enclosure.

Finally, Baron Isaac operated on the principle that the left hand ought to know what the right hand received, and had made arrangements to extend both hands; that is why the bookmaker Sem Lévy, who was his straw man, had a mission to lay Agamemnon and Salsifis with an open tap. Passing close to him, the financier asked, in a low voice: "What are the latest prices?"

"Three to one Agamemnon, seven to two Salsifis, six to one Monocle and Scaferlati, twelve to one Huit-Pour-Cent. I've already taken three hundred louis on the two favorites. But there's a strange movement going on at present, on the subject of which I'd like new instructions. It's Peau-de-Balle that's now in demand; the horse opened at twenty-five to one; it's just passed fourteen, and there's still a demand. Shall I also lay it on your account, Monsieur le Baron?"

"Oh, as much as you can. It's probably La Tafoireau and that silly fool Jérôme Thomas who've put that tip about. Anyway, if Peau-de-Balle were going to win, it's not them that would have told you."

"I'd have known it from Griffith—he owes me enough money not to be able to refuse me a little tip. But I'm sure you're right, Monsieur le Baron; in matters of horses, one can't get the better of you."

That flattery struck home; Isaac had the pretention of profound knowledge in hippic matters, and even of being a brilliant rider.

And yet, his opinion of the chances of Peau-de-Balle was not that of all competent people—far from it.

Notably, the jockeys who were to ride in the race did not remember without anxiety what had happened the previous Sunday. They had no desire to recommence the hunt that the Biennal had constituted, and were determined not to let Peau-de-Balle escape, even though, this time, he appeared to be acting as a pacemaker for Salsifis.

Tom Lane, who was not in the saddle this time, did not hide his opinion: "I think I know a little about the pace of a race. Well, I'm sure I didn't lag behind in an exaggerated fashion the other day, whatever anyone says. If I were riding today, I'd be diabolically embarrassed...I think I'd try to stick close Peau-de-Balle, but I wouldn't be tranquil, because a beast that can cover three thousand meters at that lick must have something in his belly."

"Certainly, the horse has something in his belly," Griffith replied, calmly.

The signal for the start was given; almost immediately, as expected, Peau-de-Balle took the lead. Huit-Pour-Cent, whose jockey, duly instructed, wanted to take advantage of his low weight, accompanied him, making sure of the rail. Monocle and Scaferlati, the two three-year-olds, followed immediately behind. Salsifis galloped at the rear, playing a sage waiting game; he allowed his stable companion to wear down the common adversaries, and only had Agamemnon behind him, whose action really was far from brilliant for a favorite.

At the first bend, Peau-de-Balle lost a few lengths again, but quickly regained the lead.

At the Windmill, to the general amazement, the jockeys who had tried to accompany him were seen agitating heir arms and legs, and then their whips; then the gap gradually widened between the leader and his immediate followers.

Agamemnon and Salisifis tried in vain to get closer.

At the little wood the race was over. Peau-de-Balle continued at his regular speed, in front of his exhausted adversaries.

"Oh la la!" someone in the crowd shouted. "It's a cakewalk! Go, Blight! Go, Salsifis!"

"Bloody idiot," riposted an honorable gentleman who did not know the other at all. "That's not Salsifis! That's not Salsifis! That's not Blight! You're looking through rose-tinted glasses. That's Peau-de-Balle! Peau-de-Balle! Peau-de-Balle!"

"I don't care! I don't care! I'll collect all the same—I bet the Tafoireau stable on the mutuel."

The judge put up Peau-de-Balle, the winner by a distance. Second was his stable companion Salsifis, whose jockey had persevered furiously, for reasons that will be explained later.

Gustave Louffe was radiant, Griffith too. Both had backed Peau-de-Balle to the limit of their respective means; the jockey could already see himself rising to the seventh heaven in a flying machine, and the trainer drinking three glasses of soda-water one after another at Rouzé's, which was for him a sign of prosperity.

When Griffith, with the necessary celerity and discretion, had embarked his jockey and his crack automaton for Chantilly, he went back to the weighing room, where he encountered

Madame Tafoireau. The happy owner did not have an expression as delighted as the circumstance warranted.

"Well, Madame, we've won the Cup. I told you that Peau-de-Balle was the best of your horses; I hope you bet on him."

"But no!" replied Madame Tafoireau. "Blight assured me that it was Salsifis who would win. That idiot Jérôme was also of that opinion. So I bet that that was true…and all my friends are cursing me now, because they did the same. Fortunately, I've won a lovely work of art. Come and see it—it's on exhibition. It represents Hippolyte's Chariot. It appears that it's superb."

Baron Isaac de l'Échelle-Jacob was simply furious.

The day had cost him fifty thousand francs. He had, in addition, the bitterness of being beaten by a horse he had previously owned, and, which was even harder, by a horse wearing the colors of Madame Tafoireau. He had an old grudge against that lady, compounded out of jealousy and wounded pride. In fact, in the days when Mag Iris was singing at the Boîte-à-Clous, he had manifested the desire to please her, and had made his propositions with all the delicacy that one could expect of him.

Unfortunately, the Baron had a well-founded reputation for being a very economical man, a reputation justified even by the appearance of his garments and linen. Now, an economical man was not at all to the taste of the charming artiste, who was already on the trail of the large allocation represented by the millions of Comte Jérôme Thomas. However, Mag Iris had made the Baron climb a ladder,[72] compared with which his ancestor's had only been a child's toy. She had rendered him completely ridiculous, and the conquest of a venerable actress of the Théâtre-Français, laden with glory and years, had only been a derisory compensation for the financier's self-esteem.

---

[72] The French phrase *monter à l'échelle* [literally, climb a ladder] can also signify, metaphorically, "rise to the bait."

That disastrous day reserved another disagreement for him in seeing his prestige diminished in the eyes of the bookmaker Sem Lévy and his agents. He liked to pass everywhere for a sharp operator, and a sharp operator, by definition, ought not to lose his shirt. It was extremely painful for him to hear, a few days later, a few phrases pronounced, intentionally, loud enough for him not to miss any of them.

"He's bloodied his nose, Père Isaac."

"The God of Abraham and Jacob is just."

"The excellent fellow has certainly been rolled over by someone today."

"You mean that he hasn't succeeded in rolling over someone else? That's sufficient to explain the nose..."

"Let's not worry too much on his account. The buyers of shares in De Beer's will pay him back on the day of liquidation."

There was another person who was not content, and that was the jockey John Blight.

"Monsieur Griffith," he said, "it's me who wears the stable's first colors. Why didn't you instruct the little young man, once he was master of the race, a supposition, to stop his horse if he saw me behind him? Then you thought my place was behind, on Salsifis?"

Griffith replied, in a convinced and affectionate tone: "But my dear Blight, you're an intelligent man: tell me, really, with hand on heart, how we could have divined that Peau-de-Balle would find himself master of the race?"

XI. Peau-de-Balle is a bloody good horse.

The day after that sensational victory, the commentators of the sporting press were already conceding Peau-de-Balle permission to be a good horse, without nevertheless going as far as the discern class in him. Class, as everyone knows, is only obtained by a fashionable birth in a classic stud or two consecutive victories over eight hundred meters at the age of two. Horses acquire class, as children catch measles or win a

179

medal in a baby contest. You might be a remarkable man or a cretin later; that is of no consequence; no human or divine power can henceforth alter the fact that you have or have not had measles at the age of four, that you have or have not obtained the gold medal in a baby contest at eighteen months.

Then again, in Peau-de-Balle's dossier there was an ineradicable flaw, something akin to a criminal conviction or a rejection by the draft board, which was that Ely Pauwels had declared him useless on the turf and sold him for export.

After the Cup, the newspapers did not want to stress that unfortunate detail too much.

Beni-Mora in *La Cravache*, even admired "the supple and powerful style" of Peau-de Balle, who, according to him had "visibly put on condition" since his last run. His skillful trainer had brought him to "the apogee of his form; he was a veritable picture; muscle had replaced in his the superfluous flesh, and his satiny coat testified to the completeness of his preparation." Certainly, the result of the race was "subject to caution," especially with regard to Agamemnon, whose performance was "too bad to be true"—a familiar leitmotiv—and "who was probably feeling the after-effects of the epidemic" that had been rife in the Stéphane Weiss stable five years previously. All things considered, however, "Peau-de-Balle promises to be better than a workhorse."

Brobdignac's article was impressive in its authority. Technical details abounded therein, submerging the reader, who was fatally required to stop, stunned by admiration. He demonstrated, by means of that masterpiece, that Peau-de-Balle had necessarily to win the Cup, by virtue of a predestination dating from before the Deluge, Methuselah and even *Genesis* itself. In fact that product of pure blood was "the issue" of "the cross-breeding of family 3 and family 17, which is associated, by a consanguinity of which no one is unaware, to families 23 and 52"—here followed a genealogical tree in which no pig could have found its offspring. It therefore resulted, from the currents of blood that had circulated in his noble dam's family, that Peau-de-Balle won in a style that did not come from a nose-bag. And Brobdignac concluded that he had foreseen the event a long time ago, well before the birth of Peau-de-Balle.

Le Tuyau, incorrigibly, still had reservations. For him, the jockeys of the competitors had been too keen "to run after a horse whose initial break was shattering." They had been "broken by his dash" and "if they had waited until he was at the end of his tether become coming to attack him, the physiognomy of the race would have been completely different." (The works of Monsieur de La Palisse surely constituted by the Tipster's bedtime reading,[73] and at every moment, one saw him broadly inspired by his favorite author.) Furthermore, all of that was the fault of the deplorable Bowen, who had ridden in a fashion that would not have been tolerated in an apprentice.

The same note was found in almost all the papers. The most audacious expressed the conviction that Peau-de-Balle might yet win more races.

A reporter for the *Sport du Soir*, however, who had the strange habit of seeing through his own eyes and not borrowing the ready-made phrases so convenient for use in any eventuality, wrote under the rubric "From Day to Day" these inspired, and, so to speak, prophetic lines:

Ought I to admit it? I experienced an inexplicable impression, a veritable malaise, in seeing Peau-de-Balle gallop. Certainly, his stride is long, powerful and regular; he dies not betray any fatigue at the end of a race, and nothing, thus far, permits the limit of his means to be glimpsed. But there is

---

[73] Jacques de La Palice, or Palisse (1470-1520) was not, in fact, a writer, but merely a military man whose epitaph included the line *S'il n'était pas mort, il ferait envie* [if he were not dead, he would still be envied], which jokers insisted on misreading, rendering the last phrase as *serait en vie* [would still be alive]. The misreading was incorporated into a popular song, which made his name proverbially synonymous with stating the obvious,

something artificial and staccato in his action. One has the impression of seeing a locomotive advance, or rather, a mechanical toy. The horse does not seem to be moved by a soul, but by a taut spring that one always senses ready to break.

Alone in all the press, as can be seen, the reporter of the *Sport du Soir* issued a prognosis—or, rather, a diagnosis—approaching the truth. No one paid any attention to him.

Peau-de-Balle, careless of these obscure blasphemers and fervent admirers, pursued his triumphant career. In eight weeks, the due dates specified by Fred and Tod arrived, and every one, coinciding with a victory, was settled in full. The two Yankees departed for Chicago, where they immediately began work on a stock of presidential automata ordered by various Republics in South America.

The mechanical horse always won, and his exceptional form won the admiration of the weighing room and the crowd. A rain of gold fell upon Griffith, upon Gustave Louffe and even on Madame Tafoireau, who did not attach any great importance to it, having at her mercy the inexhaustible treasury of Comte Jérôme Thomas.

Peau-de-Balle made a clean sweep of all the races to which four-year-old horses were admitted, at all distances from twelve hundred meters to four thousand. Griffith, out of dilettantism, had even amused himself winning small handicaps in which the horse led from start to finish with top weight of sixty-five kilos. The tone of the press became dithyrambic.

Curiously enough, and which must be regarded as a simple coincidence, the good form of the automaton was communicated, by a kind of contagion, to the other horses in the same stable. All of them were now earning their oats.

It's extraordinary, Griffith said to himself. *Three months ago, I was working like a dog with these damned nags, and I couldn't pick up a prize in a claimer. Today, I hardly pay any attention to them, and they're always there, of their own accord. Well, so much the better; it pleases the bosses...and Blight, too.*

One fly in the ointment, of course, was the curiosity manifest on the subject of Peau-de-Balle. It became increasingly difficult to hide him under a bushel. One day, in fact, coming back from a victorious run, some imbecile had claimed that the horse was limping. Then Ely Pauwels, whose specialty was poking his nose in everywhere and interfering with things that were none of his business, had had the pretention, while Griffith had his back turned, to see whether Peau-de-Balle's cannon-bone was warm.

Already, he had leaned over to take hold of the leg and feel it. Fortunately, Gustave Louffe was there. He had delivered, with remarkable precision, a terrible blow of the whip to the extended hand of the trainer, who had straightened up howling like a man possessed. Gustave Louffe had then said to him, in the most polite fashion in the world: "Oh, beg pardon, Monsieur Pauwels, I didn't see you there," and led his horse away.

Another story: Madame Tafoireau wanted to have a portrait of her horse made by an animal painter she had once known in Montmartre in the days when he peeled turnips and she was showing her legs in a dive at three francs a night (less fines). The artist now commanded very high prices and must, therefore, have acquired enormous talent.

Griffith trembled for twenty-four hours, and was only reassured on observing the excessive myopia of the animal painter. He installed him in one corner of his yard and Peau-de-Balle in the opposite one. The artist marveled at the patience of the horse while the sittings lasted.

"If only all models held their pose as well as that," he is still repeating today.

The painting is presently to be found in Comte Jérôme Thomas' drawing room. Its author is a member of the Institut.

XII. Baron Isaac sticks his oar in.

Since the day of the Cup, Baron Isaac de l'Échelle-Jacob had been living in a state of chronic exasperation, continually renewed by further disappointments. Peau-de-Balle, his old horse, had become a veritable enemy so far as he was concerned, always and cruelly victorious.

Three times, admirably prepared coups had been thwarted; horses specially whetted by Pauwels had run up against the mysterious crack. And that Peau-de-Balle, always the favorite now, won even when he was ten to one on. In the financier's opinion, that was spoiling the game. Oh, if he had had that admirable instrument, how cleverly he would have been able to play with him!

So, a few days before the Prix Henri-Rochefort, which was to be run at Maisons-Lafitte—forty thousand francs and a work of art—Baron Isaac declared to himself that things could not go on as they were. He had, in fact, entered in that race his horse Pancreas, whose chance, unsuspected by the public, was of the first order—on condition, of course, that Madame Tafoireau's horse was left out of account. That was the problem: eliminating that inconvenient factor.

Now, Baron Isaac had the habit of passing from reflection to action with a marvelous rapidity; that is a condition of existence on the Bourse, where the flair of the financier must be doubled with the swiftness of a conjurer, and where big fish only eat the little ones by courtesy of their greater rapidity in movement.

The idea came to him at eight o'clock in the evening, while he was dining at Champeaux. At ten o'clock he disembarked at Chantilly with the bookmaker Sem Lévy, who was at all such feasts, and fell upon Ely Pauwels, bewildered by the untimely visit

The trainer, however, amiably installed his guests in his smoking room and offered them cigars. Baron Isaac accepted without hesitation, although he had a comfortable supply of Havanas in his pocket; he operated on the principle of never refusing what he could take.

He did not wait to have inspired the first puff of tobacco to get to the heart of the mater.

"He's a nuisance, Peau-de-Balle."

The enunciation of that truth, recognized by the three individuals, immediately created an atmosphere of cordiality.

"He's a nuisance. I give myself a diabolical headache earning four sous on the Bourse, and I lose it all again at the races because that dirty beast is always getting in the way of mine!"

Sem Lévy and Ely Pauwels let the boss talk, knowing perfectly well what he was getting at, but wanting to leave the responsibility for his conclusions to him.

"So, I ask myself: isn't there any means of getting rid of him?"

Slowly, Pauwels said: "I've thought about that."

"Well?"

"There are several means. For one, you could buy the horse. But since Madame Tafoireau doesn't want to hear of it, it's necessary not to think of it. Then, I thought perhaps that one might make something of young Gustave Louffe, by paying him the price. I ran into him the other day at the station, and I thought it a good opportunity. I offered him some suggestions regarding the services than an intelligent jockey might render certain wealthy individuals...whose interests weren't necessarily the same as the interests of his bosses. I made him understand that the jockey in question could considerably augment his income, and, combining action with words, I took out in front of him, in a negligent but ostentatious fashion, a wallet that was, I can assure you, rather well-stuffed. Do you know what young Gustave Louffe did? He pretended to mistake my intention. 'Oh, Monsieur Pauwels,' he said, 'you doubtless want change for a thousand-franc bill?' and in his turn he took out and opened under my nose a wallet in which there were three times as many blue bills as mine contained. You understand that there's no means of leverage on a jockey who earns as much as he presently wants."

Baron Isaac reflected.

"But Griffith? Griffith himself? Couldn't we make him understand that it's against his own interests to let his horse win so regularly?"

185

Sem Lévy's features took on a fearful expression.

"No, no, Griffith doesn't understand anything at all. I tried to have a word with him, in vain, on the subject of the late settlement of a certain debt that he owed me. It was a matter of old and unfortunate bets. I said to him, very mildly, that I'd consent to pass the sponge over his skate if...if Peau-de-Balle wanted to have, from time to time, a little weakness, very excusable in a horse that really is being abused. Griffith threw me the money he owed me and then...then he became even more vulgar."

And Sem Lévy rubbed his lower back, which appeared to be the seat of a dolorous memory.

Ely Pauwels burst into coarse laughter.

"Yes, you returned with an injury after the race."

Baron Isaac pursued his idea.

"What about the lads? Griffith's lads?"

"I've also made enquiries of Griffith's lads," replied Ely Pauwels. "That's easy, with a glass of whisky one can find out many things. And indeed, I received extraordinary information. This is it: Peau-de-Balle isn't lodged in Griffith's stable with the other horses. He's been installed in an isolated pavilion, of which Gustave Louffe occupies the first floor, and which has a separate exit to the road, a short distance from here. The lads don't have the right to go near that building. No one has ever seen any forage go in, or any dung come out. Finally, none of my neighbor's stable lads, nor any other inhabitant of Chantilly, has ever seen Peau-de-Balle at exercise, coming or going from the training grounds."

Pauwels fell silent momentarily, and then continued in an overly indifferent tone, without appearing to be paying any heed to the effect of his words on the Baron.

"All that, in sum, is very mysterious...but those circumstances render it very easy to carry out the project of anyone who wanted to pay Peau-de-Balle a visit by night...and take him, at the same time...oh, a mere supposition...some little delicacy. That might give a few chances of victory to Pancreas, tomorrow, in the Prix Henri-Rochefort."

"I don't understand," said Isaac—who was, on the contrary, beginning to understand very well indeed.

"Pardon me!" Lévy put in. "I'm not very sure either of having understood very well the thought of the very honorable opponent, but, if the occasion were to arise, I'd permit myself to table a little amendment to the project he's sketched. Certainly, it would be interesting for us to prevent Peau-de-Balle from running tomorrow. But what would be more interesting still would be to let him run, while being sure that he wasn't in a state of win. That would permit us, firstly, to get a jolly good price on Pancreas, and afterwards to cut up a dead horse piecemeal—and what a dead horse! The unbeatable Peau-de-Balle!"

"Not to mention the pleasure of giving La Tafoireau a slap in the eye," said Isaac, rubbing his hands together.

"And Griffith," added Sem Lévy, in a rancorous tone, rubbing his kidneys again.

"Supposing…supposing that one could get near Peau-de-Balle," observed the Baron, in a meditative tone. "I don't see very clearly the means of doing that..."

Ely Pauwels smiled. "Monsieur le Baron, you know very well that every trainer is something of a veterinarian, and even a little of a chemist. I've always had around the house a few little preparations destined, either to stimulate the weakening ardor of one of our champions, or, on the contrary, to moderate their enthusiasm..."

He went out briefly and came back with a little canvas bag, which he placed on the table, between Baron Isaac's hat and gloves.

"Look, here's a measure of oats that has been…perfumed with the aid of a concentrated solution of caffeine. Suppose that a horse ate those oats. I'll go further…suppose that...."

He interrupted himself, took an enormous key out of his pocket, and dropped it into the bag.

"Suppose that someone took that key, which is marvelously adapted—oh, purely by coincidence—to the door of Griffith's little pavilion. Suppose that once inside the pavilion—tonight, for example—the person in question approaches Peau-de-Balle's box, puts that measure of oats in the manger, and then withdraws discreetly. What would happen? The horse, after having had a light supper, feels joyful, excited. He won't sleep, and prevents young Gustave Louffe from sleeping. Good...it's still a supposition, isn't it?

"After that short period of excitement, comes a period of depression. The horse's muscles become numb, his heart beats irregularly, he gets out of breath. And tomorrow, without his trainer suspecting anything, because, in normal times, the beast's gait is a trifle stiff, the crack Peau-de-Balle won't be able to overtake a cab-horse. Naturally, it will be Griffith that the stewards haul in to explain the thing, and I'd certainly like to know how he'll explain it..."

Silence fell. Baron Isaac de l'Échelle-Jacob put his foot firmly forward. "It's amusing, your supposition. But it would be more amusing if you made the experiment."

"Oh, pardon me!" said Pauwels, who, in the vein of suppositions, could see himself being driven back to the road with a pitchfork by his neighbor. "I'm a trainer, me. I occupy myself with horses, and that's sufficient for me; I don't have anything to do with the occupations of others. If the affair interests some owner or bookmaker, it's up to them to get themselves out of trouble."

"Well then, bonsoir," said Baron Isaac, rising to his feet. "Are you coming, Lévy?"

And, doubtless by virtue of distraction, Baron Isaac stuffed the little bag of hay containing the big key into the capacious pocket of his coat.

He went out, followed by Sem Lévy.

The moon was casting a silvery sheet over the forest; the June night was exquisite, embalmed by sylvan perfumes conveyed by a light breeze. The clock on the old bell-tower of Chantilly—is there still an old bell-tower at Chantilly?—gently sounded eleven chimes, the last of which expired in the nocturnal silence. Everything was asleep. Peau-de-Balle too, no doubt...

After taking fifty paces, Baron Isaac de l'Échelle-Jacob stopped resolutely.

"Here's Griffith's pavilion. It seems very tranquil. You don't want to go in, Lévy?"

"I'd like nothing better, Monsieur le Baron," Sem Lévy replied, patting his lower back for the third time, "but I wouldn't want to miss the eleven-oh-eight train. I need to be in Paris by midnight..."

Then, as Isaac remained motionless on the road, the bookmaker politely took his leave of him.

The financier was furious.

"That's disgusting! One can no longer count on anyone! Oh, damn it, I'll take care of my affairs myself!"

He approached Griffith's pavilion and, without any scruple, if not without fear, put the key in the lock. In his youth, he had successfully carried out analogous operations, and had even had occasion to open doors without having keys to put in the locks.

At that moment, there was a sound of footsteps on the road. The Baron remained in suspense momentarily, assuming that it was Sem Lévy coming back for some reason.

It was not Lévy. It was the boy who brought the dispatches from the telegraph office at Chantilly at night.

"For Monsieur Griffith!" he said holding out a telegram to the Baron, whom he could see at the door, and whom, in the dark, he mistook for someone from the house.

"Thank you, young man," said the Baron.

And as the young man seemed to be waiting for a tip, he put his hand in his pocket...in order to put the telegram into it. Benevolently, he added: "Monsieur Griffith will give you something tomorrow morning."

When the porter had drawn away, Isaac decided to act.

Ely Pauwels' key did, indeed, fit the lock perfectly.

The Baron crossed the threshold and found himself in a dark vestibule. He struck a match, regretting not having brought a lantern, and saw facing him a large exterior door that had to give access to Peau-de-Balle's stable.

He opened it, pushed it, and stood there petrified, while the match, burning down, burned his fingertips.

On a large table placed in the center of a brightly lit room, Peau-de-Balle was standing motionless and staring at him. The trainer Griffith, perched on a stool, was grooming the horse with a clothes-brush, and young Gustave Louffe was passing a paint-brush dipped in varnish over the hooves.

On seeing the Baron, Griffith leapt to the ground and advanced toward him with a menacing smile.

"Ah! Monsieur le Baron Isaac! My horse' toilette interests you, then? And you've got up at night for that? Very kind...I didn't hear you ring the doorbell, Monsieur le Baron."

Isaac had recoiled and found himself in the antechamber. He saw Griffith's jaw contracting and his fist clenching. The financier sensed that his nose, so pure in its curvature, was really in peril. But he was a resourceful man; his composure did not abandon him.

"Monsieur Griffith," he said, "I've come out of Pauwels' house. I came out of my way I order to bring you a telegram that was on sufferance at the Post Office. Here it is..."

It was Griffith's turn to be surprised. While he stammered confused thanks, the financier fled through the open door. His expedition had failed, but, in sum, he had got away with it. He did not understand anything of what he had seen, but he was far from having penetrated the secret of the equine automaton.

After his departure, the trainer opened the dispatch that had arrived in such a singular fashion and read it.

"God damn it!" he howled.

XIII. Announcement

The telegram read as follows:

Madame Tafoireau suddenly deceased. Declare forfeit everywhere. Comte Jérôme Thomas.

Griffith communicated the news to Gustave Louffe, and they looked at one another in consternation. The death of

Madame Tafoireau could, and probably would, save for a providential stroke of luck, have disastrous consequences for them.

It seemed inevitable that Peau-de-Balle would be sold at auction with the rest of the stable; he would not go to auction without being examined closely, and it would then be inevitable that the colossal deception of which the entire racing world had been the victim would be discovered.

In any case, Madame Tafoireau' heirs or the purchaser of her crack, whoever it might be, would not be as obligingly disposed as the deceased. They would not give *carte blanche* to the trainer for him to do as he wished with the horse, so carefully sequestered until now. They would at least want to look at him closely, and that would be the least of his troubles, if one gave the matter some thought.

Griffith conserved one last hope, and that was to persuade Comte Jérôme Thomas to buy the horse from the unknown heirs. Jérôme Thomas, fortunately, he could already play like a flute; he would only have to carry on doing so. But Jérôme Thomas, full Comte as he was[74]—and he did not have to fear any comparison with the night star—had already spent a million to buy Peau-de-Balle for his lover, and certainly would not shell out the same vast sum again to buy him for himself.

At any rate, Griffith could not bear the uncertainty.

"Listen," he said to Gustave Louffe. "Tomorrow, you'll take the first train to Paris, and bring me back some information."

A few hours later, Gustave Louffe had returned, and summarize the results of his enquiries thus:

Madame Tafoireau had succumbed to an attack of appendicitis. That malady was then making its debut, and was thus very fashionable; it was all the rage among the All Paris

---

[74] A *comté*, in French, as well as signifying the equivalent of an earldom, is a kind of round cheese from the Franche-Comté.

of the premières. Comte Jérôme Thomas, in the midst of his very sincere grief, poor fellow, was extremely flattered that his lover had succumbed in such a distinguished fashion. It is necessary to say that he was as yet unacquainted with the automobile.

As regards the inheritance, Gustave Louffe brought stupefying news, of which he had been in search in the establishment of Maître Dessumeaux, notary.

Madame Tafoireau had only one relative close enough to qualify for the succession. And that heir—unexpectedly, to say the least—was Monseigneur Bénin-Despalmes, the Archbishop of Caudebec-en-Caux!

PART TWO: THE MONSEIGNEUR'S STABLE

I. Conversation in the Antechamber.

In the antechamber of the archiepiscopal palace of Caudebec-en-Caux, three visitors were waiting in turn for an audience.

One of them had the aspect of a man of law, including the spectacles, the side-whiskers, the briefcase and the frockcoat, the whole sculpted in old oak. Rigid and impassive, he was sitting in a corner.

The other two, much younger, were visibly journalists and were making no secret of it. They had arrived together and were continuing an animated conversation.

"It's amazing that I didn't run into you on the train. You weren't in first class?"

"No, no, the boss doesn't permit us to travel like princes, and we don't have permits to circulate at will, as in your filthy rag, stuffed with favors by our filthy government!"

(In that epoch the Affair was in full swing.)[75]

---

[75] i.e, the Dreyfus Affair, which began with the officer's conviction for treason in December 1894 and became a focal point of sharply-divided political opinions for the next decade.

"And you've come to interview Monseigneur Bénin-Despalmes about Cardinal Capello's letter?"

"Don't play the idiot, my lad. It's not a matter of that. You've got a good tip, but I've got it too. It's a matter of the Tafoireau inheritance, and you've come, as I have, to interview the bishop about his racing stable."

"Damn! We thought we were the only ones who knew about it. It'll be a fine thing, if *Le Crépuscule* publishes an interview at the same time as us."

"On the contrary, old chap. You're going to publish authentic tips in *L'Aube*. In *Le Crépuscule* I shall publish tips no less authentic, but contradictory. The day after, we get to grips: polemics, admonitions...in sum, copy for the season!"

"Tell me, first: what's this archbishop like?"

"Oh, my dear, one doesn't joke about that! Monseigneur Bénin-Despalmes is a saint, a saint of the kind that isn't seen any more. He's not one of those ultramontane prelates, devoured by ambition, such as one sees in all the corners of articles by Jean de Bonnefon.[76] It isn't him who spends his life in the editorial offices of *La Libre Parole*, nor in the offices of the Minister of Religion. He's a saint, I tell you, and also a worthy man...because there are some saints who aren't sympathetic at all. Monseigneur Bénin-Despalmes is a saint in the genre of...let's see, do you remember Bishop Myriel in *Les Misérables*?"

"No, I haven't read it...haven't had the time!"

"Well, he's a fellow in the genre of Abbé Constantin,[77] become a bishop. He's the pastor who would not only give his

---

[76] Jean de Bonnefon (1866-1928) was a journalist specializing in religious politics, who played a major role in formulating the law that formally separated the French State from the Catholic Church, orchestrated by Aristide Briand in 1905.

[77] The virtuous protagonist of Ludovic Halévy's eponymous novel of 1882 and the 1887 play adapted from it by Pierre Decourcelle and Hector Crémieux, both very popular.

life for his flock but pawn his purple stockings to give them something to eat."

"Your metaphors are poetic."

"Perfectly justified! Monseigneur Bénin-Despalmes, by dint of helping unfortunates publicly and privately, has seen his treasury emptied—and then there was the Tassigny-la-Raclée affair, which has put him in a very unfortunate pecuniary situation.

"The Tassigny-la-Raclée affair?"

"Yes! The village of Tassigny-la-Raclée possesses a young woman named Sophie Poirier, who is favored by celestial apparitions. The Archangel Michael has appeared several times to the young woman and expressed to her the desire to have a basilica at the very place where she looks after livestock. Abbé Tronche, the curé of Tassigny, ran to the archbishop, fired up with enthusiasm. Monseigneur Bénin-Despalmes, in spite of his prudence, didn't want to disappoint the venerable ecclesiastic, who had been his fellow student at the seminary. He agreed that the edification of the basilica, on condition that there wasn't too much emphasis on the visionary, was perfectly orthodox and commendable. But as the parochial budget of Tassigny-la-Raclée was insufficient for the purchase of the first stone, a subscription was opened. The subscription wasn't a great success. Then—and this is the villain of the story—the archbishop, out of pure generosity of soul, gave personal guarantees to the architect and the contractors. The first bills are beginning to come in, and Monseigneur Bénin-Despalmes is having all the trouble in the world honoring his signature."

The journalist darted a glance at the man of law, who did not appear to be listening.

"Well," said his comrade, "it seems to me that the Tafoireau stable is arriving right on time. Peau-de-Balle appears to me, in that circumstance, to be a sort of Messiah, a delegate of Providence. If he only wins for the archbishop what he won for La Tafoireau..."

At that moment a young priest came in and headed swiftly toward the man of law.

"Monseigneur is waiting for Maître Dessumeaux... Messieurs, please excuse me for being the bearer of bad news, but Monseigneur Bénin-Despalmes has decided, as a rule of prudence before which it is appropriate to incline, not to receive any member of the press in the present political circumstances."

"Just one word, Monsieur l'Abbé—it's not about politics. What will Monseigneur do with his racing stable?"

The young priest maintained an impassive visage. "I can only tell you one thing, Messieurs. His Highness is completely ignorant, at the present moment, of the heritage to which you allude."

He left with the notary. The two journalists looked at one another, and burst out laughing.

"Come on, old chap, let's go to the local café. We can write our interview there, and it won't be a load of codswallop."

II. The Sinner's Wealth

Maître Dessumeaux, introduced into the archbishop's audience chamber, advanced toward the prelate by means of a number of adroit little skids over the bare and admirably waxed parquet. Having arrived before Monseigneur Bénin-Despalmes, who had Abbé Douillet, his senior curate, to his right, he bowed in a very pure fashion exactly appropriate to the circumstance.

"Monseigneur," he said, "I've arrived from Paris by the express, in order to inform you of an event...a sad event...that has entirely personal consequences for you."

He darted a glance at the curate, who made a discreet movement to withdraw.

"Stay, stay, Monsieur," said the prelate, smiling.. None of my personal affairs can be secret from you, thank God, or anyone else."

The notary made an amiable and vague gesture signifying: *Since that's the case*.... Then, having sat down at the prelate's invitation, he announced: "You have doubtless learned, Monseigneur, of the decease of Madame Caroline Tafoireau, your relative?"

"My relative...?" said the archbishop, surprised. "Indeed, on reflection, the name isn't unknown to me. I once heard my mother pronounce it: it was a matter of a lady, Céleste Tafoireau, a resident of Paris, who was her distant cousin. She must be very old..."

"It's the daughter of that lady who died last week." The notary hesitated before adding: "The deceased had also employed the...pseudonym of Mag Iris."

"Her daughter? In fact, she did have a daughter, who, if my memory is exact, entered a convent."

The notary did not flinch. By contrast, the curate pursed his lips in a singular fashion. It is certain that if the archbishop, whose soul was as candid as that of a little child, was ignorant of all worldly matters, his colleague occasional received echoes thereof. The sporting papers had consecrated long obituaries to Madame Tafoireau, the popular owner, and the society papers had not failed to relate the theatrical successes of the late Mag Iris. There had even been, in *Le Temps*, a first-rate lightweight Claretie on that eminently Parisian subject; it had required no less than three columns for the eminent Academician to polish off a funeral oration.[78]

The notary replied: "No, Monseigneur, no. Madame Céleste Tafoireau's daughter did not exactly enter a convent. She was an artiste. She possessed a very good voice."

"I see, I see," said Monseigneur Bénin-Despalmes. "The person sang in a spiritual choir. In my last voyage to Paris I heard a beautiful one at the Schola Cantorum..."

---

[78] Jules Claretie (1840-1913), formerly a very successful journalist, had been appointed director of the Théâtre-Français in 1885 and was elected to the Académie in 1888, but continued to dabble in his former profession.

Again, Abbé Douillet pulled a face. He had heard mention of Scalas that were not Scalas Cantorum.[79]

"My God, Monseigneur," remarked the notary, "I dare not affirm to you that the concerts in which Madame Tafoireau sang were entirely spiritual...but as my time is limited, I ought to hasten to explain the veritable object of my mission. You are, Monseigneur, the sole relative close enough to the deceased, whose notary I am, to qualify for the succession. As no testament was found, you must be considered as her heir, all reservations made in the case of possible subsequent claims, such as those, for instance, that might arise on the part of a recognized natural child."

"And did this poor Madame Tafoireau leave considerable wealth?" asked the excellent prelate, who was thinking, as always, of his poor and his good works.

"I have almost clarified the situation, which might have appeared somewhat confused. Madame Tafoireau did not leave any movable property, and the town house she owned in Paris is mortgaged for two-thirds of its value. The best thing would be to sell it at auction. The surplus of the sale price, as well as the liquidation of jewels, furniture and works of art, will serve to pay off her creditors. She had, in fact...omitted to regulate certain small debts. But one part of the succession remains intact and intangible. I am referring to her racing stable."

"Her racing stable?" said the archbishop, profoundly surprised.

"Yes, Monseigneur, her racing stable, which, since the beginning of the season, had brought in two hundred and sixty thousand francs... You'll excuse me, Monseigneur, but I need to catch the train. I shall always be at Your Highness' disposition to give him, in my study, all the complementary infor-

_____

[79] La Scala was, in the context of this reference, a music hall in the Boulevard de Strasbourg, revitalized by Édouard Marchand in 1895, where all the great names of the café concert circuit performed.

197

mation. In addition, Monsieur Griffith, senior, Madame
Tafoireau's trainer, has come to see me several times and has
told me of his intention to solicit an audience here. Will you
please, Monseigneur, communicate your decision on the subject of the inheritance to me... Monseigneur...Monsieur
l'Abbé..."

Abbé Douillet escorted Maître Dessumeaux back to the
door of the archepiscopal palace. Having arrived there, he
could not resist the temptation to say what he thought.

"Forgive me Monsieur, for mingling with affairs that are
none of my concern, but I've heard talk of Madame Tafoireau,
and the fashion in which she amassed the fortune of which His
Highness now finds himself the inheritor. I wonder whether
the acceptance of wealth coming from that source might be
badly interpreted, and whether it is appropriate to ecclesiastical dignity..."

"Monsieur l'Abbé," the notary interrupted, smiling. "I
believe that the Lord accepted the jar of perfume of a sinner
named Magdalen. You certainly recall the words that the Gos-
pel reports to us on that subject."[80]

III. A Case of Conscience

The curate, on returning to Monseigneur Bénin-
Despalmes, found the latter extremely preoccupied.

---

[80] *Matthew* 26:6-13, *Mark* 14:3-9, *Luke* 7:36-50 and *John*
12:1-8 describe the anointing of Jesus' feet, by an unnamed
sinner in the first three accounts, and a woman named Mary—
not identified as a sinner—in the last; tradition eventually con-
flated the characters into Mary Magdalen. The incident was
obviously considered crucial by the evangelists. Jesus' disciples suggest to him that the perfume could have been sold and
the money given to the poor rather than being wasted on his
feet, and he replies to the effect that: "The poor will always be
with you, but you will not always have me."

"A racing stable! The circumstance is very embarrassing. I am recalling the sacred texts and the Church Fathers in vain; I can find nothing applicable to the particular case."

"Your Highness might summon Abbé Tacot, the professor of exegesis at the Grand Séminaire. Abbé Tacot possesses a remarkable erudition in matters of ecclesiastical history. He is, in addition, one of our foremost dialecticians."

As the archbishop was issuing instructions to that effect, a visiting card was brought in.

Baron Isaac de l'Échelle-Jacob, was written thereon, *has the honor of soliciting a brief audience with Monseigneur Bénin-Despalmes, on an urgent matter.*

Please send the gentleman in," said the prelate, evidently impressed by those Biblical names.

In spite of the phenomenal aplomb that he dissimulated beneath his rather obsequious mannerisms, the Baron was really ill at ease. He was not in the habit of frequenting bishoprics, but he never recoiled when it was a matter of concluding a good business deal, and he would have presented himself at the Vatican to negotiate the purchase of Saint Peter's keys if that purchase had offered him a sufficient profit margin. That is why, unsuspectingly, he had first sought out the head of the Freemasonic Lodge of Caudebec-en-Caux, had identified himself to him as a great dignitary of the Order, and, to the great amazement of the provincial, had said to him: "You have connections in Caudebec; give me a recommendation to the Archbishop."

Not having been able to obtain the introduction—which had surprised him—Baron Isaac de l'Échelle-Jacob had presented himself, with his personal prestige alone, before Monseigneur Bénin-Despalmes.

He thought it appropriate, on finding himself face to face with the prelate, to neglect all oratory precaution and get straight to the point of his visit.

"Monsieur l'Archevèque," he said, "are you disposed to sell Peau-de-Balle for a good price?"

There was a silence. Monseigneur Bénin-Despalmes smiled with affability ad incomprehension, and turned to his curate.

"Monsieur is doubtless a foreigner and does not speak our language very well. Perhaps it would be appropriate to summon Abbé Gugussheim, who is very well versed in foreign dialects and might be able to serve as an interpreter."[81]

"No, no," protested the Baron. "Perhaps I'm expressing myself badly, or rather, you're not up to date. I'm talking about Peau-de-Balle. You don't know? No? Well, Monsieur l'Archevêque, you have inherited from Madame Tafoireau, a very charming lady...Madame Tafoireau had racehorses. Among those horses, there is one named Peau-de-Balle. Peau-de-Balle is a funny name, eh? He's a very good horse. Well, that's the one I want to buy. I'll pay you two hundred thousand francs."

Monseigneur Bénin-Despalmes, and even Abbé Douillet, were amazed by the enormity of the sum. It surpassed their comprehension that a horse could be worth two hundred thousand francs, when Bijou, the bay that pulled the archbishop's carriage, had only cost six hundred and fifty francs.

Baron Isaac, a past master in commercial psychology, understood the meaning and profundity of their emotion perfectly.

"I am in communication with Maître Dessumeaux, the notary occupied with the succession. You can ask his advice, and if you decide, he can transmit your response to me. Two hundred thousand francs, I say, Monsieur l'Archevêque; it's silly, but when I desire a horse, I'm willing to pay its weight in

---

[81] The reader will recall that I have not attempted to reproduce the eye-dialect in which the Baron's speech is rendered in the original, which helps to explain the archbishop's incomprehension. The saintly individual presumably has no notion of the less savory connotations of the phrase Peau-de-Balle at this point, although he subsequently seems to become vaguely aware of a possible impropriety.

gold. *Au revoir*, Monsieur l'Archevêque... I have the honor, Monsieur le Curé..."

As Baron Isaac was leaving the archbishopric, Abbé Tacot, the professor of exegesis at the Grand Séminaire, came into it.

Abbé Tacot was a well of knowledge in dogmatic matters. He was also a terrible man. His head was a veritable arsenal containing all the sacred texts, Papal decretals, decisions of Councils, the *Summa* of St. Thomas Aquinas—which, together with the work of Paul Bourget, constitutes the most mind-numbing load of rubbish that humans have produced in the course of the centuries—and a heap of other treasures of the same nature, drafted in French or kitchen Latin. Thus, in the most ordinary circumstances of life, whether it was a matter of making a judgment or witnessing a very simple fact, he would whip out an argument, a carefully whetted ecclesiastical law, take aim, fire, and strike you down with it mercilessly.

In every profession there are men like that. There are men like that in all the administrations, in the army, in the magistracy and even, alas, on the Turf. They are the implacable conservers of the rule-book, form and prejudice. They put spokes in every wheel, and in consequence, nothing proceeds as it ought to proceed.

Monseigneur Bénin-Despalmes had a holy terror of Abbé Tacot, who was a pitiless critic of his writs of mandamus, his allocutions and his slightest gestures. Abbé Tacot saw symptoms of heresy everywhere.

That is why it was indispensable to consult Abbé Tacot at this critical moment, when the Monseigneur found himself at the head of a racing stable.

The curate explained to the eminent exegete how the archbishop had come into an inheritance, and the nature of that heritage. He naturally passed over in the silence the pseudonym and profession of the deceased. However, Abbé Douillet did mention the visit of Baron Issac de l'Échelle-Jacob and his proposal of purchase concerning Peau-de-Balle. He even defined the individual in these terms:

"A person who had the name, exterior appearance and language of an Israelite..."

"Really, Monsieur l'Abbé," remarked the worthy prelate, "Do you think so? I would never have thought it."

Abbé Tacot frowned, and raised a dogmatic finger. "With regard to negotiations projected with an Israelite, there is no doubt. The case is specified in item VI of the fifth book of decretals: *No one, whether a cleric or a layman, may negotiate with an infidel, under penalty of a grave sin, except in the case of necessity.* Now, an Israelite must be considered, *a fortiori*, as an infidel. And the circumstance of necessity must be understood here in the strictest sense. Thus, Saint Bernard, in a letter that he wrote to Henry, Archbishop of Sens, who asked his advice on that doctrinal point, cites the case of a Christian knight lost in the Syrian desert in the epoch of the crusades. That knight, dying of hunger, encountered a Jew who sold him the aliments necessary to survive, and also wanted to sell him a horse in order to continue his journey. The holy doctor absolved the knight for having bought the food, since he would otherwise have died, and praised him highly for not having bought the horse, the necessity of which was not absolutely vital. Now, if the purchase of the horse, in the case of the knight, was not considered as a case of necessity, it is even less so for the sale of a racehorse to the Israelite that you call the Baron de l'Échelle-Jacob."

"So," said the archbishop, "it would be necessary for me to sell this fabulously valuable horse to another, Christian, individual...or have Baron Isaac baptized. But could I not keep and utilize the horse?"

"The sacred texts have not really foreseen anything in the matter of racehorses..."

Abbé Douillet uttered a sigh of relief.

"...But one can easily resolve the difficulties presented by that subject, by consulting that which has been resolved, on the matter of gambling, by the Holy Father, the Pontiffs and the Councils..."

Abbé Douillet uttered a sigh of resignation. They were not going to be able to cut the matter short this time.

"...In fact, according to the opinion of the world and the Church, racecourses constitute one of the forms, and doubtless the most reprehensible form, of gambling. Gambling has always been forbidden by the canons of the Church, whether it is a matter of games of pure chance, such as dice games, lansquenet, faro or snakes-and-ladders, or of a mixed game in which industry is combined with chance, such as piquet, trictrac, ombre, skittles and chess. The General Lateran Council held in November 1515, under Innocent III,[82] did not even permit ecclesiastics to be present in companies where those sorts of games were played: *Clerici vel aleas, vel taxilos non ludant nec hujusmodi intersint...*"

There he goes—he's off, thought Abbé Douillet, in despair.

"...and that prohibition is renewed in 1565 by Saint Charles Borromeo in his first provincial council: *Nec solum ludere vetamus, sed cos ludorum spectatores esse nolumus, aut quemquam ludentum in oedibus suis permittere.*"[83]

Monseigneur Bénin-Despalmes, anticipating that this was only the beginning of an avalanche of texts, assumed what is known in the theater as "a comfortable position" in order to listen—which is to say that he leaned back in his chair and quietly closed his eyes.

Abbé Tacot resumed forcefully. "In a particular fashion, the blessed cardinal Peter Damian is the person who fulminated must against chess, which he called a indecent, absurd and

---

[82] Inexplicably, the Abbé's remarkable memory has failed him; Julius II convened the Lateran Council in question, and it concluded after his death under Leo X. Given that, it is perhaps not surprising that his quotation seems to be both garbled and misattributed.

[83] This quotation, on the other hand, is accurate save for one minor transposition, and does indeed come from the source indicated.

infamous game: *Quam inhonestum, quam absurdum, quam denique soedum sit hoc in sacerdote ludibrium.* And he goes so far as to call it a sacrilegious game, in speaking about the severe reprimand that he had made to the Bishop of Florence, with whom he was traveling, and on whom he imposed a penance of reciting the psalter three times, washing the feet of a dozen paupers and giving each of them a coin, for having played it after supper.[84]

"And if the game of chess is condemned in such a peremptory fashion, how much more disastrous out one to consider the gambling that takes place on racecourses, the scandal being public and happening, so to speak, in the face of heaven!"

A diversion occurred, which fortunately interrupted, to the great relief of the prelate and the curate, the savant casuist's flow of eloquence. It was the entry of a lackey who announced the presence in the antechamber of T. Griffith senior.

The trainer, eaten away by anxiety on the subject of Peau-de-Balle, had decided on a personal approach to his new owner. It was necessary, at all costs, that Monseigneur Bénin-Despalmes kept the crack and ran him in his own colors; obviously, it was not the prelate who would come to palpate Peau-de-Balle in order to see whether he was alive.

The Monseigneur welcomed the visitor whom Providence had sent in such a timely fashion with an almost joyful benevolence.

"Be welcome, Monsieur. Maître Dessumeaux told us to expect your visit. We know that you give your vigilant and enlightened care to the horses that belong to us…but which will not belong to us for much longer, since Monsieur l'Abbé Tacot, here present, has just demonstrated to us that the possession of a racehorse would not be appropriate for an ecclesiastic, all the more so for a bishop.

---

[84] The quotation, dating from the 11th century, also accurate and correctly attributed, and the judgment is still remembered, not very fondly, by modern chess-players.

"Indeed," said Abbé Tacot, intending to knock out the English trainer with a single blow—the Latin punch—*"levia autem delicta, quae in ipsis maxima esse affugiant, ut eorum actiones cunctis afferent venerationem."*[85]

Griffith's church Latin was mediocre, but, surprising as it might seem, he was entirely prepared to sustain a controversy on racing, even by looking at it from the viewpoint of canon law. In fact, the previous day, he had paid a visit to the protestant pastor of Chantilly; by steering the conversation adroitly around to the subject he wanted to prepare, he had been able to make a provision of arguments and texts.

So, as Gustave Louffe would have put it, he backed Abbé Tacot into a corner.

"I don't see," Griffith said, "that anything in the Christian religion can motivate the proscription of the horse, or to have it considered as an accursed animal. I've never heard it said that Noah refused the horse entry to the Ark, or that it was a horse that presented the fatal apple to our mother Eve. On the contrary, the horse played a very honorable role in the Scriptures. The prophet Elijah was carried to heaven by a chariot drawn by four horses. According to the Apocalypse, it is a horse that transported Saint John to the seventh heaven. It was on a representative of the equine race—modest, it is true, but the thoroughbred had not yet been invented—that Joseph led his family into Egypt, and also on which, thirty years later, the triumphant entry of Jesus into Jerusalem took place. Saint Martin and Saint George are always represented on horseback, and that has not prevented them, I think, from occupying a good place in hagiography. As for Saint Paul, he was also on a horse when he emptied his stirrups on the road to Damascus."

---

[85] *Autem* should be *etiam* and *esse* should be *essent*; otherwise the quotation from the diocesan statues is correct, as it surely ought to be. It translates, approximately, as "let them [i.e., the clergy] also avoid minor faults, which in them would be great, so that their actions may be accorded the respect of all."

"Exactly!" cried Abbé Tacot, triumphantly. "The finger of Providence is found in that! Paul of Tarsus, who was simply a despicable gentile when he was on horseback, became the greatest saint of the day when he was on foot."

Abbé Tacot had noticed that Griffith's arguments, crude as they were, had made a certain impression on Monseigneur Bénin-Despalmes. He wanted to destroy that effect.

"In any case," he went on, with the objective of finishing off his adversary, "the horses of which Monsieur speaks were honest animals employed by their masters as means of transport, not instruments of diabolical gain destined to amass, in the form of race prizes, money derived from gambling."

Griffith then showed an admirable presence of mind.

"Monsieur l'Abbé, there is a parable that I want to relate to you, very poorly, but which is certainly in your gospels. It's a matter of a master who has two stewards. He confides fifty talents to each of them. He comes back a year later and asks for their accounts. The first steward returns his fifty talents, which he has kept carefully. The other, who has put his money to work, like a good Israelite, returns a hundred to him, which represents a very good interest. The master criticizes the first steward and praises the second, which proves that it is always necessary to make the gifts of the Lord fructify, and which also proves that when one has a racehorse, it is not to be sold or left in the stable, but raced in order to earn money, even when one is an archbishop."

"Money from gambling!" insisted Abbé Tacot. "Saint Bonaventure, and after him the scholarly theologian Alexander of Hales, who clarified the *Summa Theologica* by order of Pope Innocent IV, considered that one must make restitution to the poor of money won by gambling."

"Precisely!" said Griffith, with authority. "Precisely! We're in agreement. The money harvested on racecourses is centralized in order to be distributed in the form of prizes. Those prizes will be won by Peau-de-Balle, the Monseigneur's horse. And Monseigneur will distribute the money to the poor, which is entirely in conformity with the ideas of the Church and the desire of the Messieurs that you have just cited."

At that precise moment, unexpected aid came to tip the balance in favor of Griffith and decide his victory; it was brought by Abbé Tronche, the curé of Tassigny-la-Raclée.

The venerable ecclesiastic, who had the privilege of entry to see Monseigneur Bénin-Despalmes officially or unofficially at any hour, had arrived in time to hear the end of the conversation. He had humbly sat down in a corner on the edge of the most modest seat he could find, but he seemed to be in a state of extraordinary agitation and was shivering nervously while waiting for an opportunity to speak to the archbishop.

The two casuists had paused momentarily to get their breath and assemble their arguments. He took advantage of that brief suspension of hostilities to advance toward the prelate, who extended his hand to him, smiling.

"A miracle! A miracle!" cried Abbé Tronche, in a tone that reminded Griffith of the manner in which enthusiastic sportsmen on the course shout the name of the horse that they have backed when it crosses the finish line first, and even when it trails in last, well beaten.

"What news is there from Tassigny-la-Raclée?" asked Monseigneur Bénin-Despalmes.

"Our visionary, young Sophie Poirier, had a new vision this morning, manifestly come from heaven. The Archangel Michael appeared to her on a horse. That horse bore an aureole on its head and on that aureole young Sophie was able to read the words, in letters of fire: *In hoc signo vinces*,[86] Now Monseigneur, young Sophie does not know Latin, which ought to convince the incredulous."

"On saying these last words the worthy curé looked severely at Abbé Tacot. Abbé Tacot had, thus far, exhibited a regrettable skepticism in the matter of the apparitions of

---

[86] "In this sign shalt thou conquer": originally the motto of the Roman Emperor Constantine I, subsequently adopted by the Knights Templar, inscribed on their standard over a red cross.

Tassigny-le-Raclée, and had even cited texts as trenchant as razor blades.

Abbé Tronche's words produced a considerable effect. The savant professor of exegesis visibly lacked confidence; Griffith judged that he had run out of steam, and was about to collapse.

In fact, young Sophie's apparition of a horse aureoled with the prophetic words took on a very clear significance in the present circumstances; the propriety of the celestial message was evident, and its import imperious. Evidently, Providence was intimating to the archbishop the instruction to keep Peau-de-Balle, and promised him imminent victories. The involvement in the project of the Archangel Michael became so obvious that it was necessary, in order to deny it, to have eyes in order not to see: *oculus habent et non videbunt*. The construction of the basilica was to be the prize of the victories of a horse, a horse whose prizes would appease the hungry mob of creditors and constructors.

Monseigneur Bénin-Despalmes no longer hesitated.

"Thank you, my dear Abbé, for having brought us the good news, like the dove of the Ark. Monsieur Griffith, you will have the kindness to keep, in our name, the horses that you trained on Madame Tafoireau's account."

Griffith took his leave, bowing to the Monseigneur and then extending his hand to Abbé Tacot, as a polite boxer does after a fight.

Abbé Tacot, however, turned his back rancorously, muttering words in which there was mention of Luther, Calvin, Balaam's ass and Colas' cow.[87]

---

[87] "Colas' cow" was an offensive term for a Huguenot, supposedly derived from an incident in which a stray cow belonging to a peasant of that name was ill-treated by a protestant, which was featured in popular songs.

IV. The Amethyst Silks

"Monseigneur," said Abbé Douillet, "these racecourse matters are terribly obscure and complicated. I've heard it said that in order to direct a stable in the capacity of an owner, it's necessary to possess a remarkable intelligence and a great sporting erudition. One has to know the names of all the horses, their sires and dams, the color of all the silks and the weight, to the nearest ten grams, of jockeys, trainers and journalists. We'll never get through it. We ought to take advice, I order to avoid any mistakes, from a discreet and experienced person."

"One might perhaps assemble the chapter."

"The chapter is made up of eminent ecclesiastics, knowledgeable about all things, but its luminaries do not understand these purely mundane matters. It would be better to consult Maître Dessumeaux, who is accustomed to them."

A few days later the archbishop received the following letter from the notary.

Monseigneur,

I have learned with satisfaction that the Court of Rome has not raised any objection to the project formed by Your Highness relative to the exploitation of a racing stable. In conformity with your desire, after having consulted Monsieur le Comte Jérôme Thomas, who is one of the most remarkable minds of our epoch, I am able to submit to you my advice on certain matters of detail, desiring to reconcile archiepiscopal dignity with the practical establishment of a sport that certainly brings together the greatest names in France, but which is also sometimes exposed to a disquieting publicity and promiscuity.

It is thus that the color purple, which is the color par excellence of bishops, a discreet color in good taste, appears to me to be clearly indicated for Your Highness' silks. We wondered whether it would not be excellent to complete them by adding an old gold cross on the back, but that genre of orna-

mentation is a little too special; only hoops, sashes and Saint Andrew's crosses are habitually employed. As for the cap, the color red would signal, in the most fortunate fashion, the titles Your Highness possesses to a cardinal's robes.

A fortunate circumstance arises from the fact that Your Highness' jockey, Gustave Louffe, is French and Catholic, a double condition rather infrequent in professional milieux, and which ought to rejoice our hearts in these unhappy times when cosmopolitan hordes and foreign agents are striving, by the most reprehensible means, to destroy national sentiment.

I shall pass on to another order of ideas. It will be preferable that no ecclesiastic belonging to the diocese of Caudebec-en-Caux show themselves at racecourses when Your Highness' colors are represented there. The trainer Griffith, assisted by Comte Jérôme Thomas, who will graciously lend Your Highness the collaboration of his enlightenment will be sufficient for the good management of your interests.

You have also asked me whether it might not be convenient to change the name of the horse Peau-de-Balle, which appears to you to be a trifle suspect in it lightness. I shall dare to observe to Your Highness that the name has no obscene and offensive significance for the pure-minded, and that, the horse having already made that name illustrious and popular, it is better to conserve it.

Accept, Monseigneur, the respectful, etc.

Dessumeaux, notary.

As the worthy archbishop, reading this letter, was rejoicing to see things progressing as desired, Abbé Tacot hurtled into the senior curate's office, brandishing a newspaper with a vengeful hand.

"What did I tell you, Monsieur l'Abbé Douillet? The scandal's beginning!"

"What scandal? And what newspaper is that?"

"This newspaper is *Le Balai*, the organ of the Freemasonic Lodge of Caudebec-en-Caux!"

"Permit me Monsieur l'Abbé, not to congratulate you on your choice of reading material."

"Let me continue. This newspaper contains a most virulent article on the Monseigneur's racing stable. The article is visibly inspired by Baron Isaac de l'Échelle-Jacob, who, by virtue of his dignity as a Grand Mason and also by virtue of his fortune, is very well placed to drag anyone through the mud that he finds in the way of his interests. The excellent man, having been unable to obtain what he desired from the Monseigneur, seems fully determined to make His Highness disgusted with a métier that, I was the first to say, is unsuitable for an archbishop. Listen, Monsieur l'Abbé, to this article signed Léo Letaxi:[88]

"The horse, as Chateaubriand says, is in the process of becoming the noblest conquest of clericalism..."

"*Le Balai* is not very reliable from the point of view of literary sources," put in Abbé Douillet.[89]

"...Not content with having put their hand on consciences, the representatives of ultramontane obscurantism have set foot in our hippodromes, and the Bishop Bénin-Despalmes has just inherited from an old devotee..."

"*Le Balai*'s information service leaves a little to be desired," said Abbé Douillet, mildly.

---

[88] This pseudonym would have reminded contemporary readers of that of Léo Taxil (1854-1907), an outspoken author who was both virulently anticlerical and vitriolically anti-Masonic; his outrageous claims were supported by faked evidence, including forged papal correspondence. The title of his book, *A bas la calotte!* ["Down with the clergy," the name of the ecclesiastical skullcap being adapted as a slang designation of the entire clergy] (1879) is echoed later in the story as well as in the pun that concludes this fictitious article.

[89] The oblique reference is to a famous quotation from the Comte de Buffon, in his *Histoire naturelle*, stating that the noblest conquest of humankind was that of the horse.

"*...a stable whose finest ornament, an ornament that ought to be sacerdotal, bears the suggestive name of Peau-de-Balle. Let us hope that Peau-de-Balle will not devour, like a mere peck of oats, the denier of the religion and the purse of the faithful, and that the clerics, in their turn, will not have to cry out*: A bas la culotte!"[90]

"Well, that's very nice," said the curate, "but there's no point in that article falling under the Monseigneur's eyes. Put it in your archives, Abbé Tacot."

The following Sunday, the excellent Abbé Tronche, curé of Tassigny-la-Tachée, at the end of his sermon, said to his parishioners:

"My dear brethren, let us pray for the Monseigneur's horse, which is carrying our most cherished hopes. The fate of our basilica, whose walls are beginning to emerge from the ground, is intimately linked to the fate of the charger blessed by Saint Michael himself. The great archangel, appearing to one of our children of Mary, has given a certain sign of the interest he has in him. Let us therefore pray ardently today that he gives victory to the representative of the Lord's anointed."

That day, in fact, Peau-de-Balle, wearing the amethyst silks and red cap for the first time, was due to run in the Prix du Grand-Argentier at Maisons-Lafitte; and the sales of the *Sport du Soir* in the diocese of Caudebec-en-Caux were exceptional, the reading of that newspaper even distracting considerable attention from the breviary.

---

[90] Literally, "down with trousers!" but the cry obtained a special meaning in the 1789 Revolution, when the revolutionary mob consisted of *sans-culottes*. More relevant to the present citation, however, is the fact that, unlike English gamblers, who can metaphorically "lose their shirt" gambling, French punters who take a heavy loss are sometimes said to "*ramasser (or prendre) une culotte*" [pull up their trousers].

V. The Prix du Grand-Argentier

The Prix du Grand-Argentier, which is run over sixteen hundred meters on a straight course, had been founded under the auspices of a Minister of Finance imbued with strange ideas on the subject of racehorses; he thought that the interests of the equine race were intimately linked to the general interests of agriculture, and by that token to the general wealth of the nation. One can tell that the story of Peau-de-Balle is set in a very remote era.

That minister had inscribed in the budget an annual sum of twenty-five thousand francs for the allocation of that trial, an allocation all the richer for that epoch because it was a matter of a handicap: a limited handicap, since the weights, on publication, went from fifty to sixty-five kilos, and only horses that had won ten thousand francs during the years were admitted.

Peau-de-Balle had the honor of top weight, sensible aggravated by the penalties incurred following his victories since the establishment of the handicap, so his weight was seventy-two kilos.

His participation, however, was not in doubt. His owner, the saintly man, was completely ignorant of the influence of weight on races. As for Griffith, he had his reasons for knowing that the horse could carry that mountain of lead with perfect ease.

Baron Isaac de l'Échelle-Jacob, who was pursuing his campaign with the determination of his race, had decided that Peau-de-Balle would not win this time. He explained his plan to Sem Lévy on the morning of the race.

"Monsieur le Baron," the bookmaker had insinuated, "I'm wondering why you've left your three horses in this handicap. Piston, fair enough—he might gain a place with his low weight—but Échalote and Fin-Courant, who have only ever run in claimers and over a very short distance?"

"Lévy," said the Baron, "do you know how football is played?"

"Football? Yes, I have a pretty good idea what it is."

"Well, in football, you've been able to remark that, for one player who has to carry the ball to a determined place, there are four or five others, of the adverse camp, who are exclusively charged with preventing him from getting through."

"I understand, I understand, Monsieur le Baron. Piston, Échalote and Fin-Courant aren't running to win, but to prevent the enemy from winning."

"You're very intelligent, Lévy."

"At the start, they'll take the lead, come back into Peau-de-Balle's line..."

"Yes..."

"To interrupting his action, striking into his legs, boxing him in..."

"Yes, yes..."

"And the distance is too short for Peau-de-Balle, supposing he can get free thereafter, to recover from his initial disadvantage."

"Very good. So, you'll do me the pleasure of laying Peau-de-Balle with open taps. The horse is dead..."

Thanks to those instructions, the archbishop's horse started at the remunerative price of four to one, in spite of the enthusiasm of his partisans and the unusual popularity of the phenomenal crack. In any case, his heavy weight and a field of twelve competitors might have been sufficient to explain the apparent opposition.

At the departure signal, a bizarre hesitation seemed to occur. Piston and Fin-Courant, after having bounded forward, seemed to veer sideways, but that jink, well concerted, brought them hoof-to-hoof with Échalote, the third rogue—which is to say, directly ahead of Peau-de-Balle, whose initial acceleration, being mechanical and not purely impulsive, had, as always, required two seconds.

Gustave Louffe had not taken any precaution to isolate his horse; this time, in fact, he had no reason for caution, the

214

course being a straight line and not involving any dangerous bend.

Griffith was in the stand and following the race with his binoculars. He understood the maneuver."

"Oh, the swines!" he muttered, between his teeth.

But immediately, he began to smile. In fact, Peau-de-Balle, in full action, represented an express locomotive, and the danger was not to him.

"Look out!" shouted Gustave Louffe, who suddenly became conscious of what was about to happen.

In the blink of an eye, Échalote and Fin-Courant, lifted up as if by a catapult, projected to the right and left like corrida horses by the horns of a bull, were rolling on the ground with their jockeys. The third representative of Isaac's stable only received the repercussion, and was able to recover his equilibrium, but he had sustained sufficient damage for his jockey to leap to the ground and pat his shoulder anxiously.

As for Peau-de-Balle, he continued straight to the winning post in his marvelously supple and extended action.

Everyone expected to see Baron Isaac uttering loud cries, invoking the God of Israel, demanding compensatory damages, and objecting against the winner. To the general amazement, he not only remained mute, but undiscoverable.

He had slipped like a large rat into a deserted corner of the stables and found his collaborator Lévy.

"Well, it's gone wrong this time!"

"Yes, Monsieur le Baron. I'll debit you the forty-five thousand I'll have to pay out to Peau-de-Balle's backers. But aren't you going to lodge a complaint?"

"Oh, my friend you can take it for granted that if there's an enquiry, they'll discover the conspiracy. Of the three little jockeys that rode for us in the race, there's sure to be one who'll talk and spill the beans. Let's play dead; the money will come back."

However, on emerging from the weighing-room, Gustave Louffe was not surprised to be called up before the stewards.

Those gentlemen made a few observations to the young jockey on the manner in which he had frayed a passage.

"The desire to win is very praiseworthy, but you've just gambled with the lives of your competitors. It's lucky that none of Baron Isaac's jockeys was injured."

"It would be unjust to hold me responsible," replied Gustave Louffe. "Monsieur Griffith can tell you that Peau-de-Balle is a horse that's difficult to manage and brutal, who can't be stopped as one would like. In any case, I thought I saw, among my competitors, a deliberate intention to block my route; they only have themselves to blame for what happened."

The explanation was more than probable, Baron Isaac's reputation had been made a long time ago, and his acquaintance with the bookmaker Sem Lévy, who had been quoting the favorite at an excessively generous price in the circumstances, and with suspicious confidence, was well known.

The stewards therefore limited themselves to giving Gustave Louffe a warning, which was published the next day by the sporting press with appropriate commentaries.

The circumstance was underlined by a false step on the art of Monseigneur Bénin-Despalmes. The excellent prelate, having learned that his jockey had committed a sin, without at all understanding its import, had his secretary write him a letter containing three pages of excellent advice, terminated with an absolution of sorts.

On the course, as is often the case, the incident had been understood very well.

"He's got a red face, for the moment, Brother Isaac…he's fallen on to the gas tap again!"

VI. Peau-de-Balle is disturbed.

As a result of those unmerited reproaches, Gustave Louffe felt his soul fill with bitterness. As one says in racing jargon, he lost his action, was disheartened, and ended up committing a fault that was to have incalculable consequences.

Louffe was the most honest fellow in the world. He had resisted the perfidious offers of the bookmaker Sem Lévy, and the temptations that were offered to him in various, but generally feminine, forms. He had even refused, purely out of concern for his professional dignity, the awkward hand of Madame Tafoireau, which, according to his expression, wanted to "give him a send-off."

But Gustave Louffe had been possessed, since childhood, by an obsession, one of those ineradicable whims that resemble monomania in the tenacity of their manifestations. He wanted to discover and applying to humans the secret of the flight of birds.

Since he had mounted Peau-de-Balle and had been living with him, a desire always repressed but incessantly growing, had haunted him: to study the marvelous mechanism of the automaton, to analyze it in order then to make the synthesis; and then to construct a similar organism that he would adapt to a flying machine. He now had enough money to attempt the experiment.

He had resisted that desire, firstly out of loyalty to his boss, his duty consisting strictly of piloting Peau-de-Balle on the turf and watching over his incognito at the house, and secondly because the phenomenon inspired a certain respect in him, an admiration that he could not help feeling. Although he knew perfectly well what blind and purely material force constituted the crack, the cries of enthusiasm that rose up as the traveled along the track during each victory effected a kind of suggestion upon him. Peau-de-Balle was, for him, a familiar but intangible god.

However, when, having traversed the enemy lines like a whirlwind in the Prix du Grand-Argentier, Louffe had collected certain compliments that he had not sought, the automaton lost much of its prestige in his mind; it was no longer anything for him but a sort of improved bicycle, which might carry you very rapidly, but which could also get you a stinging slap in the mouth.

He gave himself the pretext that there was something inside the automaton in need of adjustment, which might perhaps remedy the excessive violence of its action, introducing an improvement that would permit him to slow down in case that momentum became dangerous. In any case, it needed looking at, and he was better equipped than anyone else to do that, given his aptitude for mechanics.

One evening, after having locked himself securely in his pavilion, he took a screwdriver out of his pocket and marched up to the automaton, which he had put back in its usual place.

He hesitated momentarily.

This is stupid! I feel like a burglar about to pull off a robbery...or a murderer. He has a way of looking at me with his glass eyes...

He leaned over, however, and started unscrewing the movable plate artfully hidden under Peau-de-Balle's belly, which gave access to the vital works.

That laparotomy was not subject to any difficulty; Louffe had, in fact, observed the fashion in which Griffith proceeded when he replaced the accumulators newly charged in a factory in Saint-Denis.

All the same, if that camel Isaac arrived now, as he did once before, he'd get a shock! And the archbishop, if he saw this...! Oh, with him, it would be simple. I'd tell him that all racehorses are built on the same model, and that one opens their belly every evening to see to their toilette. Damn it! It's a complicated affair in there! It's quite a job!

Gustave Louffe was amazed by the quantity of wheels, toothed cylinders, miniature piston-roads and dainty transmission-belts that constituted the inner workings of the very special thoroughbred.

Unfortunately, Gustave Louffe was not content to look; he wanted to touch. No child can ever resist the desire to take a toy to pieces to see what there is inside; no clockmakers, when he is brought an old watch of a special model, can resist the curiosity of taking it to pieces—to clean it, he usually pretends.

"I understand, I understand," murmured Peau-de-Balle's jockey. "It would be sufficient to displace these two pieces, to tighten that screw...give a little play to that set of gears...that will work much better...yes, that will avoid the jolt on departure and the abruptness of the stop. I'll give my screwdriver a twist. That will sort it out...there...it's nothing at all...it's no more difficult than that!"

While he was lying down, late into the night, and very content with himself, Gustave Louffe was convinced that he had put every component back into its exact place and thus contributed to the amelioration of the race of equine automata.

Two days later, Peau-de-Balle fulfilled his engagement in the Prix Tristan-Bernard. He had almost driven away all the competition, and only had two opponents unworthy of him.

He was twenty to one on.

With his customary brio, Peau-de-Balle swept ahead of his two competitors, whose ambition was, in any case, limited to the place money. Gustave Louffe was already intoxicating himself with the cheap incense of popular acclamation when, abruptly, ten meters short of the winning post, the automaton stopped dead.

The jockey, surprised, thought at first: *I must have pressed the stop lever by mistake.* Immediately, he activated the gallop lever. Peau-de-Balle did not respond.

Gustave Louffe went pale and, as the worthy Ponson du Terrail would have written—at least feuilletons were funny in those days—a cold sweat inundated him from his cap to his spurs, while a great current of air traversed his entrails. Desperately, he leaned on the lever the controlled the walking pace. The automaton started to move.

His partisans had the emotion of an anguishing handicap. The other two horses, which had not tried for an instant to make a race of it with the crack, and were following at a respectful distance, were approaching with great encouragement from the whip. Peau-de-Balle only had ten meters to cover, but he covered them at an exceedingly tranquil pace, his jockey upright in the saddle, with the lividity of a statue. If the equestrian effigy of the Commander had wanted to take part in a horse race, one would certainly have seen something similar.

At the very moment when Peau-de-Balle's head passed the finish line, his two competitors went past him like a whirlwind.

There were a few seconds of anxiety, then a sigh of relief. The judge had just put up the number of the favorite.

For the second time, Gustave Louffe was called before the stewards; he was asked to explain the incident.

"A whim of the horse. When it will take him, no one can tell."

"But in sum, you were almost beaten by your own fault. You let the beast walk, which demanding anything of him."

"Naturally!" said Gustave Louffe, with remarkable aplomb. "If I'd permitted myself to touch Peau-de-Balle with a spur or the whip, he'd have stopped completely. He's very badly brought-up; he does what he wants. Would you have the kindness to summon John Blight, Messieurs, who will confirm that?"

Blight, urgently summoned, made no difficult about admitting that the boss had put him on Peau-de-Balle's saddle one day at Chantilly, that he had gone to a great deal of trouble to make him set off at a trot or a gallop, but it had been exactly as if he were mounted on a wooden horse. He offered, moreover, to bet Messieurs the stewards a bottle of whisky that no one in that honorable company could do any better in managing that damned swine of a horse.

Messieurs the stewards declined that offer. But as, after all, Monseigneur Bénin-Despalmes' horse had won the race, they decided to close the investigation with no action taken.

Griffith, when he was alone with Gustave Louffe, sought information in his turn.

"Come on, what happened?"

"There must have been a hitch in the mechanism. I'm not in the horse's belly, it must be said."

An explanation was nevertheless required. The specialist newspapers took charge of finding it.

At the moment when Peau-de-Balle was about to reach he winning post thirty lengths clear, a female spectator on the course unfortunately opened her umbrella. The horse, frightened, veered sideways and stopped dead. His jockey, desirous of not treating him roughly, contented himself with finishing the race at a walk. He had the time to win the race literally standing still, and much more easily than it seemed.

That opinion was adopted by the majority of sportsmen, and, as happens to the majority of generally admitted opinions, was categorically belied by events five days later, when the Prix Julien-Fautrard was run.

This time, Peau-de-Balle, starting at ten to one on, remained coldly at the starting-post.

Griffith said to himself: *Damn! This is getting serious. It's going to be necessary to get Fred back from Chicago to repair the automaton. Will he consent to come? It's a pity that my Yankees have pocketed their million; otherwise, the cancellation clause would become interesting.*

Gustave Louffe said to himself: *I've definitely put the mechanism out of order. What an idiot I am! It was going so well! I'll have to sort it out; I don't see any alternative.*

Monseigneur Bénin-Despalmes sad to himself: *It's unfortunate, very unfortunate! A horse prognosticated by the Archangel Michael himself! I'll have to send our jockey the silks embroidered by Mademoiselle Benoît with our intention and the cap sent to me from Rome by Cardinal Capello, a cap blessed by the Holy Father himself and favored with a plenary indulgence.*

Baron Isaac said to his faithful Sem Lévy: "Aha! The young man's just pulled his horse! We'll soon be able to reach an understanding with him!"

The sporting newspapers said to their readers, in substance: *We foresaw this from the first day. Peau-de-Balle is a stubborn animal whose character was becoming more difficult*

with every outing; he owes that fault, as our competence per-
mitted us to observe then, to his dam Polaire VII.

And the members of the crowd said to one another: "It's all right, it's all right. They got him to stay at the staring-post this time, in order to get a better price in his next race. He's a sly one, the archbishop, but we're cleverer than he is; we won't miss out on Peau-de-Balle when he runs again."

VII. Monsieur Pigouette and Madame Subtil suffer heavy losses.

Monsieur Pigouette was a beadle at the Cathedral of Caudebec-en-Caux. He had a manner full of unction combined with a physique full of dignity. Abbé Douillet often said, not without pride: "Our beadle resembles Monsieur Félix Faure."[91]

Everyone knows that the ambition of all beadles, in that era, was to resemble Monsieur Félix Faure. Later, they wanted to resemble Monsieur Dujardin-Beaumetz; there are even some who succeed, in spite of the law of separation.[92]

---

[91] Félix Faure (1841-1899) was the President of the Republic during the last four years of his life, having been out forward for that post because he was the only man in his party who had no enemies. He died in office while allegedly being fellated by his mistress, Margaret Steinheil—which might, of course, have been a nasty rumor put about by his political opponents, but will forever remain his only claim to fame. The story is set shortly after his election, before his fall from grace.

[92] The reference to the "law of separation" [of Church and State] implies that the intended comparison is to the painter and fervently anti-clerical député Étienne Dujardin-Beaumetz (1852-1913) rather than the microbiologist Édouard Dujardin-Beaumetz (1868-1947), a specialist in the study of bubonic plague who was head of plague services at the Pasteur Institute, but the author's omission of a forename permits some ambiguity.

One would have given Monsieur Pigouette to the good God without confession. However, we can say now, since he is dead, without leaving any heirs who might be offended by the qualification, that he was the most incorrigible debauchee in the entire diocese of Caudebec-en-Caux. The cashier at the Café du Commerce had seen him, not without a scandalized admiration, playing billiards at a advanced hour of the night— eleven o'clock by the belfry—he sometimes absorbed five glasses of beer in his nocturnal orgies and lost, with a terrifying self-composure, thirty sous at auction manilla. But these debauches remained secret; the proprietor of the Café du Commerce did not boast about counting Monsieur Pigouette among a clientele that included the most distinguished members of the army and the magistracy, and the most distinguished members of the army and the magistracy did not boast about frequenting the Café du Commerce on a daily basis with Monsieur Pigouette.

Madame Subtil was the chair-woman at the cathedral. Avid for gain, as all working women are, even those who wear a black bonnet instead of a pink one, she had an apron whose insatiable pockets reminded Abbé Tacot, stuffed with classical memories, of the famous barrel of the Danaïdes, and her nose could have given rise to comparisons of the same sort, so much snuff did it absorb between the eight o'clock mass and the one at midday.

Monsieur Pigouette and Madame Subtil found themselves in obligatory and frequent communication in the exercise of their functions.

One morning in June, they were chatting in the deserted basilica.

Perhaps, if Madame Subtil had been thirty years younger and had less hair on her chin, Monsieur Pigouette, wanting to complete his resemblance to President Félix Faure in all regards, would have risked, in spite of the majesty of the location, a few words of displaced gallantry. But the chair-woman was of broadly canonical age, and had, in addition, the rebarbative air that all ladies of her métier have, except when it is a matter of passing between the chairs with the collection plate; then they put on a hideous smile and are even uglier.

The beadle therefore limited himself to observing that the weather was very good for the time of year—to which the chair-woman replied that times were hard and that one had a great deal of trouble earning a meager living.

"You're telling me, Madame Subtil!"

"Oh, Monsieur Pigouette, if I weren't a little too old, I'd certainly think about becoming a dancer like your demoiselle. There's a métier that's flattering..."

"Don't talk so loud, Madame Subtil. If Monsieur l'Abbé Tacot heard you…!"

"The other day, in the pulpit, however, he said that King David danced before the ark, and he seemed to approve of that."

"Well, yes, Madam Subtil, but there are things that are only permitted to kings, you know..."

"In the meantime, we don't have the wherewithal, like those gentlemen, to put butter on our parsnips."

"It's not only you, Madame Subtil. If you want to make a little money, I'll give you a good means. Do you know what this is?"

Monsieur Pigouette had just taken an issue of the *Sport du Soir* from his pocket.

"It's a newspaper," said Madame Subtil, without hesitation.

"Yes, it's a racing paper. Perhaps you don't know what racecourses are…read that line there."

The chair-woman put on her spectacles and read: "*Monseigneur Bénin-Despalmes. T. Griffith senior. Peau-de-Balle. Sixty-five kilos. Amethyst; red cap.* I don't understand Monsieur Pigouette. What has the Monseigneur done to be printed there? It doesn't look like a writ of mandamus."

"Madame Subtil, you ought to keep up to date; people don't talk enough in the diocese. It means that the Monseigneur is the owner of a racehorse, that the horse is called

Peau-de-Balle, that it's trained by Monsieur Griffith, and that its jockey wears purple silks with a red cap."

"How knowledgeable you are, Monsieur Pigouette," said the chair-woman, admiringly.

"Well, yes, Madame Subtil, I've had the opportunity and the honor to frequent very learned individuals, the Messieurs of the tribunal and the barracks. I meet them...hmm...over in the direction of the archbishopric...yes...and it's while talking to those people that I got the idea I'm talking about. Peau-de-Balle, you know, the Monseigneur's horse, is made to run against other horses. In those races, everyone bets on the horse they believe is going to win. And then, when the race is over, the people who have won their bets collect all the others' money. Do you understand?"

"Yes, it's presumably a lottery?"

"Not entirely, because in a lottery, no one knows the number they're going to draw, whereas, for races, there are clever people who know which horse is going to win. And me, now, I'm one of them, those clever people..."

Monsieur Pigouette winked, and tapped the newspaper.

"I know the one that's going to win tomorrow."

"I've guessed it, me too!" cried the triumphant chair-woman. "It's the Monseigneur's horse!"

"It's the Monseigneur's horse," confirmed the beadle. "Oh, Madame Subtil, how well you merit your name! Yesterday, I met Mr. Griffith, who assured me that the horse will certainly win. And besides, listen carefully, little Sophie Poirier, the visionary of Tassigny-la-Raclée has had an apparition of the Archangel Michael, and the Archangel confirmed the thing himself. And then, the Monseigneur's horse, you see, how can you imagine that he won't finish first?"

"But Monsieur Pigouette, what is it necessary to do to bet on the Monseigneur's horse?"

The beadle, seeing that he had a bite, adopted a very confidential tone.

"Listen Madame Subtil, it's necessary not to tell anyone—not even your confessor, you understand. Tomorrow, there's no mass. We'll ask for leave for the day. We'll take the train to Paris. If we met anyone we know at the station, we'll tell them that we're going to visit Sacré-Coeur in Montmartre. Once in Paris we'll take a cab to Longchamp. And I promise you that in the evening, your pockets will be too small to contain the hundred-sou pieces we'll be bringing back."

The next day, in fact, at the stroke of two o'clock, the beadle and the chair-woman passed, through one of the turnstiles giving access to Longchamp racecourse.

The chair-woman had brought her savings. The beadle had borrowed fifty francs from the proprietor of the Café du Commerce; I addition, by virtue of a thoughtlessness that he was later to regret bitterly, he had imprudently kept on his person certain funds belonging to the cash-box of the vestry that had been confided to him.

The arrival of the bizarre couple formed by Monsieur Pigouette and Madame Subtil would have caused a sensation in many public places. The beadle had brought out an implausible top hat with a shaggy nap, and his quaker coat had the very rare green streaks that one finds in the Louvre museum on certain items of Etruscan pottery.

The chair-woman had wanted to react and protest against the somber garments imposed on her by her profession. Her elegance was special and struck the impressionist mode very well; either by chance or intention, she was dressed in Monseigneur Bénin-Despalmes' racing colors: a dress of a very bright purple, and an exceedingly red and exceedingly ridiculous hat.

Funnier things had been seen on the course, however, and the members of the crowd had other things on their mind than taking notice of the costumes and appearance of passersby. Absorbed exclusively in the search for the winners, for their winners, they walked like somnambulists, wandering alive through their starry dream, under the emprise of the Problem, in the midst of the densest crowd, isolated in an inaccessible ivory tower.

Madame Subtil was astonished not to see the Monseigneur's horse as soon as she arrived on the racecourse. She had imagined, naively, that Peau-de-Balle would be exhibited under a canopy with a silver fringe, or that he would be walked with great pomp along the track, to the sound of huge organs and hymns.

"Don't be impatient," said the beadle. "We have time to see him. He isn't running until the fourth race."

Fortunately, Madame Subtil found a resource to pass the time; she recognized a compatriot, a native of Caudebec-en-Caux, who was selling licorice water to the sportsmen in the crowd.

"Better than champagne! Two sous a glass! And a hot tip into the bargain. It won't be for everyone. The winner to my clients!"

"So you know what's going to win too?" asked Madame Subtil, astonished.

"It's not difficult," replied the coco-merchant. "I give all the horses to different people. That way there are always a few who come to thank me after the race."

"Oh...!" said Madame Subtil, who had not understood.

Then, seized by the ambient contagion, bewitched by the effluvia that form the atmosphere of racecourses, she unconsciously allowed herself to give way to the need for boasting and lies that is rife on the lawns. And, instinctively, she employed expressions of which she had not had the slightest idea an hour before.

"We've got information of the first order, ourselves. We've come to bet on Monseigneur Bénin-Despalmes' horse. The proof is that the Monseigneur himself sent us to do it. You'll see."

The coco-merchant opened a mouth into which one could have poured the contents of his barrel. And immediately, seized by a kind of sacred delirium, he started howling:

"To all my clients I give the winner! Look, Messieurs, I'll tip you the wink. Come and tell me after the race whether I didn't give it to you! It's Peau-de-Balle in the fourth! Peau-de-Balle all alone, Messieurs."

Suddenly, Monsieur Pigouette started and took hold of the chair-woman's arm.

"Madame Subtil, look over there, between the two stalls...that soutane!"

"In truth, one would think that it's Abbé Douillet...but that's not possible. No, it can't be him. At that distance, all priests look alike."

The runners for the fourth race were posted. The beadle immediately disappeared, saying that he would be back in a trice and confiding the chair-woman to the coco-merchant. He was going to effect a discreet and serious punt on Peau-de-Balle; as he was not going to do so moderately, he did not want the chair-woman to see him take out a large sum of money whose origin he could not explain.

As soon as his back was turned, Madame Subtil sought information from her compatriot, who was occupied in pouring a few supplementary jugs of Seine water into his barrel.

"Tell me, Monsieur, where is it necessary to go in order to bet on the Monseigneur's horse?"

The other interrupted the baptism of the licorice water momentarily in order to develop a broad gesture that embraced the entire group of the Mutuel huts.

"At any window, Madame."

Madame Subtil disappeared for a moment and then came back, quite discomfited.

"Oh, Monsieur, I told the employee at the widow that I wanted to bet on the Monseigneur's horse. Do you know what he replied? That he didn't care and that he had a Monseigneur somewhere.[93] When I observed to him that he wasn't polite, he

---

[93] It is possible that a racecourse employee, on hearing the word "Monseigneur," would not automatically assume that it referred to an archbishop; the word had several meanings in Parisian argot, referring to various burglar's tools, pimps and large-capacity glasses.

asked me if I was drunk. A woman of my age and attached to the cathedral!"

"You didn't need to mention the Monseigneur," said the coco-merchant, who was still stretching his sauce. "It was simply necessary to ask for Peau-de-Balle."

The chair-woman made a second attempt, which was no more successful.

"The employee replied to me: 'I don't have to know Peau-de-Balle, ask for a number.'"

"Alas, Madame Subtil, you haven't understood. How much do you want to put on Peau-de-Balle?"

The chair-woman displayed four hundred-sou pieces that she had just extracted from her *profonde*—which really was the word that suited her pocket.[94]

"Well, you go to the window and you ask for four on the six as you hand over you money."

Madame Subtil, coming back from her third expedition, still had her four hundred-sou pieces; furthermore, she was furious.

"Would you believe that the Monsieur refused my coins, on the pretext that they're not good! Coins that Abbé Tacot gave me on the first of January for my new year's present, saying: 'Here, my child, here are coins with the effigy of our Holy Father the Pope. Keep them; they'll bring you good luck."

"Oh, you've no chance, Madame. If they're refusing Holy Father coins now...! Do you know what I'd do in your place? I'd present myself successively at all the windows in the row, until I finally happened upon a obliging employee who'd accept my money. Go on, have a little patience..."

The coco-merchant was right. After having suffered several humiliating refusals, Madame Subtil ended up obtaining a resounding success. In fact, one Mutuel clerk, who fancied himself a wit, had the idea of having some fun, and looked the lady up and down instead of checking the money she had.

---

[94] *Profonde* [deep] was an argot term for a pocket.

Giving simultaneous proof of his literary culture and his sarcastic wit, he leaned over toward his "pompier" and offered her this reminiscence:

Who sends us this duenna, a frightful companion
With a flourishing beard and a nose like an onion?[95]

So saying, he dropped the four papal coins in his bag. He was quite astonished to find them there that even when cashing up—which proves that one should never make fun of old ladies.

Madame Subtil returned to the coco-merchant's stall waving her tickets triumphantly. She found Monsieur Pigouette there, who had just descended a fatal slope, pushed by the demon of gambling. Unknown to the churchwarden, the vestry funds were represented by shares in Peau-de-Balle.

"Come on, Madame Subtil," said the bold speculator, "get a move on. We only just have time to get to the start if you want to see the Monseigneur's horse."

They traversed the lawns and arrived at a place where the crowd was particularly compact. Among all the backs offered to their views, there was one that attracted the beadle's attention particularly.

"But it really is Monsieur l'Abbé Douillet!" he exclaimed.

On hearing his name pronounced, the excellent ecclesiastic turned round; he seemed very embarrassed to see the beadle and the chair-woman, who were no prouder than he was. Monsieur Pigouette greatly regretted his involuntary exclamation.

Abbé Douillet thought that it was necessary to break the silence, and sought an original topic of conversation.

"So you've come to stake a stroll here, to take advantage of the fine weather. Excellent idea! Excellent idea!"

---

[95] The clerk is quoting—slightly mistakenly—two lines from Victor Hugo's tragedy *Ruy Blas* (1838).

Fortunately, an entirely predictable diversion occurred. The horses came to line up under the starter's flag, and Madame Subtil was able to admire, above the spectators' hats, the red cap of Peau-de-Balle's jockey.

A rumor...and then a sorrowful knell. The horses had set off...but Madame Subtil could still see Gustave Louffe's cap in the same place.

"But...the Monseigneur's horse has stayed there on his own! The others will come back to fetch him, surely!"

"Do you think so?" said a member of the crowd, with a snigger. "The start was good. They'll dance without him, that's all."

"But it won't count, then? We'll get our money back?"

"Undoubtedly, undoubtedly," said the worthy Abbé Douillet, who was very pale. "We'll get our money back."

"What a bunch of idiots!" cried a furious sportsman, who also had a few Peau-de-Balle tickets in his pocket. "Give us our moolah back! You have to be as stupid as swine to believe that! It's in the bucket, our moolah. It was bound to happen. When I next see a curé, I'll give him poverty! He won't be able to say his mass!"

"No one's talking to you, lout!" put in Monsieur Pigouette, who had nothing more to lose and at least wanted to put up a good show, in view of the catastrophic future events that he could foresee.

The lout in question could not let such a good opportunity to soothe his nerves go by. He fell upon the unfortunate beadle, punching and kicking. Around them, the brawl became general; it required the intervention of four policemen to extract the inhabitants of Caudebec-en-Caux.

In the train that repatriated them, Monsieur Pigouette pretended to search his pockets anxiously.

"My God! My God! I've lost all the money in the riot!"

"What money?"

"The Peter's pence money! I had inadvertently kept it on me. I shall have to confess my stupidity to the Monseigneur."

"No, no!" said Abbé Douillet, swiftly, who had no wish for his presence on the racecourse to be revealed. "I'd rather reimburse you the money—but don't mention the affair to anyone."

"And my four coins with the effigy of the Holy Father?" asked the chair-woman, bitterly.

"Ask Monsieur l'Abbé Tacot to give you some more—he's got a trunk full of them at home."

VIII. Between Scylla and Charybdis

In that epoch, a phenomenon was produced in the physical condition of Gustave Louffe that would have delighted any other jockey. He visibly lost weight, to the point that Ely Pauwels said to him one day, ironically: "Hey, Master Louffe, I can offer you a nice little engagement as a lightweight. We'll sign it soon, when you don't weigh any more than forty-five kilos and you're understood that the starter gives the signal to go when he lowers his flag."

"It'll also be necessary for me to learn to understand Sem Lévy's odds, in order to drop my hands when necessary," Gustave Louffe had retorted.

"Oh, you know those things better than I do!"

Louffe had swallowed that insult and gone away, his heart heavy.

The poor fellow was being eaten away by a worm: the remorse of having put Peau-de-Balle's mechanism out of order, and his impotence to repair the damage.

Every evening, he struggled with his screwdriver, and imagined, after long hours of labor, that he had returned the automaton to its true form, but as soon as he found himself on the track, on the hippodrome, he had to yield to the sad evidence. Peau-de-Balle was no longer himself, in the full sense of the term.

Sometimes he remained at the post, without the galloping lever having the slightest effect on him, and Gustave Louffe had to watch the disaster passively, as in the nightmares in which the worst catastrophes descend upon you without your being able to move your arms or legs, and without you being able to react to the torture of your nerves and your brain. And the patience of the starter could evidently only serve to prolong his agony.

Sometimes Peau-de-Balle departed at the velocity of his heyday, only to stop after a few hundred meters.

Sometimes, finally, he galloped with a singular gait, his front legs following the regular rhythm, while his back legs danced in syncopation. The strange horse then seemed afflicted with locomotive ataxia, and, to Griffith's great terror, it had been proposed to submit the case to the Académie des Sciences, which would certainly have delegated a natural scientist to examine him.

Peau-de-Balle's eccentricities varied infinitely, according to the manner in which Gustave Louffe, on the eve of each race, had adjusted his essential organs, with the best of intentions. As the combinations of the cogwheels, gears and levers were innumerable, also innumerable were the practical jokes that the automaton permitted his faithful partisans to encounter.

For Peau-de-Balle, in spite of the painful disillusionments that he caused every day, was still a favorite on the course at the hundred sou windows; small punters have a particularly tenacious memory.

But it was no longer sympathetic acclamations that saluted Gustave Louffe when he returned pitifully to the weighing-room at a jerky walk, the only one of Peau-de-Balle's actions that remained regular. The names of birds now alternated with the names of fish; there was also mention of household ordure and certain organs that it would have been in bad taste to mention in a drawing room.

A particularly scandalous occurrence happened one day. A drunk, having lost a hundred sous on the archiepiscopal colors, stated crying vigorously: "À bas la calotte!" which came as a surprise, because at that time anticlerical and political passions had no access to the Turf; the episcopal miter and the presidential hat were respected then.

Monseigneur Bénin-Despalmes heard about the incident, and his heart was profoundly saddened, all the more so as *Le Balai* did not limit itself purely and simply to reporting it, but aggravated it with venomous commentaries, in which the hand and style of the Baron de l'Échelle-Jacob was recognizable.

It is inadmissible, one read in that paper, *that the government will tolerate much longer the shameful scandal of which Monsieur Bénin-Despalmes, the archbishop of Caudebec-en-Caux, is presently providing the spectacle to the citizens who are, in sum, his paymasters. This, then, is the use made of the religious budget, alimented by the impositions that pressurize the unfortunate French taxpayers: it is used to promenade, in the gambling-den of racecourses, violet silks that cover all the shady schemes and all the fraudulent maneuvers by which the disciples of Loyola, since the Inquisition, have sought to appease their shameful and inextinguishable thirst for lucre. No one will be astonished if, one day soon, the enlightened patriots of the Parisian suburbs, seized by a legitimate fit of indignation, deliver good and prompt justice to Monsieur Bénin-Despalmes' horse and jockey.*

It continued in the same vein for three columns. *Le Balai* also wanted to notify its readers of the presence at the weigh-in of the reactionary lawyer Dessumeaux, and perfidiously invited the clients of the said lawyer to maintain a close surveillance on the management of any funds that might be deposited in his study. *Le Balai* also occupied itself with Comte Jérôme Thomas, declaring that for him, money had no odor—which was at least funny.

Le Balai's campaign had one result. It happened that after one race—or, rather, after an unsuccessful attempt to race—a rain of stones coming from the lawns fell upon Peau-de-Balle and his jockey. Gustave Louffe was badly bruised. As for the horse, the newspapers announced that it had come back with a limp, but that, thanks to his robust constitution, there was no reason to think that it had sustained any injury.

234

That new proof consternated the archbishop of Caudebec-en-Caux. Only Abbé Tacot was triumphant.

Monseigneur Bénin-Despalmes was overwhelmed by the weight of a profound affliction. He could already see his case brought before the Court of Rome, and struggled, uncomprehendingly, in the midst of complicate catastrophes.

He summoned Griffith, hoping to obtain good advice from him.

He was surprised o see how much the trainer had aged considerably since his first visit to the archbishopric, although Peau-de-Balle had only been wearing the amethyst colors for six weeks.

Griffith's gestures were depressed and his speech desolate.

"You see, Monseigneur, my horses are all falling sick…I now resemble a product of Le Sancy[96]…and my limbs are trembling like an old man's…"

That last circumstance might have been explained by the fact that Griffith had resumed drinking like a fish, but he did not tell the archbishop that, even though the latter had the power to redeem sins.

He continued, however: "Monsieur, I want to tell you that with regard to Peau-de-Balle, diabolical things are occurring."

"In that case," the prelate proposed, "it will doubtless be necessary to perform an exorcism."

"I doubt that that means would be efficacious. It would need something else entirely to decide Peau-de-Balle to gallop."

Having reflected at length, Monseigneur Bénin-Despalmes believed that he had found a solution.

---

[96] Le Sancy was one of the most successful racehorses of the 1880s, who went on to have a long career at stud, although he and his offspring had a reputation for being "mean."

"Bijou, the old horse that pulls my carriage, is beginning to get too old. Perhaps I could replace him with Peau-de-Balle. I don't mind having a horse that doesn't gallop."

That's what he's got! thought Griffith, in despair. "But Monseigneur," he said, "Peau-de-Balle won't consent to trot either. And then, what would the papers say if Your Eminence harnessed a fabulously expensive thoroughbred to his carriage?"

"You're right, Monsieur. So, there's only one thing for me to do: get rid of the horse, which is attracting the worst attacks on the part of the enemies of religion, without at all fulfilling the objective to which I thought he was destined by Providence. Monsieur Griffith, I received a letter this morning from a breeder who has offered to buy him for his stud."

"That's impossible, Monseigneur," said Griffith, swiftly. "Peau-de-Balle has no aptitude for reproductive functions."

The prelate did not insist. He did not want to embark on terrain in which discussion would be difficult for a prince of the Church.

"We're back, then," he said, "to the solution recommended by Abbé Tacot, on which I didn't want to settle to begin with. You know, Monsieur, that Baron Isaac de l'Échelle-Jacob is still offering a hundred thousand francs in cash for the horse."

Griffith pulled a face.

"Yes, yes," said the archbishop, who misunderstood, "I know. Abbé Tacot once saw grave inconveniences, from the viewpoint of dogma, in my dealing with that Israelite. But our eminent casuist came of his own accord to suggest an expedient that might settle everything for the repose of our consciences. I shall cede the horse to Comte Jérôme Thomas, a fictitious buyer, who will then cede it to Baron Isaac, the true buyer.

Griffith had exhausted all his energy during a month of desperate and futile struggle against fatality. He no longer had any hope, even in Fred or Tod; to his dispatch requesting help, the Americans had replied that they disclaimed any responsibility. Peau-de-Balle had been delivered in good condition, had functioned perfectly well throughout the spring, and could only have been put out of order by some fault on Griffith's part; they would not, therefore, cross the herring-pond again to come and repair the automaton, being presently occupied with things that were much more interesting.

The trainer had abandoned himself to his evil destiny. The new blow that had been delivered, unconsciously, by the excellent archbishop was, however, the most terrible that could strike him. Ely Pauwels and Baron Isaac were his mortal enemies, and the last people he wanted to see in possession of his secret.

If Peau-de-Balle had remained usable, Griffith could have hoped for their silence, based on their evident interest, but a broken-down Peau-de-Balle could only serve to doom him.

The trainer thought he was reading his death-sentence when, twenty-four hours later, two news items appeared in the sporting press, which dissipated his last illusions:

Monseigneur Bénin-Despalmes has sold Peau-de-Balle to Comte Jérôme Thomas.

Comte Jérôme Thomas has sold Peau-de-Balle, with his engagements, to Baron Isaac de l'Échelle-Jacob.

He had, however, a respite that he had not expected. Baron Isaac, to his great surprise, wrote to him asking him to keep the horse in his stable until after the Grand Prix de Deauville.

What new knavery can he be planning? Griffith wondered, pensively. *In any case, for a fellow who spends his life organizing surprises for sportsmen, he's going to take a large caliber shot in his own locker when he takes delivery of Peau-de-Balle!*

IX. The Last of Baron Isaac

You might be wondering why, in the present conditions—which is to say, in the conditions known to the public—Baron Isaac had offered a hundred thousand francs for a beast that was considered a consummate rogue.

It was because the Baron, who was in reality cunning, had the pretention of being even more cunning than he was, and in business, as everywhere else, the intelligence that one wants to have spoils that which one has. Baron Isaac had got it into his head that Griffith had been having Peau-de-Balle pulled for a month, with a view to the Grand Prix de Deauville, in which he wanted a good price.

"It's all for show, this shirking," the financier had said to Sem Lévy. "But do you know what Griffith's doing, now? His pulling is pulling my chestnuts out of the fire! I'll be damned if I can't relieve the archbishop of his horse before the Grand Prix de Deauville!"

In one sense, at least, the Baron had judged the matter accurately, and had succeeded in his objective. Peau-de-Balle was going to run in the Grand Prix de Deauville in his colors.

As the financier did not want to share the windfall with Ely Pauwels, by reason of an old grudge, and, on the other hand, he wanted the responsibility for whatever might happen, if there was a fuss, to fall on Griffith, he had left the crack with his old trainer temporarily. The latter had brought him from Chantilly to Deauville under his personal surveillance. Gustave Louffe, naturally, accompanied him and was due to ride him.

When the first prices were posted at the Hippodrome de la Touques, at the start of that memorable meeting, Peau-de-Balle was put up at twelve to one. Point by point, large bets laid by the new owner brought the price down to nine to two.

And Griffith, who was no longer anything but the shadow of a trainer, said to Gustave Louffe, who was no longer anything but the shadow of a jockey:

"What consoles me a little bit—a very little bit—is thinking about the loss that that pig is going to suffer. It's not because you're wearing his dirty silks that the mechanism is going to repair itself. We won't see his face, unfortunately, when he realizes that he's paid a hundred thousand francs for a broken-down horse. We won't see it, because by then, we'll be on our way to New York."

Indeed, Griffith had sagely judged that within the hour, the French training centers were going to become uninhabitable for him, as well as his jockey. It was preferable to get away before the bomb went off. They could always find out from the newspapers what had happened.

Gustave Louffe shook his head sadly. What had happened was his fault; he had ruined his employer, his trainer, and now it was necessary to take the road of exile!

He had spent the night yet again attempting repairs, but without any conviction, or even the desire to succeed, in order for Baron Isaac to profit—in truth, he did not want things otherwise.

The horses went down to the start. A connoisseur made the remark that Peau-de-Bale's action was smoother, and that the sea air seemed to have been profitable to the horse.

In the crowd, the usual comments were heard.

"Why is he running in Baron Isaac's colors now?"

"Because the archbishop is in mourning for La Tafoireau!"

"Shut up, you idiot. He wasn't in mourning a week ago, was he? Well, he is now! The story is that all of that's a scam: La Tafoireau, the archbishop and the baron are all in the swindle together. They're doing it to confuse you. You'll see whether he stays at the staring-post today, Peau-de-Balle! I'm going to put five francs on."

"You won't collect your imaginary money. Look at your horse, how quiet he is! While the others are passing the wining post he'll still be over there—you can admire him. That's all you'll have for your hundred sous."

However, when the flag dropped, Gustave Louffe, to acquit his conscience, pressed the gallop lever. To his great surprise—and to the great surprise of the starter and the public—Peau-de-Balle set off.

"He won't go far," said a voice.

That was also the opinion of Gustave Louffe. However, the automaton continued at its regular speed.

"He's surely not going to have the cheek to win today!" said one sportsman who had not bet on him.

Peau-de-Balle was still galloping. If his jockey had reflected, if he had thought about the certain scandal, and also of the fact that the returns of the high price were about to fall into the pocket of that old scoundrel Isaac, he would certainly have pressed the stop lever and restored the normal order of things—which is to say that events would have unfolded according to the anticipations and the desire of the majority. But Gustave Louffe was not thinking about anything—or, rather, had only one thought filling his head. The automaton was repaired! The young man abandoned himself once again to the intoxication of victory as well as to the vertigo of the race.

Without the slightest hitch, Peau-de-Balle came into the straight. His competitors were far behind.

Baron Isaac was jubilant.

"Eh! Would you believe those thieves!" he said to Sem Lévy. "I saw through them!"

Peau-de-Balle passed the winning-post in the midst of a tempest of howls and whistles. The Gospodar session was an ovation by comparison.

At the weigh-in, canes were raised; the security staff had to protect the re-entry of the equine automaton. When he came into the ring, Griffith, very pale under the insults that rained down upon him, ran forward to take him by the bridle.

The trainer had a strong desire to escape before the end of the presentation; his berth on the transatlantic from Le Havre was booked, and he no longer had anything but rotten apples to receive in his face if he stayed in Deauville. It is necessary to say to his credit, however, that he did not want to abandon Gustave Louffe in the hornet's nest, and he decided to wait a little longer, seeing that things were turning bad.

"Get down, my lad," he said to his jockey.

But Ely Pauwels came forward, followed by Baron Isaac, and shoved Griffith away.

"Pardon me," he said, in a mocking tone. "I'm in charge of the horse now."

But in his turn, Ely Pauwels had to stand aside. Two commissioners from the Societé arrived with the veterinarian Podsnap, whose expertise was habitually employed in official matters.

"Messieurs," said one of them, "would you kindly leave this animal in the custody of Monsieur Podsnap temporarily, who is charged with examining him. His race today and is previous races give rise to the suspicion that he has been drugged—doped, as the Americans say..."

"I have nothing to do with it!" shouted Baron Isaac, bravely.

"Certain large bets, of which it will also be appropriate to seek the origin...," the commissioner tried to continue.

"Pardon me! I've made the bets I wanted to! But it's not me who gave orders to Griffith to cheat and pull his horse!"

Griffith went even paler, and was visibly desirous of falling upon the Baron tooth and nail, but he controlled himself, and even put on a singular smile. His decision was made.

"If you'll permit me, Messieurs, I'll demonstrate to you here and now that my horse has never been utilized for culpable maneuvers, and that doping has nothing to do with his case. I only ask, for that experiment, that a skillful rider of indisputable honorability be put in Peau-de-Balle's saddle momentarily.

His gaze seemed to wander over the audience and settle, with apparent sympathy, on Baron Isaac.

"Monsieur le Baron de l'Échelle-Jacob, to whom the horse belongs, seems to me entirely designated for that proof, by his qualities as a brilliant rider as well as his quality as owner."

Griffith's request was both strange and audacious, but Baron Isaac, whose pretentions as a horseman were at stake and who feared, if he refused, seeing the sportsmen present smile, came forward deliberately.

"But of course, but of course! I'd like nothing better."

And, stimulated by self-esteem. He got into the saddle with more agility than one would have thought.

A gleam appeared in Griffith's eye; he had his enemy in the trap.

"Are you comfortable there, Monsieur le Baron?" he asked.

And, with the sleight of hand of a conjurer, he activated the gallop switch.

As Peau-de-Balle set off like an express train, the curious crowd scattered in panic. Cries of terror rose up from the weight room enclosure. But the automaton, after having knocked over Ely Pauwels—who was picked up with a few broken ribs—had passed through the railings.

Hooked on to the broken iron wire, various shreds of Baron Isaac's trousers were recovered. That was the only trace that was ever found of him...

Peau-de-Balle, carrying his rider, mad with terror, implacably traversed fields, roads and meadows as blind, brutal and irresistible as a force of nature. Baron Isaac, clinging to the saddle-bow, saw houses and trees flying past him, uncomprehendingly...

The runaway beast went straight ahead, without deviating, without slowing down, without flexing his hocks as he passed over obstacles...it was a veritable nightmare.

Dusk was falling; the fantastic ride might perhaps go on for hours.

It was necessary to end it. The Baron perceived the sea to his right, bloodied by the setting sun. He was about to pass over a beach. If he could steer the runaway horse in that direction, he would be saved; the beast would be forced to stop by the sea.

He let go of the saddle-bow in order to pull on the bit, sideways, with all his strength...

Victory! He felt the neck pivot and the head turn. And Peau-de-Balle was now galloping over the strand.

The horse arrived at the first waves; he did not slow down; he galloped into the water just as rapidly...

His body disappeared. For a moment, perhaps a tenth of a second, Baron Isaac could still be seen, sketching a ridiculous contortion amid the white foam of the green waves...

Everything disappeared...

Then the automaton, evidently, continued to gallop under water for a long time, for as long as its accumulators were able to function. It certainly did not emerge on the coast of England; we would have heard about that.

It must still be somewhere on the sea-bed—and Baron Isaac too.

Epilogue

Griffith and Gustave Louffe had disappeared from the weighing room at Deauville at the same time as Baron Isaac d'Échelle-Jacob, but, fortunately for them, they did not begin the sea crossing in the same fashion as the unfortunate financier.

A transatlantic liner disembarked them in New York. They immediately went to find the engineer Fred and his manager Tod, to whom they recounted their misfortune and that of Peau-de-Balle. Gustave Louffe not having confessed his imprudence, the Yankees told Griffith, in perfectly good faith, that the automaton could not have gone wrong on its own. They were right.

Even so, they were prepared to give the exiles a helping hand. Young Louffe was employed in Fred's workshop and Griffith, thanks to Tod, found a situation in a big American stable, where flesh and blood horses were trained

Today, they are both following their paths. Gustave Louffe is one of our most celebrated aviators, and Griffith has founded a thoroughbred race in the eastern Republic of Uruguay.

Comte Jérôme Thomas is a senator.

Monseigneur Bénin-Despalmes is a cardinal; he was even elected as a member of the Académie Française, on the day when his advanced age rendered it impossible for him to draft any more writs of mandamus.

And pilgrimages to Tassigny-la-Raclée are increasing all the time.

E. M. Laumann and Henri Lanos: *Aerobagne 32*

I. The Leather Bottle

On the twentieth of August last, the great daily newspaper *Le Monde*[97] published the following article, which passed almost unperceived. We are reproducing it in full here because it marked the first episode in an uninterrupted series of dramatic and mysterious incidents of which chance has permitted us to be the historians.

A leather bottle hermetically sealed with the aid of a piece of wood, which appears to originate from the handle of some implement, and sealed with dirty grease, fell on to the deck of the steamship Foch *on the first of August in mid-Atlantic, some distance from the African coast, and the latitude of Cap d'Arquin—which is to say, between the tenth and twentieth parallels, fortunately without injuring anyone. The bottle contained, it appears, a rather voluminous manuscript composed of sheets of paper of various kinds, as well as scattered notes, some of which were written on linen. The captain of the ship has taken cognizance of all of it, but is maintaining an absolute silence in that regard.*

On the other hand, on the Saharan coast, between the same two parallels, about forty of fifty kilometers into the sands, submissive Tuaregs have discovered the cadaver of man with clothing tatters. The frightful state of the body encourages the supposition that the body had landed there following a fall from very high altitude. What remains of the

---

[97] The daily evening newspaper called *Le Monde* that exists today was founded in 1944; the one featured in the story is fictitious.

clothing and, among other things, the number 32 printed on a fragment of cloth, permits the belief that one is in the presence of the unfortunate result of an attempted escape from an aerial prison. In that case, it is a matter of a German prison of which that is the official registration number, aerobagne 32.

We do not believe, thus far, that any connection can be made between the two evens, the bottle having landed on the Foch on the first of August and the cadaver discovered on the nineteenth; the state of the body does not indicate that it had been in the place where it was found for a long time.

At any rate, it is appropriate to wait for the revelation of what the manuscript contains to discover whether the two facts are correlated, and to be able to comment with any accuracy on the two events.

Le Peuple, which had long entertained a permanent petty quarrel with its rival, reproduced the same wireless dispatch the following day, making the following observations, which we also transcribe faithfully:

Our grave colleague Le Monde *appears to have envisaged these facts from a slightly romantic angle and in a manner that might surprise the readers of that organ, ordinarily so pondered. On August the first, Aerobagne 32 was due, according to its official itinerary, to pass over the place where the body was found on the nineteenth; that would therefore imply that the cadaver had lain unperceived by the Tuaregs resident in the region for eighteen days. That is impossible. On the other hand, the leather bottle would most probably have been thrown into the sea from an aerial courier whose wireless telegraph had been damaged, or whose operation had been impeded by some breakdown. That is, it must be agreed, the sole means, already employed on many occasions, to make known the nature of an accident and explain a delay that might have caused alarm.*

In any case, as our colleague says, very judiciously, it remains the case that only knowledge of the document con-

*tained in the leather bottle can provide the key to all this,
which is only mysterious to minds inclined to the romantic. As
for supposing that it is a matter of an attempted escape from
an aerobagne, such a hypothesis is inadmissible; it would require a strong dose of credulity to add faith to it even for a
minute. No one escapes from aerial prisons.*

    That commencement of polemic had no echo. *Le Monde*
did not see fit to respond, and silence fell.

    However, those few lines in an evening paper, repeated
and commented on by a morning paper, were merely the prelude to events so formidable that they were seriously to threat-
en the situation of the Ministry and for the President of the
Council only to owe the possibility of keeping his portfolio to
a fortunate diversion.

    Numerous aerial prisons are presently furrowing the
great highways of the atmosphere. Germany has thirty, France
has ten, England six and Japan two. Russia, having estimated
that its desolate northern steppes are sufficient to its coercive
needs, has not constructed any; it has kept the gibbet, that old
national relic surviving so many other relics carried away by
the revolutionary storm. China has also conserved its large
terrestrial convict prisons, which cost so little to maintain, as
well as the death penalty in multiple barbaric forms. Only the
four great powers that we have just cited have aerial prisons;
they confine their convicted criminals there, in a terrible isola-
tion, among the clouds, and any escape attempt becomes a
veritable suicide attempt. As is well-known, the other, less
important powers, confide their convicts to one or other nations possessing the penitentiary regime of aerobagnes,[98] on
payment of an annual fee.

---

[98] The French term *"bagne"* has no precise English equivalent;
it refers to a prison to which only long-term prisoners sentenced to hard labor are sent. In the late 19th century the
French moved their principal *bagnes* to its colonies, primarily
to New Caledonia and Guyana, so that they became places of

247

Economic factors were principally responsible for the adoption of aerial prisons. People will remember how difficult life was in the aftermath of the Great War, and what efforts were required to bring the land of so many impoverished nations back to full production, to reconstitute rural life and the decimated livestock. The crisis was fortunately overcome, thanks to the aid of colonies, which furnished large stocks of alimentary products.

France was the first nation to understand what advantages it could obtain from its colonial domain. Thus, it resolved not to encumber two of its finest possessions, New Caledonia and Guyana, with convicts and ex-convicts any longer. Rich territories had a more useful role to play than that of places of deportation for criminals. Once the principle was admitted, France entered resolutely into the path of realization, and created the aerobagnes.

Henceforth, murderers and malefactors of all categories were relegated to the air, in conditions that were severe but not at all barbaric. The milieu, moreover, was very healthy. The excellent results of the reform did not take long to be manifest. Escapes being impossible, the surveillance personnel could be reduced, and notable economies ensued. Finally rid of their sad guests, New Caledonia and Guyana attracted a numerous emigration composed of honest and hard-working elements, and developed in an extraordinary fashion in a few years.

Not only did the overseas convict prisons disappear, but also the majority of the penitentiary establishments in the metropolis. The Code was adjusted. As soon as a man is condemned to three years in prison, he has to purge his penalty aboard an aerobagne. In case of recidivism he can be relegated for life, in the capacity of a worker or a guard, either to an

---

long-term exile. Since the text makes the point that the first airship prisons were French, it therefore seems reasonable, as appears to have been the case within the story, that the other nations imitating that example should have borrowed the French term, which I have therefore retained.

aerobagne or one of the terrestrial relay stations of the penitentiary system.

In France, the transportation of convicts to aerobagnes is effected in the following fashion. One morning, the gates of the jail open, an autocellular emerges, carrying the convict as far as the plain of the Crau or the marshes of Sologne. There are erected the posts of resupply, rival and departure for the aerobagnes; an aircraft takes aboard its cargo of convicts and transports them to an aerial penitentiary, which has descended in response to a wireless summons. Then the great metal bird resumes its slow course in the silence and solitude of the high altitudes.

The aerobagnes were and still are divided into two categories: those which receive convicts sentenced for a limited time and those that receive convicts sentenced to life imprisonment.

A national code fixes the itineraries of each nation's aerial prisons. They must never descend below three thousand meters except to fly over their point of attachment or countries that are absolutely deserted.

The great couriers fly at five hundred meters, the sanatoria at a thousand meters, small biplanes lower down and aviettes even lower. It is with the aid of that code that *Le Monde* and *Le Peuple* were able to determine the nationality of the aerial prison that passed between the tenth and twentieth parallels at the level of Cap d'Arquin on the aforementioned date.

All the countries that have adopted the system of aerobagnes—with one exception—have made them places of detention in which the rigor of justice can be associated with humanitarian principles. Germany, faithful to its barbaric habits, has given them the physiognomy of frightful jails.

The convicts serving limited sentences who have returned from German aerial prisons maintain with regard to those places of misery a silence full of a terror with which their souls remain forever imprinted. They have the eyes of tracked beasts, fearful and suspicious. Those who seem ready to talk quickly become mute again. The little that one can get out of murmured confidences permits the imagination of frightful scenes happening aboard, and that the most frightful mental sufferings that history has known are surpassed in those hellish places.

Convicts released after three years of incarceration in German aerobagnes have been seen who have almost completely lost the power of speech and no longer employ anything more than a rudimentary language, and that incapacity of expression reveals the full depth of their intellectual degradation. What frightful memories, then, have troubled their mind?

So, *Le Monde* and *Le Peuple* had published two short articles regarding a leather bottle fallen on to the deck of a ship and a cadaver discovered in the sand of the desert. A week went by, and then events suddenly took on an exceptional gravity.

II. In which there is talk of revolution in the press, a mob in the street and a young woman.

Five days after the publication of the item in *Le Monde* regarding the fall of the leather bottle Paris was revolutionized and astounded by an event without precedent in the history of that newspaper.

At about five o'clock in the evening, under the crude light of electric lamps, a swarm of newsvendors spread out through the city selling a special edition of the great daily paper. All newspapers are cried in that fashion; it has become a necessity—from which, however, *Le Monde* had previously abstained, as much because it judged the number of its subscribers sufficient as out of pride, and because it was repelled by what it doubtless considered to be a vulgarity. Then, suddenly, that nobility went slumming, and the venerated title was uttered by the mouths of street-hawkers.

The reason for that circumstance had to be important— and, indeed, it was.

The words of a headline, in large letters, awoke all curiosities and caused hands to dip into pockets:

UNPRECEDENTED EVENT:
FRENCH ENGINEER SEQUESTERED
IN GERMAN AEROBAGNE
His torture! His cry for help! Will the government act?

And lower down, in smaller characters:

We shall commence tomorrow the publication of the manuscript enclosed by our unfortunate compatriot in the leather bottle collected at sea by the transatlantic liner Foch: a terrible story of an agony that has lasted for eighteen months. The government has done nothing
An appeal to public opinion.
Read Le Monde *tomorrow, 28 October.*

Such news emitted by any other newspaper would perhaps have left the public a trifle suspicious, but on the part of an organ that had never had recourse to any promotional tricks it took on a serious allure, and the objective at which the daily had aimed was perfectly attained. The public commented on the event and awaited the next day with impatience.

The following day, it was learned that the powerful newspaper had printed a million copies of the previous day's issue. Postal airplanes had carried them all over France; it was openly said that it was not so much the lure of lucre as the desire to impose an energetic line of conduct on the government that had led the French newspaper to act in a fashion so contrary to its habits.

Thus, on that day, the city was visibly animated as five o'clock approached, in a particular fashion.

But the time of the great daily's appearance brought a disappointment that soon changed to anger, for rancor remained keen in the depths of hearts against those who had unleashed the war; they were known to be perfidious and no

251

one was unaware that they were working, in the complicit shadows, to reach a position in which to take revenge for their defeat.

The reason for that anger was the item that *Le Monde* published, not this time as a headline but in characters like those of a poster, taking up the entire front page;

At the last moment, the publication of the manuscript thrown in a leather bottle by the French engineer Paul Ménestin, who disappeared from Neustadt in Silesia, where he was resident, eighteen months ago, has been prohibited by order of the French government.

There was an uproar followed by a popular movement. The ministry did not enjoy public favor; people were ready to demonstrate that—but that evening, the belated hour granted it some respite. The following morning, *Le Monde* once again spread placards in the streets in which it explained what had happened, thus applying, without seeming to do so, a lighted torch to the pile of straw.

This is how the newspaper expressed it:

Yesterday, at the moment of going to press, a ministerial order arrived forbidding the publication of a manuscript that the ministry judges to be apocryphal. At the same time, agents placed at the door of our offices of sales and dispatch, made certain that no copy could cross that threshold.

Either the ministry is mistaken or it is acting in bad faith. The manuscript was written by Paul Ménestin, and we have proof of that.

Paul Ménestin, a French engineer who graduated from the École des Mines three years ago, had been employed in a German metallurgical factory. Eighteen months ago our compatriot disappeared abruptly, without any investigation being undertaken by the authorities of the country to clarify the mystery of that event. Today, we are in a position to affirm that

Paul Ménestin really is, as he has written and for reasons of State, sequestered aboard the German aerobagne 32.

We have sent a reporter to Neustadt; he has carried out an investigation, consulted the mortuary registers, and has found nothing that might explain the sudden disappearance of our compatriot. We are no longer in the age of miracles, even though people have not ceased persuading us that black is white, or at least trying to do so.

How did this manuscript fall into our hands? That is our business, but in order to be precise and to prove our entire good faith, we ought to add that we do not possess the original, only a photographic reproduction of it.

We were about to print a facsimile of one of the photographic pages and publish almost a tenth of the whole story when the ministerial order arrived to stop us.

What will the President of the Council do? He has the original in his hands.

If the manuscript is apocryphal, he has no reason to forbid its publication; let its falsity be demonstrated to us and we will be the first to present the whole as a work of imagination. If it is authentic, what are the reasons for the action of the President of the Council?

We have a right to know, and we demand to know.

That article, of course, did not calm minds; on the contrary, the turbulent element of the population found therein an excellent pretext for becoming more heated. Demonstrations were manifest outside the Ministry of the Interior, and acclamations outside the offices of *Le Monde*.

In the Chambre, a député asked a question. The Minister replied that the document did indeed exist, and that it even constituted, if it was an expression of the truth, a charge of exceptional gravity against Germany, but that, precisely because of the chain of events it might sent in motion, and also by reason of the doubt that subsisted as to its authenticity, he had considered it his duty to forbid its publication. He was waiting for the investigation that he had ordered our ambassador to open to be completed and the result known.

The Chambre was content with that explanation, but the crowd did not admit it, and was agitated all that evening until the moment when the Minister announced that a wireless message from Berlin permitted the publication of the famous manuscript and that furthermore, complementary information would be given by the morning papers.

That declaration calmed the peaceful citizens, and also opinion, which wanted nothing better than to be calm. But it was palpable that everyone wanted light to be cast on the tenebrous affair.

The following day, the newspapers announced that the German government itself had taken a spontaneous step toward the French ambassador and had brought a letter from Paul Ménestin, found in the latter's room in Neustadt. In that letter the engineer declared that his life had become unbearable far from his homeland and that he envisaged the completion of the contract binding him to the German metallurgical factory as impossible. In those circumstances he preferred to kill himself, wishing that the death in question remain unknown.

It was the letter of a depressed individual; it was possible that things had happened thus.

The German government had also deposited in the hands of the French ambassador all the papers, money and effects found in the home of the unfortunate engineer, and all those poor items would arrive in Paris by diplomatic bag. As for the cadaver, it has not been recovered, and it was supposed that the desperate individual must, in a sharper fit of anguish, have thrown himself into the Oder at Kosel, only fifty kilometers way from Neustadt by railway.

Thus, the official note added, the manuscript could not be anything but the work of a romancer desirous of making a striking impact, or one of the fantasists who are not sorry to dupe public opinion and laugh thereafter at its naivety. In addition, the original manuscript was not signed Paul Ménestin, as the newspaper affirmed, but merely with a P and a scarcely legible name, which might as easily be Monestier or Bésnestier as Ménestin.

Le Monde agreed, in a small special edition issued at two o'clock, that the photographic copy it possessed bore an almost illegible signature capable of giving rose to various interpretations, but that it had opened a preliminary investigation and that its conviction remained entire.

At the same time, it announced the publication of the first fragment for that evening.

The editor-in-chief of *Le Monde*, Charles Sauter, was in his office when he was informed that a young woman, accompanied by an old lady, was asking to see him. With a brief gesture the editor-in-chief swept away, so to speak, the office boy who had disturbed him, but the latter, who was familiar with his ways, was untroubled.

"It's just," he said, "that it's about the manuscript..."

Charles Sauter's attitude immediately changed.

"Send them in right away," he said, "and don't let anyone disturb us."

A moment later, the two women were introduced. The editor-in-chief, standing up, briefly gestured toward two armchairs placed in front of his desk. The padded door closed again, and nothing could any longer be heard but the muffled and distant noise of machines.

"Monsieur," said the younger of the two women, lifting up the crepe veil that was covering her face, "my name is Mathilde Régis, and this is my mother. I was...I *am* Paul Ménestin's fiancée."

Charles Sauter, who was sketching a slight bow, raised his head swiftly and looked at the young woman attentively.

She had a strange pallor; her face, a distinguished oval, denounced a great fatigue or an extreme dolor, and her large dark eyes, with a frank but melancholy gaze, were burning with an intense fever.

"Monsieur," the young woman continued, "I am Paul Ménestin's fiancée, and I share your conviction. The note published this morning is a lie. Paul is not dead..."

She hesitated momentarily; her mother placed a hand gently on her arm. That simple gesture restored the young woman's courage.

"I have brought you, Monsieur," she continued, "An entire packet of letters that he wrote to me from out there; in none of them, even the very last, does he manifest the slightest discouragement. All of them, on the contrary, speak of the future and hope. It is only souls devoid of strength that are discouraged by obstacles and difficulties; he was not...he *is* not...a coward. I am confiding these letters to you, Monsieur, confiding them to the gallant man you are. Make use of them, publish my name if you judge it appropriate; I do not blush at my love."

Sauter bowed. "Will you permit me to ask you a few questions, Mademoiselle?"

"Anything you wish, Monsieur; once again, I have no reason to blush at the sentiment that has brought me to you."

"How long is it since you received any news of your fiancé?"

"Eighteen months, Monsieur. At that time, he suddenly stopped writing."

"And," Sauter said, with a hint of embarrassment, "you don't believe..."

"In his abandonment, a flight?" the young woman interrupted, with a dolorous laugh. "No, Monsieur—Monsieur Ménestin is not one of those who scorns a promise given."

"Then you attribute his silence to a disappearance, since you don't admit the idea of his death?"

"Yes, Monsieur. Paul is not dead, but the Germans doubtless have a powerful interest in making him disappear."

"In that case," Sauter murmured, "why haven't they killed him?"

"Perhaps they have need of him?" suggested the young woman.

"Yes, perhaps...he was an engineer?"

"An engineer and chemist."

"Aha! A chemist! That changes things slightly. In fact, if he had commenced certain endeavors, they might have need of him. One can remake calculations, but it's only with difficulty that one can reconstitute a chemical formula whose elements are unknown. Well, Mademoiselle, retain all your hope and believe that the newspaper I direct will not abandon you— neither him nor you. With your permission, we'll go up to the photographic service. I want to project before you a slide of one of the pages of the manuscript, and we'll compare one of the letters you've brought with that image. We'll know then what we're dealing with. It will be an important fact, irrefutable and established. Tomorrow, or the day after, we'll establish in the same way whether the letter in which Paul Ménestin announces his voluntary death is authentic or not. If the two proofs are conclusive, we'll go on to the end."

The young woman acquiesced with a nod of the head. Madame Régis, who had said nothing thus far, broke her silence.

"Like my daughter, Monsieur, I don't believe that the poor child killed himself; he suffered from seeing the realization of his dream postponed, but he was sure of the heart of the one he loved, and he was valiant by nature, incapable of cowardice or desertion."

Sauter rose to his feet, saying: "I'm already convinced, Madame. If you will, let's go up."

The two women got up. Sauter guiding them, allowed them to go ahead of him, opened a door and invited them to step into an elevator. In a matter of seconds they were on the terraces where the airplanes came to land, with the aid of which *Le Monde* ensured its distribution to the provinces, and even abroad.

On seeing them enter a large room entirely painted in dark red, an employee came toward them.

"Marcel," said Sauter, "you're going to project one of the slides of the manuscript and one that you're going to make of

257

one of these letters—it doesn't matter which, as long as it includes the signature. Both on the same scale. How long will it take you?"

"Ten minutes."

"Go."

The employee drew away and disappeared. Sauter had the two women sit down in front of a small screen and continued interrogating the young woman at length.

He learned by that means that Paul Ménestin was an orphan, that she too no longer had her father, a former professor of Oriental Languages, and that she lived with her mother, thanks to a little capital amassed with difficulty. The two young people had been engaged to be married for less than a year when Paul had been solicited to take up an employment at the Neustadt Steelworks. It was a unique opportunity for him to get out of the rut and to earn enough in a year to establish himself modestly in Paris and marry the woman he loved.

The young woman had reached that point in her confidences when the room was suddenly plunged into darkness.

She had scarcely had time to recover from her emotion when the screen in front of them was illuminated; then the letter addressed by Paul to his fiancée and one of the pages of the manuscript were inscribed on the white surface in identical proportions.

Sauter was about to speak, but he heard a dolorous sigh, a cry uttered by Madame Régis, and the sound of a body falling.

"Light!" he shouted.

The arc-lights fitted to the ceiling crackled, and then, under the harsh white light they projected, Sauter saw the young woman lying on the floor, having fainted.

III. Paul Ménestin's Last Letter

When Mathilde finally recovered her senses, she was lying on a divan in the editor-in-chief's office. Her mother was supporting her in her arms. Through the light curtain of her eyelashes, scarcely raised, the young woman glimpsed the tall silhouette of Sauter bending over her.

She got up, painfully, and, passing her hand over her forehead, made a gesture of driving away the last veils still obscuring her mind. At that moment, Sauter leaned further toward her.

"How do you feel?" he asked.

"Much better," she said, with a reassuring smile. "Excuse me."

"Your emotion must have been very strong to plunge you into such a profound faint."

"Oh yes! I thought I was going to die…I hoped that Paul was still alive, but a cruel doubt still tormented me, and when I saw that, thank Heaven, my unique hope was not disappointed, it seemed to me that my heart burst within my breast."

"It will be necessary to be careful of that heart," said Sauter, in an affectionate manner, taking hold of the young woman's hands. "So, like me, you're convinced that both handwritings are really those of your fiancé?"

"Absolutely."

"It can't be doubted for a second," said Madame Régis, in her turn.

"Good," added Sauter. "Then we'll be victorious, be certain of it, Mademoiselle, for a kind of instinct tells me that the letter we're expecting from Germany is fake. I'm not in the habit of letting myself go to sentiments that escape reasoning, but this time, that opinion has taken on the force of a conviction within me. So, you'll sense, I'm certain, that it's necessary not to allow yourself to be overcome by despair or chagrin. I'm going to have need of you, of all your courage. I want to find in you not merely a zealous collaborator but an energetic witness, whom nothing ought to trouble and whose certainty nothing can shake."

"You can count on me, Monsieur," said the young woman, getting up without her mother's aid. "Your support has rendered me all my energy; whatever happens, I won't weaken again."

259

Her mother helped her to adjust her hair. The old lady seemed incapable of taking any part in a conversation whose outcome made her tremble in advance.

"Of the letters that I gave you," the young woman said, "the last one will perhaps give you, as it gave me, the conviction that Paul Ménestin has been the victim of a trap. If the letter in which he announces his intention to commit suicide is not really his, as I believe, our task will be very difficult, but whatever role I might be called upon to play, I shall play it to the end, no matter what. If the letter is really his, I shall have nothing left to do but weep, alas, but I retain the intention to go to Neustadt with my mother, in order to gather the details of his life and end."

"You will not go alone, Mademoiselle, and your decision singularly facilitates what I had the intention of doing. I had decided, in one or other of the alternatives that you have just envisaged, and which I envisaged myself, to send a skillful reporter out there once again, but whom, in spite of his skill, would doubtless be suspected, which would have hindered his investigation to the point of rendering it virtually useless. He will join you, and pass for a relative of yours.

"The objective that you appear to be pursuing is too human for anyone to suppose that your journey has any purpose other than the one overtly declared. In those conditions, it will be necessary to leave right away, tomorrow, or even this evening if you can. Here, to render your task easier, I shall put on an appearance of declaring myself satisfied by the explanations, whatever they are, that the Ministry will give. When you return, furnished with the information you have been able to gather, we shall act. Then, when the moment has come, we shall light the petard—and believe me, it will make a noise."

Mathilde had regained all her empire over herself; a flame of enthusiasm gleamed in her clear gaze.

"Count on me," she said.

She was ready to leave, and extended her small gloved hand to Sauter.

"Wait a moment," he said. "I haven't finished. This evening, at six o'clock, one of the paper's reporters, Monsieur Escander, furnished with my instructions, will come to your home. The express leaves at ten past eight. You'll be in Neustadt, passing through Bohemia, the day after tomorrow, and about ten p.m.

"The next day you can start work, and be finished, unless there are unexpected complications, that same evening, or the following day at the worst. That would be longer than I expect," he added, darting a glance at Madame Régis, who was listening with a visible anxiety.

"But if I'm accompanied," the young woman out in, "my mother, who is old, can easily stay here; it won't be the first time I've traveled alone. What prevents us, then, from taking the air-express to Vienna that leaves at nine o'clock? From there, we'll catch the one that goes to Prague. We can then charter a plane, and thus be in Neustadt tomorrow evening."

"Oh, my daughter!" said Madame Régis.

"Bravo!" cried Sauter.

The two exclamations were uttered at the same time, but the young woman did not pay any heed either of them. She continued: "That's what it's necessary to do, then, if you have no objection to make. I await your instructions."

"They'll be brief, before your determination, which facilitates matters. One of *Le Monde*'s airplanes will take you to Vienna. It leaves the terrace at nine o'clock. Between now and then I'll have made the arrangements for it to accommodate you. Be here at eight-thirty at the latest."

At that moment the department heads were announced.

Sauter, who felt that it was necessary not to give Madame Régis the opportunity to intervene in the debate, hastened the adieux, giving his final instructions to Mathilde as he guided the two women gently to the door.

Less than a minute thereafter, the mother and daughter were hurrying home.

261

Needless to say, the sentimental diplomacy, tears and determination of Madame Régis, employed by turns, were utterly futile; the young woman did not yield in her resolution.

Sauter rapidly gave orders to his colleagues; he was in haste to take cognizance of Paul Ménestin's last letter to his fiancée.

We transcribe that letter faithfully here:

Neustadt

My darling, I received your letter. If you only knew what a comfort it has been for me, in this difficult exile, in which I truly see my memory of you as my unique hope!

I admire your soul, so reasonable, so serious and so loving, and you can have no suspicion of all the value that your delicate, elegant and pretty handwriting takes on in my eyes. It is a balm for me, for all the troubles that I endure patiently because it is necessary, but from which I would suffer a great deal more if I did not have your encouragement and your love.

Winter is advancing rapidly and promises to be harsh. Do you remember, a year ago, we were walking side by side through the melancholy and deserted pathways of the Petit Trianon. The trees were shedding their foliage and the wind was blowing the poor dead leaves around us in a slow waltz, but our hearts were full of sunlight? Today I feel some hope again, because I do not believe that I shall be subjected to the rigors of winter here; yes, my darling, it might be that shall return to you before the appointed time. This is the reason: the direction of the mines has caused me to pass from the engineering department to that of the chemists, and has given me for a mission a series of tasks, of researches, that I believe I ought not to accept, for reasons that I shall give you vocally.

You will understand my haste to see this year of exile concluded better when you know that I sense that I am being watched night and day. Espionage is raised here to the level of a religious dogma.

Don't be alarmed, I beg you; here, everyone is watched, the French, as you can imagine, even more than the rest. They evidently want to know whether I'm writing compromising notes. They don't know anything and won't find anything. If I didn't have the possibility of sending this letter by way of a French airplane that has just landed here because of a slight technical fault, and which is leaving again this evening, I wouldn't say a quarter of what I'm saying, because I'm convinced that all our letters are opened and read; this one will escape checking and will be put in the post directly at Colmar.

"I believe that my refusal to accept the task they want to confide to me will lead to the annulment of my contract. It's in that hope that I've already written to major factory-owners in France—everywhere, in sum, that I might exercise my profession. I only accepted this position in order to earn a large sum of money rapidly, but that necessity shouldn't lead me to exceed my duty. So, if I expect, I'm invited to leave, I'll accept, even if I have to lose a few thousand marks, I'm in so much haste to be with you, to hear your voice, to feel the tender gaze of your lovely eyes. I'm in haste, too, to be far away from the eternal suspicion by which I'm surrounded, far from the spider's web that I feel being woven around me more tightly every day, which will soon imprison all my paces, all my steps and all my thoughts.

I still have many things to tell you, but I'm being summoned to the director's office; I'll resume this letter when I return.

What follows was evidently written the same day, but at six o'clock in the evening—which is to say, a few minutes before the departure of the French aircraft,

6 p.m.
I'm sorry, my darling, but there's no question of a rupture; on the contrary, I found myself confronted by men whose courtesy surprised me. They declared themselves entirely disposed to keep to the terms of the contract, even apologizing for the excessive fashion—which I don't much like—of having momentarily thought of getting out of it. I'm therefore obliged

to go on to the end of my engagement. I'm heart-broken. I was already thinking about liberation, and now it will be necessary for me to spend another eight months here.

Eight months—an eternity—far from you, in this black and sullen city, beneath a bleak sky, among hostile people whose politeness is only a mask. Anyway, be courageous. It might be the case that you won't have news of me for some time, but don't worry. I'm going on a mission to some of the firm's factories; that will give me a great deal of work to do, and I'll always be traveling over mountains and valleys, but I hope nevertheless not to leave you for long without letters. Continue to write to me here, but be prudent. My post will be monitored.

The letter concluded with formulae of tenderness addressed to the young woman and her mother.

Sauter folded the letter slowly and put it in the secret drawer of his desk. Then he became pensive.

Certainly, reading between the lines of the latter part of the letter, discouragement was transparent, but not despair. It was a cry of impatience, not of farewell. It remained evident, however, that Paul Ménestin was suspected and watched.

Then again, if, as he had written, the engineer had been charged with chemical research that he had refused to undertake, he might have been imprisoned until he finally consented. That was quite plausible.

The hour to print the newspaper was about to chime. Sauter went down to the machine room. Passing through the editorial section, he gave Félix Escander the order to accompany him to the presses, where he was going to cast an eye over the setting of the pages.

Félix Escander might have been thirty; short, sturdy and muscular, his searching eyes behind lenses, he was a first-rate all-round sportsman. He was a redoubtable champion, for the finesse of his intelligence as well as the rudeness of his fists, courageous to the point of temerity, marvelously well-acquainted with all the tricks of his trade, and also in possession of a lively pen. He occupied a prominent position in the world of the press; Sauter held him in high esteem and only confided tasks to him worthy of his talent. The rest of the time, he left him to work peacefully in the Bibliothèque Nationale or the Archives on a history of the Valois-Angoulême, which was his great hobby-horse.

"Escander," said the boss, "I'm going to confide a delicate task to you."

"Good," said Escander, simply, adjusting his pince-nez, which always had a tendency to slide down his nose.

"I'm going to confide a young woman to you... You're not saying anything."

"In general, I don't much like transporting precious objects, but if it's absolutely necessary, confide the young woman to me. What is it necessary to do?"

"You're about to find out. Listen carefully, and make notes if you think it necessary."

Sauter leaned on the printing press; every time he stopped looking at his collaborator, his rapid glance scanned the work that was continuing in the fever of the final hour.

Briefly and concisely, Sauter brought Escander up to date with the facts we know. While speaking, he followed attentively—or, at least, tried to follow—any sentiments that might by painted on the journalist's physiognomy, but Escander remained absolutely impenetrable; not a muscle of his face budged. He listened, while delicately toying with a gilt-tipped cigarette that he taken from a silver case.

"Now, my dear, you know everything. It's necessary to help the young woman and bring me back the elements of a sensational article. Don't forget that, above all, you're an investigator on a special mission: see well and see clearly. If events oblige you to make your identity known, don't hesitate and don't prevaricate; we're a power with which it's necessary to reckon. However, only do that as a last resort. The dispatch chief will give you ten thousand francs this evening. Its aircraft number twenty-one that will take you; orders have been given to fit it out specially with a view to receiving two passengers. Number fifteen will follow you, carrying the paper. In Vienna, do everything you judge to be useful, no matter what the cost, to reach Neustadt with the minimum possible delay; the same for coming back. You have three days, get a move on. That's all—*au revoir*!"

And Sauter turned round to lean over the press.

Escander knew the boss; he knew that when the editor-in-chief said "That's all," the best thing to do was to go away without asking for further explanations. In any case, he had no observations to make. He turned on his heel and went back to the editorial offices to close the drawers in which the latest pages of the history of the Valois were sleeping.

A colleague asked him a question: "On a mission?"

"Yes."

"Far?"

"Spain."

"Lucky devil!"

Escander made it a principle never to say exactly where he was going or what he was going to do.

Mathilde was on time at the rendezvous. Clad in a black traveling costume, enveloped in a fur wrap and wearing a cap, she would be able to confront the journey she was undertaking without suffering too much from the cold.

The young woman had required a great deal of energy and will-power, not only to convince her mother of the utility of what she was doing but also to prevent the old lady from witnessing the departure. She had finally succeeded in those ends and, her mind tranquil, in that regard at least, she had hastened to the offices of *Le Monde*.

She had herself taken to Sauter's office, into which she was immediately introduced. On seeing her, the editor-in-chief came to meet her and extended his hands to her.

"Excellent, Mademoiselle," he said. "All my compliments; you're resolved—that's a trump card in our hand. Have confidence—we'll win through. We've got them, and something tells me that we shall have them still."

He invited the young woman to sit down, and rang.

"Has Monsieur Escander arrived?"

"Monsieur Escander is waiting."

"Send him in."

Félix Escander was not one of those people lacking in foresight, whom events take by surprise. He was, on the contrary, always ready to depart on any mission, and when he presented himself, he was wearing a perfectly-fitting suit over a woolen undergarment and calf-length boots, and carrying in his hand a fur-lined helmet equipped with goggles to protect his eyes. In addition, he had a leather bag slung over his shoulder that seemed to be crammed with numerous items.

The editor-in-chief made the introductions. Escander studied the young woman, who, for her part, cast a furtive but searching gaze over her companion. Was the double examination favorable or not? No one said a word,

Sauter glanced at the electric wall-clock. "It's time," he said. "Let's go up."

He led the two young people to the elevator, which deposited them on the reinforced concrete floor of the terrace in a single bound.

Two aircraft, number twenty-one and fifteen, were there, the pilots standing next to their machines. While Sauter gave them his final instructions, Mathilde glanced down into the street.

Dusk was falling rapidly, but the obscurity was not yet sufficiently dense for the young woman to be unable to see the usual feverish crowd awaiting the appearance of the paper that was going to commence publication of the manuscript that very evening. A rumor was rising from that crowd similar to the sound of the sea.

Sauter came back to join the young woman. With a broad gesture he indicated the crowd.

"That's our strength," he said. "Nothing can prevail against it, and it's with us. No dyke can stop the flood on the day when the public powers don't do their duty, their whole duty. On that day, *Le Monde* will cry: "Attack!" and the Ministry will be borne away like a wisp of straw. Remember that, Mademoiselle, and draw from this spectacle the courage and confidence you need."

"I have no need of that vision, which nevertheless frightens and delights me at the same time. Your confidence and devotion, Monsieur, have armed me." After a brief pause, the young woman added: "Then again, the day when I gave my heart, I also gave my life. It belongs to Paul Ménestin; I can, you see, sacrifice it for him, if that is necessary."

"Nothing leads me to suppose that your life will be at stake in the adventure we're launching; if I'd had the slightest fear in that regard, I would neither have solicited nor accepted your collaboration; but I'm very glad, nevertheless, to see you in this disposition—it is my guarantee that I can count on you."

"Yes, you can."

A voice rang out behind them: "All set!"

Sauter drew the young woman toward airplane 21, where the pilot was already in his cockpit.

Escander helped Mathilde aboard, and she soon found herself sitting in a narrow cabin in the midst of a heap of furs. The seats were arranged in such a manner that they could be elongated to firm a comfortable bed of sorts, garnished with a thin mattress and a pneumatic pillow. The cabin was constituted by a light aluminum framework mounted with narrow strips of silk rendered perfectly translucent with the aid of a varnish whose composition was no longer a secret for anyone.

Escander was soon installed in his turn; the electric motor was started up and, running along a plane that surpassed the edge of the terrace slightly, the aircraft took off, without any shock or any sound other than that of its propeller sweeping through the atmosphere.

A formidable clamor saluted its departure.

Mathilde and Escander were on their way to Neustadt, and perhaps toward the light of truth.

Le Monde, although it had raised its print run to one million two hundred thousand, was obliged to resume printing in the middle of the night, so far was that offering below the demand.

The first fragment of the manuscript, which we shall make it a duty to reproduce in full, was preceded by the following note:

Today we are publishing the first fragment of the manuscript of the French engineer Paul Ménestin, kept prisoner aboard the German aerobagne 32.

We have studied the whole very carefully, sorted out the sheets, and there is no significant gap between them. It really is the same pen that has written all the pages, the same mind that has dictated them; everywhere, in these dolorous lines, one senses the same soul palpitating with anguish and despair. It is that of a tracked, martyrized individual.

It is a frightful, incredible thing, but it is so. A human being, innocent of any crime, is in the hands of torturers who have resolved the defeat of his will or his death.

As is known, the entire manuscript is written on detached pages, the slightest white space of which is covered with a fine and compact handwriting; the last bears a scarcely-formed name.

The ensemble of the sheets was rolled up in a piece of cloth that might have been a handkerchief; on that fabric, in large letters, the following heart-rending appeal can be read:

"I implore, in the name of almighty God, in the same of everything sacred that a human being has in his soul, the man or woman who finds this to make a copy of it and then send the original to the President of the Council of Ministers in Paris.

"If that person does not have news of their dispatch at the end of a month, the certified copy should be sent to one of the major Paris newspapers.

"It is a prisoner sequestered on behalf of the most and most odious despotism, a Frenchman abducted from his abode

and martyrized for having wanted, in spite of everything, to remain French and not to betray his country, who, aboard the German aerobagne 32, is uttering a desperate cry and appealing to the justice of the world. Death and madness are perpetually at his sides; he is living in their shadow; have pity on him."

Le Monde added:

It is from the captain of the transatlantic liner Foch, *who has complied in every respect with the instructions of the prisoner, that we have obtained the photographic copies of which we are publishing the first extract today, and it is in the name of the immortal justice to which the prisoner makes such a moving appeal that we are doing so.*

This, then, is the first fragment of the manuscript found in the leather bottle:

IV. The First Chapter of the Manuscript: What there was in the Depths of the Ravine

It is necessary, in order that anyone should be able to add credence to this story, for me to go back for a short distance in the course of the recent events in which I have been involved. That way, it will be easier to understand the motives of those who have imprisoned me, perhaps for the remainder of my poor existence. I have only one hope, which is that this manuscript—which is, I swear, the expression of the truth—will fall into friendly hands.

But what power can break my prison of steel, wandering at an altitude of four thousand meters in infinite space?

At any rate, I still have hope, crazy as that appears. I shall hope until the last sigh...

I am twenty-eight years old. I had graduated from the École des Mines when I was solicited to come to the Neustadt Steelworks in the quality of an engineer able to speak fluent German. The contract I signed only bound me for a year—a trial period—and was worth on my return a considerable sum, which would enable me to realize a secret project very dear to me. I wanted to get married and my engagement had taken place a few days before my departure. That absence has, alas, lasted twenty-six months.

As soon as I arrived in Neustadt I sensed that I was surrounded by hostile sentiments, albeit hidden beneath a cold and stiff politeness. Then I became vaguely conscious that the work with which I was charged was not really that for which I was destined. Spies were attached to my heels, keeping watch on my actions and my words; I had evidence of that several times, and soon acquired the conviction that I was not mistaken.

The first month passed uneventfully; I received letters from France that made my life less bleak and less unhappy. Although I was engaged in the capacity of a metallurgical engineer, I was not allowed to penetrate into the interior of the factories. There were, in addition, various doors of the latter that bore notices forbidding entry, under the threat of penalties whose rigor appeared to me to be excessively severe, and out of proportion to a transgression of discipline on the part of a worker.

On the first day I was taken to a studio that had been specially allocated to me, and I was asked to depict on paper various items of agricultural machines whose broad outlines were indicated to me, as well as the purposes for which they were to be used. Their construction did not concern me; I had merely to draw up the blueprints; once those were finished, their fate became unknown to me.

The ensemble of factories affected the form of a rectangle some five kilometers long, composed of three groups separated by yards closed by iron doors in which there were not windows; all the buildings were illuminated from above and offered to nothing to the eye externally but entirely solid blank walls. The first of the groups was situated about four kilometers from the city and the last backed up to a very deep ravine whose steeply sloping sides were planted with pines and ash trees so dense and bushy that they formed a thick vault of foliage, hiding the long and narrow bottom of the gorge completely. The straightness of the lines and the orderliness of the plantations suggested an idea of artifice rather than something natural.

Access to that ravine was forbidden, not only by a series of notices repeating the imperative formula *Eintritt in diese Werkstaette streng verboten. Gefahr vorhanden. Jeder Bruch schwer gestraft*—Entry to these works is strictly forbidden. Danger. Any infraction will be rigorously punished—but also by a barbed wire fence that was probably electrified.

The place was, however, less ingrate than the arid plains that immediately surrounded the city. I chose it as the goal of the rare walks that I was able to take on Sundays when the weather permitted, to stretch my legs and saturate my lungs with fresh air. I took a book with me then and, lying in the grass, not far from the ravine, or sitting on a stone, I read or daydreamed until dusk.

I was absolutely alone, but I did not take long to discover that I was watched from a distance by a man who, hidden in a small peasant cottage, spied on me with the aid of a telescope.

Meanwhile, what happened in the steelworks continued to surprise me a great deal. After two months of discreet observation, I was convinced that the factories were laboring in the shadows on a project far more mysterious that the manufacture of any kind of pacific equipment.

Furthermore, it seemed evident to me that the quantities of raw materials that we received did not correspond to the finished products that emerged from the factories. Ostensibly, new tractors with shiny paintwork, plows, and combine harvesters were being sent forth in large numbers, but that might have masked other manufactures.

All these observations gradually led me to seek the solution of the enigma. One can easily understand how reluctant I was to lend a hand, even involuntarily, to work that I sensed to be perfidious and the deliberate violation of treaties intended to guarantee the security of my homeland.

While roaming the surroundings I had, moreover, made further discoveries. Enormous ventilation shafts, cleverly dissimulated in clumps of trees, surrounded the ravine I mentioned, and did not seem to belong directly to the factory in which I was employed. That drew me to take my investigations further; I then remarked that, although the number of workers was not excessive, the trains that brought them to the city were packed. Where, then, was that multitude going? It is true that the trains went further and passed over the ravine on the bridge forbidden to pedestrians.

To know: that was now my perpetual desire. In order to satisfy it, I took one of the trains and pretended to be engrossed in a technical brochure that I held in front of my face. The line, belonging to the steelworks, was reserved for its personnel. And I remained on it until the other side of the bridge, when I played the part of someone perceiving his mistake. I then took another train heading in the other direction—but I had been able to make a few interesting observations.

The trains that succeeded one another every few minutes were composed of a locomotive and three carriages. On departure they were filled, and a large number of workers massed on the station platforms waited for the following trains. At the factories, about a third got off; the other two-thirds only left the train on the far side of the bridge, and were swallowed up by a squat building whose doors closed behind them.

Those facts confirmed my suspicions. There were other factories, and one of them must be at the bottom of the ravine. That idea, suddenly engendered within me, was imposed more by a kind of instinct than by reasoning.

I resolved to clarity the matter.

At the restaurant where I took my meals, a man—a Polish foreman who thought he had slid far enough into my intimacy to render me a few small services—came to exchange a few words with me every evening, and soon began sitting with me at the table. I saw no harm in that; to begin with our conversations only dealt with generalities. The evening when I had decided to go over the bridge with the aid of the subterfuge I have described, however, he asked me an unexpected question:

"Do you know," he said, "that a new toxic gas has just been discovered in France, whose effects appear to be terrible?"

"I heard mention of it before my departure, but be sure that France is a pacifist country, which only ever takes up arms when attacked."

"What does it intend to do with it, then?"

"So far as I know, purify some of our colonies that are infested with mosquitoes, and combat invasions of locusts in Algeria. In any case, all the elements of the gas are known; no mystery has been made of them."

"No, all the elements aren't known; their composition and manufacture remain secret."

"I would be easy to find out," I said, imprudently.

The man looked at me strangely.

"There would be an enormous fortune to be gained," he said, playing with the crumbs scattered on the table with the tip of his knife.

And I replied, no less stupidly: "I wouldn't want to enrich myself at that price."

Scarcely had I pronounced those clumsy words than I regretted them, because, for the first time, I discovered, merely by the way that my interlocutor looked at me askance, how false and suspicious his gaze was.

I certainly have no excuse for my conduct, but it is appropriate to recall that I was there all alone, in a hostile environment, and that the man had appeared to take pity on my solitude, giving evidence of some sympathy for me.

I was not, however, the master of the sentiment I had just expressed; he perceived that and immediately changed his attitude. He looked at me frankly and said: "I approve entirely; in any case, there are chemists here sufficiently distinguished to carry that work through if they wish. I only said that to point out that a fortune is sometimes easy to come by."

The conversation was diverted, and we separated after the meal.

That man, who is certainly not Polish, was named Karl Koskutio, or at least said he was; people simply addressed him as Karl.

When he had gone, I sensed the full gravity of my imprudence, but how could I diminish its effects? If I began to avoid him, I would show him that I now held him in suspicion and that I attached too much importance to the words we had exchanged. It was better—and I hold to that decision—not to allow my anxieties to show, and to continue my relations with him as in the past, while nevertheless exercising greater prudence.

In spite of what had just happened, however, I did not abandon the idea of unveiling the secret of the factories, and, in order better to conserve the memory of what I was able to discover, I resolved to keep a journal of all the incidents that I witnessed or in which I participated.

That was all very well, but it remained for me to find a safe place to hide the document, for the woman who did my housekeeping and maintained by clothing and linen had to belong, like all the domestics, to the police spying on my movements and actions.

After long reflection I made a decision. The floor of my room was tiled, not, as in France, with octagonal tiles but with small flagstones about twenty-five centimeters by twenty, of a very pale terracotta. With extreme care, I succeeded, with the aid of a simple pen-knife, in lifting one of them, behind a curtain making a cloakroom. Then I slowly hollowed out the plaster that fixed it in place and collected the debris in a handkerchief; then I replaced everything, satisfied with my work, certain that no one would be able to discover my hiding place, so perfect did the joints seem, with the aid of the plaster dust with which I filled them.

That journal, written day by day, still exists; it is under the flagstone, in the place where I left it when I quit my room

for the last time, for I am convinced that it has not been discovered.

For the sake of prudence, even though the weather was
favorable, I let two Sundays go by without visiting my favorite
spot—which, it will be remembered, overlooked the ravine. In
any case, I had resolved no longer to go there by day, but by
night. I was waiting for a plausible reason to absent myself
one evening, when the passage of a French dramatic company
through Neustadt furnished me with the opportunity I sought. I
warned my household staff that, my intention being to go to
hear them, I would be back late, or not at all. That gave me my
night.

At six o'clock I did indeed go to Neustadt, in a suit, but I
had put an ample waxed greatcoat over it, and I took rubber
gloves.

On arriving at the theater the first person I saw was Karl,
the so-called Pole. That thwarted al my plans, reducing them
to nothing. The individual bought a stalls ticket, and I stood
there stupidly, wondering what I was going to do. They were
performing *Le Petit Duc*. I took a program and, as I scanned it,
an idea occurred to me.

The artistes were French; they were compatriots; nothing
was therefore more natural than that I should go to talk to
them. I could thus invite one of them, male or female, to supper, or at least say so, and that would render me my liberty.
The plan was simple; it only remained to carry it through.

I contrived an encounter with Karl in a corridor a few
minutes before the commencement and said to him: "I'm delighted to have come. I used to know Georgette d'Antraygues,
who is singing the role of the little Duc, and I'm thinking of
asking her to supper. Can you recommend one or two restaurants?"

He gave me two addresses, which I noted down, and the
play began.

At the entr'acte, taking Karl with me, I had flowers and
my card sent to the artiste and, at the next entr'acte, I went
into the wings.

Georgette d'Antraygues received me amicably. I solicited a moment's conversation with her, which I obtained, and I said to her: "Mademoiselle. I'm French, as you must suspect; but you don't know that I'm presently charged with an important mission that requires my freedom of action tonight. Now, I'm followed and under surveillance; it's necessary that I leave the theater without being seen. Can you help me?"

Somewhat surprised, the young woman looked at me for a long moment, and then, doubtless won over by my frank expression, asked: "Which way did you come?"

"Through the iron door that leads to the auditorium, which was opened to me without any comment."

"In that case, you can leave by the artistes' entrance. Come on—I'll show you where it is."

She went ahead of me; the scenery was being shifted. She walked every elegantly, young and pretty, with a bold attitude, in her breastplate and her powdered wig.

When we arrived at a little door, she held out her hand. "*Au revoir*," she said, "and good luck."

There were three steps to go down, a fairly long corridor, and then the street. I waited momentarily; then, when I judged that the act had begun I went to the cloakroom and collected my coat and hat. No one had seen me.

A quarter of an hour later, I left the city and, cutting across the fields, I reached the bridge over the ravine before midnight without having been followed.

There was no moon; the obscurity was profound; I would be able to operate in complete darkness.

I acquired the conviction that by going from tree to tree along the side of the ravine, not only would I be in no danger of falling, but I would easily be able to escape a surveillance that the inoffensive character of my actions ought to have relaxed.

I was taking a big risk, I knew, but I was prey to such a fever of curiosity, and was so ardently desirous of unmasking the actions of which my homeland might sooner or later by the victim, in violation of the treaties signed in 1918, that I did not hesitate.

I laid flat on the ground, face down, in order to reach the edge of the ravine; my waxed topcoat was carefully buttoned and the rubber gloves were covering my hand. I could thus avoid soiling my inner garments too much, which was the important thing.

I arrived promptly enough at the network of barbed wire; as I expected, it was electrified; I was certain of that because I had a stake supporting insulators directly in front of me. It was necessary not to think of climbing over the obstacle, and I searched for a tree whose branches extended above the wire. I found one and climbed it; then, following a broad branch, I passed over the network and let myself down without raising any alarm.

It only remained for me to act with extreme prudence.

I slid smoothly from tree to tree, under a rather abundant rain that had begun to fall, and thus reached, not the bottom of the ravine, but the crest of a wall that was absolutely sheer. At the bottom, some distance away to my left, a little red lamp was lit, under which motionless reflections extended in parallel.

What could that be?

Water? No—the reflections, as I said, were absolutely immobile. In order to find out, I started crawling along the top of the wall, and had scarcely covered ten meters when my hand discovered a piece of iron describing a curve whose two extremities were embedded in the stone. By groping along the wall, I discovered another. It was an iron ladder, like those in dry docks and the flanks of jetties. I ventured on to it and immediately went down fifteen rungs, which finally took me to the floor of the ravine. I set foot on it, and soon had the explanation of the immobility of the reflections.

I had before me an electric railway.

V. The Mysterious Factories

I was in the densest shadow one could wish for in the course of such an adventure; that assured me of an almost complete impunity, and further affirmed my resolution. I straightened up and continued my route along the track, toward the red light that was scintillating in the distance like a ruby.

I went hesitantly, at a prudent pace, but that did not prevent me from observing carefully; it was thus that I encountered, in a siding, three connected trucks, on which was resting the hull of a submarine of an absolutely new construction, so far as I could judge. Error was impossible by reason of the special, truly characteristic form that such vessels offer.

The submarine, which might have been a river submarine or designed to operate within a limited range in shallow waters, seemed to be complete, save for its deck armament, as I was able to assure myself by climbing on to one of the trucks. It was undoubtedly waiting there for the time to arrive to take to its element.

Further away, on three more trucks, lay a long slender form that had to be a cannon.

I continued my route, and soon understood. The red light was nothing but a signal planted at the entrance to a tunnel that extended underground and from which I saw coming toward me two white headlights that were reminiscent of the eyes of a monstrous beast silently charging toward my poor and paltry person. I only just had time to throw myself into the depths of a gutter, and saw a long train pass by soundlessly. I could not, alas, make out what it was carrying, but I knew enough, at least about that side of things. I hesitated to go further into the tunnel; that might be dangerous, and time was limited,

I retraced my steps. The success of my enterprise had given me a pleasure that still astonishes me. Hastening my stride, I went back along the route I had just followed. I found

279

he iron ladder that I had come down, went past it, and continued advancing.

Three or four hundred paces beyond the ladder, there was a sharp bend in the track. I crawled toward the bend, but at one moment I was in grave danger of being discovered; a motorail[99] mounted by two men, both armed with short electric rifles, passed so close to me that the wheels of their machine almost brushed my hands.

The night was pitch-black and the watchmen were doubtless only accomplishing a mechanical task; otherwise, I would have been doomed. I let the motorail continue on its way toward the tunnel and, scarcely raising myself on my elbows. I took a long look ahead of me.

I had before me a tangle of tracks that converged toward embarkation platforms. In spite of the obscurity and thanks to curious beacons that seemed to be circling in the air as a satellite orbits its planet, I glimpsed forms that were familiar to me: lifting-tackle, cranes, platforms, trucks and apparatus of all kinds, in usage in great maritime depots as well as metallurgical factories; all of it raised slender or squat silhouettes toward the black sky; further away, large iron doors were yawning. I thought I had noticed similar ones at the entrance to the tunnel but had abandoned the supposition; what I saw now confirmed my initial hypothesis; the tunnel could be closed as well.

Yes, there were high iron doors, on each side of which were red, green or violet beacons only as large as a fist, burning quite brightly, although they were all orientated in such a fashion that they could only be seen from a certain angle—from the tracks, presumably, and only beyond the bend that they followed. From the top of the slope the beacons were completely invisible.

---

[99] The French language has now informally adopted the recently-coined English meaning of "motorail," referring to trains for transporting road vehicles, but the authors of the present text probably improvised the term, evidently employing it to mean a small motorized railcar.

I was able to advance, still crawling for a hundred meters, and convinced myself that I had before me the entrances to underground factories, from which the sounds of the steel industry reached me.

Then, at a stroke, everything was explained: the ventilation shafts whose quantity had astonished me; the multitude of workers who went every morning toward a mysterious location and returned in the evening; the prohibition on penetrating into the ravine; the quantities of raw materials out of all proportion to the work that was carried out overtly. It was more than enough to convince the most incredulous mind.

But all of that was also hidden, clandestine; all of it, I understood quite clearly, could disappear at the wave of a wand, at an order or a gesture. That order given, that gesture made, the doors of the factory and the tunnel would close; the thousands of workers, abandoning the usual tools for the pick and shovel, could, in less than twenty-four hours, throw the earth of the banks into the ravine and fill the space between the two walls, cut the trees at ground level and flatten everything, at least sufficiently to hide from all eyes, even the most alert, the existence of the clandestine factories, whose work would be temporarily suspended.

On reflection, I acquired the conviction that the railways snaked underground like the Paris Metro, all the way to some city, a river, a port, where other precautions, analogous or different, had been taken—and thus, with the maximum of security, Germany was pursuing its dream of domination by secretly forging the weapons necessary to its realization.

All the surrounding populations, composed of steelworkers, were in possession of that secret, and there was not a single traitor among them. That caused me to shudder.

I had seen enough. In any case, every passing minute might bring a complication and lose me the benefit of my nocturnal expedition. I retraced the route I had followed, took the iron ladder, traversed the electrified wires by the same means and finally found myself, without incident, outside the terrain to which access was prohibited.

Day was about to dawn, but it was still raining. That ensured the almost complete security of my return. I set off across the fields, and, going in through a back door, was at home at the moment that six o'clock chimed.

As I got undressed I saw that I had torn my waxed coat; one of the belt-loops that served to tighten the garment about the waist was missing. That tormented me immeasurably, because I thought it more than likely that it would be found—and then, would I be doomed? I cleaned my shoes carefully. Similarly, I made everything disappear that might reveal my excursion; then I went to bed. By a fortunate chance, my expedition had taken place on a Saturday night, extending into Sunday; that permitted me to take the rest I needed, and also to make a few notes on the little pad that I always carried on my person rather than confiding it to my hiding place—because I wanted to know, first of all, whether that hiding place was absolutely secure...

There, the houses had eyes and ears.

When I woke up, I went over all my memories of the night, and none of the hypotheses I had formed seemed improbable to me. All the equipment disposed on the embarkation platforms had to be mounted on rails; they also had to be easily dismantled or reduced in dimensions, and, departing, would disappear either behind the doors of the tunnel or those of the factory. It was marvelously designed, and from that moment on Germany appeared to me in its entirety as a vast secret arsenal in which the program it had traced was being slowly, patiently but surely elaborated.

At midday, in the restaurant, I saw Karl again.

"Where the devil did you get to yesterday?" he asked.

"Ah, there you go," I said, mysteriously.

"At any rate, you don't go to either of the restaurants I'd identified for you."

"Neither of them, indeed. You were looking for me, then?"

"No, of course not, but as I wanted to have supper my-self, I went to the first, which was full, and then to the second; that's how I can say that I didn't see you there."

I did not reply. We separated, arranging to meet again that evening.

When I got home, the housekeeper said to me: "Give me the loop from your waxed overcoat and I'll sew it back on.

"What loop?" I said, feigning ignorance.

Without a word, the woman brought my waxed topcoat and showed me the damage.

"Why, that's curious," I said, "I must have done it board-ing the train."

The woman made no response; she headed for my bed-room, where she repaired the damage as best she could, and then left. When I was certain that her departure would not in-volve any unexpected return, I went up to my bedroom in my turn and carried out a careful inspection of the room. The waxed coat was extended neatly over a chair, and nothing re-vealed the slightest disquieting fact to my attentive examina-tion.

I had extended a piece of white thread, gummed at both ends, across the little flagstone that I had lifted up in order to hollow out my hiding place; it was intact. That proved to me two things by which I was delighted: the little redoubt had not been discovered, and the housekeeper did not sweep in the corners.

When evening came I got dressed, confided my notes to the hiding-place and went to meet Karl, with my mind singu-larly tranquil and light. As soon as we arrived at the theater I went up to see Mademoiselle d'Antraygues, who received me very amiably and told me that the previous evening, at the exit from the theater, she had been followed by a man who had emerged from the threshold of a nearby building.

"What did he look like?"

"So far as I could tell, he was tall, dressed neatly but without luxury."

"An overcoat with a touch of yellow?"

"Yes, it seemed so to me."

That was Karl. I expected as much.

But one thing troubled me; if the artiste were interrogated—as might be anticipated—what would she say? I asked her.

"Don't worry about that," she replied. "We're leaving immediately after the performance for Warsaw. The receipts are insufficient and the director has decided not to put on the third performance tomorrow. From Warsaw we go to Petrograd, and then to Sweden, Norway and Holland, all in less than a month. Afterwards, we return to France. So, you see, if they take it into their heads to question me, they'll have to decide now."

"How can I thank you for what you've done for me, and what you might still be called on to do?"

"Let it go. I'm helping a compatriot, and that's neither difficult nor, I imagine, dangerous."

"Does one ever know?"

"I'm not afraid. If I'm asked whether I've seen you, I'll naturally say yes; as for the rest, I'm a woman and it's easy for me not to give myself away."

I shook the worthy young woman's hand, and took my leave of her, but I must say that Mademoiselle d'Antraygues could never have been applauded as I applauded her that evening.

I rejoined Karl in the auditorium.

"Are you going home?" he asked.

"Certainly—why wouldn't I?"

On Monday morning, Karl accosted me at the factory gate. "Well, she's gone, your chanteuse. You didn't know?"

"No idea."

"It's bizarre."

"Listen," I said, "I don't know what reason you have for questioning me like this, but I can tell you that the person in question doesn't have to account to me for her actions, and that if she's gone, it's doubtless because her director estimated that a longer presence was unnecessary. Are you satisfied?"

284

By the way that he looked at me, I understood many things that I pretended not to, but I did not give him time to say anything more and went into the factory.

When I arrived at my studio I was summoned to the director's office. That happened too frequently for me to conceive an anxiety regarding the invitation; it probably concerned work in progress.

The director of the group to which I belonged was a fat man whose gaze was veiled completely by a pair of dark lenses. His voice was soft, full of unction. I had a profound aversion for him, without being able to explain why—a repulsion such as one experiences for a large spider or a snake.

As soon as I went in he offered me a chair politely and held out an open box of cigars. I declined the offer, not being a smoker, which he knew very well.

"I had the advantage of seeing you at the theater in Neustadt, where I too went to hear the French artistes. I adore French artistes. Ah, Paris!" He sighed. "I regret, however, that I haven't asked you to come to my office to talk about agreeable things, alas, but only matters of business."

I nodded my head slightly.

"We have, my dear Monsieur, another position to offer you. Yes, you're going now into the chemistry laboratories. The director of those laboratories will tell you what he expects from you."

"But I'm here in the capacity of an engineer, not a chemist," I said.

He raised his arms, as if surprised by my response. "You think so? It's inconceivable, however, that those Messieurs are mistaken on that point. Let's see...let's see...."

He opened a drawer, from which he took a document that I recognized as the duplicate of my contract. He pretended for a full minute to be perusing the document.

"Oh, I thought so—you've made an error, Monsieur Ménestin; I read here that you're engaged in the quality of chemical engineer"—he emphasized the word *chemical*. "So you see, those Messieurs have thought, as is the habit here, that they have bound themselves with you for the exploitation of your intrinsic…if I might put it thus, mercantile…commercial, in sum…value. Yesterday, they needed an engineer, today they need a chemist, and have sent out the call. I ought to tell you, moreover, that an associate of the laboratory has fallen ill and is in default. However, Monsieur, if you refuse, I'll inform the Messieurs."

"I had forgotten the form of my contract, Monsieur; I apologize, and I have no reason to refuse the task that you wish to confide to me."

"Ah! That's perfect, and you see me delighted!" He rubbed his pale hands together. "I'll have you escorted."

He rang; an office-boy appeared and saluted—the military salute was the only one used throughout the exploitation.

"Take Monsieur to the chemistry laboratories, to Herr Hainermann. *Au revoir*, Monsieur Ménestin, until we meet again."

In the chemistry laboratories I was received by Herr Hainermann, a tall, bony fellow with an exceedingly long neck, who wore a gold-rimmed pince-nez. He too had a sly gaze.

"Monsieur," he said, "I'll be brief, for I'm unfamiliar with the diplomatic resources of the language; I'm frank by nature and always get straight to the point I'm pursuing. This is it: France has recently discovered a formula that we need."

"Which one?" I asked.

The man, who must have been nervous and impatient, cracked his knuckles. "I've just told you, Monsieur Ménestin, that France, which has made no mystery of the fact, has discovered a composite substance from which a gas can be extracted that we want to manufacture on a large scale in our establishments."

"I still don't follow you, Monsieur."

"It's a matter of toxic gases with the aid of which your country wants to purge its colonies of the vermin that infest them."

That was very nearly what I had replied to Karl when he had mentioned the discovery in question.

"If, as you say, Monsieur, and as I believe, France has made no mystery of that discovery, nothing is easier than to obtain the formula from her."

"We don't like to ask for it; in any case, she probably wouldn't give it to us in its entirety."

"That's possible."

"Do you know that formula?"

"No."

"You've said, however, that it would be easy to reconstitute."

"Have I said that?"

"Yes. When the reflection was made to you that there was a fortune to be made—which is true—you replied that you wouldn't like to enrich yourself at that price."

"I haven't changed my opinion, but will you permit me to ask you a question in my turn, Monsieur?"

"If you wish."

"Is this an interrogation to which you're subjecting me?"

The man seemed momentarily embarrassed; he sensed that his so-called frankness was not hiding the veritable sense of his questions very well. He avoided replying to my question directly.

"However, Monsieur Ménestin, you have said yourself that France would not think of making a weapon out of these new gases; you would therefore not be betraying your country in giving us a formula that our chemists might equally discover. We need that gas in order to purify, ourselves, unhealthy regions infested with malaria. Besides which, the work would be remunerated in addition to your salary but a substantial bonus."

"I have no bonus to receive, Monsieur, and I repeat to you that I don't know the formula."

"You have, however, said that you could easily reconstitute it."

"I did say that, in fact, and I see that you're perfectly informed of everything I say, but if the doses of the substances that enter into the composition of the gas are easy to find, it doesn't follow that I'll consent to search for them."

"We can, I repeat, find them without you, and your refusal would not be taken kindly."

"I'm sorry about that."

He cracked his knuckles again, and took a step sideways, as if to give himself time to think of better arguments; then he turned toward me again.

"Come on, Monsieur Ménestin, render us this service; we're in rather a hurry to utilize the regions that I mentioned to you, and thus render them appropriate for habitation. On the other hand, we've obtained information, and we know you have a sufficient competence in this matter of gases. Germany has made an honorable peace with France; furthermore, she's ruined, completely ruined—there's nothing more to fear from poor Germany."

For some time I had seen things as they were; it was more necessary than ever to play a tight game. I also knew that I was incapable of being as cunning as the people who surrounded me and that on that terrain I would surely be beaten. I resolved, therefore, to cut the matter short.

"It's possible that the branch of chemistry in question is sufficiently familiar to me," I said, "but to my great regret, that would be all the more reason for me to believe that I am not authorized to carry out the task that you're requesting of me."

"You're going to find yourself in a difficult situation."

"What, pray?"

"Breach of contract. Anticipated forfeit."

"In that case, Monsieur, I'm ready to pay the stipulated penalty."

The man hesitated momentarily, drumming his fingertips on his desk.

"That's your final word?" he said, eventually.

"That's my final word. However, Monsieur, you can write to Paris to request the formula, or for authorization to carry out research here under my supervision."

"We'll see, Monsieur; I'll inform the Council of your refusal."

"You have no further need of my presence here, Monsieur Director?"

"No, Monsieur; you can return to your occupations."

We saluted one another and I returned to my office, where I found myself almost isolated. I remained alone with my thoughts, wondering what would result from that interview and the refusal I had opposed to the strange proposition—a refusal that I did not intend to take back.

Leaving momentarily the plans of a combine harvester, I concluded a letter for Paris—a letter in which I could say a little more about things than usual, a French aviator being in Neustadt for the moment, retained by a slight engine fault; I wanted to ask him to take the letter with him. That way, it would escape the gaze of an occult censor of whose existence I was sure.

An hour later, I received a visit informing me that the management had abandoned its plans, out of respect for my scruples, of which it approved, but that I was designated to make a tour of inspection in a mining district whose yield left something to be desired; I was to depart the next morning for Lignitz.

That tranquilized me completely. Could I believe in so much duplicity? Could I suppose that all those men were planning to deliver me to the most frightful and longest of tortures?

Poor insensate that I was!

I went to Neustadt, gave my letter to the aviator who was kind enough to take charge of it, and went back to the town. I went into a restaurant and went to sit down next to Karl, as if nothing had happened.

There was nothing unusual in his attitude, and we separated in the usual way. Having returned home, I jotted down a few notes on my pad, which I then enclosed in its hiding place.

And, fool that I was, I went to sleep, content to see things turning to my satisfaction and cradling the hope that my annoyances were over.

How long did I sleep? I don't know. I was suddenly woken up by a sentiment of anguish, like that one experiences after a nightmare. However, I had no memory of any dream at all.

I was trying to go back to sleep and to chase away the painful impression, when I became certain that someone was moving in the house.

Footsteps had just paused outside my door.

Footsteps? No, a scarcely perceptible rustle—but I had heard it, though.

Was I the victim of a hallucination, or had I been duped by some noise from outside?

No; I had the intimate conviction of not being mistaken about the cause of my awakening.

I listened carefully, holding my breath.

Nothing was moving any longer; I could no longer hear anything—but I was certain nevertheless that there was someone behind the door.

So convinced was I of the reality of a presence that I could have counted the nocturnal visitor's heartbeats, as I could also have noted the regular sound of his muffled respiration.

In the distance, a clock chimed one.

VI. A Strange Court Martial

I surprised myself, while listening attentively, calculating how much time had passed since that moment I had gone to sleep and my abrupt awakening.

I knew all the sounds that occur in a dormant house: an item of furniture creaking; an insect scratching in a wall; the wind gently shaking a door; the thousand frictions on which the nocturnal silence confers an extraordinary intensity. I had heard them many a time, and it was none of those that had woken me up. Only a mysterious divination had warned me that someone else was there, separated from me by a wall or a door: and the idea that he might appear, from one moment to the next, terrible and murderous, had overexcited my nerves.

I was lying on my bed, my eyes fixed on the door behind which the unknown visitor was standing. An irrational fear was beginning to grip my throat.

My awakening must have made some sound, and, by scarcely perceptible signs, I divined that the man had paused anxiously, listening and hesitating between action and flight.

Gently, I disengaged an arm from the covers, slowly opened the drawer of my night table and took out my automatic pistol. I had the habit of sleeping in pajamas, so I did not have to get dressed. I turned the commutator of the electric light, but there was no current. Then I reached for my pocket torch, and lowered my feet to the floor.

Then I had a very clear perception of a hasty flight. I leapt toward the door, but when I opened it I heard the one downstairs closing. I had not been duped by an illusion, for when I went downstairs in my turn I perceived, by the light of my torch, the damp trace of a human foot.

It was still raining. I went rapidly to the door opening on to the street. It was only on the latch, although I was sure that I had locked it with the key. I opened it and took a step over the threshold. To the right, the street was absolutely deserted, but on turning my head to the left I almost fell over in surprise. Karl was standing before me.

I shone the light of my torch in his face; it was tragically pale.

He took a step backwards. "You're blinding me, damn it!" he exclaimed.

"What are you doing here?" I asked him.

"I'm going home. What about you?"

"I'm running after a burglar. Didn't you see him running away?"

I had the conviction that he had just been in my house, but I did not want to let him know that.

"I haven't seen anyone."

"That's surprising—but it appears that the police are every efficient here; they'll find the burglar. I'll ask them to do so in the morning."

He uttered something like a stifled snigger, and as I was going back in he said: "Good night."

I stood there considering my lock. It had not been forced. When I went back upstairs I examined the footprint on the step; it was still visible. It was that of a big heavy man—like Karl.

When I was lying on my bed again, with the intimate conviction that I would be undisturbed for the rest of the night, I reflected on what had just happened. Two hypotheses immediately presented themselves to my mind: someone had wanted to rob me, or to kill me. Rob me of what? Documents? I had never let it be known that I had any in my possession. Murder? Yes, that was it. I was now almost certain of it, and Karl, whose lividity had struck me, must be certain of it too.

Following the chain of events that had unfolded since the morning, I arrived logically at the conclusion that, having refused the mission they wanted to give me, they had every interest in rendering me mute forever regarding the strange proposition of which I had been the object.

Admitting that, I sensed that my life remained in constant danger and that it was necessary for me to take measures to safeguard it, but I was exhausted by fatigue and put off until later the examination of what I ought to do. With that, I went to sleep.

The next morning, I went to the factory as usual, leaving my notepad in the hiding-place as a precaution. I was wary. At the factory gate a guard I did not know informed we that I was wanted in the administration.

I followed the man. After taking a few steps in the first courtyard I noticed that instead of taking me to the technical director's office, as I expected, the guard was taking a different route.

"Where are you taking me?" I asked.

"To the Administrative Council, as I was ordered."

"I thought I was going to see the technical director."

"No."

"Damn it, friend, you're not very talkative."

"I'm not your friend, and, as you say, I'm not talkative— here, only the imprudent are."

I was on the point of reprimanding his insolence hotly, but I did nothing. I had been wrong to speak to the man; it served as a lesson, and I shut up.

It was the first time I had penetrated into that part of the factory. The man opened a low door, took me up the steps of a short staircase, and then introduced me into a vestibule where there was no other furniture than benches attached to the walls on three faces. One might have taken it for the antechamber of a dispensary.

The man disappeared through a door opposite the one that had let me in and I went, while waiting, to a narrow window that only opened with the aid of a key. That opening, through which a man could not pass, overlooked a courtyard closed by an iron door.

I did not have time to see any more; the man reappeared and, holding the door open, said to me: "This way, if you please."

I obeyed, and went into a strange room. It was painted entirely in dull gray, lit from the left by two windows. On the far wall was a portrait of Wilhelm II in the full dress uniform of a field marshal, and above it, the two-headed eagle. Beneath the portrait there was a long table draped in black cloth; the German heraldic bird was embroidered on its face. Behind the table were three chairs in which the three directors of the factory were sitting, in the uniforms of colonels in the German army. Finally, facing the table, there was a wooden stool, which my guide indicated to me.

I went to the stool but remained standing. My guide, a colossus, stationed himself behind me. I stood there, in the expectation of what was about to happen, determined to defend myself, if necessary, until the end.

The technical director, who was sitting in the center of the table, looked at me silently for a minute, his forearms placed on the table, his eyelids half-closed. One of the assessors got ready to write down what was said.

Finally, the president spoke. "Monsieur Ménestin," he said, in a curt voice. "You have been engaged in the capacity of a chemical engineer in the Neustadt Steelworks, not in the quality of a spy."

Immediately, I saw that I was doomed, but that affirmed me in my resolution to sell my life at the price I estimated its worth, and I held my position, wanting to know, before anything else, to what extent they were informed.

"I don't understand," I said. "Please speak clearly."

"I shall. On the night of Saturday and Sunday last, after having cleverly given the man charged with your surveillance the slip, you penetrated into the forbidden zones and explored the ravine."

I merely made a gesture of vague significance.

"You deny it?"

"I'm waiting for your evidence."

The president allowed something resembling a smile to show on his tight lips; then, very solely, managing his effect, he lifted a piece of paper and uncovered two objects on the table that I recognized immediately. They were the belt-loop from my waxed coat and my notepad.

"This is yours, is it not?"

"It's mine."

"Then you no longer deny it?"

"I never denied it; I was waiting. Yes, I penetrated into the zones that you qualify as forbidden, because it was my duty to do so. You have betrayed the solemn engagements that you signed in order to obtain peace, and in consequence, my country is under threat. That, I had divined, but I needed certainty; I went to search for it at the bottom of the ravine. I acted as any Frenchman would have done in my place, as you would have done yourselves if the roles had been reversed."

"We do not have to judge what we would have done in similar circumstances, but we do have to judge you."

There was a brief pause, in which the president seemed to collect himself. Then, still with the same smile, he continued: "You might believe, Monsieur Ménestin, that we have been punished because we have sinned and, as you say in your country, we have introduced the wolf into the fold by permitting you to draw, from a good source and easily, information that you consider precious."

I made another evasive gesture.

"You would be wrong to remain in that belief, which would be humiliating for us," the president of the tribunal continued. "We knew that, sooner or later you would attempt to discover things that ought to remain secret, and we have, so to speak, led you by the hand in all your hidden steps toward what you wanted to know. It was necessary for our projects, Monsieur Ménestin, that we were guilty in your eyes, in order for us to impose our will upon you, and we have succeeded."

"Less than you think," I said. "A man who exists today cannot cease to exist tomorrow without those who love him becoming anxious and seeking information, without their moving heaven and earth to know what has become of that living man."

The smile straying over the man's thin lips became frightful.

"You're quite wrong, Monsieur Engineer," he went on, "to think that your life is in danger. It is precious to us, as it is to you, and to the fiancée who is waiting for you. We have no designs on your life, and, if you will give us your word of honor—which you will keep, we are convinced—to maintain an absolute silence about your discovery, we are prepared to render you your liberty."

"I have no oath to make."

"Who knows? In any case, that solution, which remains at your discretion, is nevertheless subject to certain conditions. Would you like to know what they are?"

"I don't believe there's any point. What I want to know is what you're going to do with me."

"You'll know when the time comes, Monsieur Ménestin…believe me, you'll know when the time comes. So, Monsieur, since you have guessed it, Germany is preparing the vengeance for her defeat, every day, patiently. You will understand—at least we hope so—that a grain of sand, in the form of a human life, cannot count for very much if it were to hinder the realization of our projects. That is to tell you that is necessary not to constrain us to extremities that we would like to avoid. Yes, Monsieur, your sagacity has seen clearly; Germany is no longer anything but an immense clandestine factory; her seas already shelter redoubtable invisible fleets beneath their surface; her population is no longer anything but an army ready for any sacrifice, and the day is not far off when our ever-glorious eagle will extend its wings again in a sky of battle and revenge."

That heroic and grandiloquent ode was followed by a brief silence; then the man continued: "Now, Monsieur, it follows from all that that your existence would be nothing in our eyes if its suppression could be of any utility to us. If we let you live—weigh my words carefully—it is because we have an interest in doing so, and we would be heart-broken if you mistook our decision for an evidence of interest or sentimental weakness."

I had resolved not to interrupt the man, but anger was making my blood boil, and at that moment I put my hand to the pocket that contained my automatic pistol.

"Leave your pistol tranquil, Monsieur Ménestin, it no longer contains its cartridges," said the president.

There was a minute's heavy silence, which I did not break.

When the colonel understood that I did not want to speak, he continued: "I was saying, Monsieur Ménestin, that we have need of you. We have already alerted you to that fact, yesterday, but you turned a deaf ear. When we hired you, it was in the quality of a chemist rather than an engineer; we knew that you had studied toxic gases, and had even written a paper on those that had been employed in the Great War. Having you with us, it only remained for us to put you in a situation of being unable to refuse to work for us. You are in that situation today, and these are our conditions.

"You are going to take charge in one of our establishments of a laboratory that has been prepared for you. No escape, and no communication with the earth and those who inhabit it will be possible for you. There, you will have to hand all the means necessary to reconstitute gas KBI. As soon as you have given us the true formula—for we know that the gas that France is employing to sanitize its colonies is not the real KBI but a derivative thereof—you will be set free, on the condition of maintaining silence. In any case, we shall monitor your silence.

"If, as reason commands you to do, you obey, your salary will be paid in full, as well as a bonus."

"And if I refuse?"

"In that case..." A menacing gesture completed the sentence.

"What if, as is the truth, I am completely ignorant of the composition of the gas KBI about which you are talking?"

"That would be very unfortunate for you, but we know that you're not unaware of it."

"Then, I repeat, what if I know it, but I refuse to divulge it?"

"We will constrain you to do so."

"Never!"

For the first time, the light veneer of politeness that covered the nature of the colonel cracked and split, and the brute's true face appeared. He struck the table with a violent blow of his fist, his pallor was accentuated, and the muscles of his jaw tautened under the influence of a furious anger.

"We need that formula, do you hear!" he vociferated. "We need it, and we know how to obtain it."

I tried to take possession of the stool before which I was standing, in order, if necessary, to make a weapon of it, but it was riveted to the floor.

One of the assessors—the one who was not acting as a stenographer—spoke in his turn.

Softly and paternally, his hands benevolently crossed over his breast, he spoke with compunction.

"You'll reflect, Monsieur Ménestin, we're convinced of it. We'll give you twenty-four hours, during which, you'll understand, it will be necessary for us to watch over you, but nothing will be done to you, you won't be molested in any fashion. In twenty-four hours, you'll give us a response, which, I hope, will be dictated by your reason."

Oh, the treacherous face, the miserable hypocrite!

The president had calmed down under the unction of his aide's words. He recovered all is dignity and addressed me. "You're going to be taken, Monsieur, to a place where you can do nothing against us or against yourself. In twenty-four hours, you'll let us know your decision."

The guard who was still standing behind me placed his hand on my shoulder. The three judges of the infernal tribunal stood up and left through a little door.

"Follow me," said the guard, in a curt and mocking tone.

I followed him.

VII. Twenty-Four Agonizing Hours

My guard did not say another word during the twenty-five or thirty paces he made me take in a corridor whose extreme narrowness was calculated, it seemed to me.

By means of a secret mechanism, the man opened a small door that I made out vaguely in the gloom, and said: "Go in."

"And if I refuse?" I said, pushed by a sentiment of curiosity rather than revolt.

He did not hesitate; abruptly placing his heavy hands on my shoulders, he shoved me with so much brutality that I stumbled two or three times before being able to recover my equilibrium.

I head the click of a lock behind me. I was a prisoner. I found myself in a cell constituted by walls of a soft, elastic substance, against which—I carried out the experiment—one could make every effort without the slightest chance of breaking the resistance or ripping a hole therein.

In one corner, a bed had been fixed to the wall, devoid of sheets or blankets: a small mattress thrown on a block, all of it made from the same substance, which I was encountering for the first time. In another corner there was a lavatory. Daylight was entering from above, through a round opening sealed with the aid of striated glass and an armature of steel wire. I explored the cell hastily. There was nothing that could serve as a weapon, against oneself or anyone else. It was also in vain that I searched for the door through which I had been thrust into the lair; it was so perfectly dissimulated that it could escape the finest sagacity.

I fell on to the bed; I needed to calm my nerves, which were dolorously overexcited, in order to be able to reflect sanely.

What were they going to do to me?

That was the first question that I posed to my anguish. I did not have many hypotheses to envisage in that regard, alas. The wretches would never release me if I persisted in my refusal. Yield to their orders or die: such was the dilemma.

If I obeyed, I would extract myself from their claws—but was that certain, in spite of their promises? And was it not still my duty, in any case, to refuse what they expected of me, and to oppose to them, no matter what, the force of inertia?

Nothing remained, therefore, but to await events.

The time passed drop by drop; the wan daylight dispensed by the cupola gradually diminished in intensity, and then a strange phenomenon occurred; the walls, the floor and the ceiling became luminous, not by virtue of transparency, but in themselves. They emitted a light analogous to that of phosphorus, and that luminosity increased by reason of the disappearance of the daylight. Finally, it became fixed at a moderate intensity. I understood. Thanks to that light, I was observed, as everyone must have been who had occupied that cell temporarily for some reason. None of my gestures could escape the inquisitive eye that I sensed fixed upon me from the other side of the partition.

A slight noise attracted my attention; it was a very soft rustle, which my ears perceived in the surrounding silence. And I saw a kind of tower appear, pivoting, bringing into the cell a tabletop on which there were two covered plates, a bread roll and a small pitcher. There was a large envelope on top of it, which I opened.

It contained a piece of paper stamped with an eagle, only bearing the words: *Twenty-four hours have been accorded you to make a decision.*

I accepted the nourishment that had been thus presented to me, not wanting to weaken myself.

Is it necessary to say how many plans of escape agitated in my poor head? But no, no resource presented itself to me, not even that of throwing myself, in a moment of rage at a guard, because I understood that none would come.

Finally, day dawned. Another tower had appeared opposite the first, which had disappeared. It bore more nourishment and a second letter. That one informed me that I only had eight hours left to decide. I had decided.

I wrote two lines of protest at the bottom of the letter, which I replaced on the tower. I broke the bread, drank a mouthful of water, and returned to lie down on the bed, no longer wanting to think about anything but the past and the person I had left behind, desperate.

Toward evening, I had the intuition that something was about to happen. I heard a soft hiss, and, indeed, something changed in the ambience of the place where I found myself. It seemed to me that the atmosphere became blue-tinted; furthermore, a slight odor, quite pleasant, floated around me.

Then, by degrees, but fairly rapidly, I sensed myself becoming torpid, my mental faculties weakening.

That happened painlessly; I even felt a kind of relief in feeling myself sink into unconsciousness. I made an attempt to get up, but did not have the strength.

Well, I thought, *it's death by asphyxia*. I was preparing myself for that, when a voice rang out in the cell.

"If you consent to obey, raise your hand or say yes."

Certainly movement as still possible; I could still speak—but a residue of will caused me to remain motionless.

The wretches had counted on my weakness, on the anguish caused by the approach of death, but they had misjudged me. My last thoughts were for the woman I loved. A violet veil extended over my sight; my ears were buzzing; it seemed to me that I was falling indefinitely. Then I lost consciousness.

What happened between the moment when I no longer had a sentiment of things and the one when I recovered consciousness? I don't know, but it seemed to me that I was emerging from a long and very profound sleep when I sensed once again that I was alive. Gradually, the faculties that had abandoned me under the influence of a powerful anesthetic returned, and I had the sensation of lying on a kind of mattress, bound so tightly that any movement of my arms and legs was impossible.

A particular noise had been striking my ears for some time; it was a kind of purr, like that made by large nocturnal insects in flight. Above me extended thick darkness, but cold air was striking my face.

In spite of the frightful dolor that any mental labor provoked in me, I understood—and was confirmed in that idea by the sudden appearance of a star that scintillated momentarily before my eyes—that I was aboard an airplane and that the plane was rising through the night air.

The night might have been well advanced when I recovered the use of my senses. Slowly and by degrees, I saw the darkness brighten. I know not what delight, what sentiment of joy, invaded me at the sight of that nascent light; at a stroke, I felt penetrated by a new strength, a greater courage, and my entire soul, in a sentiment of gratitude and joy, rose up toward the sky, whose limpidity announced the fulgurance of the first blaze of dawn.

Light fleecy clouds were rising toward the zenith; a gold stripe lit up in the orient; everything was vibrant; and the sun, the divine sun, leapt, so to speak, into space.

We were rising very rapidly. I had understood everything. I was a prisoner, tied up, put aboard a fast airplane: a military aircraft, because I could see the stock of a machine-gun at my feet, and under one of the wings, in the course of a swift bank, I glimpsed German colors.

Suddenly, in the confines of the horizon, which my gaze could reach, I saw an object scintillating, on the metallic surface of which the sun ignited dazzling flashes. From then on, my intelligence was focused on the thing in question, which I saw growing rapidly, because it was coming toward us, as we were going toward it.

Its form became distinct. It was an enormous airship, very long, a monstrous biplane of an aspect with which I was not yet familiar. I had the leisure to observe it. Ten or twelve propellers must assure its propulsion; they were sweeping through the air so rapidly that one could not count the number of blades composing them; but they ceased momentarily to be spinning suns and were immobilized; I saw then that they had two sets of blades, differentially geared. As soon as their movement stopped, the giant aircraft began to rise up vertically; I concluded that another ascensional system must exist on board. Then it became motionless and its wings commenced palpitating, like the wings of a bird hovering above its prey. Our airplane headed toward it, in such a fashion as to remain beneath the great metallic bird.

Then the keel appeared; it was singularly powerful, with its two sets of landing gears, one fitted with wheels, the other with floats.

Beneath the keel of the great aerial vessel I saw a trapdoor open, through which a stout steel cable descended supporting magnetic slings. Then a man, whom I had not seen and must have been stationed immediately behind the pilot at my feet, came to my mattress; the latter, I understood by the rapidity of the maneuver, must be fixed to a light metal frame, to which, guided by the aforementioned man, the slings were attached. Then the man whistled stridently.

Immediately, I saw him disappear, as if swallowed by the void beneath.

Tilting my head slightly, I realized what had happened; the airplane that had brought me was letting itself drop, and was now fleeing through the air; it was soon no more than a dot in the ultramarine sky, and then disappeared.

Looking up, I saw that the stout steel cable was drawing me toward the trap-door of the gigantic biplane, which had resumed its progress, albeit very slowly. I went past the keel, full of iron struts and articulated organs: apparatus for lifting the enormous anchors that were asleep at their post, and was absorbed by the trap-door, which closed again. Finally, I was deposited on the airship's metallic deck.

Immediately, two men—two soldiers as silent as shadows—approached, bent down and removed my bonds. They took me under the arms, stood me up and dragged me away.

I did not say a word, convinced of the pointlessness of resistance, but I was biding my time. Sooner or later, the moment would come.

VIII. Aboard the Aerobagne

The men who were supporting me guided me to one of the sides of the airship, to a small door overhanging a kind of gallery, access to which, possible by climbing, was prevented by a mesh of steel wire. On that gallery I perceived a man on sentry duty between two machine-guns mounted on pivots. That was all that I saw on board. My conductors opened the door, pushed me across the threshold and closed it behind me.

The place where I found myself resembled both the cabin of a ship and a cell. A hammock with an inflatable mattress, a table and a lavatory constituted its furniture. All the objects composing it were fashioned from tubes or sheets of aluminum.

The cabin was brightly illuminated by squares of translucent silk and a sheet of a more solid transparent material that must have been set in the floor of the gallery I mentioned. The cell was, like everything on the biplane, constructed of riveted sheets of aluminum; the framework was tubing of the same metal.

I was a prisoner aboard an airship.

They left me there for about an hour. Apart from the purr of the propellers, no sounds reached me. Three strokes were sounded by a bell. Did that indicate the hour, or was it the signal for same maneuver? I had stopped pacing back and forth in my cell; my head was still heavy and prey to a strong desire to sleep. Perhaps they were speculating on that state of lesser resistance. That was credible, for the door opened and a feldwebel appeared on the threshold.

"Come," he said.

He stood aside and saluted. I went out.

I had decided to obey, not to put up any physical resistance to their orders—could I have done otherwise?—but I was still determined not to surrender the formula that they wanted.

I followed the man. The door let out into a place that resembled the fore or aft decks of a first class battleship. The floor was constituted by woven aluminum wire; one could see the void through the inferior structures. The area was dominated to the right and the left by the gallery I mentioned, which ran around the airship. The third side, toward which we were heading, was constituted by a metallic partition pierced by a door and two portholes. Above the door, below the Germanic eagle, was inscribed the word *Kommandant*. On the fourth face, a similar partition with a low door above which I could read *Bagne* and the number 32.

So I was in an aerobagne!

When my guide arrived at the commandant's door, he knocked, spacing out the raps, and then opened it.

I went in.

I immediately found myself confronted by a man who was standing in front of two other officers—a lieutenant and a second lieutenant—and a military physician.

"Approach," said the man I assumed to be in charge—and who was, in fact.

The door closed behind me. I took the two steps necessary to place myself at an appropriate distance from the individual and waited. Fortunately, I was bare-headed, which dispensed me from saluting.

"You are the Frenchman Paul Ménestin?"

"I am Paul Ménestin."

"Good. Know, Monsieur, if you do not know it already, that there is a judicious choice to be made between the actions of life. On earth, you have not judged wisely, and you will suffer the consequences for as long as it is deemed necessary. I have received orders to consider you as a unit lost among the other units that I command, and you will henceforth bear the number seven."

He paused momentarily, as if to await what I had to say; then, before my silence, he added: "I will add that, with an objective that I do not know, I am to put at your disposal, at your request, a chemistry laboratory installed especially for you; you will be taken there every day, and you will meditate your imprudence there if you do not want to do anything else—but remember, Monsieur Frenchman, that at the slightest infraction of discipline you will be treated like the other convicts and subject to the same penalties. Go."

I did not "go" as the brute ordered; I remained standing before him, and I replied: "Whatever fate you and yours reserve for me, Monsieur, a day will come when you are called to account for it."

The commandant made a gesture; the feldwebel, who had remained behind me, as rigid as a pikestaff, took my by the arms and dragged me out.

We had only taken a few steps when the youngest of the officers joined us. "Weber," he said to the feldwebel. "Leave the prisoner on the deck for an hour. He can see everything— but don't let him out of your sight."

Then he turned to me. "You're going to be able to convince yourself that you cannot count on any human aid, and that any escape is completely impossible. It's necessary that you have those two certainties in order not to waste your time nursing stupid hopes."

He turned on his heel and drew away.

Of those I had just seen, that one was the least disagreeable. He was still very young, very blond, with large blue eyes, and a warm resonant voice. He left me the hope that he was not as sly and cruel as his companions, and that one day, perhaps, he would not be devoid of pity.

The feldwebel drew away at a leaden pace to take up a position in a corner, where he waited.

Then, followed at a distance by my companion, I set out to visit the immense vessel. This is what I discovered.

The airship is approximately a hundred or a hundred and ten meters long; its supportive surfaces, of which there are two, are about seventy. At the far rear is the steering apparatus. To either side, port and starboard, near-horizontal ladders lead to posts where two small aircraft, their wings folded, are suspended from the sides of the monster, like launches aboard a transatlantic liner. To judge by their dimensions, they are both reserved for the officers, and only accessible, given the point of departure of the ladders, to the officers. They are aerial lifeboats.

Other similar ladders lead to the propellers, and almost half way along each of the wings. In the bow and around the cockpit, two wireless telegraph installations are installed, along with a crane and lifting-tackle.

The aircraft is powered by electricity, without the aid of internal combustion engines. It employs, I subsequently learned, the recently-discovered ABK accumulators; the electrical energy stored aboard is considerable, and exceptionally long-lasting. Those accumulators only require recharging once every two or three months, they retain so much force.

Six tractional and propulsive helices and two further ascensional helices, all differential, ensure stability and progress, under normal circumstances, at a rate of twenty kilometers an hour.

As I have said, the aircraft is circled by an elevated round-path with machine-gun posts. I conclude in consequence that the number of warders must be relatively small.

The aerial vessel is subdivided into five compartments or sections. The first, in the bow, encloses the propulsive apparatus, the lodging of the mechanics and the men on watch. Immediately afterwards, but separated from the first section by a gap in the hull and linked to it by a bridge, is the command post, the dining room, the office and the bedrooms; then the deck or platform on to which my cabin, a firmer solitary confinement chamber opens; and finally, the largest of the sections, the gehenna, the bagne.

How many people are suffering therein? I've never been able to obtain a precise number. They sleep in hammocks, are dressed in gray, and live like animals.

Add, in order to have a complete vision of the giant aircraft, that the hull and superstructure appear in a tangle of guy-ropes, nets and lifting-gear, like a city enveloped by an immense spider-web.

That is where I was to live henceforth. That is where I have lived for eighteen months.

The hour that had been granted to me must have elapsed, for my guard took me back to my cell. I saw that someone had taken advantage of my absence in order to stick a piece of paper on one wall, I which I read the following in beautiful Gothic script:

ORDERS

1. The most absolute silence is imposed on everyone.
2. Obedience must be passive.
3. All offenses will lead to punishment that no one can escape.

Punishments

1. Solitary confinement; privation of nourishment.
2. Flogging.
3. Suspension in the void by the hands, for a duration in proportion to the offense committed.
4. Suspension and maintenance in front of a moving propeller, for a duration in proportion to the offense committed.
5. Perpetual sequestration in the strait box.

I learned subsequently that the "strait box" in question was situated under the hull In the midst of the landing gear. A hammock with a hole above it through which nourishment could be thrown, and a mobile plank to dispose of the body when death ensued: that was what they had dared to imagine for a human being. The man thus punished as permanently enclosed in that box, which was more reminiscent of a coffin than a habitable structure, even for a convict.

I had just sat down, in a state of discouragement and dolor that is easily imaginable, when my attention as attracted by a soft, rhythmic sound, like that produced by a continuous friction on the metallic floor. The feldwebel came to open my cell, as ordered.

The convicts! All clad in iron-gray trousers and jacket, barefoot, placed one behind another three abreast, were slowly circling the deck. It was the exercise period.

They were all similar. The same stigmata of misery and despair had fashioned their features, hollowed out their eyes, blanched their faces. They all had the same gaze of fearful beasts, eternally tracked: a bleak, lifeless gaze; they all seemed to have lost the faculty of thinking and acting other than by instinct, innate or developed under the blows of an iron discipline.

Nameless creatures, whose crimes almost disappeared under the rigor of punishment: one could not see them without being struck by terror.

A brutal blast of a whistle stopped them. They made an about-turn and stood still. A second blast of the whistle made them sit down on the floor; then, each of them took an aluminum bowl out of his jacket and waited. Four more convicts appeared then, carrying a large receptacle containing a thick brown substance, a kind of soup made from purely chemical elements. Each convict received two ladlefuls of the mixture and a biscuit. After they had absorbed that pittance, two other convicts, bearers of a large leather bottle, distributed water.

That was all.

A third blast of the whistle brought the members of the frightful taciturn crowd to their feet, and they resumed their slow movement. For half an hour they circled, heads down, arms dangling, without exchanging a glance; then a signal caused the door through which they had come to open, through which they disappeared.

Dante had not imagined anything more terrible.

How long did I remain without being able to write, and what ruse was it necessary to employ for me to succeed in doing so?

For months I remained confined to my cell, my sole distraction being the exercise that I was obliged to take; then, one morning, the feldwebel came to find me and took me to see the commandant.

The latter was waiting for me standing up; he was accompanied by the junior officer.

"Monsieur," he said to me, "Although the relations that have been able to exist between us have necessarily been devoid of cordiality, I am going to ask something of you that I cannot impose on you."

"Why not call me *Seven*," I asked him, "since that is my number?"

He uttered a snigger in which the anger was palpable. That was what I was seeking.

"You can impose an order on me—it remains to be seen whether I shall obey it—but do you think you have the right to ask me for a service? Don't you find that humiliating for yourself?"

I saw him go white with rage; he raised his closed fist over the frail table that supported bottles and glasses, but the fist did not come down.

The second lieutenant, who never left the commandant's side, made a brief salute and intervened.

"Monsieur," he said to me. "Our engineer—or, rather, our chief mechanic—has just been struck by a congestion. The medical officer is with him. When he was struck down, he was examining the apparatus of starboard propeller number two, immobilized for three hours, which obliges us to proceed with an uneven number of propellers. The vessel cannot maintain that progress easily and is suffering considerable fatigue. If you have no concern for the lives of the warders and officers, we have human debris here that perhaps interest you more. Those lives, Monsieur, might be threatened at any moment, because if the wind rises, it will be necessary to lighten the vessel...to *dispose of ballast*, you understand? We're too far from any relay to hope to be able to reach one without resorting to that measure. You're an engineer..."

"You ought to be one too," I told him.

"I'm not; it's a lacuna in our professional education."

"The cabin has no mechanic?" I said.

"Yes, but he's being punished; he's to be flogged this evening. It's his negligence that caused the damage."

"All right," I said. "I consent...for the sake of the human debris, of which I am one at present. Lead the way—I'll try to help you."

"Follow me," he said.

The commandant had slumped on to a divan and was fuming, with a malevolent smile.

IX. A Hellish Existence

The second lieutenant led me to starboard cabin number two, and, for the first time, I set foot on the near-horizontal ladder that led to the engine-rooms and the wings.

It was frightful!

As soon as one had surpassed the hull one found oneself with the clutching void below: a gulf of three of four thousand meters in which the clouds were floating. A terrible vertigo made me dizzy and caused my limbs of vacillate. However, I had the courage to overcome any weakness, and I followed the officer as deliberately as if we had both been on the ground.

When we were in propeller chamber number two, the two guards stood aside and, leaning over the machine, I examined it. The damage was serious; the entire apparatus had jammed. I had to take it apart completely. I studied the pieces one by one; the second lieutenant looked at them with me.

As I have said, he was not absolutely antipathetic to me, by reason of his youth.

When my examination had concluded I showed him the cause of the damage and indicated what it was necessary to do. While I spoke he took rapid notes. When I had finished he said: "Thank you, Monsieur."

I went out of the propeller chamber first and, without bothering to see whether I was being followed, went back to the hull. The second lieutenant stopped me with a gesture and then, going on ahead, he took me to the commandant's bridge and paused.

"Are you still intent on opposing the same refusal to the proposition made to you?" he said.

"Still."

"But you're placed in a situation of *force majeure*, which could silence many of your scruples, and don't forget that those here and those down below are incapable of pity."

"I'm not asking for any from anyone."

"You're wrong, Monsieur Ménestin. No one can say that he's scornful of pity; you'll realize that when you know this hell better."

"What forces you to live in it, Monsieur? The profession of jailer is a wretched one for a man of your age."

He stared at me, his eyelids lowered, and then he replied: "You're not the only one to have a secret, and perhaps mine is as respectable as yours."

I made an evasive gesture. He was about to draw away.

"Pardon me," I said. "It appears that a laboratory has been put at my disposal. May I see it...and work in it?"

"On what is asked of you?"

"On anything except that."

He reflected momentarily.

"We'll see, Monsieur," he said. "I'll mention it; we'll need to take orders from below. But it seems to me that it's not impossible. We'll add your request to the radiogram that we send to the ground tonight; you'll have your response to-morrow."

He saluted me with a brief movement of the head and in-dicated another ladder, which led to the deck.

I went back to my cell—but at five o'clock the feldwebel brought me out to witness a barbaric spectacle that the second lieutenant had announced to me.

The convicts were kneeling in three rows. Their eyes, this time, were lit up by a gleam of ferocious curiosity; a kind of joy was legible in those gazes of mastered beasts. The wretches found in the scene that was about to unfold before them a means of emerging, for an all-too-brief moment, from the dismal state of mental immobility in which they were maintained by the silence and the uniformity of their existence as the damned. It was an event that tickled their evil instincts.

On the round-paths and in the blockhouses I have mentioned, the guards stood with their electric rifles, and the machine-gunners were at their posts, with their weapons aimed at the silent crowd. The officers were standing on the bridge. Only the noise of the propellers, a soft purr, was perceptible.

The guilty man appeared, his torso bare and his mouth gagged. He was thrown to his knees. One of the guards approached and placed himself half a pace behind him to the left. The man was armed with a whip with three leather thongs.

Impassively, the commandant raised his white-gloved hand.

The whip whirled through the air and fell, whistling. The first blow scarcely made the man quiver. All the convicts, craning their necks, watched avidly. Thirty times the whip struck the back of the wretched human rag. The flesh turned blue, swelled up, then burst. At the tenth blow it split, and the blood began to flow; the man was agitated by a great shudder. At the twentieth blow he fell unconscious and received the last ten strokes of the flogging thus.

The motionless officers watched the torture; only the second lieutenant had turned his head away, and his gaze was lost in the sky; I counted it to his credit that he avoided an ignoble spectacle that I only glimpsed intermittently myself.

The man was carried away; then the convicts returned to their abode, having resumed their bleak expressions.

Yesterday's execution has had consequences that were to bring other punishments in its train. It appears that incoherent words traced in blood have been found on one of the metallic walls of the prison:

To die! To see the earth again ! Trees! The odor of soil! Death! Death! Death!

The investigation has demonstrated that a convict has dipped his finger in the blood that the tortured man shed and traced that inscription in the dark, which summarizes all his dolors and all his hopes.

"If the investigation doesn't discover the guilty party," the feldwebel told me, when he reported the incident to me, "the entire camp will be punished."

I had believed that, at least during the night, braving the written prohibitions, the convicts could talk to one another in low voices, exchanging a few words, hearing their voices, or at least that of their neighbor. In fact, that is impossible; each convict is isolated in a closed bed, a kind of crate that resembles a coffin, and is sealed; the latticework floor supports a leather mattress inflated with air.

Two guards patrol the central corridor, and as soon as they perceive raps or scratchings that might constitute a kind of secret language, they intervene, in such a fashion that the communication ceases immediately.

The convict is alone, without ever being able to exchange a thought, a hope or a word with one of his companions in ignominy. Can one imagine such a torture?

I've learned today that it is the second of April; I must have been here about two months.

The laboratory installed in the doctor's consultation cell has finally been opened to me, and I've been given the feldwebel as a watchman. Although small, the laboratory is fairly complete, and at least I can write there without awakening the suspicions of the junior officer. All the materials have been brought at night by airplane, as I was myself.

The feldwebel has seen me stuffing pieces of paper into an earthenware retort, but he imagines that I'm putting formulae on them, and that in consequence, they will only have to search that retort to collect the precious documents. He's a Pomeranian who doesn't know how to read; he's enormously stupid and as chatty as a magpie. He has so few opportunities to spout his stupidities that he catches up when he's alone with me; it's therefore easy for me to learn many things about this strange world I inhabit.

When I expressed astonishment one day at seeing him at his age—between fifty and fifty-four—still in the army, he made this strange response:

"In the special army that I'm in, age has nothing to do with it; it's the point of departure that's everything. Some are in it for five years, some for two, the convicts forever."

"Do you know why I'm here?" I asked him.

"No, but your case is serious. What did you do? Me, I stole from the regimental treasury."

Thus, I've been led to conclude—and the conclusion has been verified since—that all the creatures living on aerobagne 32 are expiating a sin, some falling under the force of military law, others under the rigors of the penal code.

The convicts are guarded by prisoners who are purging a penance and pursuing their rehabilitation; that is always accorded to them if they fulfill the duties of their functions resolutely.

Lieutenant Eitel has become almost familiar with me; he comes to keep me company frequently. It's thanks to him that I've been able to obtain the sulfuric acid and certain ingredients that I need to attain a goal that I'm secretly pursuing.

The fellow is strange: a bizarre composite of sensibility and egotism. He is indifferent to the misery that surrounds him, but his own, to which he believes he is submitting, appears to him to be the only great and respectable one. He has, however, often deigned to sympathize with mine.

Like the man who traced the bloody inscription, he regrets his homeland—not Germany, but the ground, wherever it might be. For all these exiles in the sky, the earth is their fatherland!

"Oh, to see the ground again," he said to me this morning, "to smell the good odor of trees and freshly-opened furrows, to hear running water! When I go back down, Monsieur Ménestin, it seems to me that my first concern will be to throw myself face down to embrace and kiss the ground."

"Like you," I replied, "I experience that sentiment. I know a corner of my country where the sea murmurs in the sonorous cup of a little inlet; all around, the landscape extends, blond with wheat or brown when the soil is newly plowed, planted with apple trees with heavy fruit…it's toward that corner that my memory most frequently wanders…"

He quit me with his soul full of melancholy; he's still a child.

Yesterday, he told me that I was free to go anywhere on the airship, except for the prison, in the strict sense, and offered me his hand. I could do otherwise than take it; he shook mine for a long time, with an insistence that embarrassed me

From Weber I've learned that the officers are not without anxiety; the convicts are becoming restive, and two are to be punished tomorrow. They've spoken—fifty lashes to punish that sin! Weber also said—the amity that the second lieutenant seems to have for me has loosened his tongue singularly—that the convicts are seized by a kind of contagious folly annually. They start to utter cries, all talking at the same time. Nothing can stop them. It's necessary then, he added, to have recourse to powerful means. What powerful means does he mean? That frightens me.

My relationship with the commandant has remained the same; however, he comes to the laboratory sometimes, in passing, always to ask me whether I'm working on my liberation. One day he seemed alarmed by the quantity of blank paper that I employ, without him knowing precisely how, and he informed me that, from now on, the sheets will be rationed and I'll have to justify their usage.

Yesterday evening. I had a conversation with Second Lieutenant Eitel that it's necessary to report. I was standing on the bridge; the weather was clear and I was contemplating the constellations. Thousands of stars were scintillating; we had the sensation of flying among tremulous gleams. Eitel came to join me.

That evening, his soul was inclined to reverie by the sublime spectacle of the nocturnal sky, and our conversation took a rather intimate tone. I recited a few of the French verses I knew for him, and he started singing, very quietly, Schumann and Schubert. The purr of the propellers sustained that singing, which didn't surpass the bridge.

Under the powerful charm exerted by that splendid hour, I sensed that Eitel and I were united by profound affinities, and I couldn't help telling him so.

"I'd like to be your friend," he replied, "and my friendship for you would astonish you, if you knew its extent."

I was embarrassed by that statement, as I had been by his handshake; he sensed it.

"Perhaps, one day," he went on, "you'll understand why I've just let you glimpse a little of my soul, Monsieur Ménestin, and then everything will be explained to you; but for now, tell yourself, for you might doubt it by virtue of what you see here, that I do have a heart beneath my soldier's uniform, and that that heart can suffer, as all hearts suffer."

"Why do you stay here?"

He kept silent for a minute; then, seemingly making a decision, he said, in a low voice: "The Kommandant is my father..."

Then—I don't know whether I was obeying some secret and despicable desire to make the man suffer or whether I didn't have time to reflect—I said: "Your father! But I've been told that all the people living here were subjected to a punishment!"

I saw him shudder and go pale; to hide his distress, he turned up the collar of his greatcoat.

"Yes," he said, after a pause, during which he seemed to be sustaining an internal struggle. "Yes, my father is subject to one, like everyone here. My father committed, as an officer...an unworthy action. He's expiating it by five years in the bagne, but while conserving his rank. He's already done two years, the first alone, the second with me. I came voluntarily, to try to prevent him from drinking and degrading himself. Thanks to my presence, he's mastered his vice somewhat."

I remained mute with confusion. In spite of the hatred that I had amassed against everything German, the second lieutenant's conduct was so generous that I couldn't help feeling sorry for him.

"I didn't want to hurt you," I said, "or to make you suffer."

"I have more to mourn than you think, Monsieur Ménestin. Do you remember that I told you that no one has the right to scorn pity? My pride was already dead, and I no longer ask for anything but commiseration."

"You have all of mine."

"Perhaps I'll need it one day. Promise me that when that day comes, it won't be in vain that I hold out my hands to you."

There was only one response I could make. I made him that promise.

X. The Investigation at Neustadt: A Camouflaged Landscape

Escander and Mathilde, whom we left in mid-air, landed at Neustadt after the expected interval. Instead of setting down at the official landing-ground, the airplane descended very gently in a field on the edge of the city, that being what Alexis had decided to do.

Alexis, the pilot of airplane 21, was not an ordinary man. Born in Paris, the middle of a faubourg, he retained the spirit and something of the mores of that faubourg. Beneath the veneer of education that covered his true nature to some degree, the soul of a street-urchin still showed through. Accomplished in all sports, including English boxing, of which he had a thorough knowledge and practiced for pleasure; he was also a champion swimmer, jumper and foot-racer. In addition, he was endowed with an imperturbable self-composure, fearing nothing and ready for anything, and a facile tongue, which brought delight of the different societies to which he belonged. Twice before, he had accompanied Escander on long-range missions; he took a great deal of pride in that, and had vowed an unalterable amity to the *Monde* reporter. Small but well-

proportioned, the proprietor of a shock of hair with no defina-
ble color but coiffed in an aviator's helmet, with a perpetual
smile: such was Alexis.

"Why are we setting down here?" Escander asked.

"To show what can be done, Boss. These people take us
for bumpkins, with their landing-field as big as the Sahara. It
makes me dizzy."

"We'll get arrested."

"No fear, Boss—I'll put them to sleep."

In fact, a policeman ran forward as soon as the plane
touched down, and started jabbering something no one understood."

Alexis, steady on his feet, only responded with the few
German words that he knew. Those words, in fact, he knew in
almost all the languages of the world: "Engine trouble...fuel...oil...eat...drink..."

"Halt!" he said to the agent. "And Madame Boche and
the little Boches? All well? Go on, too bad. Halt...engine
trouble, I tell you. Outside your routine, understand? Be good.
Open up, dear chap!"

Escander came to the assistance of the two interlocutors;
in bad, but sufficiently comprehensible German, he explained
that engine trouble had forced the airplane to land

The policeman contented himself with taking down the
international identification number of the apparatus and went
away.

Immediately, Alexis, who had started rummaging in his
engine for form's sake, took to the air again, and by means of
a savant maneuver, came down on the landing-ground.

Escander and Matilde had themselves taken to a hotel,
where they registered as Monsieur Escander, commercial traveler, and his cousin.

The great *Monde* reporter had explained to the young
woman the program he intended to follow. He had read Paul
Ménestin's manuscript in its entirety, and had been able to
draw up a plan of attack.

"My intention," said the reporter, "is first of all to have a look around, to see things that, knowing the avowed objective of our visit, they might have an interest in hiding from us. In that regard, you'll be very useful to me. Our presence is already known, without a doubt, but that's of little importance, since no one knows the reason for our arrival. It's necessary not to let them know that reason until the last moment.

"They'll monitor us, have us followed, keep us under surveillance. Until the moment when they know what's going on, let's give them the impression, so far as we can, of people who are only concerned with one thing: collecting information about the death of someone dear to us."

"We'll act as you desire, cousin; I don't want to hinder you in any way, even by a personal opinion that might trouble yours. I merely count on being useful to you by virtue of my feminine intuition. Women have delicate senses; they notice the little things, and understand them, when they want to."

Mathilde Régis was no longer the plaintive young woman who, in Paris, had been overwhelmed by chagrin. She had been suddenly transformed by the crack of the whip that had given her hope, and now resolute, she was no longer showing anything but the grace of her smile and the brightness of her gaze.

"Good," said Escander. "We understand one another, I'm certain. Now, if you have no objection, we'll take a little walk in the country; perhaps it will tell us something."

That remark was overheard in part by the waiter that was prowling around the table where the two young people were having a light meal. He immediately presented himself.

"If Monzieur an Matame are making an exurzion in the guntry, zere is a garage nearpy, a ferry cood garage, ferry cood vehigles, ferry cood drivers."

"If everything is as good as that," said the reporter, "show us the way."

The young woman was ready in a minute.

On the threshold of the hotel they found Alexis smoking a cigarette.

"The airplane?" Escander asked.

"In a garage."

"You've left it alone?"

"The door's locked. There's only one, and I have the key in my pocket."

Escander could not help smiling at Alexis, who made himself at home everywhere. The waiter gave them directions to the garage and the reporter gave him a tip.

At the garage the three companions found an obsequious individual; it happened, as if by chance, that he spoke French. The reporter explained to him that they wanted to undertake an excursion, and wanted a car that he would drive himself. The man, without ceasing to execute little bows, told him that he was absolutely heart-broken, but that it was absolutely impossible for him to satisfy that desire, because police regulations did not permit automobiles without chauffeurs to be hired to foreigners.

"But at least," the reporter asked, a trifle sarcastically, "those chauffeurs take you where you want to go?"

"Why not, Monsieur?"

"Who knows? Perhaps the police regulations impose itineraries on tourists."

The garage proprietor did not reply.

"Prepare me a vehicle with a docile chauffeur—I'm in a hurry. Here's the deposit."

The vehicle was ready in less than five minutes

"Will you permit me to go with you, Boss?" asked Alexis.

"If you're certain that the airplane isn't at risk."

"No more so than the apple of my eye."

"Come, then."

"Shove over a little, clumsy," said Alexis to the chauffeur, and, in spite of the latter's ill-will, installed himself comfortably in the front seat. The vehicle set off toward the Steelworks, which Escander had designated as the objective of the trip.

The bleak silhouette of the buildings stood out against a gray sky. Soon, they were six feet from the walls devoid of openings, surpassed by tall chimneys slowly pushing a heavy and dense smoke into the atmosphere.

"It's frightful," said Mathilde. "It's more like a prison than a factory."

"Perhaps it's both," said the reporter."

"You're visiting?" asked the chauffeur, turning round.

"On the way back," said Escander. "Drive on."

"Where?" asked the chauffeur. "There's no more road."

"What's that?" demanded Alexis, indignantly.

"A path that ends in the fields."

"*Into paths full of drunkenness,/Let's go together at a slow pace...!*" sang Alexis, pretending to seize the chauffeur around the waist.[100]

"What?" said Escander.

A heavy silence fell in the vehicle; the two young people looked at one another anxiously.

"But there are trees and hills over there," said the reporter. "Can't one go as far as that?"

"It's of no interest," said the chauffeur, leaning on is steering-wheel."

"I'd like to go there, though."

"What if I damage the car?"

"I'll pay."

"But..."

"Come on," said Alexis, pushing the chauffeur away. "I'll drive the old banger like a demoiselle. Where do you want to go, Boss?"

The chauffeur, seeing that he was not going to have the last word, gave in. "At your orders," he said.

---

[100] The song quoted is one that Maurice Rollinat used to sing in Le Chat Noir in the 1880s, when Laumann used to hang out there.

He started his vehicle moving again, but carefully steered it toward the deepest potholes and the most chaotic places that appeared in front of him.

Escander leaned toward he young woman, and spoke to her in a whisper.

"I'm singularly troubled," he said. "We've passed the Steelworks, undoubtedly. Now, according to your fiancé's manuscript, the railway goes along the northern edge of the buildings, and then heads into the country, toward a ravine. That railway no longer exists, if it ever did."

"However…," said the young woman, unable to admit that Paul had not told he exact truth.

"I understand your doubt," the reporter continued. "You wouldn't be a woman, or a woman in love, if you didn't have an absolute confidence in what your fiancé wrote, but..."

The chauffeur braked abruptly. "Impossible to go any further," he said.

"Perhaps we're mistaken," Escander murmured in the young woman's ear. Aloud, he said to the chauffeur: "Let's go back."

Mathilde's hand descended on Escander's sleeve, and in a rapid voice, quietly enough for the chauffeur not to overhear: "No, not yet, I beg you. Let's go as far as the trees; if the vehicle can't go any further, let's go on foot."

Escander hesitated, but the young woman's tone was so imperious and imploring, at the same time, that he said abruptly. "As you wish. Chauffeur, wait for us. Alexis, come!"

Then, helping the young woman down, he took her by the arm and drew her away swiftly.

Alexis followed, without understanding—which caused him to grumble a little.

The trio went past the first curtain of trees. It was a plantation of pines, not very dense; then there was another stand, much thicker. Between the two plantations the terrain dipped slightly.

Escander stopped; he rummaged in his pocket and took out a piece of paper. "This is an approximate map I drew up according to the data in the manuscript," he said. These are the buildings that we've passed, over there. The track ought to bend here, and the ravine should be here or here...

"According to the estimates I've made of the car's speed, we're five or six kilometers from the Steelworks, and thus at the very location of the ravine, but look—there are no ventilation shafts, any more than a railway or a ravine."

Alexis had listed to the reporter's explanations without saying anything.

"It's frightful," said the young woman. "Perhaps we've made an error—perhaps there are other steelworks in the vicinity?"

"In any case," said Escander, "let's not leave the place without making a thorough examination. Let's search, auscultate the ground, interrogate the stones. You've heard and understood, Alexis? We're looking for a ravine. You go that way, Mademoiselle; I'll go this way, and you go on ahead, Alexis. Can that damned chauffeur see us?"

"No, Boss—there's a bend in the road. No danger from that direction."

"Ah!" said Mathilde. "We're here!" Her voice took on a joyful tone. "Haven't you told me that Paul was watched when he came here to rest?"

"Yes," said Escander, "by a man in a small building."

"There it is."

In fact, less than fifty meters away, there was a little cottage, like the ones that shelter the employees of railway companies—but it appeared to be deserted; the shutters of the two windows were closed, and from a distance it seemed completely abandoned.

XI. The Place Where the Ravine Was Excavated

It was, in fact, to a veritable auscultation of the ground that, for his part, the reporter devoted himself, searching for an indication or a vestige from which he could draw a conclusion, but he discovered nothing that could really put his sagacity on the alert. With the aid of his "pocket detective," however, he took various photographs to note movements of the terrain and also, in order to prove, if necessary, that the manuscript might be held to be suspect—a sentiment that as beginning to impose itself upon him again.

He looked for the young woman, and found her some distance away with Alexis, making signals for him to come and join them. As soon as he saw the gleam in her eyes, Escander understood that she had discovered something.

"Look!" said Mathilde, when he had joined her—and she pointed with her gloved finger at a clump of leaves, withered but still green, partly buried in the soil, which appeared to have been trodden down.

"Well?" said Escander.

"Those dying leaves," said the young woman, whose eyes were shining with a profound joy "are last summer's, and they're the leaves of a tree already old, as you can see by their tissue and their dimensions. Furthermore, they're still on their branch."

"I confess that I don't understand," said the reporter.

"I'm saying that they're still on their branch; now, branches are attached to a trunk; that trunk is underground— the tree is buried.

"Great gods!" exclaimed Alexis, falling to his knees and beginning to dig in the ground. Escander did likewise, and the two men worked with so much energy that the young woman, glad to have convinced them, burst out laughing. Escander turned his head toward her, raising his head, and a broad smile illuminated his face, ordinarily not very cheerful.

"It's marvelous! Truly marvelous!" exclaimed Alexis, throwing handfuls of earth around.

The hole that they had just hollowed out very easily, so friable was the earth, had laid bare the extremity of the branch of an ash tree as thick as a finger. It was in vain that the two men tugged on it from above to detach it from the soil; it would have given way if it had only been plunged into the ground, accidentally or deliberately, but they could not break it. Escander stood up, while Alexis, who had taken a large knife from his pocket, made the hole deeper.

"It's evidence itself," said Escander to the young woman, "and you're worthier than I am to be the great reporter of *Le Monde*; I'm nothing but a donkey compared with the penetration of your intelligence. That branch, as you say, is attached to a trunk, and that trunk is entirely buried in the soil."

Alexis stood up; he had cut the branch fifty centimeters from its extremity, and the branch was still ornamented by two small clumps of leaves, still alive. Thus, Escander observed, their burial was recent.

"We're witnesses," said the young man, presenting the branch to the young woman. "Here, Mademoiselle, this branch belongs to you, and never, I believe, has a more beautiful bouquet been offered."

More emotional than she wanted to appear, Mathilde held her hand out to the reporter. Alexis wiped his knife, without saying anything.

"What they've done is formidable," the reporter said, "and it's easy to comprehend. As soon as *Le Monde* signaled the existence of Ménestin's manuscript, these people sensed the danger and they've taken their precautions. Yes, Mademoiselle, thanks to you, and you alone, your faith, we've just had the revelation that the terrible danger identified by your fiancé really exists, and what they've done shows its extent. For the moment, let's keep searching. One proof leads to another; let's turn over the soil with our fingernails, if it's necessary to carry out the task. We need more and better!"

Neither the young woman nor Alexis had any need to be encouraged, Mademoiselle Régis sensed that she had just grasped the thread that might lead, first to the truth, and after that to the man she loved—and even if she had to march toward the cruelest of certainties, she was more resolute than ever to go to the end of her mission with the same firm heart.

As for Alexis, he had too much taste for adventure in his blood not to be delighted.

As before, the three young people each went in a different direction, in quest of further discoveries. They came together again along a depression with a gentle slope and were about to climb the opposite slope of the depression when Escander, who was leaning on his cane, nearly fell over. Abruptly devoid of solid support, the cane had just sunk into the soil by twenty or thirty centimeters, and then stopped as it collided with a hard object.

On any other occasion, no one would have been troubled by such an incident, but in the present circumstances, everything was of interest. On his knees again, Alexis attacked the soil energetically with his hands. Escander, and even Mathilde, joined him. Feverishly, their hands dug, throwing back the earth. A joyful exclamation from Alexis brought the other two to their feet.

"Ah! Damned Boche! They like iron so much they sow bolts, and this one has already taken root."

While speaking he showed his two companions the head of a bolt, perfectly visible at the bottom of the hole. In a matter of minutes the two men cleared out the bottom of the hole made by Alexis, and a metallic plate appeared in the form of an elongated hexagon, riveted to another piece of metal by fifteen large bolts.

Escander could not suppress a cry of triumph. "The bridge!" he exclaimed. "It's the bridge! If we could keep digging, we could lay the whole thing bare. Oh, the bandits! At the first alert they've filled in the ravine. Bu don't worry—we have them!"

Alexis listened open-mouthed. As for Mathilde, radiant, she was hanging on the reporter's lips.

"Yes, certainly," the later continued, his fever not yet calmed down. "Oh, certainly—we're going to unmask them and we'll clip the wings of the two-headed raptor that serves as their emblem."

Escander took four photographs of the excavation and the bolted plate.

"Alexis," he said, afterward, "fill that in."

"That's a pity," said Alexis, already at work, "Because it really is work well done."

They returned to the chauffeur, who enveloped them with a gaze charged with suspicion.

"Nice countryside," said Alexis, resuming his place in the automobile. "One could spend one's life here."

But Escander wanted to have the last word. "Tell me, chauffeur, this place isn't bad, but it but seems better still on the other side of the ravine?"

"What ravine?"

"The ravine."

"There is no ravine—at least, I don't know of one."

"Perhaps you're not a native?"

"I was born here."

"That's curious. We have, however, been told that there's a pretty ravine near here."

"You've been misled. There is no ravine; there never has been."

"Take us back to town then," said Mathilde, "to number eight Wilhelmstrasse."

That was the address where Paul Ménestin had lodged.

The chauffeur started the vehicle. The two young people looked at one another with evident satisfaction. They had no need to speak to translate the sentiment of joy that gripped both of them. Had they not, in fact, attained, and even surpassed, the objective they wanted to achieve?

When the vehicle stopped it was the young woman who got out first. By virtue of a sentiment of exquisite delicacy, Escander allowed her to go into the house on her own, to which she had come as if to a pious pilgrimage.

A correctly-dressed old woman presented herself; sly and hypocritical, she waited. Mathilde explained the object of her visit. The old woman then hastened to be obliging, offering a seat and refreshments, which were refused; but she declared that it was absolutely impossible for her to give any information whatsoever, as she had only been in the house for three months and came from far away. As for the woman who had served as housekeeper to the former tenant she was dead, poor thing.

Mathilde was shown the bedroom and the small drawing room; nothing there reminded her of the man she loved.

The two young people went to the police, where they wanted to know what they could be told about Paul Ménestin. A functionary declared that he could not tell them anything except that: "One Saturday morning, Monsieur Ménestin went to the factory, as he did every morning, but he was not seen there, and did not reappear. A letter was found in his home in which he declared his intention to end his life; a search was begun then, but in spite of the zeal deployed, had no result."

At the factories, they were given an absolutely identical response. As for Karl, the Pole, he had returned to Warsaw.

"No matter!" said Escander. "One thing remains: Ménestin is alive, imprisoned, as he says, aboard one of their aerobagnes, and we're carrying away tangible proofs that everything he recounted in his manuscript is accurate."

They rejoined Alexis at the hotel. It was about five o'clock; the worthy fellow seemed anxious, and he drew Escander into a corner.

"Boss," she said, "I'm worried. Since we got back people have been prowling around us. There might be a squabble before long."

"So?"

"So I think that as soon as the demoiselle has had a rest, we'd better go."

They no longer had anything useful to do in Neustadt, for Escander was convinced that they would learn nothing more by staying longer, so he consent to the departure. When consulted, Mathilde declared that she was ready.

The three young people set out, and reached the landing-ground rapidly, but without affectation.

No one attempted to prevent Alexis opening the hangar; two or three men, probably wardens or mechanics, watched them from a distance. He drew out his apparatus, which he inspected rapidly. Mathilde and Escander installed themselves within.

Certain that his apparatus was in good condition, Alexis was also about to take his place when two policemen ran up, out of breath.

"Get down! Get down!"

Escander allowed them to approach.

"What do you want?" he demanded.

"You haf a votogravic abbaratus' It is vorbidden. Must gome to the bolice station to open it. Come! All come!"

"Don't move, Boss, or we're cooked!" shouted Alexis.

The policeman turn to Alexis. The young aviator possessed all of Carpentier's[101] best punches, and knew how to make use of them. With a triumphant straight right he sent the man flying three paces, got rid of his acolyte, who attempted to intervene, with a left hook neatly placed on the jaw, leapt into the apparatus and set it in motion.

The docile bird gathered speed and suddenly reared up, rising rapidly. Gunshots rang out behind it.

XII. Escander Has Recourse to Powerful Means

The investigation undertaken in Neustadt satisfied the editor on chief of *Le Monde* in every respect. As soon as he had assimilated the results he telephoned the Minister of the Interior to bring him up to date. The Minister recognized that Escander's discoveries confirmed Paul Ménestin's story, but asked the newspaper to limit itself, for the time being, to publishing the engineer's manuscript, without taking a hand in the affair. France was anxious about the gravity of certain events that were happening beyond her frontiers; it was necessary not to add to the excitement of public opinion.

Very worried, Sauter summoned Escander.

---

[101] In 1920, the boxing champion and war hero Georges Carpentier had not yet suffered the crucial defeat by Jack Dempsey that sent his career into a steep downward spiral.

"They're gagging us, my dear friend," he said. "We can continue to publish the manuscript, but without commentary. Our readers will end up believing that it's a romance."

"However," said the reporter, "Ménestin exists, and the clandestine factories too, and the author of the manuscript really is aboard German aerobagne 32."

"That's my conviction, but it's necessary to wait. That's the order."

"It's humiliating."

"Yes, but what can we do?"

"Will you give me three days, my dear Boss? In three days, I'll submit a project to you that I've been studying for some time."

"Agreed—I'll give you three days."

"I also need Alexis, the pilot who took us to Neustadt, and a substantial amount of money."

"How much?"

"Maybe a hundred thousand."

"Damn!"

"I also need airplane 21."

"What are you cooking up, Escander?"

"I want to bring you Paul Ménestin, within a month."

"Escander, if you can do that..."

"You'll get me the Légion d'honneur—thanks, but I've already got it. No, Boss; if I succeed, you'll publish at your expense my history of the last Valois-Angoulêmes."

"Agreed—a luxury edition, with reproductions of iconographic documents—but I want to know..."

"You shall—but whether I succeed or not, *Le Monde* will never have had, and never will have, a story as sensational to announce in headlines."

When he left Sauter, Escander went up to the platform on top of the building, from which the machines of its aviation service took off.

"Alexis! Where's Alexis?"

"He's about to leave, Monsieur."

"No, he isn't leaving. Tell him to come. At the same time, I'm informing you that airplane 21 bas been mobilized for my service. Get a move on—at the trot!"

After having invited Alexis to dinner in a small restaurant on the left bank, Escander took him along the quais.

"Tell me, Alexis," the journalist said, when they had reached a deserted spot, "do you know twenty resolute fellows who'd like to earn a round sum by taking a few risks?"

"Do I! Heaps—and first class fellows, you know, who won't back away from a dust-up—as long as everything's proper, of course."

"I'm incapable of proposing anything else to you; there'll be fighting, but with Boches."

"In that case, I know thousands of them."

"Twenty or twenty-five will suffice...for a month, all expenses paid, fifty francs a day and good work to be done...but it'll be hard."

"Pardon me, Monsieur Escander, but has it to do with the business at Neustadt?"

"Yes."

"Then it's all right—and those I bring with me, I'll answer for as for myself."

"But once again, it'll be necessary to fight, to stick it out...perhaps to the death."

"They'll stick it out."

For an hour, Escander talked. Alexis listened in a religious silence; then, gained by a joyous enthusiasm, he destroyed one by one all the objections that the reporter raised before him.

It was very late when the two men separated, with a handshake.

The next day, at three o'clock, the reporter presented himself at the home of Mademoiselle Régis. Without concealing any of the audacity of his project, he explained all its details. When the two young people separated, it was agreed that the young woman would agree to take a short sea cruise.

Escander then had himself taken to the Boulevard Ney, where he had no difficulty finding the garage that Alexis had designated as a meeting place. The pilot was waiting for him on the threshold.

"Are they here?" was the reporter's first question.

"All present and correct—twenty-five, as you requested, the best there are when cunning's required."

They went into the hangar. As they came in the twenty-five men who were waiting for them formed a line, and all conversations ceased. Escander contemplated them momentarily in silence, and then, with his hands in his pockets, he spoke to them.

"My friends, Alexis has told you that I need twenty-five brave lads, resolute and devoted. The work for which you're being hired is important, dangerous but perfectly honorable. There will doubtless be blows to deliver and receive. If you're killed, your heirs will receive a sum of ten thousand francs; the wounded will be cared for, and pensioned if necessary. There will, of course, be a contract to sign. Those who want to come with us raise our hands."

All the hands went up.

"In a few days," said Escander, a train will take you to Le Havre, but between now and then, I need you to be discreet. If you have curious wives, tell them that you've enrolled to search for treasure buried at sea. That's all. *Au revoir!*"

Saluted by acclamations, Escander took Alexis away to ask him for additional information about the personnel he had recruited. The majority of the men lived by various industries on the margins of society—handymen, street-hawkers, improvised mechanics—but they all had clean records, legally speaking, and were relatively scrupulous in their honesty. Escander declared himself satisfied. Alexis was to keep in constant contact with them and make sure that they were kept in hand.

From the Boulevard Ney the journalist went to *Le Monde*. When he came out again, he had *carte blanche*, and Sauter was rubbing his hands joyfully.

Escander's day was not yet finished. At six o'clock, in the Avenue du Bois de Boulogne, he rang the doorbell of the great chocolatier Laverdy, whose friend he had been since their schooldays. Laverdy had only had the difficulty of coming into the world to find a fortune of forty millions in his cradle and a prosperous business that he allowed hands more expert than his own to manage. He was a charming fellow, but he had one grave fault: he was perpetually bored, no matter what. Only Escander amused him, precisely because he did not take the ennui of the idle man seriously. He welcomed the journalist with open arms.

"You're going to have dinner with me, and then you'll take me to see something capable of amusing me."

"Old chap," said Escander, "I'm bringing you something that would cure a neurasthenic abandoned by all the faculties in the world. Do you still have your yacht?"

"The *Étoile polaire*? Of course—but what can I do…?"

"You're going to do something with it. Is it ready to sail?"

"A dispatch to the captain and she can put to sea tomorrow."

"Perfect. Let's have dinner, then, and listen to me."

Throughout dinner, Escander talked. By dessert, Laverdy as exultant; he was no longer taking about ennui or the desire to die; on the contrary, he was burning with a fever of activity, and if the journalist had listened to him they would both have left that same evening. Escander left him in that disposition, and while going home, as he expelled the smoke of a magnificent cigar toward the September sky, he said to himself: *This is definitely turning out even better than I hoped. The Boss will be pleased.*

Two days later, he introduced Laverdy to Mathilde, and the chocolatier took the young woman to Le Havre in his powerful automobile.

XIII. The Manuscript Continued:
The Revolt

For a fortnight, the second lieutenant has hardly quit my laboratory. I've succeeded in devising an explosive that produces a considerable force of expansion from a very small volume. I've enclosed it in six medium-sized metallic flasks; with the aid of a single inversion one can obtain, by mixing the elements, an almost instantaneous deflagration. I've hidden four of the flasks at different points on the airship and kept the other two—after which I had the commandant notified that I've concluded my initial research and that I'd like to show him the results.

He summoned me immediately.

"In the course of my work," I said, "I've discovered an explosive that deploys a hitherto-unknown force."

He smiled skeptically.

"I'd like you to give me the opportunity to experiment with it in your presence," I went on. "One cubic centimeter of the product could reduce the room we're in to smithereens; I'd like to convince you of that."

He was no longer laughing.

"In sum, what do you want, Monsieur Ménestin?"

"That you place me above some target—a rock, for instance. You'll see that I'm not exaggerating."

"All right. Tomorrow we'll pass over a group of rocks at sea level; you can take your choice—but don't hope that your discovery can modify in any way the conditions of your sojourn here; it's a gas that you're supposed to reconstitute, not an explosive."

I inclined my head to show that I'd understood and left. Second Lieutenant Eitel joined me on the bridge where I like to stand.

"At six o'clock tomorrow," he told me, "when the convicts come out, there'll be two executions...punishment number 3 and punishment number 4. You'll have to watch. Summon up your courage; they're said to be terrible punishments."

"But aren't you revolted by such cruelties yourself, Lieutenant?"

"My own misery causes me to scorn that of others. However, the contemplation of the spectacle will be odious to me."

The last remark astonished me, but I was not at the end of the surprises that Lieutenant Eitel had in store for me.

That evening we found ourselves in the same place, and we spent the evening chatting about a thousand things. As we separated, he took my hand and shook it, with a long, embarrassing grip.

"If you only knew how I'd like to be your friend!" he said.

"But aren't you, to the extent that you can be?"

"Not enough for my liking, Monsieur Ménestin. If, at the price of a treason, I could conquer your...affection, in order to obtain it, I'd betray my father and my country."

He did not wait for the effect of his words. Confused, he got up, uttering a kind of dolorous groan, and drew away rapidly. I saw him take one of the ladders and go to one of the engine rooms, almost at a run.

I remained disconcerted by those words, so grave or so ill-considered. After a while, the lieutenant came back, sat down, and, with his face turned skywards, appeared to deliver himself to a profound meditation.

He uttered a long sigh, and turned toward me. I remained standing beside him.

"Life is cruel, Monsieur Ménestin; there's little we can do to make it better. It's necessary to encounter a soul that understands your own... I'm very unhappy.... Excuse me... Just now I said something that must have seemed strange to you, but if you knew how troubled I am, how miserable my poor existence is..."

He bowed his head and held it between his hands. I addressed a few comforting words to him, but they were futile. I held out my hand; he took it, and shook it effusively. Then I saw that he was weeping.

"Come on," I said, "be reasonable; I sympathize sincerely with your troubles, even though the true reason for them escapes me. I'd like to see you happier."

"Good night," he said, abruptly.

The next day, at four o'clock, we were at sea off the Saharan coast. The commandant informed me that the airship was about to fly over a group of reefs, and that the time had come to try out my explosive. Dawn was beginning to break on the horizon.

I took one of my flasks and went to the bridge. The officers were all there. Eitel greeted me with a smile.

The airship descended rapidly, in a faintly tight spiral, around the red head of a rock, which put something like a large bloodstain upon the glaucous immensity of the waters.

We were about five hundred meters from the waves. At that moment, on his father's order, Eitel came toward me.

"You're going to give your device to the spotter," he said. "He's the one who has the order to drop it."

The spotter was the man in charge of all landing maneuvers; he was very skilful. On the other hand, I understood perfectly that the commandant wanted to relieve me as soon as possible of the redoubtable flask that I was holding in my hand.

"When he lets it go," I said, he has to turn it upsidedown. "It will only require ten seconds to provoke the mixture of the liquids."

Eitel nodded his head, smiled at me, and then, taking the flask he went to give it to the spotter, who was standing motionless at the prow of the airship, above the void.

The 32 was still descending; never, except when landing, had it flown so low. Scarcely a hundred and fifty meters from sea level, a whistle-blast immobilized the propulsive and tractional helices; only the ascensional helices were functioning to maintain the biplane at that height.

"Dispatch!" Eitel commanded.

The man inverted the flask and let it go. We were able to follow its fall through space for about twenty meters, and then we lost sight of it, but a second or two later, we where whipped in the face by a great displacement of atmospheric waves. The aircraft had started moving again when the noise of the explosion reached us, weakened by the distance. With the aid of prismatic binoculars, we were able to observe that the effect had been formidable; the rock was almost leveled, and the sea was foaming all around it.

The commandant ran toward me.

"That's perfect, Monsieur—but you intend, I hope, to give me that formula?"

"Indeed," I said to him, holding it out. "Here it is."

"Very good. Do you want anything in return?"

"No, Monsieur," I said. "It's not in your power to give me what I'd like. Know, however, that that explosive is known to your compatriots; I've only manufactured it. Know, too, that I have four similar flasks…well hidden, I assure you. On the day when I'm weary of the life I lead here, or simply of your company, I have the wherewithal to liberate myself from it. It's you, Monsieur, who are my prisoner henceforth. I have the honor of saluting you."

He looked at me open-mouthed, not yet understanding—but when he had grasped the meaning of my words, he suddenly turned crimson. I thought he was about to explode. He clenched his fists, and then put his hand to the hilt of a small dagger, an insignia of his grade, which was beating his left flank; but all those manifestations left me cold.

"I'll have you put in solitary confinement!" he howled.

I took a flask full of explosive out of my pocket and showed it to him. Then, I calmly went down from the bridge.

My intention was to go back to my cell, but the door of my cabin and that of the laboratory were locked; I was forced to remain there.

Orders had been given to all the guards to search every corner of the airship for the flasks I had mentioned. They searched everywhere, scrupulously; neither my cabin, nor the laboratory were spared. They found nothing, of course—which visibly augmented the commandant's rage.

At six o'clock—for it was necessary that it be daylight in order that no detail of the tortures should be lost—the convicts were brought out.

The former, previously condemned for murder, was to be suspended in front of a propeller moving at top speed, and thus exposed to such a blast of air that the skin split and bled as if scored by a knife. That was further complicated by the suspension, by a steel wire, which dug into the flesh.

That torture lasted a quarter of an hour; that was enough, it appeared, for the man to emerge from it permanently insane.

That one escaped the fate that awaited him. The steel wire snapped and the man, absorbed by the void, uttered a frightful cry as he fell. Leaning over the guard-rail, I saw him disappear. At that moment we were over sand-dunes, level with Cap d'Arquin, at an altitude of two thousand feet.

That frightful fall was greeted by a burst of laughter on the commandant's part. He must have been drunk.

There was a brief agitation in the gray mass of the convicts; that was all.

Not a word had been pronounced.

The man who was to suffer punishment number three was condemned to three minutes of suspension by the hands above the void. Like the first, he was led forward by four guards. His torso was bare and his legs were tied at the knees and the ankles. He was placed above a kind of trapeze installed a few moments before, which was swinging with a regular movement at the end of its steel wires.

The man, who would thus have to preserve his life by the strength of his resistance, put on a brave face; for the moment, he had more hatred than dread in his eyes. The bar of the trapeze was placed in his hands, but he kept them open and did not grasp the bar.

Then, without a word, and as if they had anticipated that resistance, the two guards tied his wrists to the bar with a thin

339

thread, incapable of supporting the man's weight but sufficient to keep his hands in the position in which they were put.

The guards let him go; a blast of the whistle resounded, and two of the plates of the metallic deck, on which the patient's feet were resting, flexed gently with the aid of hinges.

The convict went frightfully pale, but his hands remained open. The hinged flaps continued to open, only offering an increasingly slippery purchase to the man's feet.

The patient clenched his jaws; his eyes filled with an atrocious terror, and he closed his hands desperately.

The floor disappeared completely beneath him, and the bar of the trapeze descended slowly, until the man's waist was level with the floor, his legs in empty space.

Suddenly, the terror was effaced from his visage; his face, although its pallor was livid, maintained a kind of mocking impassivity. Twice, he raised himself up by the force of his arms, as gymnasts do, until his face was level with the metal bar—which made the commandant snigger.

That snigger changed into a laugh, and, in spite of the discipline that ordered the most profound silence, he spoke.

"Look! Clever man! What vigor! He's splendid! It's not three minutes he needs, it's five! What biceps! What strength! What courage! Bravo!"

A rage seemed to succeed his sarcasm.

"I've seen stronger men than you let go, out of strength! What are you going to do, wretch?"

I could not hold still any longer. I ran toward the commandant.

"It's you," I told him, "who are a wretch! That man is suffering in silence—he has more dignity than you."

"Be careful, Frenchman," he howled, "that I don't hang you from the trapeze!"

"Try," I said—and I showed him the little flask that I had in my pocket.

He was a coward. He mumbled something else, and went down to his cabin, to hide his fury or drown it in alcohol—but he would come out again soon, more furious and more brutal than ever.

When I returned my gaze to the torture victim, I saw that from livid, he had become crimson. His muscles were standing out and moving beneath his skin like snakes; his breast, horribly taut, seemed ready to burst; his hands were clenched, and once again, an unspeakable terror filled his eyes.

It was necessary for him to endure the torture for another minute. He closed his eyes; a frisson shook his entire body; I sensed that he was about to let go.

Eitel saw it too. He raised his whistle to his lips and blew.

Immediately, the trapeze came back up, the floor closed, and the man, whose wrists were untied, collapsed. The first lieutenant took out his watch, impassively, and consulted it.

"The duration was thirty seconds short, lieutenant" he said, addressing Eitel. "You'll stand guard in the prison for forty-eight hours."

Eitel was about to respond when a formidable clamor broke out. It was the convicts.

They were all on their feet, with a murderous gleam in their eyes, howling incomprehensible words and uttering cries. A furious wind of folly was carrying them away. They were a demonic host, screaming for the sake of screaming. Some were singing, others ran around, howling; the most reflective attempted to invade the bridge, but it did not occur to any of them to band together for that enterprise, so their efforts remained vain.

It was obviously one of the revolts that had been mentioned to me: a fit of collective madness. One of the guards had been seized; he disappeared into an eddy; his screams were mingling with the others when the commandant, his jacket unbuttoned, appeared on the bridge. In spite of his drunkenness, he understood the terrible danger that as threatening everyone's existence.

Launched against the guard-rail of the bridge, he leaned over the tumultuous convicts; his appearance provoked a renewal of cries and fury. The commandant howled something that no one could hear; the first lieutenant joined him and shouted something in his ear.

Eitel, very bold, having recovered his original attitude, all pride and rigidity, came toward me.

"You don't belong here, Monsieur Ménestin." Then, to temper the harshness he sensed in that order, he added: "I beg you."

"Thank you," I said, "but I'm all right where I am."

The commandant had seen me; he came toward me.

"Your flask, Monsieur, quickly!"

I shook my head negatively. He stamped his foot angrily.

"Throw your flask at that rabble!"

"No, Monsieur."

Down below, the display of madness continued. The guard who had fallen into the hands of the convicts could no longer be seen, but his fate was not in doubt.

Suddenly, two detonations rang out. Eitel collapsed, uttering a cry, at the same time as the ship's doctor, who fell face forward.

Then the commandant blew three blasts on his whistle, which dominated the racket; the machine-guns crackled. Then there was a terrible turbulence in the delirious crowd, still howling; bodies were stretched out; others were writhing on the floor. But I did not see any more; abandoning the battle, I went to the two officers lying nearby. The doctor was dead, his head traversed by a bullet. Eitel was bleeding abundantly from the left shoulder and had lost consciousness. Hastily, I unbuttoned his collar and his tunic.

Then I stopped.

He was a woman!

I picked him up—what should I call him now?—and carried him to his cabin. A rapid examination of the wound convinced me that it was slight. I put a dressing on it with the aid of napkins, and, unclenching his teeth, I made him absorb a few drops of gin that I had found in a bottle.

He soon recovered consciousness.

His gaze, on perceiving me, did not reveal any disturbance; on the contrary, an interior joy was manifest therein. Then her womanly nature betrayed itself, and her first gesture was one of modesty; with her sound arm she covered her face.

"Now you have my secret. Only you and my father know it. You'll know later why I'm here. Go now—it's necessary that they don't find you with me. I'll say that I was able to drag myself here on my own. Thanks...Paul."

I left her, full of perplexity and anxiety. Outside, the battle was over. The convicts, mastered, had been shoved back into the prison and the guards were busy throwing the cadavers cluttering the deck overboard.

The commandant, sobered up, advanced toward me.

"Eitel?" he demanded, anxiously. "Where is he?"

"I think he's in his cabin. I saw him heading in that direction."

Without saying anything more, he ran in that direction, went into the cabin, and came out again very shortly to run toward me again.

"You know therapeutic substances—give me something to stop the blood!"

While speaking, he dragged me into his cabin. He put a campaign medical kit in front of me, where I found all that was necessary to make up an adequate hemostatic. I gave him the medicament, informing him as to how it ought to be employed, and offered to apply it. As I expected, he refused, and drew away rapidly.

I sent back to my laboratory in order to note down the events I had just witnessed, and then I set out in quest of a means of getting the journal I had been writing for six months to the ground. In the commandant's cabin I had seen a kind of leather bottle in which he kept his brandy; I resolved to take advantage of the circumstances to take possession of it.

I succeeded in my enterprise and, without having been seen, I went back to my laboratory with the product of my larceny. After having poured out all the liquid it still contained, apart for half a liter that I put to one side, I hid the bottle carefully behind jars and retorts, where no one would look for it.

Thanks to Eitel I had requested and obtained an internal bolt for my door. I pushed it, and started filling the bottle with the pages of my journal. I had no great expectations of that means, alas, but I took the chance because no one has the right to bow his head beneath adversity and, while breath of life remains, hope and struggle are imposed upon him as the primal duties.

I was still occupied in that task when someone rapped brutally on my door.

It was the commandant. He did not ask me any questions.

"Eitel is better," he said. "He's asking for you. Go."

Then he headed for the prison, accompanied by well-armed guards.

I answered the invitation. The person who had been Second Lieutenant Eitel was lying down. She smiled at me and indicated with her gaze a folding chair set beside her bed. An awkward silence followed.

It was me who broke it. "Your father's just confirmed that your wound isn't serious. You'll need to be careful though. If he were still alive, the doctor would certainly oblige you to be quiet and rest."

"That's of no importance; the doctor could prescribe whatever he liked, but I'd be much less obedient to him than my desire to see you and talk to you."

"But your health is important to me, and I'm going to leave."

"No, I don't want that! Why delay what has to happen? Stay, I beg you."

The imperious officer and the imploring woman had spoken through the same mouth.

Since the occasion could not be deferred, I resolved to regulate the equivocal situation immediately; obediently, I took the seat that was indicated to me.

"An explanation between us is necessary," she said. "I owe you one, and I owe one to myself. I'm the only daughter of the Kommandant of this aerobagne; my mother is dead. When my father was...embarked, I obtained his agreement, after a certain lapse of time and at the price of a great many tears and prayers, that he would let me join him—but it was necessary that no one knew. He succeeded in passing me off as a young officer, a deserter condemned to detention. He obtained his papers, facilitated the officer's fight, decked me out with his identity, and embarked me with him. It was simple, and no one perceived the deception. Since then, I've been Second Lieutenant Eitel, and I pass for a distant relative of my father.

"Your arrival left me indifferent at first but, alas, it didn't take long to exercise an influence on me that I combated, and at which I blushed. In spite of my efforts, it had an effect on me that modified all my ideas and all my tastes. Your presence soon became necessary, indispensable, to me. That's what led me, irresistibly, to tell you that for you, in order to be linked to your life, I would almost be willing to go as far as treason. Today, I can affirm to you that I would go that far. Now, it's no longer as anything but a woman that I'm speaking to you, Paul, and that woman is forced, by the sentiment that has taken possession of her, to make you these confessions... Now that everything equivocal is dissipated... That language must surprise you, but tell yourself that exceptional circumstances give rise to exceptional events, and what I dare to say now, at an altitude of three thousand meters, I certainly wouldn't say on the ground, dressed as a woman ought to be dressed..."

I was about to interrupt, but she silenced me with a slight gesture of the hand.

"So, now, you know the full extent, the full force of the...affection"—she was about to say love, but did not dare—"that I have for you. That affection has inspired me to form a project."

She maintained silence momentarily, while her gaze searched mine.

345

"I have," she continued, "envisaged and prepared our escape. This is how. We'll take advantage of our passage over an inhabited center to take possession of one of the emergency aircraft—the starboard one. I've checked its equipment, and it's now ready to receive us. I know how to fly it; it's child's play. During a dark night, we'll slip out to it, free it from its moorings, and in less than an hour we'll be on the ground."

"All that," I said, "does indeed prove to me the force of a sentiment whose full value I appreciate, but you have a right to demand its price. What is it?"

A cloud passed over her face. Wanting to temper the cruel aspect of my words, I took her hand. She fixed her large eyes on mine and said: "Everyone has the right to seek to achieve their happiness."

"Yes, without harming that of another."

"Too bad for the other! Who worries about me and my suffering? This is what I ask of you, then: that as soon as we land, I become your legal wife. A wife takes the nationality of her husband, and you've destroyed in me everything there could be of the German. You can't hold that against yourself. As soon as we're married, we'll return to your homeland, or any other you choose, and I can say, before God, that you'll be unable to wish for a more docile, humbler, more loving wife than me."

She had spoken in a single burst, very rapidly, as if to get her explanation over as quickly as possible. As for me, I had never been so unhappy, for I was reluctant to make the poor woman suffer. I tried, however, to bring her back to reason, to make her envisage all the consequences of our action.

"What about your father?" I said

She laughed disdainfully. "He'll still have alcohol—and believe me, that will be sufficient for him."

"The esteem that I have for you," I continued, "the profound amity, even"—she frowned—"makes it a duty for me to be as frank as you have been yourself. When I was abducted and sequestered by your people, for refusing to betray my country, as you know, I was getting ready to return to France to marry a young woman there who has my promise and my love. I don't intend to betray her, even at the price of my liberty, any more than I would have betrayed you, had I made the same promise to you."

Contrary to my expectation, she did not manifest either anger or despair. She simply smiled.

"I knew," she said. "Except, Paul, there's one thing you don't know, and which, when you know it, will silence your scruples, of which I approve. Everyone in France believes that you're dead; it has been officially announced. Your death certificate has been published, because the people holding you here have decided never to release you, even if you submit to their conditions. You know too much, Monsieur Ménestin, that it's necessary not to know. Hence, you're here for life.

"In those circumstances, your fiancée must believe you dead—dead for more than a year, and morally, you are. There's no dolor so bad that time can't reckon with it, and don't you think that after your fiancée has mourned you, she'll allow herself to be loved by someone else?"

I had risen to my feet. All of that, which I did not know yet, distressed me. All the hatred I had accumulated against those people burst forth. I forgot that I had before me a woman that I had already bruised.

"Whatever an action might be for which you are responsible as well as yours, Mademoiselle, I shall leave time the care of attenuating in you the memory of what it remains for me to say to you. You belong to a race that I hate and despise too much ever to see anything in you but a foreigner and an enemy."

She looked at me, devastated; then, with an exclamation of furious rage, she hid her head in her pillow, biting it in order not to scream.

I went out, prey to a thousand various sentiments, but anger and indignation were dominant. Enough reason remained to me, however, for me to understand that I had just made an irreconcilable adversary, and that the tolerance that had been shown to me in recent months was at an end.

This very evening, I shall throw the bottle into the sea. With the door bolted, I shall slide the manuscript through the neck, and seal it hermetically...

It's finished.

Go with God.

8 August...

XIV. In which it is proven that Escander has no lack of initiative

Laverdy's yacht, the *Étoile polaire*, was sailing rapidly toward the western coast of Africa., after calling in briefly at Lisbon and Tenerife, where food supplies for two months had been embarked.

The vessel was thus fully laden, but was traveling rapidly. In addition to the crew, composed of twenty men, there were twenty-five robust fellows aboard, all dressed in white and quipped in the manner of colonial soldiers. The rear section was reserved for Escander, Mathilde, Laverdy and Alexis.

One evening, Escander resolved to make his final confidences.

"My friends," he said, "you know the goal that we're pursuing; it can be summed up in a few words: to get Paul Ménestin out of German hands. For that, I've envisaged several means of which you, Laverdy, are unaware, and of which Mademoiselle Régis is similarly ignorant. Only Alexis knows them, for I had need of his devotion, his cunning and his courage from the very outset."

"You're overdoing the ignition, Boss—that's sufficient, don't go on," said Alexis, who was lying on the deck.

Escander did not make any retort, but continued: "It is, alas, the case that we can't count on anyone but ourselves, for the French government remains convinced, until more amply informed, that the Germans are acting in good faith.

"Few means are available to us. The first that comes to mind is that of a direct attack, with the aid of a squadron of armed aircraft, but, in addition to the fact that the success of such an attempt would be very dubious, we have no way of knowing whether the Germans, if they saw themselves on the brink of being caught, wouldn't simply murder Paul Ménestin, in order not to leave any proof of their crime behind. They could pass him off as one of those killed in the skirmish, and that would be that."

"That is, indeed, to be feared," said Laverdy.

"It's therefore necessary, without further discussion, to set that first means aside as offering too few chances of success. There's little left to examine; only one thing seems practicable to me, and this is it:

"It's now the twenty-eighth of September. According to the international tables that regulate the circulation of the great penitentiary aircraft, aerobagne 32 is due to pass over Cap d'Arquin and the dunes of Iguidi between the first and the eighth of October. It's in that zone that we ought to try to reach it. But where, exactly? In what fashion can we act, forced as we are to act alone; there must be no witnesses to this affair. My choice has therefore fallen on the point when the bagne, ceasing to fly over the Atlantic, arrives over the sands before continuing over the dunes of Iguidi, where I want to make it land."

"But that's quite simple," said Laverdy. "One fires a cannon shot, and breaks a wing."

"A poor means," Escander retorted. "The 32 can rise up to six thousand meters, and be no more than a dot in the sky. However skillful our gunners are, I doubt that any of them could hit it at that range—and then, as I said just now, the life of the man we want to save is in their hands; we need to think only about that. This, then, is what I've decided to do:

"We'll disembark our contingent of fighting men in the dunes of Iguidi; they'll set up camp. Our fellows, installed under tents, will wait as tranquilly as possible. They'll remain under your command, Laverdy. You're a reserve officer; that gives you a certain competence."

"I'm at your disposal, old chap," said the chocolatier.

"Mademoiselle Régis will disembark with you; she has a series of written instructions, of which I'll give you a duplicate. Now, listen!"

The journalist lowered his voice, in order that neither the man at the helm nor the officer of the watch could hear, and what he said then was so extraordinary that there were exclamations of surprise and fright.

Laverdy leapt to his feet. "It's madness!" he said. "I'll never permit that."

Escander felt Matilde take his hand. The journalist squeezed her small, frail hand gently and fraternally; then, laughing frankly, he went on:

"My dear Laverdy, you'll permit anything I want, for two reasons. The first is that you're my friend and, in consequence, you don't want to cross me; the second, which will appear more serious to you, is that you've surrendered to me, in writing, all your authority aboard ship. I am, therefore, the sole master here, and can, if it suits me, send you to the bottom of the hold to keep our airplane company."

"But you'll kill yourself, you idiot!" howled Laverdy.

"That's not at all certain. In fact," the journalist affirmed, "I believe that I won't."

"And once you're among the Boches, will you be any further forward? What are you going to do, alone against an entire crew?"

"Don't worry—I won't be alone. I'll have two good automatic pistols with five shots each. And then again, if chance turns against me, you'll still have the duty, my dear Laverdy, of continuing the work with which you've generously associated yourself. You'll reckon with the Boches, and you'll return Mademoiselle Régis' fiancé to her."

"Get away!" cried Alexis. "We'll succeed, and what a triumph! They'll give M'sieur Escander the Légion d'honneur...no, he has that already...anyway, they'll give him something useful and agreeable—a tobacconist's shop, for example; there's nothing better. Ma'mselle Régis will marry M'sieur Ménestin; M'sieur Laverdy will occupy himself with his chocolate plantations, and I'll hand in my resignation as a bird and set myself up as a restaurateur at the sign of the Anti-Boche. All right! All right!"

XV. A Dot in the Sky

Forty-eight hours later, in the dark of the night at the end of September, the *Étoile polaire* dropped anchor off the dunes of Iguidi, in very favorable weather. Escander, the yacht's first mate and six sailors embarked in a launch and headed for the coast, whose lines were discernible in the moonlight. At the prow, a sailor took soundings and directed the route in accordance with the depth; the launch reached the shore and ran aground gently.

The following morning, the disembarkation as effected. The tents were set up and Laverdy was introduced as having supreme authority in Escander's absence; a former sergeant-major, artful and intelligent, was appointed as his second-in-command; the doctor was also disembarked. At Escander's request Mathilde stayed aboard. The men were then informed of what was expected of them. For some time, Alexis had given them hints regarding the objective of the expedition; not only were they not surprised but they manifested a genuine enthusiasm. Automobile machine guns were set up, the catering organized, and everything seemed to be going as well as possible.

The night passed peacefully; although a tornado burst forth at about eight o'clock in the evening, it was not very violent.

In the morning, Laverdy, on the point of quitting the *Étoile polaire* to go ashore, was in a very bad mood. On the deck, in a rather sullen tone, he said to Escander: "I don't know what's stopping me from giving the order to go back to Le Havre."

"Impossible," said Escander, coldly. "I need you and the boat more than ever; you can go back to Le Havre later, my lad."

"When you extorted the on-board authority from me, I didn't know your insane plan."

"Now you know it, it doesn't change anything."

"But..." Laverty, sensing that the struggle was futile, took two steps toward the ladder, but did not step on to it. Fundamentally, he was a brave man with a heart of gold, under his appearance of indifference; a sob caught in his throat. He turned to Escander and hugged him.

Mathilde, who witnessed the departure, drew away, distressed. She was found later, weeping in her cabin.

Laverdy embarked in the launch, but could not help shouting to Escander: "You're mad, you hear? You're mad, mad, mad!"

The boat carrying him drew away, and the *Étoile polaire*, in conformity with Escander's plan, moved slowly away out to sea.

Two days passed without anything being signaled. Escander gave orders for airplane 21—which, thanks to Alexis, had been painted blue, like all the machines in the air force of French Occidental Africa, was installed on the foredeck, solidly moored. The wings had not been mounted, as an extra precaution, but putting them in place, with the expert personnel that he had aboard, would only require two hours of work. Everything as ready and anticipated; they were waiting.

A tornado burst forth every evening at the same time, augmenting in intensity every time. There was nothing surprising about that, because it was the beginning of October, in the middle of the rainy season, but it annoyed Alexis. By contrast, Escander was delighted; the elements would be his accomplices.

"However unfavorable the hour is to me," he said, when he made allusion to his plan, "I'll tell the Boches that it's the tempest that provoked an engine failure."

The *Étoile polaire* sailed thus, at reduced speed, Escander's design not being to stray too far from the camp, with which he kept in constant touch with the aid of the wireless.

Toward mid-afternoon on the third day, a minuscule dot, which the sun caused to sparkle, was spotted. It was German aerobagne 32, flying at an altitude of three thousand meters.

Aboard the *Étoile polaire*, Alexis had the wings fitted to his airplane, checked the controls, the steering and the engines; after two hours, the 21 was ready to take off.

Escander went to see Mathilde; he had a carefully sealed letter in his hand.

"It's time for action," he said, with a good humor that he exaggerated in order to tranquilize the young woman. "I've never been more certain of success, but if, however—it's necessary to anticipate the worst, without believing in it—I don't come back, deliver this letter to its address."

Already, for two days and nights, the young woman had been asking herself whether she had the right to accept the journalist's sacrifice, and for a long time, her conscience and her heart had been saying no.

Her lips were trembling; her eyes were full of tears. Escander guessed what was about to happen and armed himself, not with courage but with severity.

"I can see by your emotion," he said, "that you're about to ask me to abandon my project, that you'd a hundred times rather sacrifice your hopes than see me run a danger, and that you'd prefer the ruination of your happiness to a remorse. Don't worry: your happiness and your fiancé's liberty will only be the consequences of an action I'm undertaking in order to unmask the enemies of my country. That alone is important and that alone is making me act. Forgive me for speaking to you like that, and let's part; too much time has already been lost."

The young woman had not expected such curt language. As Escander drew away, she launched herself forward.

"No, no! I beg you, abandon your unrealizable project. I don't want you to go! I don't want it!"

But Escander pushed her away gently and ran toward the bow, leaving the young woman sobbing.

The journalist rejoined Alexis, already solidly strapped into his seat. Escander took the place reserved for him. The 21, set in motion, glided smoothly over the foredeck and immediately took flight. It banked steeply at low altitude, and, returning along the course traveled by the ship, flew over the sand. At that moment Escander gave a signal agreed in advance, and then the aircraft gained height, designing a great semicircle that was to take it above the aerobagne.

At sea, the captain of the *Étoile polaire* ordered: "Hold the helm! Engine full ahead! Three hundred revs!"

The *Étoile polaire*'s hull shuddered in its entirety, and cut through the swell more rapidly.

XVI. In the Air in Mid-Storm

The airplane rose up, no longer seeming anything but a dot in the sky, but at the same time, in the south-west, the black clouds of the daily tornado were accumulating.

Only Escander, sitting in the cockpit, was visible, looming over Alexis, who had had his seat lowered in such a fashion as only to have his eyes above the propeller housing.

The journalist, full of confidence in his pilot's mastery and coolness, occupied himself buckling around his waist the straps of the lifebuoy, to which was attached the retention system of a silk parachute with an automatic safety-release. An extreme confidence animated him; certainly, he had a reputation as a daredevil, he knew that, but at the moment he felt much more tranquil and sure of his nerves than the day when, dressed as a dervish, he had entered the shadow of a forbidden temple in the depths of India, not far from Tibet, and each of the other times that he had risked his life.

When he had checked all the attachments of his safety-harness, he adjusted his leather helmet on his head and adapted the voice amplifier in order to be able to exchange a few words with Alexis—who, coiffed in a similar helmet, with earphones, was attentively supervising the progress of his aircraft.

"Can you hear me, Alexis?"

"Very clearly, Boss."

"How long before we're over the Boches?"

"A little more than an hour; we need to climb a lot further; we're only at five hundred meters, but the wind's beginning to get up and it's against us…that's a hindrance, and then again, it'll carry you away in the fall. It's therefore necessary to drop you behind the 32 to have any chance of falling on it."

"That's what I calculated."

"Have you made certain of the straps?"

"Yes, don't worry."

"I'm afraid that the wind might ball up the parachute."

"We'll see."

"While falling, hold your breath, don't open your mouth and squeeze your legs together. There are two compartments in the buoy; one contains cordials and food concentrates, the other rockets. If you fall into the sea, don't forget to send one up as soon as you return to the surface. You light it by popping off the tinplate capsule that covers one of the ends and dipping it in the water."

"All duly noted, my dear Alexis. I'll remember everything."

Above all, don't forget to release the parachute cord; the catch is just above your head. Do that two or three meters from the sea and you'll slide in like velvet; the wind will carry the parachute away—otherwise, it might cover you and prevent you from getting back to the surface."

"Yes, I have all the recommendations engraved in my memory, but it's not into the water that I'm going to fall but on to the Boches. As soon as my fall commences, Alexis, you do exactly as I've told you to; it's necessary to give them the certainty that there's no one aboard the plane. As soon as you're out of sight, set a course directly for the dunes of Iguidi, where you go down, alert the camp and await events."

"You'll be obeyed, Boss, but if the Boche aircraft doesn't come down, it'll be because you're dead—then I'll go up again in my cuckoo and stick my beak in; we'll bring the company tumbling down!"

"I forbid you to do that."

"Go ahead!" said Alexis. "I'm like you—when I have an idea, I stick to it, and as you won't be there to prevent me, I'll do as I like. Look out!"

A violent clap of thunder had just shaken the entire sky. The silhouette of aerobagne 32 was becoming more distinct, but Alexis, hampered by the wind, still had to climb to get above it.

"Need to hurry," said Alexis. "We're going to be caught by the tornado."

He turned a handle; the propeller rotated with a crazy velocity, and the 21 continued to gain height more rapidly.

Would he have time to reach a calmer region? The valiant little bird was performing admirably, but the tornado burst.

The 21 was surrounded by an ocean of fire. Detonations, rumbles and rips succeeded one another, formidable and fearful, with no discontinuity. Under the action of the wind, the 21 went off course, recovered, and then, driven away again, bucking and rearing, continued the struggle.

For an hour, Alexis fought, his arms weary, his head buzzing. Finally, he succeeded in lining up with the 32, two hundred meters above it and slightly behind—about a hundred meters.

At that moment, a formidable flash of lightning seemed to envelop the frail aircraft, accompanied by a furious gust of wind, and the 21, performing a backflip, was turned completely upside-down.

Escander, projected, as it were, into the void, fell...

Paul Ménestin, who was coming out of his laboratory, stepped back in terror. The immense aerobagne, in the heart of the storm, seemed to be ablaze.

Half of the crewmen were at the emergency posts; the other half were at battle stations; the commandant and the first lieutenant, standing on the bridge, were exploring the sky, which seemed to be on fire, with their gaze. The airship was pitching, and large raindrops were already beginning to fall when, after several attempts, Ménestin was able to reach a favorable observation post. An airplane of a tiny model was perceptible, entirely blue. The poor little bird, carried away by the tempest, was behind the bagne and higher up.

Suddenly, abruptly, its wings dipped and it cartwheeled. The pilot was then seen waving his arms in distress, in falling, sustained by a partly-opened parachute.

As for the aircraft, it began to execute a series of loops, flew through the air like a projectile, and disappeared. In any case, no one was any longer paying attention to it. All gazes were following the man with the parachute, which had finally opened broadly, and as beginning to moderate his vertiginous fall.

The wind pushed the unfortunate fellow directly toward the bagne, and in spite of the maneuver that the commandant ordered to remove his vessel from the line of the fall, the pilot in perdition was bowled on to one of the supportive planes of the 32. People ran to help him; he was brought unconscious to the deck, and then taken to the commandant's cabin.

XVII. Escander at Work

When Escander recovered his senses, he found himself extended on the floor of the cabin. Two men were leaning over him: the commandant and the first lieutenant, who were watching for signs of life. A third officer, dressed in a second lieutenant's uniform, was standing to one side.

Never, since the day when Ménestin had discovered the secret of the woman who was posing as an officer, had those two individuals encountered one another again. Ménestin avoided the young woman, who similarly avoided him, and the French engineer had seen the withdrawal, one by one, of all the petty liberties that had been accorded to him.

Escander was not one of those who leaps into immediate action; he had a delicate cunning, which did not take a risk without mature reflection, which left nothing to chance and which, for the moment, was causing him to pretend to be in a worse condition than he actually was—for, although he was still completely shaken up by his terrible fall, he retained all his mental faculties. His jangled nerves, overly taut, had lost their spring, but his mind, fortunately, conserved all its lucidity.

The first lieutenant unclenched the teeth that he was holding tight deliberately, and slid a few drops of cordial into his mouth. Escander did not budge. The officer lifted his head and then released it. The patient let it fall back heavily.

"Who the devil is this intruder, Lieutenant?" asked the commandant, whose perplexity was translated by the stupid question.

"I don't know, Kommandant, but we're about to find out."

So saying, the lieutenant had opened Escander's flying-jacket, and found a card in his pocket bearing the inscription:

Aviation de l'Afrique Occidentale Française
Alexis-Charles Blin
Pilote

The lieutenant passed the card to the commandant, who, after having examined it, dropped it on to a table. It was obvious that neither of them understood French very well.

The two men fell silent. The tempest could be heard raging outside.

"Hmm!" said the commandant.

The first lieutenant perceived his superior's embarrassment. "I think the best thing to do," he said, "is let him recover his senses; afterwards, we'll see. If we have any anxiety in his regard, we can always reattach his parachute to his shoulders and throw him overboard."

358

Escander felt himself carried away. The rain wet his face again; then he divined that they were penetrating an enclosed space and he was laid on a bed. He was left alone. He opened his eyes. He was in a narrow cell, which he recognized, by the clutter, to be a miniature chemistry laboratory. A metal bed, equipped with a leather mattress, was the only furniture in the strange redoubt. He had some difficulty getting to his feet, because his aching limbs were making him suffer, but he finally managed to take a few steps.

An immense satisfaction filled his soul; the most difficult part was over; the rest depended on his ingenuity and his courage. He lay down on the bed again to get a little rest and reflect at his ease.

To begin with, one problem was posed: how to find out whether Paul Ménestin was really aboard. Few means presented themselves: a direct question in that regard would surely be answered by the reattachment of his parachute. Could he prowl round the airship? He would not be permitted to do that. Only one thing remained possible: to pretend ignorance of the German language. That would doubtless lead the commandant of the aerobagne to have him interrogated by the prisoner; but for that, it was necessary for none of the officers to know French. Would he be so lucky?

Calmly, he awaited events. Fortunately, he had not been searched thoroughly, and he still had his two automatic pistols.

Outside, the tempest had calmed down; only the rain was continuing, heavy and regular.

After an hour or so, a man suddenly came into the cell. He found Escander still recumbent, but his eyes were open. He immediately went out, and Escander heard footfalls running through the downpour. Ten minutes later, the two officers, enveloped in their cloaks, came into the cell.

The commandant approached the bed, the first lieutenant respectfully remaining a step behind.

"Who are you? Where do you come from?" interrogated the senior officer, in German.

Escander put on a profoundly bewildered expression, and risked: "I don't speak German. I'm French."

Then the first lieutenant approached and repeated the two questions in what he believed to be French. The result was pitiful. Escander pretended to be making superhuman efforts to understand, and then adopted a contrite expression, while rubbing his legs, which appeared to be causing him considerable pain. After much effort, he repeated: "French, I'm French. My name is Alexis-Charles Blin, pilot."

The two officers looked at one another, nonplussed. To acquit his conscience, Escander continued: "I was going from Conakry to Amative. I was caught by the tornado. I had to gain height to try to find more manageable weather, but my cuckoo took a tumble and I only just had time to get out with my parachute. It's lucky you were there."

While speaking, he continued rubbing his legs, but he had just furnished a plausible explanation for his presence aboard the 32, and he promised himself not to depart from it.

The two officers looked at one another again. Their embarrassment was visible. Finally, the commandant seemed to make a decision; he murmured a few words to the first lieutenant, who deigned to acquiesce with a nod and went out—but he came back a minute later, flanked by a third person, whom Escander devoured with his eyes.

When I think, he said to himself angrily, *that Mademoiselle Régis certainly has a photograph of her fiancé, and that I never thought to ask her to show it to me...*

The commandant spoke for some time to the newcomer, who, for his part, gazed at Escander with feverish eyes

Mademoiselle Mathilde, the journalist thought, *told me that Ménestin doesn't wear a beard. This fellow has one that could serve as an apron. Still, we'll see.*

The bearded man spoke. "I've been instructed to ask you who you are and where you've come from."

"And you, who are you? French?"

"Yes."

"Tell them that I'm a pilot in the Senegal-Madagascar service, that my plane was damaged during the journey by the tempest and that I had to bail out...but what's your name?"

The bearded man repeated word for word what the journalist had just said, but did not reply to the question he had been asked.

The two officers shook their heads and looked at one another in silence.

The bearded man took advantage of that brief moment to put his finger over his lips.

It's him! thought the journalist, his heart leaping with joy.

"It's necessary to separate them," said the commandant, "and prevent them from communicating with one another. "As soon as we're close enough to a center of habitation we'll drop anchor and get rid of the intruder, by confiding him to his parachute."

It was the commandant who, in response to the first lieutenant's affirmative nod, committed the formidable, unexpected gaffe: "Stand down, Monsieur Ménestin."

A discreet smile brushed Escander's lips. He had suspected the truth. Now the name, even pronounced in a German accent, confirmed his conviction.

The bearded man saw the smile, and his gaze lit up with a fugitive gleam.

The officers conversed for a few moments more in low voices, and then the first lieutenant said to Ménestin: "Follow me." The two men went out. On the threshold, they bumped into Second Lieutenant Eitel.

"What are the orders?" he asked.

"To lock this one up"—the first lieutenant pointed at Ménestin—"and post a sentry at his door."

"Do you want me to take charge of that?"

The first lieutenant, wet and worn out with fatigue, had only one priority: to get to bed as soon as possible.

"Gladly," he replied. And he drew away.

361

Eitel watched him disappear, and then turned to Ménestin.

"You must know, Monsieur, that it requires a powerful motive for the person who owes her greatest dolor and greatest humiliation to you to address speech to you. Know that you're a prisoner here for life. If my government decided to return you to your people, or if, eventually you found some chance of escaping, you couldn't do it. I've discovered, one after another, your flasks of explosive, and, as true as I hate you and am weary of living, I'll blow up the airship."

"With your father?"

"With my father and all the others, as long as you're one of them."

"I recognize the spirit of your race there. Is that all you have to tell me?"

"That's all."

Eitel took a step back. Ménestin went into his laboratory, and the second lieutenant, uttering a dull exclamation of rage, went to wake Weber in order to confide the guard of the prisoner to him.

Apart from Weber, who was pacing up and down outside the cabins to which Ménestin and Escander had been relegated, in a very bad mood, everyone aboard the 32 seemed to be asleep.

However, without making any noise, Escander's door opened, so softly that Weber did not hear anything. The two men on guard at the prow and the mechanics in the engine rooms could not see anything that was happening on the deck.

The feldwebel, lost in his sullen reverie, went past the door that stood slightly ajar and continued his route without seeing anything. Then the door opened fully. Escander, his feet bare, an automatic pistol. In his hand, appeared on the threshold. He advanced stealthily, and positioned himself directly in front of Weber when the other made his about-turn.

When the feldwebel saw the barrel of a pistol between is eyes, he did not utter a cry or make a gesture. Escander collected the electric carbine that the German was holding in a weak hand.

"March," said the journalist, in a German as correct as could be. "Take me to the French prisoner, or you're dead."

The feldwebel obeyed, heading toward the laboratory door, on which he knocked. Escander stood behind him, pistol in hand. Finally, the door opened. Escander shoved his guide into the cell, brutally, and closed the door behind him.

"You're Paul Ménestin," said the reporter to the bearded man, who, not knowing what the other wanted, had grabbed a glass pestle as a weapon and was holding it defensively.

"Yes, I'm Paul Ménestin," the man said, putting down the pestle.

"Finally!" said Escander, radiant. Then briefly, he explained: "I've come to rescue you. Your journal has made a lot of noise, but you'll know that later. Your fiancée is at sea at this moment, a few kilometers away. For the moment, let's act. Do you have any rope. We need to start by tying this man up."

With the barrel of his gun he indicated the feldwebel, who, thinking his last hour had come, threw himself to his knees, his hands joined.

"I've got something better than rope," said Ménestin. "Wait!"

He went to a drawer, took out a wad of cotton wool, which he saturated with a liquid, and, returning to Weber, whom Escander was still holding under the threat of the pistol, placed the tampon abruptly over his nostrils. The man tried to defend himself. But it was only an attempt; he soon collapsed to the floor. Ménestin leaned over him, applied the soporific for a second time, and then stood up.

"He'll be out for two hours, at least."

Escander handed the electric carbine to the engineer. "I assume you know how to use this?"

"What do you intend to do?" asked the engineer, taking the weapon.

"Get into the commandant's cabin, stick our weapons under his nose and oblige him to descend into the dunes of Iguidi, where an ambush is set up."

"That's impossible," said Ménestin. "Such a maneuver would inevitably provoke the arrival of people who would question the orders, worrying for them and contrary to the laws of aerial navigation. Believe me, we'd certainly fail."

"There are the convicts. Let's free them and set ourselves at their head."

"Before they'd understood the situation we'd be captured, even if we succeeded in freeing them, which is impossible."

"What then? Remember that we only have two hours of night ahead of us; we'll be trapped; the sleeping man will be discovered..."

"Listen to me. We might, perhaps, with a great deal of determination and luck, be able to take possession of an emergency aircraft, detach it and let ourselves drop."

"Explain."

"There are two emergency aircraft reserved for the officers in case of disaster. It's easy enough to reach them. Two switches put the wings in position; two bolts and powerful magnets hold them in place, and there's a third and last mechanism to release the apparatus from the flank of the bagne, where it's attached. I know the maneuvers well enough to attempt the adventure. The two aircraft are provided with two landing skis; the hull, moreover, is constructed like a boat. If we can't reach the ground, we still have a chance of coming down in the sea, unless..."

"Yes, unless...," said Escander, "but since we have no other means, let's go, and let's hurry."

Ménestin's only response was to open the door. The deck was deserted. Escander had taken back the carbine, whose functioning Ménestin explained to him, because he needed both hands free to be able to work on the aircraft—but he slipped one of the two pistols into his pocket.

Rapidly, Ménestin climbed one of the ladders leading to the starboard wing, which sheltered the aircraft that Eitel had chosen.

The aerobagne was pitching markedly and the reporter felt a frightful vertigo grip the back of his neck; the frightful attraction of the void blurred his vision. A cold sweat moistened his temples, and his legs seemed to be disappearing under him. In spite of his fear, though—for he was afraid—and in spite of the horror of the tragic night and his position, he continued to advance, without looking, following his guide instinctively. The latter was marching with a firm tread.

Finally, the two men reached the aircraft. The hardest part was over. Another five minutes of easy work, and the liberated aircraft would take flight.

At the very moment when they thought they were saved, however, they heard the metallic sound of a door, which was banging its frame at every pitching movement.

It was Ménestin's door, left open by Escander, that was banging.

"Press on," said Escander. "That damned door will get us caught."

"A bolt won't slide," said Ménestin, his voice low and his teeth clenched with effort. He could not, in fact cause one of the release mechanisms to operate.

Escander slid into the cockpit to help him, but at that moment, a strident whistle blast dominated all the other sounds.

"We've been discovered," said Ménestin, redoubling his efforts.

Escander stood up in the cockpit, rifle in hand. Above them, in the giant aircraft, a tumult burst forth; whistle-blasts succeeded one another, and searchlights lit up, inundating the gigantic airship with dazzling light.

Suddenly, above them, a black, elegant silhouette appeared, strangely magnified by the lights.

Escander saw it distinctly lean over, and he heard words shouted into the wind: "Remember my oath! Come back aboard, or you'll die!"

Escander aimed the rifle.

Ménestin, who had recognized the voice, cried: "Don't shoot! For God's sake, don't shoot!"

But Escander did not hear, and the abrupt detonation rang out. A cry like that of a wounded beast sounded, and then they perceived the heavy fall of a body, immediately followed by a mighty explosion.

Eitel had been faithful to her oath. As soon as the young woman had realized that the escape was under way, she had taken one of the flasks of the explosive manufactured by the engineer. At the moment when, in her rage and despair, she had perhaps been about to hurl it, Escander's bullet had struck her, with the flask in her hand, and the terrible explosion had been triggered.

The supportive plane surface under which the emergency aircraft was moored disappeared, torn apart, ripped away with a tremendous din, and the two refugees could see what had been Lieutenant Eitel suspended by one leg from an aluminum beam.

She was still alive.

"Paul! Oh, Paul!" she said—and then the beam gave way and the body disappeared into the night, at the same time as a heart-rending scream rang out.

The two fugitives looked at one another, sweat on their brow.

The great and sinister bird that had been aerobagne 32 was also mortally wounded. Dragged down by its weight, in the direction where support was abruptly lacking, it was no more than a wreck, slowly spinning.

What remained of the damaged wing caught fire; then the fire reached the other wings, and everything else that offered an aliment to its combustion, and the giant aircraft fell, an ardent torch gliding through the darkness, dragging its entire crew with it...

XVIII. In Search of Survivors

The *Étoile polaire*, skillfully maneuvered, had been able to remain level with the 32; in spite of the tornado, the airship had never been entirely lost to sight. Mathilde, dressed in a sou'wester, was standing beside the captain on the bridge, her lips taut, her gaze staring into the darkness, where only the fulgurance of the lightning revealed the presence of the aerobagne, brutally, at intervals.

The minutes went by slowly. It seemed, at one moment, to the young woman and the captain, that an aircraft flew over them—but it was only a fugitive impression. Had not Alexis promised to drop a flare, if everything had succeeded?

An hour went by, then two—two interminable hours of mental agony for the young woman, exhausted by fatigue, whose garments were soaked. She did not weaken, though.

Night fell.

Suddenly, Mademoiselle Régis uttered a cry, pointing to a dot in the sky—for the poor child could not articulate a word. The commandant looked up. Aerobagne 32 was clearly visible.

With all its searchlights illuminated, it was resplendent in the night, like a great winged beetle.

All of a sudden, and immense flash of light enveloped the entire upper part of the airship, unveiling all its details, and then, for two or three seconds, everything went dark again. Then, a little flame was perceptible; it grew and spread, following geometric lines, grew further, and was finally resplendent and victorious. The airship was seen to turn over, like a ship at sea taking in water through one side.

Then, everyone aboard the *Étoile polaire* understood that there had been an explosion aboard the aerobagne. The incandescent mass began to fall, first rather slowly, and then vertiginously...

Mathilde Régis had thrown herself to her knees, her hands joined, her eyes full of horror.

367

And suddenly, nothing could any longer be seen. The sea had just swallowed that which had been aerobagne 32.

Dawn broke, but over the turbulent surface of the Atlantic, the watchmen could not see anything to guide a search. The captain of the *Étoile polaire* did not even set a course for the presumed location of the sinking. The *Étoile polaire* began to describe large circles around that point, but its search was in vain; nothing, over the extent of the waves, revealed the place where the airship had been swallowed; no wreckage was floating.

Two hours passed thus. The captain turned to Mathilde Régis, who, sitting in a folding chair armed with a pair of binoculars, was gazing anxiously.

"Mademoiselle," he said, emotionally, "our research, unfortunately, can be considered to be concluded. I'm going to set a course for the dunes of Iguidi."

At first the young woman looked at him uncomprehendingly, and then passed her hand over her forehead several times.

"What are you saying, Monsieur? I don't understand."

The officer repeated his statement, in a soft but persuasive voice, and added: "There isn't one chance in ten thousand that anyone was able to escape the disaster."

Finally, the poor child understood; she leapt to her feet, her face ardent, animated by an expression of violent tenacity.

"What, Monsieur! You're abandoning the search?"

"It's futile, alas. All hope is lost."

"No, Monsieur, it's not futile and all hope must not be abandoned. There would be no more justice in heaven and on earth if those you must try to recover were lost forever."

The officer had not expected that language and those purely sentimental reasons."

"As you please, Mademoiselle," he said, more coldly. "I am at your orders. Nevertheless, I must add that in rallying to the dunes of Iguidi after a fruitless search I would only be conforming with the instructions that I have received."

"I still hope, Monsieur, I repeat. How far are we from your rallying point?"

"Approximately ten marine miles—eighteen or nineteen kilometers."

Mathilde maintained silence momentarily, and then gazed fixedly at the sea, "You have received imperative orders, Monsieur," she said, after a few seconds, "to which you must conform, but nothing permits you from obeying them while permitting those who conserve a hope to continue searching."

"How?"

"With the motor-launch."

"I can't permit that. The sea, as you can see, is still turbulent; the barometer is falling; it would be putting the lives of others in danger. Be sure, Mademoiselle, that if the search already carried out has had no result, those made by the launch could not be any more so."

"But Captain, who ought you to obey?"

"Monsieur Escander, under whose authority Monsieur Laverdy placed me."

The young woman smiled with joy, perhaps for the first time since she had left Paris. "Would you please read this," she said. At the same time, she handed the officer a piece of paper.

The captain read: *The commandant of the* Étoile polaire *is to put himself at the orders of Mademoiselle Mathilde Régis in everything she demands that can reasonably be executed. Escander.*

"Very well, Mademoiselle. There is, however, a restriction here—'that can reasonably be executed.' Now, I do not believe that it would be to expose a mere launch to this swell; however, if two men volunteer to accompany you and if the first mate will take responsibility for the expedition, the launch will be put to sea."

"I'll take that responsibility," said the mate.

The captain blew a brief, strident note on his whistle. The sailors of the crew came to line up at the foot of the bridge. Mathilde, getting ahead of the officer, leaned toward them.

"My friends," she said, vibrantly, "you know what happened last night. I believe that my fiancé has been able to escape the conflagration and death, and that he is lost at sea. The motor-launch is being equipped for me. I shall search until nightfall. The first mate will command the vessel. I need two men: can they be found among the brave men that you are?"

"Yes! Yes!" All arms were raised.

After the mate had chosen two sailors, the captain came to Mathilde. "I disapprove, Mademoiselle, but I congratulate you. I shall tack here until you return, ready to come to your aid if necessary."

The launch had been put to sea and the mate had put a few provisions, including cordials and drinking water, aboard. Everything was ready; the ladder was lowered and Mathilde descended into the boat.

The swell was heavy; the small craft plunged into the hollows of the waves or scaled their foamy summits, but held up valiantly. In the prow, Mathilde turned toward the sea, interrogating its surface every time her gaze was able to look out over the waves.

Finally, at about three o'clock, a white patch appeared on the dark blue surface. They headed toward it. The launch advanced swiftly. The patch became more distinct. It was long and narrow; finally, no more doubt was permissible; it was one of the supportive planes of aerobagne 32.

The launch accelerated. Finally, it came alongside one of the edges of the gigantic wing and slowly circled around it. At one of the extremities, half-submerged, two forms were lying. The launch drew closer. A man leapt on to the wreck and fixed a mooring-rope there. The young woman leapt on in her turn, and clinging to the ribs, succeeded, with great difficulty, in reaching the two bodies. She leaned over them, and then, standing up with her arms raised, she uttered a cry of triumph and collapsed.

At six o'clock in the evening, the *Étoile polaire*, having picked up the castaways, was heading toward the dunes.

The force of the explosion produced by the flask that Eitel had been holding in her hand had freed the aircraft in which Escander and Ménestin had taken their places. Obedient to the law of gravity it had fallen vertically, but Escander had leveled out its flight and it had reached the sea gliding.

The two men thought they were saved, but they perceived that the hull of the plane, constructed like that of a boat, had been split by the explosion and that it was taking on water.

At the moment when all hope seemed lost, however, the aerobagne fell into the water, scarcely two hundred meters from the place where they were; at the same time, one of the monster's wings had settled, so to speak, on the water a few brasses away.

They had swum to it and had reached it, but both of them, out of breath and out of strength, had lost consciousness after reaching the raft, which the wind and the waves had dragged nearly four miles from the *Étoile polaire*, outside the search area.

The publication by *Le Monde* of Paul Ménestin's manuscript had impassioned public curiosity; the articles that Escander sent to his newspaper following the deliverance of the engineer made an enormous impact. The daily's print run reached prodigious proportions, and Escander's name, suddenly popular, became a kind of rallying cry: that of France entire, united in the struggle against German knavery and barbarity.

SF & FANTASY

Adolphe Alhaiza. *Cybele*
Alphonse Allais. *The Adventures of Captain Cap*
Henri Allorge. *The Great Cataclysm*
Guy d'Armen. *Doc Ardan: The City of Gold and Lepers; The Troglodytes of Mount Everest/The Giants of Black Lake*
G.-J. Arnaud. *The Ice Company*
André Arnyvelde. *The Ark; The Mutilated Bacchus*
Charles Asselineau. *The Double Life*
Henri Austruy. *The Eupantophone; The Olotelepan; The Petitpaon Era*
Barillet-Lagargousse. *The Final War*
Cyprien Bérard. *The Vampire Lord Ruthwen*
S. Henry Berthoud. *Martyrs of Science*
Aloysius Bertrand. *Gaspard de la Nuit*
Richard Bessière. *The Gardens of the Apocalypse; The Masters of Silence*
Chevalier de Béthune. *The World of Mercury*
Albert Bleunard. *Ever Smaller*
Félix Bodin. *The Novel of the Future*
Louis Boussenard. *Monsieur Synthesis*
Alphonse Brown. *City of Glass; The Conquest of the Air*
Émile Calvet. *In a Thousand Years*
André Caroff. *The Terror of Madame Atomos; Miss Atomos; The Return of Madame Atomos; The Mistake of Madame Atomos; The Monsters of Madame Atomos; The Revenge of Madame Atomos; The Resurrection of Madame Atomos; The Mark of Madame Atomos; The Spheres of Madame Atomos; The Wrath of Madame Atomos* (w/M. & Sylvie Stéphan)
Félicien Champsaur. *Homo-Deus; The Human Arrow; Nora, The Ape-Woman; Ouha, King of the Apes; Pharaoh's Wife*
Didier de Chousy. *Ignis*
Jules Clarétie. *Obsession*
Michel Corday. *The Eternal Flame*

André Couvreur. *Caresco, Superman; The Exploits of Professor Tornada* (3 vols.); *The Necessary Evil*
Camille Debans. *The Misfortunes of John Bull*
Captain Danrit. *Undersea Odyssey*
C. I. Defontenay. *Star (Psi Cassiopeia)*
Charles Derennes. *The People of the Pole*
Georges Dodds (anthologist). *The Missing Link*
Charles Dodeman. *The Silent Bomb*
Harry Dickson. *The Heir of Dracula; Harry Dickson vs. The Spider*
Jules Dornay. *Lord Ruthven Begins*
Alfred Driou. *The Adventures of a Parisian Aeronaut*
Sâr Dubnotal *vs. Jack the Ripper; The Astral Trail*
Odette Dulac. *The War of the Sexes*
Alexandre Dumas. *The Return of Lord Ruthven*
Renée Dunan. *Baal; The Ultimate Pleasure*
J.-C. Dunyach. *The Night Orchid; The Thieves of Silence*
Henri Duvernois. *The Man Who Found Himself*
Achille Eyraud. *Voyage to Venus*
Henri Falk. *The Age of Lead*
Paul Féval. *Anne of the Isles; Knightshade; Revenants; Vampire City; The Vampire Countess; The Wandering Jew's Daughter*
Paul Féval, *fils. Felifax, the Tiger-Man*
Charles de Fieux. *Lamékis*
Fernand Fleuret. *Jim Click*
Louis Forest. *Someone is Stealing Children in Paris*
Arnould Galopin. *Doctor Omega; Doctor Omega and the Shadowmen* (anthology)
Judith Gautier. *Isoline and the Serpent-Flower*
H. Gayar. *The Marvelous Adventures of Serge Myrandhal on Mars*
G.L. Gick. *Harry Dickson and the Werewolf of Rutherford Grange*
Raoul Gineste. *The Second Life of Doctor Albin*
Delphine de Girardin. *Balzac's Cane*
Léon Gozlan. *The Vampire of the Val-de-Grâce*

Jules Gros. *The Fossil Man*
Edmond Haraucourt. *Daah, the First Human; Illusions of Immortality*
Nathalie Henneberg. *The Green Gods*
Eugène Hennebert. *The Enchanted City*
Jules Hoche. *The Maker of Men and His Formula*
V. Hugo, P. Foucher & P. Meurice. *The Hunchback of Notre-Dame*
Romain d'Huissier. *Hexagon: Dark Matter*
Jules Janin. *The Magnetized Corpse*
Michel Jeury. *Chronolysis*
Gustave Kahn. *The Tale of Gold and Silence*
Gérard Klein. *The Mote in Time's Eye*
Fernand Kolney. *Love in 5000 Years*
Paul Lacroix. *Danse Macabre*
Louis-Guillaume de La Follie. *The Unpretentious Philosopher*
Jean de La Hire. *The Fiery Wheel; Enter the Nyctalope; The Nyctalope on Mars; The Nyctalope vs. Lucifer; The Nyctalope Steps In; Night of the Nyctalope; Return of the Nyctalope*
Etienne-Léon de Lamothe-Langon. *The Virgin Vampire*
André Laurie. *Spiridon*
Gabriel de Lautrec. *The Vengeance of the Oval Portrait*
Alain le Drimeur. *The Future City*
Georges Le Faure & Henri de Graffigny. *The Extraordinary Adventures of a Russian Scientist Across the Solar System* (2 vols.)
Gustave Le Rouge. *The Dominion of the World* (w/Gustave Guitton) (4 vols.); *The Mysterious Doctor Cornelius* (3 vols.); *The Vampires of Mars*
Jules Lermina. *The Battle of Strasbourg; Mysteryville; Panic in Paris; The Secret of Zippelius; To-Ho and the Gold Destroyers*
André Lichtenberger. *The Centaurs; The Children of the Crab*
Maurice Limat. *Mephista*
Listonai. *The Philosophical Voyager*
Jean-Marc & Randy Lofficier. *Edgar Allan Poe on Mars; The Katrina Protocol; Pacifica 1, 2; Robonocchio; Return of the*

Nyctalope; (anthologists) *Tales of the Shadowmen 1-12; The Vampire Almanac* (2 vols.)

Ch. Lomon & P.-B. Gheuzi. *The Last Days of Atlantis*

Xavier Mauméjean. *The League of Heroes*

Joseph Méry. *The Tower of Destiny*

Hippolyte Mettais. *Paris Before the Deluge; The Year 5865*

Louise Michel. *The Human Microbes; The New World*

Tony Moilin. *Paris in the Year 2000*

José Moselli. *Illa's End*

John-Antoine Nau. *Enemy Force*

Marie Nizet. *Captain Vampire*

Charles Nodier. *Trilby and The Crumb Fairy*

C. Nodier, A. Beraud & Toussaint-Merle. *Frankenstein*

Henri de Parville. *An Inhabitant of the Planet Mars*

Gaston de Pawlowski. *Journey to the Land of the 4th Dimension*

Georges Pellerin. *The World in 2000 Years*

Ernest Pérochon. *The Frenetic People*

Pierre Pelot. *The Child Who Walked on the Sky*

Jean Petithuguenin. *An International Mission to the Moon*

J. Polidori, C. Nodier, E. Scribe. *Lord Ruthven the Vampire*

P.-A. Ponson du Terrail. *The Immortal Woman; The Vampire and the Devil's Son*

Georges Price. *The Missing Men of the* Sirius

Edgar Quinet. *Ahasuerus; The Enchanter Merlin*

Henri de Régnier. *A Surfeit of Mirrors*

Maurice Renard. *The Blue Peril; Doctor Lerne; The Doctored Man; A Man Among the Microbes; The Master of Light*

Jean Richepin. *The Crazy Corner; The Wing*

Albert Robida. *The Adventures of Saturnin Farandoul; Chalet in the Sky; The Clock of the Centuries; The Electric Life; The Engineer Von Satanas*

J.-H. Rosny Aîné. *Helgvor of the Blue River; The Givreuse Enigma; The Mysterious Force; The Navigators of Space; Vamireh; The World of the Variants; The Young Vampire*

Marcel Rouff. *Journey to the Inverted World*

MYSTERIES & THRILLERS

M. Allain & P. Souvestre. *The Daughter of Fantômas*

A. Anicet-Bourgeois & Lucien Dabril. *Rocambole*

A. Bernède. *Belphegor*; *Judex* (w/Louis Feuillade); *The Return of Judex* (w/Louis Feuillade); *The Shadow of Judex* (anthology)

A. Bisson & G. Livet. *Nick Carter vs. Fantômas*

V. Darlay & H. de Gorsse. *Arsène Lupin vs. Sherlock Holmes: The Stage Play*

Séamas Duffy. *Sherlock Holmes in Paris*

Paul Féval. *The Black Coats (The Parisian Jungle; Heart of Steel; The Sword-Swallower; 'Salem Street; The Invisible Weapon; The Companions of the Treasure; The Cadet Gang); Gentlemen of the Night; John Devil*

Émile Gaboriau. *Monsieur Lecoq*

Goron & Émile Gautier. *Spawn of the Penitentiary*

Paul d'Ivoi. *Around the World on Five Sous* (w/Henri Chabrillat)

Rick Lai. *Shadows of the Opera: Retribution in Blood; Sisters of the Shadows: The Curse of Cagliostro*

Steve Leadley. *Sherlock Holmes: The Circle of Blood*

Maurice Leblanc. *Arsène Lupin vs. Countess Cagliostro; Arsène Lupin vs. Sherlock Holmes (1. The Blonde Phantom; 2. The Hollow Needle); The Island of the Thirty Coffins; 813; The Many Faces of Arsène Lupin* (anthology)

Gaston Leroux. *Chéri-Bibi; The Phantom of the Opera; Rouletabille & the Mystery of the Yellow Room; Rouletabille at Krupp's*

Richard Marsh. *The Complete Adventures of Judith Lee*

William Patrick Maynard. *The Terror of Fu Manchu; The Destiny of Fu Manchu*

Frank J. Morlok. *Sherlock Holmes: The Grand Horizontals; Sherlock Holmes vs Jack the Ripper*

Jean Petithuguenin. *The Adventures of Ethel King*

Antonin Reschal. *The Adventures of Miss Boston*

P. de Wattyne & Y. Walter. *Sherlock Holmes vs. Fantômas*

David White. *Fantômas in America*
Pierre Yrondy. *The Adventures of Thérèse Arnaud*